myrna dey

E X T E N S I O N S

a novel

✄ ✄ ✄

NeWest Press

COPYRIGHT © MYRNA DEY 2010

Library and Archives Canada Cataloguing in Publication

DEY, MYRNA, 1942–

EXTENSIONS / MYRNA DEY.

ISBN 978-1-897126-68-4

I. TITLE.

PS8607.E9848E98 2010   C813'.6   C2010-903639-5

EDITOR: ANNE NOTHOF
COVER AND INTERIOR DESIGN: NATALIE OLSEN, KISSCUT DESIGN
COVER IMAGE: Untitled Twins, 1992, toned silver print *by* DAN ESTABROOK
AUTHOR PHOTO: CEDRIC DEY
PROOFREADING: PAUL MATWYCHUK

 Canada Council for the Arts Conseil des Arts du Canada   Canadian Heritage Patrimoine canadien   Alberta Foundation for the Arts   edmonton arts council

NEWEST PRESS ACKNOWLEDGES THE SUPPORT OF THE CANADA COUNCIL FOR THE ARTS, THE ALBERTA FOUNDATION FOR THE ARTS, AND THE EDMONTON ARTS COUNCIL FOR OUR PUBLISHING PROGRAM. WE ACKNOWLEDGE THE FINANCIAL SUPPORT OF THE GOVERNMENT OF CANADA THROUGH THE CANADA BOOK FUND FOR OUR PUBLISHING ACTIVITIES.

NeWest Press
201, 8540 – 109 STREET
EDMONTON, ALBERTA T6G 1E6
780.432.9427
WWW.NEWESTPRESS.COM

No bison were harmed in the making of this book.

PRINTED AND BOUND IN CANADA   2 3 4 5 13 12 11 10

EXTENSIONS

To the memory of my parents and brother, Gil, Marian, and Warren Williams, for their love of words and of me

✂

I ONLY SPOTTED THE PHOTO because Gail stopped to talk to her son's hockey coach. He was a moose of a guy, like one of our regulars in cells who required three men to restrain. Or, as the joke goes, one woman.

While they discussed Mighty Mite registration, I busied myself in a dark corner of the garage. A shoebox full of pictures was going for three dollars — cheap gold plastic frames with calendar prints of kittens, flowers, babies, plus the one that caught my eye. It was an old sepia photo of twin girls, about four or five, dressed for a formal pose in long ruffled dresses with big bows in their ringlets and black lace-up boots. It looked exactly like one my grandmother had given me of her and her sister. Hardly possible coming from a home here in rural Saskatchewan, but I couldn't resist the urge to compare them.

"I just want the one picture," I said to the large woman sitting at the cash table. "Here's three dollars for it."

"Three dollars for the whole box."

"I don't want the whole box." I thought I was doing her a favour by allowing the box to sell twice, but her expression told me I knew nothing about garage sales.

Seeing us, Gail pulled away from the hockey coach and came to my rescue. "She's flying, Joyce. She doesn't need any more baggage. This is my friend Bella from Vancouver — Constable Dryvynsydes. She and Monty trained together."

I winced that Gail had to work in the "Constable," but kept a friendly smile on my face. Joyce nodded without returning the smile. When she accepted my three dollars, I felt I had cleared customs with an undeclared pair of shoes on my feet.

"Whose stuff is this?" Gail asked.

"Multi-family, looks like Cindy Mingus," said Joyce, distracted by a woman behind us who seemed eager to transfer a Crock-Pot and an armful of jigsaw puzzles to the table.

Gail and I moved out of the garage and down the driveway as fast as we could, leaving the carton of gilt-edged pictures behind. Before we reached the safety of Gail's minivan, Joyce bellowed, "Don't forget the bake sale!"

Gail let out an exaggerated sigh. "You didn't have to buy anything. I just wanted to give you a sample of local colour. What we do for recreation here in the boonies."

I studied the picture again. "I wanted this. It looks like one Sara gave me — you must have seen it. The only evidence she had of a twin sister. I'll dig mine out when I get home, if I can ever find it." I stared at the bows on the girls' heads — one straight and neat, the other floppy. Sara said her floppy bow was the only way she could tell herself from her sister. "But there's no way they could be the same. Sara's was taken in Nanaimo."

Gail nodded. Old friendships spared a lot of explanations. She had known my grandmother since we started kindergarten together in Vancouver and, like me, had called her Sara. All through elementary school, Gail and I were known as the Gold Dust Twins because of our fair hair, but in Grade Seven the nickname ended when my hair darkened to khaki brown. At the same time, I shot up like a space needle and Gail grew curves. By the time we graduated from high school, I had come to rest at 5'11" and had a few mounds of my own. Gail never did make it past 5'2", but she stayed blonde and was always the cutest in any group. When she came to visit me in training at Depot in Regina, Monty, one of my troop mates, fell in love with her at first sight, and not much later, she reciprocated. I had to sign a prenuptial agreement promising, for my part in this match, to visit them in whatever isolated place Monty ended up. Willow Point, Saskatchewan, was the third such outpost, but his corporal's hooks came with this move, an impressive promotion for someone with his years of service. All the while, I was swallowed up in the lower mainland, where the RCMP acts as the municipal force for several cities surrounding Vancouver. I served with the Burnaby detachment and rented an apartment on the Vancouver side of Boundary Road. It could have been worse — I could be working in Surrey.

Gail pulled into the driveway of their grey vinyl-sided, split-level home. It was more or less like their other quarters provided by the RCMP, and more or less like all the houses on the short crescent. Monty greeted us with baby Macy in one hand, a barbecue brush in the other, and their son Clancy whooping around him.

"What do you think of our town — *enchanté, non?*" Monty grinned, as Gail took Macy into the house, Clancy following. Monty's grin had won over everyone at Depot, staff and recruits alike. Back then, he had a Québécois accent, now almost extinct under Gail's influence. He must have inherited his sense of humour from his mother who named him Montcalm and his twin brother Wolfe.

"Terrific place. For sure you'll want to retire here." I followed Monty to the deck where spicy meat cubes were cooking on skewers.

"Put your feet up." He gestured toward a chaise lawn chair and handed me a glass of cold beer. "This is recuperation time for you."

The best mirror is an old friend. That line was used to introduce one of the many eulogists at Mom's funeral, and never had anyone confirmed it more than these two. Here they were propping me up again. Macy was born six weeks before Mom's crazy death on Valentine's Day, but that didn't stop Gail and Monty from flying out for the funeral. I raised my glass. "Here's to your new home."

Monty raised his bottle from the barbecue. "Life can start for us now that you're here to baptize it. How are you? And your dad?"

"Confused. Both of us. Six months haven't made it any more real. Dad's still at a loss. He's practically given up golf without her, and crosswords just don't fill the days for him. I think I've persuaded him to take a course in cartoon drawing."

"Cartoons?" Monty almost lost a mouthful of beer.

"He needs a project and has always been creative. Even though

Mom was the art teacher, he was the one who drew the most wonderful comic strips for me as a kid. Great fantasy stories, lovable characters. He even made up songs for them to sing." Monty smiled, sliding the kabobs easily from their skewers into a stainless steel bowl. Whenever I tried that, they ricocheted into the barbecue lid. "And I might take a history course. Get started on the academics both my parents wanted me to take instead of becoming a cop. Aren't I contrary? Now that Mom's gone, I'm ready for the course she would have died to have me take."

Mom and *died*. I still could not speak that combination of words without a choking feeling starting in my throat and ending up in my eyes. I saw death regularly and remember my first next-of-kin notification two weeks into the job, when I had to tell a mother her sixteen-year-old daughter had been killed in a car accident. Tears fought to get out then, but within a couple of days, more sad files had pushed that memory aside. I could not bury my mother's file so easily. I was barely getting used to the idea that Sara was gone and that was already seven years ago. Dying seemed such a secretive betrayal, a covert operation. Each on her own, no consultation with Dad or me.

Monty shook his head. "I still can't believe it. I'll never forget Retha jiving with your dad at our wedding. She looked like a teenager."

"How do you think it felt being mistaken for sisters when your mother is in her fifties and you *are* a teenager?"

Not that we looked alike. I was a Dryvynsydes in height and fine hair, whereas the petite Retha had a thick, manageable blonde bob all her life. Her size four had not changed since she was fifteen, even after she had me at age thirty-six. In her fifties she started running, first half marathons, then full, always ending up in the top ten for her age division. Perfection did not stop with her body. She regularly won awards for imparting a love of art and music to her students in an innovative way. To which could be added: first-class hostess, patient mother, uplifting wife. After Dad retired as high school principal, she made sure they took at least one enlightenment trip a year — a museum tour of Spain and France, an archeological dig in Egypt. She would never go for the idle beach vacation in Mexico or Hawaii, though she did accompany

Dad on a golf holiday to Palm Springs every year, and learned enough of the game herself to challenge him on the odd hole. Efficiency on every front. Her supreme act of efficiency was to outrun, outexercise, and outstep old age by dropping dead on her treadmill just after she turned sixty-seven. The only role Superwoman Retha Dryvynsydes could not have played was a feeble old lady, so she added an early death to her list of achievements. Congratulations, Retha.

"You ready with the meat, honey?" Gail bounded onto the deck with two bowls of salad and a basket of rolls, Clancy behind her. Two sweeps of her arms and the cedar picnic table was transformed into something out of *Chatelaine* — fruit-spangled tablecloth, glasses, plates, and napkins in assorted solid fruit colours. By the time the adults sat down, Clancy was eating quietly and neatly at one end of the table, and Macy was cooing contentedly on a blanket nearby.

"You're another Retha," I said.

"I wish," said Gail, "but not with these thighs." Monty gave her bare tanned legs an approving pat.

"So how's Willow Point so far?"

"Pretty quiet at work," said Monty. "A few impaireds, B&Es, gas theft from farms, vandalism. Hey, it's a service town for farmers — the better criminals go elsewhere. Last week we got called to get a cat out of a tree."

Gail shook her head as Monty spoke. "That garage sale is about as lively as it gets. Maybe once Clancy is in school and I start teaching skating, I might find some kindred spirits tucked away. So far it's only been hockey mothers — Joyce was one of those. As usual, I'll end up on more committees than I want, because there are too few women to go around."

I thought of Gail and me as teenagers, both of us privileged — no, make that pampered. She concentrated on figure skating and I spread myself thin into everything. As an only child I was encouraged to sample both parents' passions: dancing, figure skating, piano, art, sports, along with decent grades, which I barely and lazily maintained. In our own ways, Gail and I had both rebelled from a life where rebellion was not necessary. Though never forced upon us, a university degree was certainly encouraged, so what did I do? Waited tables at the Cactus Club for a couple of years while waiting for my acceptance into the RCMP, which, after waitressing, was the second most unexpected line of work either parent would have considered for me. And Gail's parents, both pharmacists, had envisioned a profession for their daughter in pro skating, journalism, or pharmacy, where bake sales, hockey camps, and community skating lessons were on the edge of a rewarding career and family life, not the focus. Not that they were disappointed with Monty as a son-in-law, but they had not expected Gail to find him so soon.

"We won't be here forever, thank God," said Monty, helping himself to a second plate of food.

"If we ever get close to a large centre again, I'm going to take some courses." Had Gail heard us talking? She had started an arts degree before she got married. "In journalism. Amazing how raising a family brings out the urge to do something for your own development. Seems you're always tending to someone else's needs." She wiped Clancy's face with a napkin and released him to play in the back yard.

Monty escaped from this discussion into the house for more beer. RCMP spouses make as big a commitment to the force as the members, and he knew it.

"I wouldn't know about that," I said.

"No one setting your heart aflutter?" Just as Macy was about to fall forward on her face from a sitting position, Gail scooped her up and plunked her on her knee.

"Only as in 'How do I get rid of this loser?' There are lots around, and I could be a magnet if I don't watch it." One way I had not let my parents down was in marrying too early. In four months I would be thirty-one and had lost my only prospect.

"Is Ray still on your mind?"

"Yeah, with all the other creeps. He doesn't stray into my good thoughts anymore, but he has left me with a healthy suspicion of his gender."

Ray Kelsey was my first and only love. In high school I hardly dated and like to think it was because I was too tall for all the boys. Ray Kelsey was 6'4". He came to my rescue when I was a rookie cop going to court for the first time. He was a rookie Crown Prosecutor and helped me through my jitters. We did not get together then because he was going out with a woman he had met in law school. Too clingy, he told me when they broke up. "What I like about you, Arabella, is your independent spirit." Three of the best years of my life later, my future was all planned in my head. We had even lingered at the ring section in jewellery stores not long before he dropped the bombshell about the blonde bombshell in his office. "The problem with you, Bella, is that you're too independent."

Monty reappeared with two bottles of beer. "Spoke to Chad Simmons last week. He got a corporal's posting in Porcupine Plains. Asked how the best-looking member of our troop was doing."

Trust Monty to give me a lift.

"Your best-looking troopmate bought something at the garage sale today," said Gail.

"What could Willow Point offer a woman from Vancouver?" asked Monty, then looked at Gail and wished he hadn't.

"An old photo. It looks identical to one I have of my grandmother and her twin sister."

"Maybe it is."

"How could it be? She told me her mother had it taken when she and her sister were four. It's the only picture of them in existence. Just before their mother died of the flu, she gave them each a print. The girls were only eight and were sent to live with different relatives. Her sister died of the flu a year after that."

"It still could be a match."

I shook my head vigourously. "What are the odds of that? Both sisters ended up with aunts who didn't want them, so there's little chance either would keep a photo of a dead girl. These were poor families. Besides, this all happened on Vancouver Island, around Nanaimo. Almost a hundred years ago. This is Saskatchewan."

"You're talking in terms of odds. I took a course last month in Regina on the patterns of criminal behaviour. There are a few maybe, just enough to confuse you. More weird things happen than anyone could ever make up if he wrote a book. I guess we need guidelines to get our leads, but at the back of my mind I'm always thinking, the solution to this case is going to be something we least expect."

"So that's why you're such a young corporal."

Macy had fallen asleep on Gail's knee, and she rose carefully to slip into the house with her.

"You'll get there," Monty said.

"I'm not sure I want to. I'm not sure about anything anymore." I had written the corporal's exam and my mark was mid-range, like all the other marks in my life. The next step was to apply for a corporal's position when one became available. Experience, references, and other qualifications played as much a role as exam results, but I was still missing one important requirement: the motivation to put my name in.

"Then you're headed in the right direction."

"Seriously. I often wonder what I'm doing on the force. Lately I feel the way I did on the basketball court in junior high." Gail returned with a tray of strawberry shortcake and whipped cream just as Clancy arrived panting at the deck. "Gail can tell you about that. The coach made me centre, captain even, because I was so tall. I was terrified when the ball came to me, because I didn't know what to do with it. Possession of the ball brought the opposing guards, waving their arms in my face, threatening me with B.O. fumes, trying to freak me out. Finally, I pretended to be busy guarding someone whenever I thought the ball might come my way. My back was always to the passer. I should never have been there in the first place."

Monty laughed and heaved Clancy and two plates of shortcake onto his big knees. "Must be a slump. You seemed a natural at Depot. In scenarios, we hated following you because you had such good instincts dealing with people."

"Maybe since Mom died I've been questioning everything. Did I join for the right reasons? I can't even remember why now."

"I can," said Gail. "I remember the exact day. It was fall. We were in Grade Eleven, walking home through dry leaves. We came to that old house with all the junk in the backyard, and a crowd of people were standing along the sidewalk. The ambulance was already there and two police cars drove up. A male and female officer jumped out of one and went into the house; a third man kept the crowd away. A few minutes later the paramedics brought a covered body out on a stretcher and we heard someone behind us say, 'Suicide. She blew her brains out.' The female officer went back and forth between house, car, and ambulance, and you were awestruck. You said, 'That's what I'd like to be, because you get into places no one else does.' You wanted to know what the dead woman was wearing, what was in her fridge, if she had left dishes in her sink. You hoped she had at least spared herself some housework."

"What recall. You should be a reporter," I said, setting my empty plate down. "Or a chef."

Monty slid Clancy off his knee and came back with a thermos pot of coffee and three cups. "And I'm witness to another reason you gave at Depot. You were the only one in our troop who said you had joined to help lost children."

I covered my head in my hands. "Right. Aren't those two solid motives for upholding law and order: nosiness and pity. Remind me to watch what I say around you two."

The sun was casting carnival-coloured flames in the evening sky, so brazen you wanted to stop talking — even breathing. Gail lit a citronella candle at our feet. I almost said I had joined the force so I could meet Monty, and Gail could marry him, and I could nourish myself forever with moments like this in the company of these two. But my tear ducts had been working overtime recently so instead I said, "Whoever said the most beautiful sunsets in the world were in Saskatchewan and some corner of India was at least half right."

⚹ ⚹

WHEN I GOT BACK TO MY APARTMENT in Vancouver, there was a message waiting. "Bella, hope you had a good trip. Call when you get in. Love, Dad."

My father so seldom phoned for fear of disturbing me, that he signed off on my answering service as if he were writing a letter. In response to this rare occasion, I called immediately.

"Hi, Dad. Everything okay?"

His Hello voice lifted. "Fine, fine. How's Gail?"

"Doing well. They send their love."

"Monty? Does he like his new posting?"

"Their town is small and remote, but they're making the most of it, the way they always do."

"You must be tired. You on the early shift tomorrow?"

"No, I'm not really tired at all. Do you want me to come over?"

"Oh no, nothing like that. I probably should not have bothered you with that message, but your Aunt Janetta had a heart attack. She's okay, so don't worry. I thought I might go over to Nanaimo on the weekend to see her. I don't imagine you have the time off."

I wondered lately how a man in full command of a large school for twenty-five years could be so hesitant and apologetic. Since my mother's death, he made me think of a collapsed drawstring bag, requiring someone to tighten the straps to give him a purpose again. I had to remind myself he was ten years older than Mom, and a surprise blow like that would leave anyone close to eighty helpless. "As a matter of fact, I do have Sunday off and I'll be happy to go over with you. How is Janetta?"

"Still in hospital, but Lawrence said she is recovering steadily. Well, thanks. I'll let you get back to your unpacking now."

"Bye, Dad."

Unlike my parents, I did not require absolute order, so the notion of unpacking my suitcase before I needed the items inside had not occurred to me. I thought about Aunt Janetta instead. Considering the fact she was Dad's only sibling, we did not see much of her and her family.

Mom planned the few get-togethers we had when I was young, and they were always on the island. The only time I remember seeing Janetta in our home in Vancouver was after Sara's funeral, and then Mom's. She and Uncle Lawrence and their two sons and wives were all in attendance for those. Aunt Janetta was nice enough in her reserved way, but I could never get over the letdown of her looking just like Sara but not acting like her. Not fair of me, because no one acted like Sara.

Sara had named her daughter after her lost twin Janet, who was named after their mother Jane. I thank my mother for insisting on my name — awkward and old-fashioned as Arabella is in its full form — or Dad might have tried to wring out one more version. He admitted later he had Janine in mind. He argued that Arabella was too long for Dryvynsydes, having been stuck with a mouthful himself all his life. He pointed out that Llewellyn Dryvynsydes contained only one "y" fewer than that long Welsh place name with fifty-eight letters. And if it were spelled the Welsh way, "Llewyllyn" or "Llywyllyn," it would have been tied or had even more. From what Sara could recall of her eight-year-old sister, Janetta had carried on the name in a fitting manner. Janet was always quiet and careful, Sara said — she was the defiant one who spoke her mind.

I thought of the picture and fished it out of my handbag. The wide-eyed curiosity of the floppy-bowed twin did contrast with the stoic look on the face of the girl with the neat bow. Or was I just imagining this now, thinking about Sara and the two Jane derivatives? And what was the original Jane like? I would have to look for that picture to see how far off I was. A quick survey of my sparsely furnished one-bedroom apartment told me it wasn't here.

Being at Gail's confirmed how much of a homemaker she was and

I wasn't. Within minutes of her arrival anywhere, she surrounded her family with pottery, candles, pictures, cushions, fluffy quilts. On the contrary, I realized I had gone for the prison-cell look. Why else had I chosen the striped mattress ticking sofa from Ikea years ago? And the block end tables to go with it? My one item of elegance was Sara's gold brocade love seat I had claimed when her apartment was dismantled. Janetta had taken a few things and Dad had her Queen Anne chair in their little den.

Three posters hung on my living room wall — Serengeti zebras (more stripes), *Cats* (the first big musical Mom took me to as a teenager), and a colourful Caribana poster I had picked up in Toronto when I went there once with Ray for a law conference. In my bedroom I displayed my photo collection — Mom, Dad, Gail and family, my graduation, party shots with friends making faces. Those were the trappings of my present life. All my other belongings, including the photo from Sara, had been left in the family home, which Dad still occupied. Was I poised all these years to move back?

I realized I had lied to Dad: I was exhausted. I had also lied to Gail. Ray Kelsey was still an open wound. The dumpee often said it wasn't the breakup itself that hurt, it was the way the dumper handled it, yet I had never heard anyone complimented on his breaking-up skills. As if there could be an easy way to receive such news. I remembered Ray picking me up from my shift to take me to a bar in downtown Vancouver, but beyond driving out of the detachment parking lot, the evening was a blank. I could not really say how he handled it. I do know that later in the elevator going back to my apartment, I could not understand how the other passenger — a teenager with a baseball cap — could stand there so calmly when the entire world had suddenly become a disaster zone. Why wasn't someone screaming for help?

And then when my mother's relentless encouragement had almost convinced me there was a reason to keep on living, she dropped dead. So I had probably averaged three or four hours of sleep a night for the past nine months, not enough when it comes to cuffing a two-hundred-pound guy who doesn't want to be cuffed. Especially the one last week who decided to take all his clothes off in his car before surrendering. A delicate procedure, to say the least. And one where there was no question of back or front cuffs. I fell into bed hoping to feel functional by 4:30 AM.

Strange dreams filled the night. I was in uniform in a coal mine to protect two little girls in frilly dresses from disaster. While we waited for the cage to come down the shaft to take us out, thunder from collapsing tunnels raged around us. The lively twin became quiet and curious, ready for adventure. The quiet one began wailing because she was getting coal dust on her best dress. Their faces then turned black, and although I knew it was from soot, I also knew it was permanent. I woke up feeling powerless and full of terror because I realized we would not get out of there. As haunting and disturbing as it was for the rest of the day, the dream served a purpose: everything at work was lessened by comparison. While taking statements at two domestics, and from a hype with stolen goods, flashes of that mine scene kept coming back to me. The trouble at hand seemed almost refreshing. Even Jake, the most annoying person on our watch, made only one reference to his Volvo and abstained from his contempt for domestic vehicles when we went for breakfast. All of us felt sorry for anyone Jake stopped who was driving a Dodge or Chev. He believed they should be given a ticket for stupidity.

My four twelve-hour shifts went quickly. Sleep, work, supper with Dad twice at Wendy's on Cambie and Broadway — his kitchen since Mom died. No more upsetting dreams. I wanted that picture, but was resisting the memories that would come from the search. When I pulled up in front of the house early Sunday morning, I was verging on rested. Dad was pacing back and forth on the sidewalk, always ready an hour early.

"The ferry leaves at eight forty-five," he said, opening the door of my little Mazda before I came to a complete halt. He had given me that information at least once each of the past four days.

"We'll make it with time to spare, Dad." I sped away, screeching my tires, partly to make a point and partly because sometimes off-duty, I got unexpected impulses to act like the people I arrest.

"Did you have breakfast?"

"I'm fine."

"I brought you an egg and some toast." Carefully he unwrapped a paper napkin from the pocket of his jacket and handed me a peeled boiled egg. He opened another napkin, which I spread across my capri pants and set the buttered toast on it. He had taken over where Mom left off trying to change my habit of not eating for three hours after I got up. I nodded thanks and pointed to the two travel mugs of coffee in the holder. "Yours is in front."

As anticipated, we were first in line at the ferry and had forty-five minutes to walk around the parking lot. Once on board, I calmed down. When you drive all day for a living, it's a break to have someone else at the helm. Dad suggested we walk around the deck. We watched the Gulf Islands loom and recede, the sea breeze bringing new light and colour to Dad's face, causing his nose to drip. It was as if his island bloodline surfaced when he got close to Nanaimo, even though he was a born and bred prairie boy until he moved to Vancouver in his late teens. I took a tissue from the pocket of my pants and handed it to him. I always kept a supply for my own chronic nasal drip, which I had inherited from him, and he from his mother.

"When did you last speak to Janetta?"

"Easter maybe. And Canada Day. She called to see how I was doing."

"She isn't much for keeping in touch, is she?"

"No worse than I am. When your grandmother was alive, she was the pipeline to both families. She did such a good job we never learned to do it for ourselves."

"Sara's been gone for seven years."

"In other words, Janetta never felt totally comfortable with your mother. She intimidated her or something, though I don't think your mother intended it that way." Dad had a habit of starting explanations with "in other words" even before he had offered any on the subject.

"A lot of people are intimidated in the presence of perfection. I know I was at times. Especially as a teenager."

Dad grinned wistfully. "She couldn't help herself. We would never have lasted if I had tried to match those standards of hers, so I decided early that I had to be my own lackadaisical self."

"Hardly. Don't forget you're the one who did last."

A gull groomed itself on the railing next to us. "The only one in my family who could hold a candle to your mother's drive and passions was your grandmother. Whatever she had got diluted in Janetta and me."

Dad was slipping into his cozy cove of inadequacy. "Some people accomplish just as much as others, only not with the same intensity. Sara is remembered as the flamboyant one, but that doesn't mean she outdid Grandpa never missing a day of fifty years working at the bank." I then switched to diversion tactics, as I had seen Gail do with Clancy when he had his mind set on something hazardous or unnecessary. "Do you remember that picture of Sara and her sister as little girls?"

"Vaguely."

"Do you know where it is?"

"Probably in one of those boxes in the bedroom closet. Your mother looked after those things."

That's what I thought. The memory corner.

I brought two more coffees from the cafeteria and by the time we finished them, we were pulling into Departure Bay. A wave of vertigo hit me as we descended the steel staircase to the vehicle deck and I grabbed Dad's arm for balance until we reached my car. I hoped it wasn't a killer headache coming along for the ride, because they often struck when I was supposed to be relaxed. We drove off the ramp onto roads unknown to me, but Dad said he knew how to get to Uncle Lawrence's house, and in his usual prepared fashion, held a Nanaimo street map as backup. He had called his brother-in-law to say which ferry we would be taking, and the front door opened the minute we pulled up to the neat green and white bungalow. I had a hazy recollection of the place when I was last here as a teenager, but a family room and extra bedroom had been added, changing the shape of the house.

Uncle Lawrence met us on the front steps. He was a short, bald, pudgy man who laughed too quickly and too long to have a real sense of humour. He shook Dad's hand and went to shake mine before I gave him a polite hug, squeezing another laugh out of him like an accordion. "Doug and Lenny were here yesterday with their families. Too bad you missed them."

"Lenny too?" I asked, immediately regretting I had shown my preference for one of his sons. Lenny piloted small planes out of Prince George and had an easy way about him. Besides Dad, he was the only relative on either side who made me feel short. Doug was foreman of a sawmill in Campbell River and a replica of his father, so by standing here talking to Uncle Lawrence I had not missed seeing Doug. Because Mom and Dad had waited almost ten years for my arrival, I was much younger than all my cousins — a grand total of four. Doug and Lenny were in their forties, and the two daughters of Mom's older sister were more like fifty. They each had families and successful careers as a lawyer and bank manager in Toronto. Of course.

"Best to go to the hospital about 12:15," Lawrence said. "She'll have had her lunch and they'll be done their procedures. We can get something to eat at the cafeteria partway through the visit. She can rest that way."

We declined Lawrence's offer of coffee, but accepted his tour of the garden. A retired electrician, he kept busy in winter making Christmas candles out of fluorescent light bulbs for friends and in summer and fall, experimenting with prize-winning pumpkins. Janetta's pansies, gladioli, roses, and marigolds rimmed his rows of corn, peas, beans, carrots, and potatoes, and he walked us around the whole plot. "I killed a hundred and twenty-seven potato bugs this morning. Three hundred and fourteen yesterday."

Back in the house, I looked at the photos on the dining room wall. A close-up of me in a brown Stetson and red serge hung among duplicates we had of weddings — Sara and Grandpa, Mom and Dad, Janetta and Lawrence, Lennie and Doug and wives. Sara's antique tea wagon and silver tea service had ended up here as well as some framed petit points and Royal Doulton figurines that were once part of her apartment. Besides these pieces, the order and organization of this household were familiar to me. Filling my nostrils was a special aroma I had not inhaled since Sara died — a clean, yeasty mixture of freshly-baked bread and Sunlight bar soap. My head insisted I did not have the connection with this house my senses were transmitting. For one thing, the large puffy sofa and recliner in patterned velvet were completely alien to the contemporary furniture I had grown up with or the period style Sara liked. And the absence of original paintings on the walls got rid of any further notion of déjà vu. Uncle Lawrence broke into my thoughts, reminding me among other things that my dizziness was gone.

"Might as well get going. They eat early in the hospital. We'll take our car." He led us through the kitchen to the garage. Dad sat in the front seat with him and I sprawled in the back, a luxury for me. As he backed out, I waited for the usual joke from someone new. "I'd better watch my speed, eh? I hope you won't give me a ticket." I managed a laugh for the ten thousandth time.

We reached the hospital in less than ten minutes so I did not get much of an impression of Nanaimo. Vancouverites have to fight the urge not to feel superior to their island cousins — or to anybody anywhere — and I had opened my mind to a task that never presented itself. Dad and I marched through the polished corridors behind Lawrence to Aunt Janetta's doorway; we entered slowly, passing a nurse carrying a lunch tray on her way out. Aunt Janetta was sitting up, a smile on her pale face.

We each gave her a careful hug, then pulled up chairs and sat at the side of her bed. Lawrence perched on the edge of the vacant bed in the room, cap in hand, feet barely grazing the floor.

"How nice of you to come, Lew. And for you to take time from your busy job, Bella."

She recounted the story of her heart attack. How she finished the supper dishes, how she felt tired, how she pushed herself to water her posies because it had been so dry lately instead of sitting down to watch the news as she normally did. "She could have asked me, but oh no," said Lawrence on cue. Then she described her indigestion, thinking it was because she had met a friend for lunch and ordered her first Thai salad, which was spicier than she liked. Then the heartburn got worse, so she went and sat in the kitchen. "He was putting the lawnmower away when the pain really started. I could barely get to the door to call him."

"Fortunately, the ambulance came right away or the damage could have been a lot worse."

The two of them had relived these details so many times they were now in slow motion and perfect unison. Ordinary events that would not bear repeating except for their consequences. Something like my dream where those underground tunnels were collapsing while every-day life went on above. I sat captivated by the story, mainly because Jan-etta became Sara in the telling. They had always looked alike, though Sara was considered pretty, feminine, and vivacious, and her daughter, neat and pleasant-looking. Today Janetta's grey hair, not yet fastened into a roll, fell around her thin face and shoulders and transported me back to the Vancouver General and my final visits to Sara. Maybe it was because I had so recently lost my mother that I suddenly saw Janetta as a necessary member of my world. A woman I hardly knew became my mother and grandmother. "You have to get better," I blurted out. At the same time my nose started dripping and it probably looked as if I were crying.

"Thank you, dear," she said, surprised. "Don't worry. I'll be fine. They want to do more tests and then I'll be released."

Dad appeared oblivious to this blurring of identities going on in my head. He knew this was his sister and not his wife or mother and continued talking to her about Lenny and Doug and how he had been doing on his own for the last six months. "Don't know how I would have managed without her," I heard him say before realizing he was talking about me.

"We're both starting courses in the fall," I said. "He's taking cartoon drawing and I'm taking history."

"We'll see," said Dad, embarrassed. "She wants me to start a course so I don't drive her crazy."

"That's perfect, Lew. You know, Bella, I used to love it when we were kids and your dad had to look after me if Mother and Dad were out. He'd draw fantasy figures the whole time. Better than the funnies, by far. What did you name your comic strip again? The Ratchet Fam-ily, that's it. They all looked like tools. Mrs. Ratchet had curlers in her hair, so her head looked like a ratchet wheel. Her husband was Hatchet Ratchet and he had a hatchet jaw. The son was Hammerhead and the daughter was Naillie, thin as a nail. The town they lived in was called

Latchtown, and all the doors and windows of all the houses had huge latches. The province was Patchton, so everything anybody owned was covered with patches."

"How come you didn't draw the Ratchets for me?" I demanded. "But I was pretty happy with Cedric the Cockroach and Thump the Butterfly."

Janetta began to shake with laughter, more relaxed and merry than I had ever seen her.

Dad too laughed in spite of himself, then pointed out the absurdity of thinking he should attempt cartoons when there were so many young talented artists and animators in this digital age. He said he was going to work on a children's book instead, using cartoon-type illustrations; he already had a rhyming text in mind. The courage to make this announcement to me when I had other plans for his grief therapy obviously came from having his sister and her husband in the room with us. Mob mentality — I saw it all the time on the streets. To make his point, he got up and started toward the door. "We're tiring Janetta. We'll go to the cafeteria and let her rest."

Janetta looked wistful as Lawrence, Dad, and I filed out, but when we returned later, she was asleep. Her eyes opened at our approach, her face drained of the liveliness it had held earlier. Lawrence rolled up her bed so she would not have to lift her head from the pillow.

"We'd better go," Dad said, reaching over to take his sister's hand by way of goodbye.

"You just got here," she murmured.

"We don't want to undo all your treatment in one visit."

"I wish you lived closer. It's so good to see you both."

"When you're feeling better, we'll come back again."

The resemblance to Sara continued to amaze me and I told her so. She smiled and said Lenny had said the same thing yesterday.

"Do you have any pictures of Sara as a child?"

"The only one I've seen is of the two sisters with bows in their hair. Don't you have it?"

"Somewhere. I have to search." I decided not to bring up the look-alike photo.

"She wanted it handed down through the girls in the family and I didn't have daughters."

"I don't suppose there are any photos of her mother."

"Not that I remember. I have some of Jane's letters — Mother gave them to me before she died. They were written to Jane's sisters in Wales, so I don't know how Mother ended up with them." Janetta put her hand to her mouth and shook her head the way Sara did. "Isn't that the limit? They're in a trunk downstairs and I haven't even looked at them. There was so much to sort I forgot about them."

I could feel Dad pacing around the room behind me, a signal to get going. "I'd like to read them some day. I'd like to learn more about my great-grandmother."

"Jane Hughes had a short, sad, hard life, that's all I know about her. Why don't you come back and we can go through them together."

I kissed Janetta on the forehead and followed Dad into the corridor. Uncle Lawrence lingered a moment to inform his wife of the potato bug count and the Sears bill amount. He wanted us to stay for an early supper. He had steaks to barbecue and new carrots, peas, and the potatoes he had rescued. I was agreeable because I could see the empty house was torture for him. Dad, however, did not hesitate.

"Next time," he said as Lawrence pulled into his garage and he headed straight for my car. "Bella has to be up by five tomorrow. Morning shift, you know."

"I'd like to hear more about your job sometime," Lawrence said.

Instead of looking at my uncle's disappointed face, I stared at my lying father. I had just come off my block and he knew that. I was to be the fall guy. When I saw him take a cigar from his shirt pocket for the ferry ride home, I remembered where those cigars were most enjoyed. Douglas Park. Dad was planning to watch a recreational baseball game this evening while sitting with his pocket radio tuned into the major leagues. I gave Uncle Lawrence an extra sympathetic hug because I did not want him to know his brother-in-law's real motive in getting away so quickly. It brought no laugh this time.

And as we pulled away, my mind too was on the mainland: wondering which box of photos in Dad's closet would hold the two little girls.

✂ ✂ ✂

FOR THE NEXT FEW WEEKS I was too busy at work to go through the boxes. After hours there were barbecues. Our watch was pretty tight despite some squabbling that went on behind backs. Being non-confrontational myself, I had come to the conclusion that this method was as good as any to deal with a grievance. Eventually it disappears, and you haven't left two parties with words in their heads they won't forget.

When I was free and not too tired, I'd meet Dad for a quick meal at Wendy's. Keeping my distance from the kitchen where Mom ruled was becoming selfish and impractical. Sometimes I would go back to the house with him and watch *Jeopardy!* until the emptiness was too much to bear. How could Dad sit and watch TV in the basement room surrounded by Mom's exercise equipment?

"I'm going to put a sign up at work to sell this stuff," I announced suddenly after we realized we were watching a rerun of a show we had seen with Mom when she guessed the final answer none of the contestants knew. "You'll never use it."

"You don't want it?"

"It wouldn't fit in my place."

"You could use it here."

"It's too much Mom. As soon as it's gone, I'll probably buy myself a set."

"Do what you want." Dad shrugged, rightly confused by my logic.

By the weekend, I had sold Jake on the deal, and he swapped his precious Volvo for a friend's truck for an hour to pick up the works — treadmill, trampoline, bicycle, Ab Master. After he left, I stayed to watch a baseball game with Dad, but now I couldn't stand being there because the equipment was *gone*. What kind of daughter was that? I reminded myself Dad was faced with this empty house all the time; at least he was in it when I was there.

For me, it was more than missing Mom. In fact, I was often so aware of unspoken standards in her presence that I couldn't deny a certain freedom, much as I hated to admit it. What I had lost was a sense of what to do next. She always knew, even when I didn't want to follow. She provided distractions for me when pieces of the future I had planned with Ray Kelsey kept coming back like demonic homing pigeons. A brisk walk — make that a brutal march — around Stanley Park, a movie, lunch in Kitsilano. She was always upbeat, and as annoying as that could be when I wanted to feel sorry for myself, her mood eventually dominated mine. She even died on Valentine's Day to make sure I was surrounded by flowers when there would be no more from Ray. This house was hollow without her.

To prolong my visit with Dad, I made up my mind to look for the picture of Sara and her sister. I got as far as the walk-in closet in Mom and Dad's bedroom, where boxes of overflow photos, letters, and yearbooks had been stored since I was a kid. I opened one and saw two or three alternate poses — the best photos had gone in an album — of Mom looking radiant holding me as a big bald baby. I had to get out of there right away, so I deserted Dad again and went back to my apartment.

The next time I saw him was registration night. After supper at Wendy's, he decided to accompany me to the college, so he would have a new sidewalk to pace while he smoked his cigar. As I was experiencing a sudden case of jitters walking into the building, he remained cheery outside. I felt conspicuous in a skirt worn for the occasion, a long batik wraparound that brushed the top of my sandals. As if I were taking this too seriously, the other registrants, all ages and sizes, hurried in and out in shorts, accustomed to the procedure. I suspected they were all more studious than I was. Other than the RCMP depot, the last exams I had taken were Grade Twelve departmentals. But I had been accumulating black book time for these classes, so I was not about to throw my bonus hours away. My B.C. history prospectus covered three single-spaced pages of reference material and I suddenly wished I had signed up for English as a second language. When I came out, Dad was irritating. He was singing "Up a Lazy River" and held out his hand to see my book list.

"I guess courses don't change that much. You might have to buy one history book. I think we've got most of the others."

"Show-off. I know what you're thinking."

"I don't even know what I'm thinking."

"You're thinking I should have taken a course like this a long time ago."

"Why would I think that?

"Because it's true."

He lit another cigar and we set off into the soft evening air. When he continued singing, I decided not to hold my own insecurities against him. He hadn't sung like this for a long time.

The following Wednesday I sped straight from work to my history class. The enrollment was small, composed mainly of visible minorities. At work we had to classify people according to race, and my mental pen noted them automatically. I ended up sitting next to a young guy probably in his early twenties, a mixture of Caucasian and Black, who smiled as if he knew me. I wondered if I had ever picked him up. No, he appeared too genuinely friendly to be a shit rat — you get to know their type.

"This your first course?"

That's getting personal, I thought as I answered: "For a while, anyway."

"I mean with Barnwell. You ever had him before?"

I shook my head just as Barnwell walked in and introduced himself. Early fifties, small and slight, with long curly hair like Howard Stern. As soon as he opened his mouth, all heads straightened to attention. For the next hour and a half his booming voice brought the Haidas, Captains Drake, Cook, and Vancouver to life. His lecture made me think of the Disney films I saw as a kid where a paintbrush creates an entire scene with a few brushstrokes. I noticed my neighbour taking detailed notes. At the end, he turned to me with a "So how did you like him?" grin and I spoke without thinking: "Will you be coming to all these classes?"

"I never miss Barnwell."

"Would you mind doing me a favour? I work shifts and might have to miss a class. Would you share your notes with me if I do?"

"You a nurse?"

I nodded because I could see this guy putting up his hands and joking, "Anything you say, officer," if I told the truth.

"Sure, any time." He stood up from the desk and towered a good four inches over me. I was not expecting that.

I thanked him and walked ahead since he seemed to be waiting for me to go first. At the door I turned back to say: "You're right. He really is good."

Next day I was off to a bad start at work. Walking from the locker room to the cars, I came face to face with Ray Kelsey. He was at the main desk getting some information about one of his clients in cells. I had not seen him since he showed up uninvited at Mom's funeral.

"Hello," I said, rushing past him. I tried to keep the sound of my heart drumming against my bulletproof vest as background accompaniment instead of a solo.

"Hi, Bella." He gave me a big crocodile grin showing all his treacherous capped teeth. He was tanned, and handsome as ever in his lawyer's suit. "How ya doin'?"

Cut the street talk, I said to myself. "Very well."

"Your dad? He's okay?"

"Fine." I was not about to share Dad's welfare with Ray, so I left it at that.

It was clear Ray wanted to chat, but his phone rang from his pocket, rescuing me. I fluttered my fingers at him and hurried on. His eyes followed me with a confused look. I heard him speaking sharply as I walked away — probably Blondie wanting him to pick up some nail polish on his way back to the office. I found my cruiser as fast as I could and exited the parking lot as if I'd been called out on a high-speed chase.

In sight, in mind. Thanks a lot, Ray, thanks a lot, Retha. You've joined forces to ruin my life. For a second I saw my mother as the little blonde co-conspirator sitting in Ray's office. I had counted on them cherishing me forever, and they both dumped me. I held back the tears until I was alone in the car writing up the file from my first B&E of the day. When I left, the female whose house had been burglarized was still wailing over her stolen jewels. *Get a grip, woman,* I felt like saying. *You can get more of those gold bangles when your sister goes to India next month, just as your husband said.* I had to get used to losing an engagement ring myself. Instead of the one Ray Kelsey almost bought me, I ended up with my mother's.

I put the plastic bag containing the woman's cheap jewel case in the trunk. I had taken it simply to give the woman some hope, though I knew no clues would result from it. People felt better when you mentioned the word "fingerprints," but they didn't realize how difficult it is to get a good print from a crime scene; you must get the points to connect on six or seven circles of the print and the clearest surface is glass or metal. Besides, I wouldn't be surprised if this case was a set-up. The suspect had left an upturned crate under the open window of the Hindu prayer room, where, for security reasons, the woman had moved the jewels from the master bedroom just the night before. She had no insurance, so she probably did not stage it herself, but I didn't rule out the husband. He seemed like the moocher type who might come up with the idea of fencing his wife's jewellery. No proof, of course.

As I wrote up the file in the car, tears plopped like summer raindrops. I blotted my eyes and the paper with a tissue. I don't know how long I sat there with my chin bobbing uncontrollably, but I pulled myself together when I saw a P.C. approaching from the other direction. Dave drove up, rolled down his window and said "Denny's?"

I nodded and he cruised on. Usually I looked forward to breakfast with the guys. I enjoyed being the only female on our watch. Not that I wasn't comfortable with female members, but I liked knowing what men thought when they were together — I didn't always like what they thought, but I liked knowing. This morning I did not have much of an appetite when Dave, Jake, Sukhi, and Emile squeezed further into the booth to make room for me. Dave had hot chocolate, the other three

ordered coffee, and as soon as I sat down, the waitress arrived with plat-
ters of eggs and pancakes. She looked to me for my order.

"Toast and coffee, please."

"You okay?" Dave asked. "You seemed a bit shaky back there." Dave
was a big guy, a Mormon. We called him Rudder because he insisted
on taking the steering wheel if anyone drove with him. He also believed he was ordained to steer everyone in the right direction, including his wife and four kids, and all the lawbreakers he picked
up. I pitied anyone who had to listen to one of his sermons from the
back seat.

Emile was the brains of our group. We called him Mr. Know-It-All
because he did. Ask him a simple question like the difference between
condominiums and co-op housing, and he would go on for fifteen minutes. We learned to ask him things at the beginning of a meal and not
when we were running out of time. He had an anthropology degree
from Concordia and, as a native French speaker, he delighted in correcting our English. He was the one we consulted about the Criminal Code whenever doubts arose. At least I did. Dave and Jake believed
they knew it all too.

Sukhi was my favourite partner. His full name was Sukhwinder
Ahluwalia. He was slight, strong, quiet, and alert with the best sense
of humour of all of us. If we took calls together, we often burst out
laughing before we got back to the car. It could be anything that got
us going — the person's hair, something that was said, even the wallpaper. I remember the first time it happened. We were called to a Sikh
household and I commented later about how rambunctious the little girl was.

"That was a boy," he smiled.

"No, the little one, the one in white pyjamas with the bun in her
hair tied back with lace."

"That was a boy," he insisted. "I had one of those myself."

I had cracked up, as much with embarrassment as anything, and
when Sukhi joined in, it started a long series of laugh attacks. Last year
he got engaged to a girl his parents had picked out for him. Conveniently, he was madly in love with her.

In spite of their quirks, these guys felt like the brothers I never had. They knew something was bothering me and each comforted me in his own way.

"You should eat more than that, Arabella," Dave said, "or you're going to get a headache. Have a bowl of porridge."

"Porridge would just make her hungrier an hour later," said Jake.

"It's a good start to a day. I make sure my kids have it before they leave for school."

"Yeah, and I bet they have pop tarts on the days you're working."

Emile explained: "Porridge is the perfect breakfast. Especially eaten with plain yogurt. You get your fibre, vitamins, and minerals."

"If she gets hungry before lunch, she could take a bagel with her," said Dave, finishing the last of his pancakes and syrup.

"As long as it's a multi-grain spread with peanut butter instead of cream cheese," smiled Emile, taunting us now.

"Anything would be better than these sausages today," said Jake, pushing his plate away. "They taste as if they've been cooked in axle grease."

"Hope it's a Volvo axle," said Sukhi.

I caught his eye and we exploded. Everyone did, including Jake. By then, breakfast was over and the waitress arrived with our bills. When Jake explained about the sausages, she tore his up.

"Thanks, guys," I said. They knew what I meant.

Back in my car I cleared for a file with Sally the dispatcher.

"Two bravo fourteen stand by to copy a priority. Son attacking mother with knife." She gave me an address in the Edmonds area. "Complainant's surname, spelled Delta Echo Alpha November; Given name Wanda, common spelling."

"Copy. I'll be responding Code Three."

"I'll be sending two bravo six for cover."

"Copy." I turned the siren to wail and wheeled out of the parking lot. The address was in a slummy neighbourhood I knew all too well. In fact, I'd attended a call last year at this very address. Wanda Dean and her son had hysterical fights regularly; her first reaction was to call the cops. Last time the boy said he would only talk to me alone, and since he didn't pose a threat, Sukhi went and sat in the cruiser. I started writing up the file in my mind as a woman stood waiting at the door for me. *Complainant greeted me in state of agitation. Race: Aboriginal/ Caucasian.* Emile pulled up just as I was entering the house.

"He threw down the knife and now won't come out of his room. He don't listen to nothing I say." Wanda was probably in her thirties and still pretty despite the alcoholic's puffiness that generally precedes skin and bones. Her hands were shaking as she took a drag on her cigarette. I sensed Wanda was overreacting as usual, and waved Emile away.

I stepped inside to a thick, stale, sour smell — years of dirt and smoke layered on every surface. Something like a cheap motel, only worse, because cooking odours were mixed in. Piles of newspapers lined the entry and corridor down to a closet whose doors were held permanently open by an avalanche of old clothes, shoes, and broken toys. A thought struck me: a leaky ceiling could turn this passageway into a papier mâché tunnel — the kind you see on model train sets. I reminded myself to e-mail Gail and Monty and tell them the novelty of being in other people's homes had definitely worn off. "Where's the bedroom?"

She led me through the living room, the sofa's back and arms stained from greasy heads, its cushions littered with potato chip crumbs and torn bags. Across the partition to the kitchen another woman and young boy were standing among the ruins of a week's meals.

"They'll tell you what he done," Wanda said, waving her arms in their direction. "He took that knife and started swinging it around and said he was going to use it on me." She picked up a bread knife from the top of the partition; it too was caked with some kind of matter. The two witnesses nodded enthusiastically.

Wanda tried the knob of the bedroom door, then banged. "The police want to talk to you, Terry. It's the lady again."

"Terry?" I said, knocking. "May I come in?"

Wanda lit another cigarette and banged again. "Terry, get out here. You're embarrassing me." After the next silence she turned to me: "You gonna break it down?"

I ignored her question and said softly: "Terry, I'd like to talk to you. Will you please let me in?" I tried the knob again and it was unlocked. I stepped into the room. Terry's eyes took me in, but he did not raise his head. He was a stocky boy with brown hair and a pasty complexion, much lighter than his mother's. He was sitting on his bed among rumpled, discoloured sheets. He had been crying.

"What's the problem, Terry? Why did you take the knife to your mother?" I spoke slowly.

"She keeps after me is what."

"That's because you won't listen to me. You keep doing wrong." She stepped closer to the bed, but I blocked her off.

"How old are you now, Terry?"

"Thirteen."

"You know you can't go threatening people with knives without getting into trouble?"

He wiped his tears with a dirty hand and stared straight ahead.

"That's not all he does," wheezed Wanda, taking a drag. "The neighbour behind us say he steal his hose." The two witnesses had joined us in the bedroom, both speaking at once. "That's true," said the mother. "He try to get Freddy to go with him and steal some drinks and pretzels from the 7-Eleven, but Freddy's a good boy, he won't do it. He come and tell me."

"That's true, that's true," Freddy repeated like a parrot.

"How old are you, Freddy?" I asked.

"Twelve," he and his mother said in unison.

I thought of Sukhi and what we would have made of this pair later. "Why aren't you and Terry in school today?"

"The principal committed suicide at Terry's school so they took a holiday," said Wanda.

"Where do you go to school, Freddy?" I bit my tongue before adding "Tattler's Elementary?"

"He got a doctor's appointment today," said his mother, while he nodded on cue.

"So you decided to take the whole day off." I spoke more harshly than any of us was expecting.

"He steal all the time," Wanda continued, bringing the focus back to her son. "Last week he bring me flowers for my birthday and I find out he steal them from the flower shop. Look at this room." She gestured toward some old crayon drawings on the walls that might have been done by a five-year-old. She picked up a dirty sock from the floor. One sock. From a floor covered with clutter. "How can I keep the place nice when he throw his socks around?"

Terry began to cry. "I come home last night and she's passed out again. I thought she was dead. How you think I feel?" He sobbed noisily. "I had to call my dad to come and take her to the hospital but then she woke up. My sisters do anything they want and she loves them to death. She want to put me in jail."

When his shoulders stopped heaving, I spoke quietly but firmly above Wanda nattering "They're good girls."

"Terry, you can't keep stealing or threatening people with knives or you will end up in jail. I don't want to see that happen, because I know you're really a good boy at heart. And I believe you'll try your best to prove it. Because you know it too, no matter what anyone says about you."

Terry stared at me and the other three looked disappointed as I turned to go. Wanda followed me through the house, pointing out Terry's caked soup bowl that would otherwise not have been noticed on the coffee table among empty beer bottles and overflowing ashtrays. In the paper passage she stopped me and whispered: "I know he's doing drugs too."

"Wanda, you'll have to try to sort things out with Terry. Maybe give him some praise when he does something right." Our job was not to play psychologist, so I handed her a card. "Here's the name and number of a counsellor you might want to talk to. I don't think it's the police you need."

"Oh, thank you, officer. I write down everything he does wrong so I can take that sheet along with me." She smiled, as if we really did understand each other.

It was drizzling when I finally escaped. I gulped a breath of fresh wet air to cleanse my lungs of the stench. Just before I reached the car, Wanda came running after me. "He's swearing at me again. What should I do?"

"Call the counsellor." I got inside as fast as I could. My hands were shaking more than Wanda's. The rain was pouring down now, and I knew I had to drive somewhere or she would come running out again. I turned the corner and parked in front of another house that probably had the same things or worse going on inside it. I had gone to hundreds of domestics in this area, seen a hundred Wandas and Terrys. Why was this different?

Seeing Ray this morning proved how vulnerable I was myself. I had attended the former calls as if they were part of a world to which I never could belong. Today the connection triggered a thunderstorm in my head. I felt as if I had skidded to a halt at the edge of a dangerous precipice. Retha and Ray could easily become my Terry. If you took away my security on all other fronts — financial, professional, family —, I might be seeing Wanda when I looked in the mirror. It was not only her addictions, her squalor, or her poverty that made her helpless. It was her need for a scapegoat.

A counsellor would never untangle what was happening in that house, because Wanda needed her son to be the obstacle to her happiness. As if removing one dirty sock from a trash heap would make the trash heap fade into the background. The comfort of blame right there for the taking. For Wanda, for the witnesses, for Terry. And for me.

I was not sure if my limited visibility was due to the pounding rain on the windshield or the pounding now going on in my head. I told Sally I was coming in. As I crept along the streets to the detachment, I muttered, *Thank you, Wanda, for leading me where you will probably never go yourself.* One look at me, and my corporal advised me to take the rest of the day off.

When I got to my apartment, there was a message from Dad. When I called, he said he had been going through boxes and found the picture of Sara and her sister I was looking for.

"I wondered if you wanted to meet for supper at Wendy's and I could bring it. But you don't sound too well."

"Headache," I said, fighting the nausea mixing in with the

painkillers. "I'm going to lie down now and should be all right by supper time."

"We can make it another time."

"No. I'll see you tonight. But let's not go to Wendy's. Let's eat at home. We can fix something together. In Mom's kitchen. Hot dogs, eggs, anything. I'm ready to go through those pictures."

✄ ✄ ✄ ✄

DAD HAD SCRAMBLED EGGS, sardines, and toast ready for me when I arrived. I had not eaten anything besides the toast and coffee at Denny's and was hungrier than I thought. I hated to admit Dave might be right about breakfast and headaches. Mine was now in its phantom stage, the hangover still there but the throbbing gone. Dad insisted I take a mug of camomile tea with me to the living room where he had set a large shoebox — his, not Mom's — on the footstool. He was excited about something.

"The picture is here," he said, opening the box, "along with some old letters from your great-grandmother."

There they were. Sara and Janet as young twins in long dresses and ringlets, one bow neat and one bow floppy.

"Damn," I muttered. "I forgot to bring the other one." When I left the apartment all I could focus on was finding my car keys and keeping my head still while my body moved. "Maybe I'm not seeing clearly right now, but I'm sure this is the same picture." The angle of the girls' little black boots was the same. Both in third position, I knew from ballet classes. The hand of the floppy-bowed one was on the arm of the neat one.

"And the other picture came from Saskatchewan?" Dad asked in disbelief.

"Not just Saskatchewan — Willow Point, Saskatchewan. Point Zero."

"You'll have to put them together to make absolutely certain. Maybe there are traces of DNA on the back of each photo."

"You're always a step ahead of me."

I lifted the top letter from the pile in the shoebox. It was written with blue ink on vellum paper that was beige now, if not originally. Its folds had begun to wear through, so I opened it very carefully. The date at the top read April 4, 1894, Nanaimo, B.C.

Dear Brother and Sisters,

Just a few lines in answer to your letter, trusting they will find you better than when you wrote. We were glad to hear that Margaret and Gwynyth were pretty well but sorry to hear that Evan has been so sick. La Grippe is a terrible disease in this country. Gomer has been laid up with it for two weeks and Tommy is not feeling well but he never misses work at the mine. It is all the worse here for it is so wet — cold rain much of the time. We were also very sorry to hear of poor Catherine so sick. We wonder if she wouldn't like to come out here. We would so much like to see her and all of you. Tommy said he would send money at once. He is making our home here in Chase River comfortable and Mama would brighten at a visit. She is still weak but has her good days. There is never a day passes that I am not thinking of you. I wish I had enough money to carry me back to Wales. I would leave tomorrow.

I miss school very much, especially the small library in our classroom where I often borrowed books to read. Miss Maasanen gave me a copy of Tess of the D'Urbervilles on my last day there and I treasure it. I have to remind myself that the little money I bring in washing clothes adds to Tommy's wages. I have two customers now, one is a miner's wife and the other is a Negro gentleman who lives in a cabin not far from us. He has an orchard here and another farm on Salt Spring Island where his wife and family stay. He is a kind, hardworking man. I am sleepy now. Mind to write back by return mail, addressed to me. I remain your loving sister

x x x x x x x x x x x x Jane x x x x x x x x x x x x x x

I stared at the letter in my hands. Why was I surprised that X was not a modern symbol for kisses? Words from more than a century ago as fresh as if they had just appeared on my e-mail screen, though much prettier in their careful, elegant script. The clear circles and swirls made me think of penmanship exercises when we first switched from printing to writing in Grade Three.

"Did you read these?" I asked Dad.

"A thrill, isn't it? A hundred-plus-year-old letter from the mysterious Jane Owens. Judging from her handwriting, her spelling and grammar, she seems to be, shall we say, a refined woman. Call me a snob, but I'm relieved about that. She must have had her own standards, because she could not have had much of an education. Sounds as if she was a teenager here, quitting school reluctantly to do laundry."

"Do you know these other people? Catherine, Tommy, Gomer, Evan?"

"Catherine and Margaret were her sisters, but I don't know the name of the brother in Wales. Tommy and Gomer are her brothers in Canada. Evan and Gwynyth are Margaret's children, I gather. Uncle Thomas and his wife took Sara to live with them when Jane died." Dad said Sara for my benefit — in case I wouldn't understand if he said Mother. "She wasn't happy there, mainly because of Aunt Lizzie. She was a discontented, jealous woman; Sara was prettier and worked harder than her own two lazy daughters did when they were at home."

Yes, I remembered that account from Sara, especially when she called herself pretty. It was the truth, but at my early teenage stage you always put yourself down, so her honesty surprised me. "Where did Janet go?"

"To Gomer, I think, Jane's younger brother. But she died a year later, also from the flu. Sara told Janetta and me that the day Lizzie informed her Janet was gone was worse than her mother's death. At least she had her sister to share that with. And for a year she'd had hope of finding her again. What saved her after that was Laura, a baby born late in life to Thomas and Lizzie. Mother was able to swallow her tears when she took care of Laura. She came to think of her as a baby sister until Lizzie's jealousy got in the way. She would wait to have Laura to herself to play games and tell stories."

"What about Uncle Thomas?"

"He was always kind to Sara, but didn't stand a chance against Lizzie, from what I understand. I wish I had paid more attention."

I was thinking the same thing, because I spent a lot of time with Sara growing up. Grandpa died two years after I was born, and I remember her saying that as much as she missed him, nothing would equal the grief she felt from losing her mother and sister. Her words were: "It was so deep it served as an inoculation against all future suffering." Weird how you remember certain phrases.

Sara stayed on in their apartment, not far from our house and even closer to my school. A convenient halfway house when I was a teenager. Mom told her friends that Lew's mother had turned into an eccentric as a widow, but to me she was just the way a grandmother should be. She let me call her Sara because Grandma and Nana were too stodgy for the new age into which I was born and she was reborn. She began consulting psychics, teacup readers, and Ouija boards, much to Mom's alarm. Retha thought her mother-in-law should be beyond searching for the beyond. Sara also started smoking in her sixties, which really bugged Mom. She was afraid it might have the wrong influence on me, but little did Mom know I needed no help. Gail and I and most of our friends were smoking every chance we could get. It was Sara who called me on it, when I stopped in one day reeking of nicotine. "It's a nasty habit, Arabella. Not one thing going for it — health, cost, smell. You've been blessed with a beautiful smile, so why ruin it with yellow teeth? Set yourself a goal: hold off until you're my age and then you can smoke all you want." She got through to me.

Sara talked a lot about her mother and how she wished they had had more time together. Unfortunately, it often did not get past my ears because my brain was filled with more pressing issues, like what to wear to the freshie dance — the slacks that made me too tall or the skirt that made my hips too wide?

"Whatever is good in me came from her," Sara said of Jane Hughes, "but I'm afraid I ended up with a lot of my father." She must have meant her bone structure, for she said he had small, fine features, and her mother had a larger open face with a pronounced chin, and big hands and feet that Dad and I inherited. Otherwise, I could not imagine any of Roland Hughes in Sara, when she described him. He was usually drunk, he was mean, and when his wife took ill with the flu, he did nothing to help. Reading Jane's mention of La Grippe in her letter made me feel odd. Here I sat knowing she would die of it before she did, but after she did die. Where's the before and after in that?

Maybe I had not been totally deaf, because Sara's words started coming back. I now remembered her telling me that when Jane got sick, Roland assigned his two eight-year-old daughters as nursemaids. Sara said it was a task they had undertaken willingly and did not need his accusations that they were lazy. She knew even then his outbursts were from fear, but they hurt just the same. Their brother Llewellyn, ten years older than they were, had already left home. He had lied about his age to join the army. Sara said he would have joined the circus to escape the mines and his father's drunken rages, so the First World War came along at the right time. "Except it was the wrong time," she had added, "because he never did come home. Our brother's life was even shorter and sadder than our mother's."

Funny, how my mind was clearing through the fog of the headache. I recalled being shocked when Sara said she was thankful her mother and brother had died at the same time until she explained that they were connected cosmically now through death as well as birth. As a kid, I liked listening to Sara's theories of reincarnation: that we are surrounded by the same souls in every lifetime, so we should work things out with them during this one. If a husband acted too much like a baby, for example, he might end up as his wife's son next time around until he learned to mature. I had not thought much about it since then, but could now see Sara sitting in her Queen Anne chair, making a steeple of her fingers, as she suggested her tall son — my father — might be her brother. And — with the letter still in my hand — I could hear her saying that I just might possess the spirit of her beloved mother. I would be nearby to usher her out of this existence just as she was there to assist at her mother's departure. She believed it was almost a holy rite for which she was chosen. Janet had gone to an outside pump for fresh water, and their mother called Sara to her bedside. She spoke so softly that Sara had to climb onto the cot. She told her that if she had a son, she should name him Lew, because he was a fine and gentle man with no one to help him at the end. Then her mother squeezed her hand and died with a smile on her face.

For Sara it was the moment she grew up. She was certain Jane had sent Janet out deliberately, so she could be alone with her. When her sister came back and saw Sara sitting next to the bed holding their dead mother's hand, she screamed and dropped the glass of water. Then their father came crashing through the curtain, wailing about his dear wife. Sara said she thought he was going to hit her for letting her mother die, but he crumpled in a sobbing heap at the foot of the cot.

Later Sara insisted that because Jane Hughes said, "he was such a fine and gentle man," she knew her son was already dead, although the news had not reached them yet. She also called him a man for the first time because she was able to see him dying like a man on the battlefield. Sara had heard many stories about dead relatives coming to guide you over to the other side.

I looked up at Dad watching me. "You were named after your uncle Llewellyn?"

"The request from my grandmother's deathbed? Yes, I do know that story."

"Any pictures of him?"

"Not that I know of. In other words, Mother could only remember him as tall, dark, and melancholy. On account of their father, she said. But he was always helpful to his mother. Sara was six when he was shipped overseas." Inching his way to the dining room where his paper and paints covered the table, Dad stopped and said seriously in his teacher's voice: "You know, the influenza pandemic killed more people than any other disease outbreak in human history. More died of the flu than were killed in the First World War. In Canada alone, during one month in 1918, a thousand people died every day, close to 50,000 total. Worldwide estimates are between forty and a hundred million, statistics from other continents being unreliable." He shook his head. "No memorials and very little space given in the history books to such a catastrophe."

It was reassuring to see Dad had not lost his confident, professional manner, so I kept him going. "How did it start?"

"No one is sure, but they do know the mutability of the virus is what made it so deadly. One theory says it started from a pig in China. Does the swine part sound familiar? Probably the one today developed the same way. Flu viruses could be passed from pigs to humans and vice versa. In this case the pig might have contracted a bird flu virus at the same time as it held the human flu virus. Inside the pig, the bird flu strand would humanize, allowing it to keep birdlike features that make it so infectious, yet at the same time acquiring properties that allow it to grow in the lung cells of a human being. No doubt I'm oversimplifying."

That's simplifying? I rolled my eyes to myself, and decided not to ask any more questions.

Silenced, Dad proceeded to his artwork. "Have a look at some of the young Jane Owens' other letters."

I picked up another one dated May 17, 1894. I was hoping for more specific names, but it too was addressed "Dear Brother and Sisters."

I take the pleasure of answering your letter we received last week. Dear Catherine, I don't think you can wish any more to see us than we do to see you. It upset us so much to hear of you being sick. Mama has been more sick than usual for three weeks, keeping to her bed the whole time. She is stronger now but still not well. Gomer has the flu, Tommy has a very bad cold, but work is steady in the mines and he will have 26 shifts this month. Now that I am chief cook and bottle washer, it wouldn't do for me to be sick. I am only troubled at times with catarrh in the head, causing my nose to drip.

My work at one household is hard. The mistress is only two years older than I am and is a common girl from Nanaimo. We were in the same grade at school last year. Her husband is from here too and worked with Tommy until he was somehow made tram boss. Now they think they are royalty and the rest of us are servants. The good part is holding her baby while the nappies are rinsing or when she goes out.

My other customer makes up for working at that place. When he brings his clothes to our house to be washed, he usually leaves apples or peaches or a piece of fresh lamb with us. I often deliver the clean clothes back to his cabin for the sake of a walk in the fresh air. Last week I met his younger son and a daughter at his cabin. They are golden in colour with smiles all over their faces. When you come, I will introduce this dear friend to you.

Tommy sends $20 and more next time. He will roast a bullock for you and I don't know what he isn't going to do. I will make coconut cake, sponge cake, custard and lemon pies. We are expecting a great arrival. Mind to write.

I remain

x x x x x x x x x your loving sister, Jane x x x x x x x x x

In the middle of the letter a wave of grogginess hit me. A warning from headquarters that the ache had not quite run its course and I was to show it some respect by resting. Or was it the word *catarrh* in Jane's letter tickling a gene trail that led from her sinuses to mine. Eerie, seeing your destiny in front of you. I wanted to know more about them. Were Margaret and Catherine the only sisters? Did they live together? The "2" in "$20" had been written in different ink. "Can I take these letters home with me?"

"Take everything." Dad was completely engrossed in the task of drawing a cat pushing a piece of sponge up a staircase. A grey tabby with a bobbed tail that looked a lot like Mister, our first pet. "It's the children's book I'm working on," he said apologetically. "About a cat named Sissipuss." When he saw the reference was lost on me, he added. "I'm going to see if he'll get along with our old friends Cedric the Cockroach and Thump the Butterfly, or if they're too outdated for him. He's a postmodern cat."

My head wasn't up to anything intellectual, so I said, "Thanks for supper. I'll call you tomorrow."

Back at my apartment Drill Sergeant Headache had taken full command of the blood vessels in my head again. Left, throb; right, throb. You win, I muttered, popping two liquid gels and slithering out of my jeans and sweatshirt into a loose nightgown. One more thing before I shut all systems down. I took the picture from home and carried it to my dresser where I had left the other, still in its ugly gold frame. I looked at them together, blinking away the pulsations blurring my vision.

They were a match.

Using a knife, I pried open the rusted prongs holding the frame against the backing and removed the photo. Measured one against the other, they were exactly the same size. If I closed my eyes and mixed them up, I could not tell which was Sara's and which came from the garage sale. No need for forensics to prove these pictures were identical. But I did have need of sleep right now and fell onto my bed, pulling my duvet around me. The letters and pictures stuck behind my eyelids like flyers pasted against a lamppost by the wind.

Who was Jane Owens? Could I read her life between the lines?

✂ ✂ ✂ ✂ ✂

JANE IS NOT SURE WHAT has wakened her so early. Was it the sudden rush of rain on the roof, Mama's moaning in the bed next to her, or Gomer's croupy cough from Tommy's room? In the darkness, she slips from under her warm comforter and shivers at the sting of the cold wooden floor on her bare feet. She pulls on her housecoat and slippers with a cougar's stealth, practised for a year through a sick or sleeping household. She tiptoes to the kitchen, the aroma of yesterday's roast lamb infusing the cool dewy air. Carefully removing the iron cover from the stove, Jane ignites the kindling she laid out last night. The fire will be just right for Tommy's bathwater and breakfast when he comes home from his shift, giving her enough time for a letter. She lights the coal oil lamp at the far end of the table where its glow will not waken the sleepers. At the back of a curtained shelf under a pile of tea towels, Jane keeps her few treasures: the fine vellum paper and fountain pen Cassie gave her as a parting gift, and two sterling silver bangles Mama and Father presented on her confirmation into the Methodist Church when she was twelve. She slides out the pen, a sheet of the paper, and a bottle of ink from the store.

"Dear Brother and Sisters..."

She begins by telling them how much she misses them, though the three sentences she writes cannot possibly explain how much she longs for Cassie's company. Oh, to be back in Wales or have her here with them on Vancouver Island. She misses Margaret and Gilbert too, but they both have families, and she knows Catherine is the one who will snatch her letter from the postman and read it to the others. Margaret will continue what she is doing even while Cassie reads — pickling, sewing, scouring floors, or scolding her two young children Gwynyth and Evan. She is like Tommy, always busy, not the kind to sit down and talk the way Catherine does. Jane could tell Cassie what she cannot tell Mama because she is too occupied with her sickness; or Tommy because he is always too tired from the mine or from fixing the house and saves his few words for friends at the Whistle Stop; or ten-year-old Gomer, who is too young to talk to about anything except to mind his manners.

Families belong together, Jane is about to write, as she listens to the crackling swoosh of kindling burning down. She waits for the fire to settle into a gentle whisper before rising to touch the kettle to make sure she filled it the night before. Back at the letter, Mama's voice enters her head and she hesitates. Mama gets impatient whenever she complains of being so far from the others. "You stir up discontent with that kind of talk. There are so many worse off than we are." She uses the Monmouths back in Wales as an example. Mr. Monmouth lost both legs in a mine accident, and Mrs. Monmouth has to look after him as well as two children without normal brains who can't walk or talk and have to be fed. Some sickness in the family that gets passed on. And all without money. That is true bad luck, Mama says.

Jane tries to remember the Monmouths whenever she thinks about her own father and Margaret's husband being killed in the same mine explosion, forcing her two older brothers, each in a different country, to look after the rest of the family.

It happened so fast. Mama, Jane, and Gomer were suddenly on a ship to Canada last year to set up housekeeping for Tommy on Vancouver Island so he could provide for them. And back in Wales, Gilbert and his family shared his meagre wages with Catherine and Margaret and her two children. At least Margaret was able to keep her own little mine cottage where there was room for Catherine. Margaret's fine sewing brings in a little more now, and Cassie started teaching children in first standard, so that will help. Who would have counted on Mama taking ill with a lung ailment on the boat and hardly having a day of strength since? They have to be thankful both voyages to British Columbia, their own and Tommy's five years earlier, had taken place after the completion of the Canadian Pacific Railway through the country.

Before 1885, Tommy told them, men would spend six months on a ship going around the tip of South America to get from Britain to the west coast. How would Mama have managed more than the two and a half weeks their journey took? Hard as the wooden benches in the train cars were, she felt less sick from the motion on rails than on waves.

"'Tis the shock of all that's happened causing Mama's illness," Cassie wrote, but Jane is still trying to figure it out.

She tries so hard not to complain that tears squeeze out of her eyes from the effort. What can she write? She tells Cassie that today she will go to Cruikshanks to do laundry. But will she say that Stella will probably ask her to make two or three pies; that she will leave Jane to mind her new baby when she goes to the fire boss' house for tea; and that she will snatch the baby from her when she comes back, because she thinks Jane is getting too close to him? And she cannot tell that Stella has become so high and mighty she even puts her own underwear in for Jane to wash. For which of them is that a greater disgrace? She will write that Stella is only two years older than she is and that they were in school together last fall in Chase River. Can she add that they were both in the same grade, because Stella was repeating and Jane had been put forward after the first week when the teacher saw her skills and ability? Those things make her sisters and brother proud of her schooling in Wales. No, she cannot worry them in every letter about how much she misses school.

She can still feel the way her stomach twisted the day Mama said, "Things are getting left undone at home." She knew what it meant. If only she did not have the long walk to and from school every day, she would have more time for her chores. For a while she got up in the dead of night to bake pies and make soup, and have Tommy's meal ready to warm up when he came home from the mine. She even managed to wash clothes quietly at the same time, boiling white laundry in kerosene cans on the stove, while using a washboard in a galvanized tub for the pit suits outside in the dark. But the extra coal needed to heat the stove so early went beyond Tommy's quota, so that was that.

Jane never did tell her sisters or anyone else about her last day. How Stella left at the same time, gleeful because she was with child, knowing

Lance Cruikshank would marry her and that would mean the end of school forever. Through Stella's giggles, Jane had to fight back tears because school was her favourite place in Canada so far. She was top student in all subjects and dreamed of becoming a teacher herself some day. In the classroom she lived in a different world, away from scrubbing coal dust from stiff work clothes until her fingers bled. When she carried out her books on the final day with her stomach bilious, she felt fifty years old instead of fifteen. The teacher, Miss Maasanen, almost cried herself when she gave Jane a copy of *Tess of the D'Urbervilles* because she knew how much she liked to read. Looking back, she is thankful she did not also know on that unhappy day that she would soon be washing clothes for the girl cackling in front of her.

Her sisters and brother have enough to worry about without her whining, so she will tell them instead about Mr. Louis Strong. Yesterday he brought them another piece of lamb along with his laundry. The lamb comes from Henry "Butch" Hargraves, whose cabin and meat sheds Jane passes on the way to Louis' place. Jane does not like the way he looks at her, but Louis seems friendly with him, so she always says "Good day" before hurrying on. When Louis pays for her services, he always compliments her on the fine way she presses his clothes with the flatiron and folds them neatly. This makes her smile because it does not take much to smooth out overalls and iron sheets and a few flannel shirts. What a difference between a farmer's and a miner's clothes, especially a farmer as careful and orderly as Louis Strong, who spends his days among fruit trees.

She could tell them how she has never heard an accent like Mr. Strong's — soft and easy, from the southern United States. Maybe when both families save enough to bring Cassie over to live with them, she will have enough time to tell her all about Louis Strong's life. How he was a slave, even though his father was the white plantation owner. How he bought his freedom twice and still was not allowed to leave. How he finally fled to California only to learn Negroes were not welcome there, any more than they had been in Mississippi or Tennessee. (An excellent speller, Jane likes writing those words with their clusters of double letters, so she might have to include this information before she sees Cassie in person.) Mr. Strong told her that Governor James Douglas, a mulatto himself born in a South American country called British Guiana, invited Negroes to come and settle in his new colony of British Columbia, so that's how he and his family ended up here. He had bought some land on Vancouver Island a few years ago to experiment with apple trees, to continue grafting various strains. But he did not want to give up the other farm and cattle he owned on Salt Spring Island, so his sons Maynard and Adam stayed behind with their mother to run it. His daughter Ruby is a schoolteacher in the Cedar district, not far from Chase River.

Jane pulls all of this out of him with questions, when she delivers his clothes to him. By nature, he is a quiet man who does not like to talk about himself. His cabin has become the schoolroom she misses so much, where she can dwell in visions from realms other than her own. She grieves to think of him as a young lad wearing only one garment for night and day, sleeping on a straw mattress on a dirt floor in a shack with rags for covers. One pot of stew set in the middle of the floor fed all the children, eating from their knees. In fact, whenever Mama mentions the Monmouths now, Jane thinks of the young Louis Strong instead. And she no longer takes her family's covers for granted; they are quilts that Mama and Margaret sewed back in Wales, threadbare now in places, but more than adequate to keep everybody warm. Probably Margaret and Catherine are stitching new counterpanes at this very moment to replace the ones sent to Canada. Jane lifts her pen from the paper and can almost hear her older sister scolding Cassie to stay at her task and stop daydreaming so much or playing with Gwynyth and Evan.

A snort from Gomer reminds Jane it is time to move him from Tommy's bedroom to the couch. Bundled in blankets, he wheezes as she guides him, still asleep, the few steps to the front room. When Tommy finishes the two small bedrooms he plans to add, Gomer and Jane will each have a sleeping space. She would gladly share hers with Cassie, as she did in Wales. On her way back to the letter, Jane checks to make sure Mama is still sleeping. And as if someone else might be looking over her shoulder, she swivels her head before writing: *Last week I met* his younger son and his daughter at his cabin. They are golden in colour with smiles all over their faces. She could never record that she spent half an hour alone in the company of Louis' son Adam after Ruby rode her horse back to her schoolhouse. Even putting his name on paper feels bold, and she omits it.

Jane cannot reveal that she considers Adam Strong to be the most beautiful boy she has ever laid eyes on. Standing next to him in Louis' yard caused all kinds of sensations she has never felt before: pounding heart, light head, and gibberish coming out of her mouth. At eighteen, he is almost three years older than Jane, who will be sixteen in December. She once met Mrs. Strong when she came over to help her husband make apple cider; Adam is not as dark as his mother but darker than his father who carries the imprint of his own white father. Louis, in fact, could almost pass for someone of Spanish or Greek descent, though he would never have tried such a thing in the United States. She thinks of Adam's shade in terms of the old dressers and tables Tommy picks up from other miners, then sands and revarnishes to a gleaming finish. Light oak is the colour of Adam's face in the sun; his neck, polished maple, and his arms, a rich mahogany. He seems as strong and still as an oak himself, just like his father, whom he shows respect and affection at all times. He works hard tending his parents' cattle and farm, because his older brother comes to Salt Spring Island only on his time off from prospecting for gold on the Skeena River in the north. With Maynard away so much, Adam has become the one his mother depends on. Jane smiles to think of Gomer taking on such a load when he cannot yet build a proper fire in the stove. All this she will tell Catherine when they are finally together again. For now she closes with kisses, inserts from a can on the shelf the $10 bill Tommy has instructed her to send, and seals the letter in an envelope.

The sun has begun to break through the morning's haze, and Jane fills an enamelled basin with water now heated in the kettle. In the scullery off the kitchen, she slips quickly out of her robe and nightgown and washes her strong young body, gooseflesh rising from the cold air not insulated by the blanket curtain. Two freshly cured hams and a slab of bacon hang from the ceiling; Tommy gets their pork from a fellow miner—not from Henry Hargraves, to Jane's relief. Back home, their father did the curing, and Mama kept chickens whose necks she wrung herself. That is all past.

She pulls a shimmy over her head, then a white blouse, and steps into a petticoat and a grey woollen skirt, all warming in a bundle next to the stove. As she fastens her lisle stockings to her garter belt, she notes the grease tins are full. Time to make more soap. On the way home she will stop at the store for lye. She leaves the curtain open to insure warmth for Tommy's bath, stuffs her feet into Gomer's boots, and flings a cloak over her shoulders. She exits quietly, two empty pails in one hand, a chamber pot in the other. After a brief stop at the privy, she steps quickly down a lane to a pump shared by a cluster of dwellings.

Tommy did well claiming this parcel of land. Lush with alder, poplar, maple, pine, and hawthorn trees, their large lot slopes gently down to the Chase River flowing through the bottom corner. Sometimes she thinks of the fugitive native murderer in his canoe, whose chase years ago by Hudson's Bay Company scouts gave this sparkling stream its name.

Tommy had rented a small shack on his own until just before his family arrived, when he purchased a larger one for $50 to move here from the declining Wellington mine. Mama contributed her small compensation from Wales for furniture and housekeeping. Many miners rent company cottages, partly due to the greed of the owners, but also because homes can become worthless if the mine dries up, unless they are moved to a new site. Tommy believes they are well located in Chase River. If his work at the No. 1 Nanaimo mine ceases, he can sell or move their home again. He learned the value of owning and maintaining property, no matter how modest, from their father. Even their outside cedar shingles are weathering evenly, in contrast to the unsightly bleeding wood on some of the smaller, shabbier cottages built or rented by others around them—mainly Finnish farmers and miners.

Jane sees Gertie Salo turn into one of those cottages now with full pails. She is relieved to be spared stories of school at the pump from her former slow-moving classmate. Complaints about the studies she craves. The mine whistle jolts her into a quicker pace, still careful to keep the water from overflowing. Back in the warm house, she fills oil cans with water to boil for Tommy's bath and scoops lard from a tin into a cast iron frying pan. Mama sneezes from the bedroom.

"Thomas home?" she calls in a weak voice.

"Not yet," Jane says, looking in on her mother propped up on pillows. She is a small woman whose curly black hair has turned a steely grey since her arrival in Canada and now matches her eyes. Her skin bears a hectic flush, but is surprisingly firm, especially on her arms and neck, considering she has not had the benefit of much fresh air and exercise. "I've started his meal. How are you feeling?"

"Could be better. Water boiled yet?"

"I'll bring your tea just now." Gomer coughs and shifts on the couch as Jane stops to pull the blankets over his shoulders.

"Hakie," he mutters through a crusty nose and parched mouth.

Jane takes a handkerchief from her skirt pocket, checking to see that it is clean before exchanging it for a wadded-up cloth, which she drops into a pail of cold water. She postpones the thought that in an hour or so she will be rinsing out Lance Cruikshank's slimy handkerchiefs in a similar pail, then boiling them on the stove. At the sound of the mine train whistle at the Chase River stop, she hurries to fill the galvanized tub in the scullery with hot and cold water. By the time she has added strips of roast lamb, cold potatoes, and onions to the hot grease in the frying pan, her brother's heavy steps sound on the path.

Soot-faced, Tommy enters wearily, discards his boots and tosses his lunch pail next to them. On the way to his bath he passes behind Jane drizzling beaten eggs through the hash, which she will dish onto a plate at the sound of his coal-stiff clothes dropping to the floor. A scrubbed Tommy emerges from the washroom, more ready to sleep than to eat. He never speaks until he has completed this ritual, and sometimes not until after his meal. Or sometimes not at all.

Jane spoons out a small plate for herself and takes the chair across the table from her brother. He is tall and, she thinks, quite handsome, but too shy and retiring to encourage anyone to look at him for long. When he left Wales for Canada five years ago, she remembers him boarding the ship in Cardiff, his greatcoat so large only his head protruded from it — no hands and just the ends of his feet. His hair was sandy-coloured then and now it is dark. She is not sure if it has been dyed permanently with coal dust or if it is just the natural deepening of colour almost everyone in her family experiences. She glances at Gomer's tousled head, still blonde but once white. She alone was born with the same brown hair she has now. When Tommy pushes his empty plate to the side, Jane sets a dish of preserved plums and a mug of tea in front of him.

"Shift go well?" She takes a sip of tea.

"Nobody killed."

"You off for a while."

"Sunday noon."

"Going to the dance tonight?"

"Might. Rollie wants to go."

Tommy's friend Roland Hughes often ends up at their house. He lives with his father, a moody, mean man, and admits he likes being in a house run by women. Jane welcomes Roland only because he is more talkative than Tommy, and she gains news about people in the mine and Chase River. But he drinks too much and she is certain he will end up like his father. "Stella is sure to go on about what she's wearing when I get there."

"If Lance takes her."

"What do you mean?"

Tommy glances at his young sister protectively. "Lance sometimes talks as if he's single."

Jane stifles her surprise so Tommy will not think she's too innocent and stop talking. "How can people become so different because of a new position? Stella told me herself his uncle got it for him."

Tommy pushes his chair back from the table, nodding. "Not so long ago he was a mucker, cleaning up while our crew laid timbers, and complaining about all the orders. Now he gives more as tram boss than he ever took."

Jane likes to see her brother smile, a triumph that often comes from speaking two or three sentences at once. She loves the soft cadence of Glamorganshire he tries so hard to lose. Whenever their mother speaks in Welsh, he answers in English, so Mama has stopped. Tommy possesses the sweetest voice in the family and, like Papa and Gilbert, has a whole choir in his throat when he sings. Even Gomer is developing a fine singing voice, more the pity he won't have church to practise it the way the rest of them had back home. Mama's illness has robbed them of many traditions. As for Jane, Mama says her voice is too full of shrill curiosity to be musical, but she does love to sing to Stella's wee baby when she is alone with him.

"Da bore, Thomas. Time for another cup of tea with your mother? And a slice of bara brith."

Mama shuffles from the bedroom, wrapping her dressing gown snugly around her. She sits down on the chair Jane vacates to make porridge. Jane has noticed Mama regains her health most in the presence of her oldest son. Tommy, who had risen to retreat to his bed warmed by his little brother, sits back down and pours himself more tea. Gomer, draped in his bedcovers, struggles from the couch to join them at the table. His voice is thick. "Dno porridge for bme."

Jane serves two bowls, along with the current bread requested, and leaves her little brother for her mother to discipline for a change. From the cloak cupboard she takes a long green woollen cape and umbrella. "I'll be back whenever Stella's through with me," she says, then remembers the letter to post on the cupboard. "I wrote to the others."

"Again?" says Mama. "You just wrote last week."

"If it's not sealed, here's another ten dollars t'ward Catherine's passage," says Tommy, pulling a bill out of his shirt pocket.

Jane's heart leaps at the prospect. She rushes outside for a welcome gulp of fresh air and rain on the short trail between workplaces. She will correct the amount in the letter at the post office.

✂ ✂ ✂ ✂ ✂ ✂

BETWEEN THE FIFTH AND SIXTH BLASTS, the foghorn on the Departure Bay ferry turned into my alarm clock. Or maybe it was the fifth or sixth snooze button. I was not aware of the alarm buzzing until my dark bedroom swallowed up Uncle Lawrence standing on the dock; he was still looking sad because we did not stay for supper. Cold toes told me I was badly swaddled in my quilt. I raised my head slowly, then sat up carefully. Nothing. I jumped to my feet. Hallelujah. The disappearance of a headache almost made that skull rattling worthwhile in the first place. Almost.

When I turned on the light, I saw the identical pictures of Janet and Sara on the night table. But the clock next to them said half an hour to briefing, so I yanked on my jeans and sweatshirt from the floor and grabbed my pants and last ironed shirt from the closet. I'd take a quick shower at work. Times like this made me thankful I had a short haircut that required no curling iron or gel. I used the rails of the staircase to the underground parking lot to propel me downward four steps at a time.

At the detachment, I was showered and in my uniform in record time and almost crashed into Emile entering the briefing room. He handed me the cup of coffee in his hand. "You look as if you need this more than I do."

Our corporal asked if I was feeling better, and I nodded.

"Well enough for a stakeout?"

I nodded again.

"Put your jeans back on. There's a video store off Boundary we suspect is a fence for a convenience store in Coquitlam. Hang around and see what you can come up with. Sukhi will go with you."

Sukhi smiled, cool and organized already in his plain clothes. We had a couple of hours before the video store opened so once I'd changed, I suggested we get some breakfast. I was so ravenous, Sukhi wondered if I were the same person he had eaten with yesterday. Had only twenty-four hours passed since then? I felt as if I'd been thrown into a cauldron containing Ray, Retha, Wanda, Terry, and Jane Owens, then agitated on one of those paint-stirring machines. Dad was the only one who had not shaken me up.

When we got back to the car, we had a call to go to a supermarket. We still had time before the stakeout, so we pulled into the parking lot in our unmarked car. It was a monster food store, the kind thieves like best. Especially when no loss preventions officer was on duty and they knew it. We talked to the manager in bulk foods, while Sukhi scooped out a bag of chickpeas. They had their eye on a man who had been coming in twice a day recently. He was a young Vietnamese, spotted by a Vietnamese employee who had a hunch about what he was doing but did not want to confront him without grounds. We agreed to our roles.

At the moment, the suspect was filling his cart in the canned vegetable section. Sukhi pushed his cart casually behind him. I lingered at the other end of the aisle. He moved along toward me and we both reached for the sesame rice crackers at the same time, his hand pulling away politely until I had taken my package. From there he pushed his full cart to the express checkout counter at the far end without giving any of the closer cashiers a glance. I followed at a distance to where Sukhi was already browsing through a magazine rack at the checkout. The man's back was to us during this transaction, which was much too brief for so many items. From the other direction, the manager approached and nodded at me. Sukhi followed our man through the automatic doors and I caught up in the parking lot. I hung back, within earshot, when Sukhi confronted him at his own car.

"Do you have receipts for these goods, sir?"

"Right here." The man held two bills in one hand like playing cards. "This for the big order — you see, mushroom soup, rice, tuna fish." He pointed meticulously to each item, then to the first bill. "See date." He waved the second bill. "This for crackers only. I forget crackers and go back. I show cashier first bill."

Sukhi took the bills from him. "The date might be right, but you had your thumb over the time. You bought your first big order two hours ago and I'll bet it's in your trunk. You thought you could get away with a duplicate set of free items using the same receipt." When four more bags of groceries were discovered under a blanket in the trunk, Sukhi asked: "And where are the receipts for all this?"

I stepped forward, as the man dug nervously in his pocket for the non-existent bills. "Here somewhere," he kept repeating.

The manager arrived as I cuffed him and guided him into the back of our car. "Pretty nice scam you had going for a while." He pushed the cart with the stolen goods back to the store.

"Where do you sell your stuff?" Sukhi asked on the way back to the station. "Who's your fence?" The man retreated into silence, pretending he didn't understand a word we said. We left him in a holding cell and headed back out on our main file.

The video store was part of a little strip mall that housed a copy shop, a dry cleaner, and a Vietnamese takeout restaurant. From a glance through the windows, I figured the tenants were probably all Vietnamese, including the man we were watching. Sukhi picked up two coffees from the takeout place and we cruised around the block once. We saw a woman dressed in a business suit go in and out quickly, a man in a bus driver's uniform drop off a pile of DVDs, and three teenage boys in baggy pants and baseball caps spend half an hour inside before bouncing out with an armload of movies. No one suspicious yet. I was getting hungry again. I had not brought my usual sandwiches due to my late rising, and much as I tried to avoid the extravagance of buying two meals, I would need something soon to prevent the headache's return. I told Sukhi so and he stared into space.

"Do you mind — listening?" I asked sarcastically.

"Look."

A scruffy-looking guy with a plastic bag in his hand was pacing around the traffic light across the intersection. He was watching the video store. Just as another car pulled up in front of it, he lit a cigarette and changed direction. A few stores down the street he turned around, saw the car leave the video store, and started back toward the intersection. He crossed this time — quickly, I'd say, considering how he had been sauntering back and forth on the corner.

"Feel like a movie?" Sukhi asked, and I was out of the car in time to reach the entrance right behind the fellow. He eyed me nervously, but I gave him a convincing look of indifference and headed straight for the Comedy section. He went to New Release DVDs. The man behind the counter was aware of us both, but did not look up from the computer. I moved to New Releases and for a few seconds we pulled movies off the shelves together. I recognized the shaking hands of an addict, the right missing its index finger, causing his cigarette to tremble between the middle two.

I would give him his chance. I walked behind him and busied myself in the sale bin, the corner farthest from the counter. My back was to both men as Sukhi walked past the front window with another cup of coffee from the restaurant. I winked. My peripheral vision was well-developed, and while I studied the selection, I could see the guy make his way to the counter. He had two DVDs in one hand and the bag in the other. The owner, or whoever he was, opened the bag without looking at the man. He reached under the counter and handed him some cash, at the same time slipping the plastic bag out of sight. The man turned quickly to leave, the DVDs now the only items left on the counter. I stepped in front of him at the door and showed him my badge. Sukhi came in.

"What just happened here?" I asked.

"What do you mean?" He reached to scratch his nose with his whole hand, which shook now more than ever.

I knew he had been through this ritual a lot, and he knew that I knew. We still had to say our parts as if they had been scripted.

"What did you sell him?"

"I don't know what you're talking about."

"What's your name?"

"Steve Rutherford."

Something so humbling about confessing your name at a time like this. As if it's all you've got left and you're surrendering it. Rutherford was a refined English name. I had a vision of him saying both names shyly to his kindergarten teacher, and running home in short pants to Mrs. Rutherford with a crayon picture he had drawn. Full of pride and promise. How did he get from there to here?

The man at the counter called out in a heavy accent: "Your bag. You forget your bag." Steve did not know where to look, so he stared at the floor.

"How about the DVDs? He forgot those too," said Sukhi, walking to the counter and taking the bag from the man waving it. He looked inside, then handed it to me. Three baseball caps with Vancouver stitched on them, six cans of Fancy Feast, four packages of Hamburger Helper.

"How much did he pay you for this junk?"

"Nothing. I forgot it, just like he says."

"You must have receipts for it then, if it's your bag."

"It's not really my bag," Steve sighed. "I mean it is now, but I found it in the park over there. Was sitting on the bench having a smoke when kids came running out from behind the bushes. Later when I went into the bushes to take a leak, I found this bag on the ground."

"Give me a break," I said.

"Honest."

"But what brings you to a video store with this bag of treasures?" Sukhi asked. "How much did he give you for it? Five? Ten at most?"

"Nothing. He didn't give me nothing."

"How much cash you got on you?"

Steve took a ten-dollar bill from his pocket. "I had this when I came in."

Sukhi turned on the other man and established he was the manager. "Where's your store?"

"Right here is my store."

"Your convenience store? Where you take all this stolen stuff to sell? We've got a friend of yours at the station. I think he's ready to tell us where your store is. Coquitlam ring a bell?"

I watched the man's face for telltale signals. None. Steve would probably tell us everything he knew when we got him to the station, but it wouldn't be much. We hung the Closed sign on the front door and led them both to the car in handcuffs as curious eyes from the other shops in the strip mall looked away. The Plexiglas partition — our silent patrolman — was hardly necessary. The two men sat separate and quiet in the back seat, one unreadable, the other hopeless. My stomach growled and churned. Sometimes my job made me sick.

At the station, we left Steve in a holding cell and took our two Vietnamese for questioning. It turned out they were cousins. No help from them, of course, just a hunch of Sukhi's. The same last name did not mean too much since it was a common one in Vietnam, according to one of our members who was born there. We dug into the computer a little deeper and found immigration information, including the fact that they had the same grandparents. Their Uncle Tan did own a convenience store in Coquitlam and used his brothers' sons to round up inventory for him. He had already been charged once with no conviction.

While they were vigourously denying any connection to each other, I was the only one who thought they might be telling the truth. Even if they were cousins, it seemed possible to me they didn't know it. The old uncle could easily have kept these young immigrants in the dark to prevent them from uniting against him. But when I heard them later laughing like brothers, I was glad I had not spoken up. The guys at work welcomed every chance they got to call me naïve.

I used the rest of the day for reports to Crown Counsel, sustaining myself on a bagel and cream cheese and dreaming about the steak in my fridge. Within half an hour of getting home, I would have a baked potato, broiled steak, and salad. My shift finally over, I hurried to the locker room to lock up my gun. On the way, I noticed the date on the wall. The same date I had been writing on reports all day.

Wednesday. My history class.

I barely had time to get there. I had left my notebook in the car, useful now, though not so useful for studying. The steak went on the back burner, so to speak, and I slapped the steering wheel as I made an abrupt turn into a McDonald's drive-thru. Poor organization, Arabella. Retha's voice was so strong in my head that I didn't hear the voice on the other side of the drive-thru speaker until she repeated herself.

I gobbled down the last of my French fries order just as I pulled into the college parking lot.

Barnwell was at his lectern when I dashed in. My young friend from the first class was grinning. Not to sit next to him would be bad manners.

Barnwell started: "Having discussed some of our First Nations in this province, I would like to talk about the immigrant groups who made British Columbia their home."

My neighbour had his pen to paper before I could wrestle mine from my purse and turn my notebook to the right page. Barnwell's strong voice spun around me like a CD before it hits its first cut. I tuned in at "Welsh coal miners on Vancouver Island" and immediately thought of Jane Owens and her brother Thomas, and everybody sick in that house she so desperately wanted to fill with more family from Wales. Barnwell spoke of the Douglas seam of coal, which was discovered by an Indian chief and was responsible for enticing European settlers to Nanaimo. James Douglas arranged for the purchase of twelve miles of waterfront land in exchange for 688 blankets. Not long after that, he left the Hudson's Bay Company to become governor of the Crown Colony of British Columbia and Vancouver Island.

"Douglas' mixed heritage is sometimes forgotten," Barnwell went on. "His mother was a Creole woman from British Guiana, his father a Scotsman who had gone down to run a sugar plantation there. When he returned to marry a Scottish wife, his father sent for him to be educated in Scotland. Young James set off for Canada at the age of sixteen to work for a colonial company, ironically following in his father's footsteps. He was tall, rugged, and fearless, perfectly suited to our inhospitable landscape. Like his father, he mated with a native woman, legally this time."

I glanced at my neighbour and wondered if he and everyone else in the room were thinking about his colour and size at the mention of James Douglas.

"Sir James Douglas' leadership often verged on autocracy," Barnwell continued, "but he was probably the only man capable of holding the Crown Colony against an American takeover. Especially once word got around that there was gold in the area. To replace the scant population of Fort Victoria men who had gone prospecting on the mainland, he invited the Negro community of San Francisco — and I use the politically correct parlance of those times — to settle on Vancouver Island. Even freed slaves had been denied citizenship in the United States and would not be loyal to that country."

Jane's Negro gentleman. I wondered if the warm flush on the back of my neck was as visible as the flush on my neighbour's face. I had never really thought about personal letters as part of history. History came from museums, from libraries, from someone sitting in dusty rooms going through yellowed newspaper clippings, documents, and letters of people who were already historical figures. How could Sir James Douglas be connected to my great-grandmother writing heartsick letters back home to her family? Or to this guy sitting next to me who might be thinking the same thing about his ancestors? Maybe I should quit daydreaming and take some notes. I had only asked him to share his with me if I was absent, after all.

Barnwell had moved on to the Chinese workers, who suffered even more from the white man's prejudice. "These immigrants continued to work harder and longer in the mines and on the land for less pay. In 1887, the famed Number One coal mine exploded in Nanaimo. One hundred and fifty men perished, and close to half were Chinese. Their casualties were listed by number, not by name. They carried on with their burden like Sisyphus."

My pen lifted on the word. I had written Sissipuss. I smiled, thinking of Dad. This history class was teaching me more than I bargained for. But not enough. Sisyphus had ended the lecture, and Barnwell was now passing out sheets with term paper topics on them. I cringed at them all. Indians and Explorers; The Contribution of Sir James Douglas; Chinese or Black Immigration in the 19th Century; American Influence on the Crown Colony; Effects of the Gold Rush.

"Which will you do?" My neighbour asked.

"No idea. How about you?"

"The immigration one sounds interesting. Maybe because it's fresh today."

I nodded. My notebook was still open, so it was worth a try. "By the way, how do you spell the man with the burden? S — ?"

"S-i-s-y-p-h-u-s. Strange, Barnwell should mention him. My classics prof was just talking about him last week."

And? Come on.

"Imagine rolling that rock to the top of the mountain all your life just to have it roll down and you start over."

Thank you! Now I wouldn't have to ask Dad. I might even test Emile with it. I was so engrossed in these thoughts I did not hear "Are you on duty tonight?" until he repeated it.

"No, I just finished my shift."

"Are you in the ER?"

I hesitated, until he said, "You probably get asked that a lot."

I was thankful he had reminded me of my lie, but not so thankful I had told it in the first place. "Yeah, I'm sort of in triage — sending people where they're meant to go."

"Care to have a coffee?"

I thought of the steak at home, my stomach rumbling. "Sure, why not."

He told me his name was Crane Reese as we crossed the street to Starbucks. Something about the way he pulled out my chair automatically made me think this guy was genuinely gallant. Had I become too conditioned to men in uniforms and lawyers' suits to spot a gentle soul? He ordered a regular coffee and I asked for a frappuccino topped with whipped cream and chocolate. I was hungry, not thirsty. "You a full-time student?"

"Pretty much. I'd like to get into filmmaking some day. In the meantime, I work as a movie extra to support my lavish lifestyle." He smiled big, treating me to a mouthful of the most glistening teeth I had ever seen.

"Is there enough work?"

"Plenty. There are lots of career extras out there. Much of it is standing around, but it's okay when you're paid and fed for it."

"Very interesting," I said, truthfully. I had never met a movie extra. They must be law-abiding citizens. Then I asked, "Where are you from?" and immediately regretted the implication that he had to be foreign.

"Born and raised in Vancouver. Supposedly some of my relatives came from Salt Spring Island, part of that scene Barnwell was talking about today. Maybe I could do a family tree as my term paper."

"You too? My ancestors were Welsh coal miners there, but there's not a topic on them."

"Barnwell will let you do what you want, if you talk to him."

"I'll think about it." The mocha had made my appetite for solid food worse, and after some exit chat I stood up and said I had to get going.

He insisted on paying the bill, despite my protests at having consumed the glutton's share. He walked me to my car. "See you next Wednesday. Unless you're stitching somebody up."

As I drove away, I decided there was no reason why I should continue this charade, because the longer I kept it up, the harder it would be to backtrack. Then again, in three months I would never see this guy again, so it really did not matter what he thought I did for a living.

My impatience to eat caused me to undercook both steak and baked potato, so the whole supper was a letdown. I wondered what I would have done with the potato in pre-microwave days when I was this hungry, but, as Dad liked to say, that was purely academic. Or he would have said: in other words, that was purely academic. For a change, I did not turn on the TV. I slipped into my sleep shirt and settled on the bed under my quilt with the box of Jane Owens' letters on my lap.

✂ ✂ ✂ ✂ ✂ ✂ ✂

"ONLY DON'T FORGET TO SAIL, BACK AGAIN TO ME."
Jane stops singing, thinking little Norman is asleep, but then his eyes
open for more. "Baby's boat a silver moon, sailing in the sky." She continues stroking him with her soft voice and fingers until she knows for
sure he is in dreamland. She tiptoes away from the crib, eager now to
finish the lunch dishes. At the sound of the back door opening and
closing, she stops. It is a loud slam, not Stella's quick entry. Two male
voices accompany feet stomping across the kitchen floor.

Glasses clink. "I'll get us a drink."

Jane freezes on the spot. Lance is home? In the middle of the afternoon?

"Your wife here?" A distinct Irish brogue.

"She took the baby to Thurstons for a tea party. How do you like
this? I can't even find a clean glass. Goes out and leaves dirty dishes in
the sink. First one there, last to leave. Stupid bitch."

The bedroom door is slightly ajar and Jane eases herself behind
it. She says three prayers: that the baby will not wake, that Lance will
have no cause to come into the bedroom, that she can suspend all
breath and movement in her body for the length of the men's drinking session. Stella told her Lance must never know she leaves Norman with her sometimes. He believes a mother's place is with her
child and that place is in the home. Jane loves having the house and
baby to herself and does not advise her employer otherwise. Not that
she would share any of her true thoughts with Stella anyway, though
after hearing how her husband speaks about her, she feels less harsh
in her opinion.

Chairs scrape the floor. "Whoa, that's enough, Lance. We've got a shift to finish."

"Too many ears there. I heard some news today." Pause. "New seam's been found."

"That's nothing new."

"True this time. Very reliable sources, if you know what I mean."

Jane supposes the other man's silence is breathlessness.

"Mount Benson," Lance goes on. "Southern slope."

A low whistle. "Who's going to get it?"

"We are. If we can keep it to ourselves, you know what I mean."

Jane understands why the other man is doing more sighing, blowing, and whistling than talking. She has heard Roland Hughes talk to Tommy about the Mackie mines. The Wellington pits are showing signs of being worked out. The rich coal seams that brought miners to Vancouver Island from all over are nearing exhaustion, and their jobs could be gone within a year or two. Roland always tells Tommy that Mackie is such a smart businessman he will have something for them once these pits are finished, but Tommy never seems convinced. If what she is hearing now is true, her judgment of Roland will have to go up a notch. A small one.

"Hargraves found it. Fallen tree with coal clinging to it. Good thing he knows an outcropping when he sees it. Someone else might have left it for grass to grow over again. Another drink?"

"I'd say so. News this big needs washing down. Whose land?"

Jane's nose starts dripping. Her handkerchief has fallen from her apron out of reach under the crib and she must use the hem of her skirt.

"Now that's the problem. The land belongs to an ex-slave called Strong. He's got two farms, one on Salt Spring Island and an orchard right on top of our new coal mine. They're saying Mackie himself talked to him, and he's not interested in selling. Says he spent a lot of time breeding the fruit trees he's got growing there. Says it's all he's got to leave for his family." Lance curses under his breath. "How about our families? Who'll take care of them when we're out of work?"

Jane stiffens. The tone of Lance's voice adds nausea to the area enclosing her pumping heart. She imagines him grinning, his teeth slanting backward like a shark.

"Does he know the value?"

"No one knows for sure, but it's the best thing Mackie's seen since he opened up the Wellington seams, I hear. Even better, it's close to the railroad."

The Irishman whistles again just as the baby rolls over in his crib. He lifts his head and looks around. Afraid to take a step on the creaky floorboards, Jane reaches toward him, mouthing her hushes. His father's voice from the kitchen turns out to have a soothing effect and his head drops back on his blanket, eyes firmly shut. Jane wants to drop to her knees in thanks, but Lance's words are too compelling for her to move a muscle.

"Hargraves knows this Strong. Got a cabin he uses for butchering close to the fellow and they sometimes hunt wild boar together. Both keep sheep. He was getting firewood from Strong's property when he discovered the coal. Told Mackie not to worry, that he'll be able to persuade the darkie to sell. He's already bragging about what's in it for him. Not a word to anyone, you understand."

"I don't know a thing."

"Better get back." Scraping chairs are followed by another sound of glass breaking. "Let her cut her hand when she finally cleans this place up."

Jane still cannot move, even once the back door has slammed and the men's voices and footsteps on the path disappear. Gradually, the paralysis seeps out of her and she walks softly to the kitchen. She sees the broken tumbler and throws the pieces away before filling a basin with water and soap. How does a man speak so cruelly of his wife, even one as silly as Stella? As if to remind her, Stella hastens through the back door just then, giggling like a tardy child. She is pleased with herself for having been included once again in a party with women she believes to be important. She recounts a story of how two fine china teacups were put with the wrong saucers, and she was the first one to notice it. Jane stops Stella's giggling by telling her Lance was home.

Stella freezes, as she stares at the dishes Jane is just finishing.

"The baby and I kept quiet in the bedroom," Jane says quietly, watching her face release some of its fear. "He thought you had taken Norman with you and never did find out I was here."

Stella's shoulders remain rigid. "Why was he here?"

Jane shrugs. "He had another man with him. I think they had a drink. The bedroom door was closed so I couldn't hear much." She mumbles, as much to cover up the event for herself as for Stella. She unties her apron, stuffs it in her cloth satchel. "He might tell you why."

"He'll tell me something, all right. You hadn't done the dishes when they came in?" Her voice begins to rise in accusation until a sharp glance from Jane causes her to look down guiltily. When she raises her eyes, they plead not to be left alone. But Jane has her long cardigan on, her hand on the door.

"Oh," she says before stepping outside, "a tumbler got broken when the men were here. I found it in the sink and threw the pieces in the waste pail." It was the kind of thing Stella would blame her for when she found it missing.

Jane says goodbye without looking back and bounds down the path like a deer, hardly touching the ground. She chooses the forest trail rather than the main road home to avoid meeting anyone, her heaving chest forcing her to pause in a grove of arbutus trees to catch her breath. The information is like a lump of coal smouldering inside her. If she hangs onto it, it will burn, but she must be careful where she lets it go, for it will also cause cinders wherever it lands. Mama would scold her for repeating hearsay, so she will not tell her. Maybe Tommy would do well to know, for it might take away some worries about future work. No, unlike Roland Hughes, Tommy always says he wants no part of secrets until they're not secrets anymore. And he would think she was wrong being hidden in the Cruikshanks' bedroom, regardless of her explanations.

But it is not the talk of new coal causing agitation — that goes on in shops, school, at her own kitchen table all the time — rather, the words about Louis Strong hang heavy on her heart. He looked tired when she returned his clothes last time, but nothing in his manner or words hinted that Edgar Mackie had personally paid a visit to his cabin. Have the mine bosses been threatening him, or is it Lance's rough tone of voice making everything bigger than it is, the same way he thinks of himself? Butch Hargraves is supposed to be Louis' friend. What can she tell Louis that he does not already know? She does not want to give him more worries, especially when she is not even sure if they are justified. The word of Lance Cruikshank is nothing to take such a risk for, so she must keep this news to herself, carry on as if she has never heard it.

Scratched by brambles she has not bothered to sidestep, Jane at last reaches home. Feathers of smoke greet her from the chimney. Tommy should be sleeping — is Mama tending the fire herself? Inside the back door, Louis Strong has deposited his bundle of clothes to be washed. Her mother is clearing the kitchen table in her good skirt and blouse with rouge on her lips and more than a normal flush on her cheeks, all signs of visitors. Mama never has callers, being too sick to have made any friends in Canada. At the sight of Jane, her shoulders slump and she sits down abruptly on a chair.

"Louis was here?"

"He brought the clothes. Said there was no rush, as usual."

"How was he?" Jane asked.

"What do you mean, how was he? Tired, same as ever, far as I can see. He's an old man."

"I just wondered. He seemed a bit under the weather last week. How was your day, Mama? You look fresh."

"Well, I don't feel fresh," she sighs. "Unexpected guests are enough to tire the likes of me."

"Who was here?"

"After lunch, Tommy went in to sleep — he was working on the cupboard all morning, poor lad — and Gomer came running in from school. He told me two of his friends' mothers were coming to pay me a visit in an hour's time. Not a minute to gather my strength, and you not here to help me clean up or set out tea and cake before these strangers arrive."

"What did the women want?" Jane forces herself to keep her voice down, as much to prevent it from becoming shrill after all the other surprises as to respect her older brother sleeping in the next room.

"They started out saying what a fine boy we have in Gomer and that he is welcome to come to their homes with their sons after school. Then they said the teacher, Miss Maasanen, was getting married next summer. I knew married women were not allowed to teach, but why were they meeting with someone like me, too sick to take part in the community?"

As she speaks, Jane remembers this same glow on her mother back in Llantrisant after church when friends would come in for tea. Seeing it, she realizes how much she longs for Mama's full presence in the family again.

"Soon they come to their point. These two ladies, wives of businessmen in Nanaimo, are also members of the Southfield school board and early as it is, they want to think about hiring a teacher for the new school next year. The daughter of Louis Strong has applied for the job."

"Ruby?" Jane says enthusiastically.

Her mother pauses, then speaks deliberately, illustrating how to restrain eagerness and impatience. "Yes, Ruby Strong. The one who teaches in the Cedar district. Seems she wants to be closer to her father — him alone and all — and she could be if she lived in the teacherage."

Jane's feelings scramble. She wonders if Ruby would do the laundry and take away her reason to see Louis and his son.

"Gomer told them you do work for Mr. Strong, so that's why they were here. They want to know my opinion of the family. I told them you consider Mr. Strong a gentleman. I told them that you have met his wife and his children, and you came home full of praise for them."

"Thank you, Mama. You did the right thing."

Mary Owens fans herself with her hand, feeling the heat from the stove as intensely as she feels the cold, aches, and pains — always more than anyone else. She moves her chair closer to the door. "These ladies welcomed your recommendation. They knew of Miss Strong's fine reputation at Cedar School and were building a case against one or two fathers who might be disinclined to hire a Negro teacher."

Jane explodes in spite of herself. "Do they know Ruby? Do they know how hard-working and how kind she and her father and mother and brother are?" At the word "brother," she reddens, as if speaking it will give her feelings away. "Do they really know how well-loved she is at Cedar School? That she takes children to board, gives them food and shelter there, sometimes gives them rides on her horse? She took her training at the Nanaimo Normal School, same as the other teachers, and probably learned better because she cares more about doing a good job." At these words she feels a twinge of disloyalty to Miss Maasenen, who treated her so well.

Mama is becoming tired and stern again. "I said what I could in favour of Miss Ruby Strong. I can't do anything else and neither can you, Jane. I have to lie down now." She rises from her chair and walks, slumped, to the bedroom.

"Gomer would be blessed to have Ruby as a teacher. He might even learn something for a change." Filled with shock and anger from the day's events, Jane strides outside to cool her burning cheeks. She hears uneven strokes from an axe somewhere in the maple trees behind their house. It must be Gomer chopping wood. Badly, as usual. She hides behind a cedar bush and watches him. Sweat pours from his brow onto the school clothes he has not troubled himself to change. Jane considers stepping out and scolding him for causing extra washing for her, and then showing him how to chop wood properly. In the end, she decides her little brother must stick with something long enough to figure it out for himself. If only his fingers survive. Soon he tires of the effort and throws the axe down in disgust. Jane stays hidden as he marches back to the house, kicking everything in his path. Today Gomer's carelessness is too familiar to stir her as it usually would. At the sound of the back door slamming, she picks up the axe and carries it to the outside shed where Gomer knows it belongs. Since they moved to Canada, axes and hatchets have become familiar to Jane, but this time the primitive tool feels dangerous in her hand. A shudder passes through her, as she throws it into the shed as fiercely as Gomer had thrown it on the ground. The sound of Tommy's heavy footsteps on the other side of the wall reminds her he will want something to eat before he sets off for his night shift.

Tommy is testing the hinges of the new cloak cupboard as she enters.

Even if he is occupied at the same task, Jane can tell instantly from her brother's manner whether his shift lies before him, or if he has just finished. On his way to the pits he has the edginess of a hawk, easy to snap with impatience at any interruption. After work, the same impatience is restrained by exhaustion and withdrawal. Gomer prattles on about a friend from school who has a newer and better axe that makes wood chopping easy. Jane is not surprised when Tommy snarls, "Nothing wrong with our axe but the person using it."

She quickly sets the table before Tommy sits down, stirring the thick soup of beef, barley, and vegetables she had made before she left this morning. Within minutes, the family is sitting down to a meal of Scotch broth, homemade bread, and bread and butter pickles, made from their own cucumbers in the summer. Jane lingers at the counter filling Tommy's cylindrical lunchpail with roast beef sandwiches. She pours hot tea into the bottom and snaps the flat compartment containing sandwiches on top, just as her mother takes her chair in her best blue woollen housecoat. Jane has no appetite, and explains that she has sampled too much at the stove and is in need only of a cup of tea. She steals glances at Tommy to see if his face or movements will reveal that he knows or thinks the kinds of things Lance Cruikshank knows and thinks. Does the mine create cruelty like Lance's, or is it miners like Lance who create poison gases in the mine? Has her brother been shaped by the darkness and the coal damp? He is bothered by the horses and mules going blind underground, something that would never trouble a man like Lance. No, Tommy could not be part of this threatening thing that has escaped, whatever it is.

The meal over, Tommy changes to his miner's suit in the scullery and tests the hinges on the cupboard once more before opening the door. Mama says, "Come you home safe, Thomas." He nods, but does not answer as he leaves. Mama goes back to bed and Gomer flips pages of his school text loudly at an unreadable clip. Jane cleans the kitchen and slides the oil lamp to the end of the table. She pulls out her pen and paper from under the tea towels. Cassie, Cassie, please come over soon. What can she write to her brother and sisters without telling them all that happened today? A letter can easily go astray and Jane

Owens, responsible daughter and sister that she is, could never be the bearer of such news.

October 25, 1894

Dear Brother and Sisters,

It has been three weeks since Catherine's last letter and I long to hear from all of you. Are Gwynyth and Evan over their colds? I am not surprised by the praise from the parents for Cassie's conduct in the schoolroom. She has a loving manner with all children and with adults alike.

Mama had two ladies from Gomer's school for tea this afternoon. We do not have many guests in our home on account of Mama's illness and I think she was the better for it, though she is resting now. They said Gomer is a fine lad and a welcome friend for their sons. Our little brother must have a different face outside, because he complains every day about walking so far to school and then about every minute inside it. He would be happy to stay home and do nothing. I would gladly trade places with him, but he would not want my jobs. The school needs a new teacher because the present one is getting married. How I wish you could be the teacher here, Cassie.

Tommy is over his cold but does not get enough rest between shifts. There is always something for him to tend in the house and, of course, he likes a little time at the tavern with his friends on weekends.

My hours at the other miner's house get longer and longer, though my pay remains the same. I am tired and upset from being there and will go to bed after I put the clothes of my other generous customer to soak.

Stay healthy, dear Brother and Sisters, until we will be together again and can talk freely.

x x x x x x x x Your loving Sister, Jane x x x x x x x x

✂ ✂ ✂ ✂ ✂ ✂ ✂ ✂

"HULLO," I croaked.

"Oh no, did you work nights? I'm sorry, I thought you'd be up by noon."

"It's okay, Dad. I'm off. If it really is noon, I must have slept over twelve hours."

"That's because you need it. I just wanted to tell you Janetta called yesterday. She's back home and doing much better. She can't go very far and wondered if we would like to go over again. She seems moved by your visit."

I remembered sitting over her hospital bed with my nose running. "Sure. When?"

"You're the busy one. You decide."

"Maybe after my next block. Thursday?"

"Sounds fine. She mentioned the letters. Wants you to see them. I'll let you go back to sleep."

"Don't rub it in. I'll talk to you later." I rolled over on the bed, cordless phone in hand. I was still groggy. After ten months of insomnia I now did nothing but sleep. Both signs of depression. I knew I was having wild dreams, but could not hang onto them in the morning. All that was left was a somber, overcast feeling. Of mines, misty forests, a foggy ocean. Jane Owens was haunting me. My knee knocked against the box of her letters where I had stopped reading last night with only three left. I pulled one out, and without lifting my head, began to read:

October 2, 1894

Dear Brother and Sisters,

Your letter last week was a treasure to me, Cassie. Mama
thinks I spend too much on postage, but I cannot wait any
longer to reply. When you write, I am back in Llantrisant
with you, playing with Evan and Gwynyth, hearing you
and Margaret chatter. Margaret, Mama is proud that
your handiwork is making a name for you, especially since
it was she who taught you to sew. Cassie, by the time you
get here, you will be hired as a teacher because of your skills
with children. Evan and Gwynyth are lucky to have you in
the home as a tutor. I am so in need of your company that
sometimes I believe I will not last. Since I left school I do
not meet with any girls my own age except my employer
and she is not a friend. I would stop working at that
house this very day but Tommy is building on more rooms,
and materials take more of his wages. He is hoping to be
made timber foreman soon. He has worked hard for this
promotion and deserves it.

My only friend is my other customer. I would trust him
with all my secrets except those that might hurt him. I wish
more people knew how kind he is but he keeps to himself
mostly. The person he sees most is the one he should not
trust. Next week his younger son will be over helping him
to finish off the harvest.

Dear Sisters and Brother, I am tired and must go to
bed. Tomorrow I have ten pies to bake for the harvest fair.

x x x x x x x x x Your loving sister, Jane x x x x x x x x x

Ten pies. I was twice my great-grandmother's age in this letter and had
never made one. And I had certainly never done anybody's laundry but
my own. I cringed to think that at fifteen, I did not even do that; I left
it to my mother to push the buttons on the washing machine. Even

worse, I would pout if the jeans I wanted to wear were still in the wash. As for fighting to walk to school, I grumbled when I had to get up to catch a five-minute ride with Gail and her dad. I must have inherited Gomer's genes.

I propped myself up against my pillows, which, speaking of laundry, could do with a wash. I thought of Jane wringing sheets out by hand and hanging them on a line to dry. Was she pretty? Was she tall? My height certainly didn't come from my mother. I had to confess that until now I considered Jane's life boring and pitiable, because housework all day was not my idea of fun. For the first time, I felt the full weight of her responsibility as a fifteen-year-old. Of the thousands of houses I had been in, I had seen few where a teenager was in charge. Sure, lots of kids survived drunken, addictive parents by doing laundry or cooking Kraft Dinner and pizza, but teenagers who quit school these days usually did not do it to support their family or bake pies. Social Services were just around the corner. What astonished me was the way Jane accepted her lot. You did what was expected of you back then. I still found it hard to believe that I was holding actual testimony in my hands from that century and not just reading about it in a book.

And what *was* going on with her other customer, the Negro gentleman? What were Jane's secrets and who was the person he should not trust? She had my attention now. I reached for another letter and the phone rang again. I tried to answer with enthusiasm this time.

"Arabella? It doesn't sound like you."

So much for cheerfulness. It was Megan. When I joined the force, I decided my full name sounded more professional. An alias, you might say. Megan was on another team, but we often had barbecues and baseball games with them.

"You busy this afternoon?"

"Depends."

"Lonnie's brother is here from Calgary. We wanted to take him to Stanley Park, walk the seawall, go for a drink later. Thought you might like to come along?"

"Trying to fix me up?"

"Nothing like that." Then Megan's famous three-minute laugh. How would she and Uncle Lawrence get along? "But you never know."

Before I could stop myself, I had said: "Sure. Why not?"

"Great. We'll pick you up in an hour."

As soon as I hung up, I remembered what I really had planned for the day. Study. I had still not picked a topic for my history paper. Being a mature student had not made me any more mature about study habits. How did I ever agree to a blind date today? Mom always said, if you don't fill your life with what's important to you, other people will fill it for you.

I showered and changed into jeans and a turtleneck, cursing as I did so. Myself, mainly, though Megan came in for recriminations as well. For having the nerve to treat me like a friend, was that it? At times Megan was the human equivalent of fingernails on a blackboard for me. I felt guilty thinking this, because she always included me in her circle and for all the world, we got along. But her voice was like a power drill and she bared upper and lower teeth in such a forced smile that I sometimes had to look away, especially when people were taken in by it.

Maybe I was jealous. Not because she was small and dark, because Gail was small and blonde, and I loved her. Maybe because every inch of Megan's taut little body was a cop. For all the doubts I had about my career choice, she was filled with rock-solid certainty. And to seal her fate, she married Lonnie, another member who was tall, stable, and devoted, so they could patrol the streets together on their days off looking for something to report. Lonnie was a dog man, and whenever I was at their place for a party, I spent as much time with the dog as Lonnie would allow to avoid Megan's screechy performances. I wondered if his brother would be as single-minded as these two about his field.

Turned out to be an oilfield. His name was Hank and he was a geologist with some big oil company in Calgary. When I got into Lonnie's spotless Jeep Cherokee, I had persuaded myself to be carefree, to allow nothing to ruin the splendour of this sunny Vancouver day. But Hank managed. Tall and good-looking like Lonnie, he made lots of money and offered excellent prospects as a boyfriend or husband. He also was an authority on everything. Not opinionated like Dave or a know-it-all like Emile, who both invited teasing. No, he took himself and his information very seriously. At first I thought he was joking when he said, "Ocean currents? A fascinating subject." But then he held us captive for the next fifteen minutes with a slow, detailed explanation. Even a comment about Vancouver's lovely greenery brought on a lengthy monologue about how flowers on the west coast bloom longer and are richer in colour, but fragrance on the prairies is stronger because of the air. If you tried to distract him by pointing out a pair of seagulls fighting, he nodded quickly then returned to the exact place in the sentence he had stopped. By the time we finished our walk around the park, I was afraid even to sneeze, in case a lecture on the origins of "Gesundheit" would follow. The only good thing about Hank was that Lonnie and Megan did not get a single chance to mention their files.

Following our drink at the Sylvia Hotel, the other three were ready to move to a Greek restaurant, then back to Megan's and Lonnie's for more drinks. My survival instincts kicked in.

"Sorry, but I promised my dad I'd see him tonight. If you plan to stay in Vancouver, you can drop me off and he can drive me home later."

"Party pooper," said Megan in her buzzsaw voice. "Your loss, girlfriend."

Hank stopped short in the middle of an explanation of shale varieties, visibly disappointed to be losing two new ears. They were going to a restaurant in Burnaby and insisted on taking me back home for my car on the way. "Maybe another time," Hank said brightly as I exited the Jeep as if it were in flames.

Inside my apartment, I kicked my shoes off and screamed: I hate you, Ray Kelsey, I hate you! What I should have screamed was: I hate this dating game! But I did mean it about Ray Kelsey too.

I made myself a sandwich and flopped on the couch in front of the TV. I had to study. I had to get started on my paper because I was working every day between now and then. Move, feet, and take me into the bedroom to pick up those books. My finger listened instead and roamed through twenty-five channels of dull programs. I settled on the least interesting one I could find — *Cathedrals in Portugal* — and watched the entire show, imagining Hank as tour guide. Then Retha's voice cut in on my procrastination as it had in high school: If you finish your assignment, give yourself a reward, preferably not food (right, Retha). Do something you look forward to doing, but only if you have honestly done the work. If you achieve results from this process, you might discover the reward is in the study itself. Nope, I never did discover that, but I knew what I could use as a lure. My great-grandmother's letters. I was eager to read those last two when Megan interrupted. I would get through the history text for the sake of Jane Owens.

✂ ✂ ✂ ✂ ✂ ✂ ✂ ✂ ✂

NOVEMBER MUST BE Vancouver Island's bitterest month. Jane pulls her cloak tighter against the gathering storm. She thinks of the same leaden skies and wet winds that drenched her last year on the way to school when she had to tell her teacher she would not be returning after Christmas. A cedar bough whips a spray of water onto her head; she pulls up her hood and presses the faded red plaid bundle of clothes against her waist under two overlapping layers of cape. Louis' laundry bag is made from an old shirt she stitched together, its sleeves serving as ties. She is thankful she pulled on Gomer's rubber boots at the last minute, for this sudden downpour would surely have soaked her own thin leather ones through.

To her right, black smoke from a stand of alder trees tells her Henry Hargraves is in his cabin. Though he lives with his wife in a house in Nanaimo, he keeps a cabin here for eating and sleeping, as well as two sheds at the back for cutting up carcasses and curing. If she is to believe Lance, he must do some work for Mackie, though it is easier to imagine him with bloody hands than coal-blackened ones.

Jane moves as far to the left as she can, thankful that an overgrowth of Oregon grape on his path prevents a clear view from his cabin to the road. At least the slashing rain will keep him inside today, for as much as she flinches at the thud of his axe on animal sinews and bones, even worse is silence between the blows. That is when Jane inches like a deer in the forest, dreading the roar of a brushed branch or the thunder of a broken twig. Last month she did not escape soon enough and Butch Hargraves met her on the road.

"You're Louis' maid, aren't you? Jane, is it?" He had grinned at her with a face that made her think of a harvest basket — knobby gourd nose, beet-coloured lips, and teeth like dried corn kernels, yellow alternating with navy and grey. He stepped close enough for her to smell a stale blend of pipe tobacco, sweat, sour breath, and curing smoke on his clothes. "Would you do my laundry for me? Wash my underclothes?" His laugh was dry and crude. She edged away from the big bearded man with the axe, grasping the packet of clothes more tightly to control her trembling hands. "Maybe you only want Negro slave men like Louis? Or is that the only kind who wants a plain Jane like you?"

Plain Jane. Hurrying down the empty path now, she is pelted with water bullets drumming out the name. The only good thing about reaching the meat shacks is that she is almost at her destination.

Less than half a mile away, the cabin of Louis Strong stands on a hillock in a clearing of arbutus trees. He built it himself from fir logs, about the same size as her house now that Tommy has almost finished the two new bedrooms. As Jane steps into the open yard, sunlight shines through the veil of rain. She sees Louis watching from the porch outside the rough-hewn door; a smile streams across his face at the sight of her.

"Come, chile." From the edge of the stoop he ushers her in. "Come in out of the rain, Miss Jane. Why you insist on bringin' my clothes you'self? Ah would gladly come for them."

Smiling as she always does when he says this, Jane leaves Gomer's boots just inside the door on the polished floor made of split logs. She follows Louis inside. The large main room holds a stove, cupboard, table and two chairs at the far end; closer to the door, an old couch and chair face a blazing fireplace, the perfect welcome to her shivering body. Two bedrooms have been partitioned off on the other side, their walls not reaching the ceiling. Modesty has always overruled Jane's curiosity about glancing into that space, and today she notices the blanket curtain is pulled.

"Sit awhile until you get warmed up. Let me dry that cloak for you." He spreads the wet cape over a wooden chair near the cookstove and pulls the padded chair closer to the fireplace. "No need to brave the rain for me. Clothes can wait."

Jane sinks into the worn cushions, the chill draining from her. "When I started out, it was dull but dry. The storm came up just before the butcher's place."

Jane thinks she sees a scowl on Louis' forehead at the mention of the word "butcher," but cannot be sure it is not her own thoughts she is reading. Louis scowls more often now. His old eyes, ringed by darker skin, are betraying him, and his strong shoulders hunch when he bends forward to see an object better. He once told her he believed he was eighty or so. He laughed when he said no one kept a record of him. His father wanted no proof of him on his plantation and would have sold him for less than a horse if he had an offer.

"Look like the rain lettin' up a bit, but you sit and rest to make sure. My wife send some fresh apple butter, some fresh bread too. Ah'll gi' you a slice wit' some tea. And take some apples back with you, 'fore ah forget." He lifts up the edges of two logs in the floor, extracting a burlap bag of apples from their storage bin. He sets it next to her boots.

The room shelters Jane like a cave. Is it the natural log walls and flooring instead of painted wood partitions that are in her house and every other building she knows? Or is it Louis' soft accent removing her from sickness, from the mine, from the Cruikshanks, from the crudeness of Butch Hargraves? Being here with someone even more foreign to this rainforest than she is makes her feel at home. "Was your wife over again, Louis?"

"She sent it with my son." As he sets a mug of tea and a plate of bread and apple butter on the flat arm of the chair, he nods toward the bedroom. "He still here, lying sick in the bed."

Jane's shivers return, now of a different origin. "Adam's here?"

"Caught a fever last night and ah tole him best not to take the boat back to Salt Spring until he can lift hi' head from the pillow. Ain't no complainer, that chile o' my ole age. When he don't get up to help his mother or me, ah know he sick."

Jane's fingers shake on the cup. She had not counted on seeing Adam again until the new year. "Will he be all right?"

"For sure he stronger than a fever unless it the kind that wipe a whole people out, but ah don't think so this time." As he speaks, the bedroom door opens. Adam steps out quietly, his eyes not fully open, his face as pale as his father's.

"You remember Miss Jane, son."

Adam and Jane exchange shy smiles. Born in this new province, Adam sometimes cannot conceal his amusement at his father's formalities. Jane blushes, thinking about the last time she saw him in October during the harvest. She carried water to him in the orchard while he was picking fruit, because his father was busy sorting apples. Louis protested it was not her job to serve them, even when Fan Mah, Louis' Chinese helper, was away for the day, but Jane insisted. When Louis came with the cart for the apple baskets and found them sitting on the ground together, he told Adam gruffly to put his shirt back on in front of a lady. She wonders now if that moment took his appetite away for a week, as it had hers.

"You still feel sick?" Louis lays the palm of his hand on his son's forehead until Adam moves away.

"I'm better, Papa. I'll be leaving soon to catch the boat back home." He ladles water into a cup from a pail on the cupboard.

"You feel warm yet. Why not stay one more night with me? Tomorrow is Sunday. A day of rest."

"You mean church."

"Church is all your mother think about. She prayin' all the time." Louis turns away and stares out the front window.

Adam does not answer, so Jane rushes in. "Sometimes I miss church. We used to go in Wales and I liked the singing."

"Singin' fine, prayin' fine too. Prayin' in private, just between you and God. Not talkin' all the time about prayin' and scriptures and God's work."

"Mother does God's work," says Adam.

"Sure, she do God's work. Nobody on this earth a better woman than your mother. But so do you do God's work, so do Miss Jane, even a old sinner like me try to do it. No need to keep talkin' about it every minute." He sees the discomfort on his son's face. "How about some soup before you catch that boat? Miss Jane, would you have some soup with us? You need warmin' up too."

"No, thank you," says Jane, knowing she will not be able to swallow a mouthful in Adam's presence. "I must be getting home before the rain starts again." She rises from the chair.

"I'll walk you part way," says Adam. "It's getting dark."

Her legs weaken and she grips the back of the chair. "Thank you, but it's not so far. I know the path."

"We'll both take you as far as the butcher," says Louis. "He has some pork and lamb to send back home with Adam. Ah got a piece for you too. We went huntin' yesterday." Jane believes she sees disappointment in Adam's eyes, but she must be mistaken. Why would he be interested in a plain Jane? Louis mumbles, "Meat's all ah can trust with that man."

"What do you mean, Papa?"

"Dunno for sure. Catch him watchin' me sometimes when we're out huntin.' Though ah feel safe wi' a gun in my hand. Ah know ah'm a better shot than he is, and he know it too."

Jane does not dare speak.

"Last night we playin' cards at his place and ah see that same look. It come since he talk about my land. Ax me if ah want to sell. Ah say no, ah spend years workin' with my trees, graftin,' tryin' new things and ah ain't about to gi' everything up."

"What did he offer you?" Adam's eyes are no longer sleepy.

"No price come up. He tell me someone would pay a lot of money for my land, but ah got no interest in that. Ah been workin' hard since ah take my first step and before that, ah was on the back of my Mama stooped over in the cotton fields. Ah drive cattle all the way from California up to this country so we can have a better life. And we have a better life. And them fruit trees, them's my best work."

Jane is thankful neither man looks at her.

"Why does Butch want your land?"

"Butch don't want it. Coal people want it, though nobody but him come forward.

So Lance made up the conversation with Mackie, thinks Jane.

"Coal. There's coal here?"

"On the slope, they say. But if there's coal on my property, it must carry through land they can buy. Ah don't own much."

Both men put on worn jackets, and Louis hands Jane her cloak, testing it for dryness.

"When did this come up? Mother know?"

"Few weeks back. Nobody know, excep' you now, and Miss Jane. Ah try not to think about it too much, just get on with my work. The butcher don't say no more about it, excep when he watchin' me, ah pretty sure what he thinkin.' Always was a coarse fellow, especially with the ladies."

A snort escapes from Jane without warning. She pulls a handkerchief from the pocket of her skirt and pretends to stifle a cough. She has never known Louis to talk so much without the aid of questions. It is as if he wants these things said.

"Forgive such talk, Miss Jane. Ah've no right to burden you wi' my worries."

Louis slips Jane a dollar bill and pats his clean clothes lying on the table. "Such a fine job you do. But ah do believe it not safe for a young woman to be out in the forest with cougars roamin' around. Next time ah pick them up."

"No," says Jane, too quickly. "I like the walk and fresh air. Sometimes when it's warm, I take the long way home by the bluffs. The wild pansies and oxeye daisies remind me of the slopes of Wales." She bends quickly to pick up her bag of apples and to pull on Gomer's boots, while Adam is drinking more water. She hopes they will be hidden by her long skirt.

"Bluffs? So far from here? Ah can't remember when last ah been in that direction."

Adam holds the door for her and his father. Her oversize boots cause her to trip against him, and he steadies her back with his arm. Cool, moist air saves her cheeks from catching on fire. Through the rain-freshened fragrance of moss, cedar, arbutus, and fir she walks between the two men, never feeling safer in her life. They reach the butcher's hut too fast. Jane stops on the road, as Louis turns down the path.

"I'll go on from here."

"Ah want to gi' you a piece o' pork for your family. Then Adam and ah will walk you home."

Free meat is not worth standing face to face again with Butch Hargraves. "You've given us a lot already. I must get home now."

"Ah need my son to help carry the meat, but ah could wait for him here while he accompany you home. He seem strong again to me, but your cheeks so flush, ah believe you catch his fever."

Jane and Adam look away before their eyes lock. "I'll be all right. And Adam has a boat to catch." She starts walking backward.

"Well, if you're sure, Miss Jane. We'll watch you awhile."

"Goodbye, then, Louis," says Jane, and nods toward Adam, not trusting herself to speak his name. Gomer's boots prevent her from running, but she breaks into a clumsy skip to be out of their view as quickly as she can. What a foolish girl to be caught up with such feelings. And how does she rid herself of them now? She reaches home without knowing how she got there. Her skirt is torn at the bottom. Did a cougar attack her or was it another branch of holly she missed seeing again? Her mind is too full of silly thoughts to notice anything around her until she is outside her house. Fearing she will be late for supper, she bursts through the door. She is surprised to see Roland Hughes sitting at their kitchen table playing gin rummy and drinking beer with Tommy.

"Good day, Jane." Roland puts his cards down to greet her.

"Hello, Roland."

Tommy seems relaxed. Gomer has pulled up a chair behind him, fidgeting and watching his big brother's cards. Even Mama is in the sitting room knitting, glancing up between her stitches with a contented view of the young men. "Looks like you got caught in the rain," she says, referring to Jane's hair.

Jane touches it, wondering how she had appeared to Adam. "A little. Louis made me a cup of tea and I warmed up."

"Why doesn't the old man pick up his laundry here?" asks Roland, showing no sign of resuming the card game now.

"He has offered many times. And besides I like to get out for a walk in that direction," Jane says defiantly. "When the flowers are in bloom, I walk to the bluffs on my way home. The heartsease" — she uses her mother's term for wild pansies — "on the hills take me back to Catherine and Margaret, and the way things used to be." She steps out of Gomer's boots, no longer caring if anyone sees them, hangs up her cloak, and sets the apples in the cool lean-to.

"The bluffs?" Mama says sharply. "Be you careful on those bluffs. Moira McPherson's son was playing with another boy up there and fell over and broke his neck. And this is your home now, no use pining for what once was."

"Jane's a big girl, Mama, she can take care of herself," smiles Tommy. "As long as she doesn't wear Gomer's boots to the bluffs. She'd be sure to stumble then."

Everyone laughs, including Jane. Roland watches her as she brings the pot of soup from the shelves in the lean-to and sets it on the stove. She is careful not to glance too long at him for fear of comparing his pale thin face and slight body to Adam. She is able to breathe more easily now, relieved for the calm. How could she feel such comfort in the company of Louis and Adam, when now from the familiarity of her home, that world seems off limits?

"Maybe Roland would like to stay for supper," says Mama. Tommy clears away the cards and beer glasses.

"Thank you," says Roland. "And maybe your sister would like to go to the dance with us tonight."

Tommy looks as surprised as Jane. Mama is the only one who speaks. "Not yet. She might think she's an adventurer, going to the bluffs, but she'll be only sixteen next month and that's still too young for a dance hall full of miners."

"I'd look after her," says Roland, with a conspiratorial smile, "in case her brother is too busy with Lizzie Carter."

Tommy reddens. "Quiet, Hughes."

"Lizzie Carter?" Jane turns quickly from the stove. "She's been over to Stella's. How do you know Lizzie, Tommy?"

Tommy mumbles, "I've seen her at the store. And she brings lunches sometimes when her father and brother forget."

Roland leans back in his chair, his eyes darting from Tommy, to Jane, to their mother, amused at the reaction he has provoked. Jane stirs the soup vigourously. Lizzie Carter. Big and bossy. Not as silly as

Stella, but not as pretty either. She refuses to imagine her shy, moody, hardworking brother in the clutches of Lizzie Carter. Roland likes to tease, so maybe that's all there is to it, but Tommy is not denying knowing her. At least the talk has shifted from her going to the dance. She is thankful Mama said no, so she would not have to do it herself. Tonight she wants to be home alone.

She sets out plates and bowls on the table and pulls up another chair, wishing it were for Cassie. They would go for a walk later and she would tell her all about today. In the meantime, she will share their meal with Roland Hughes whose eyes are still watching her every move. She remembers Adam's eyes — also alert but with a soft detached merriment — and again, she resists a comparison. Later, when Mama has gone to bed and Roland and Tommy are at the dance, she will write a few lines to Cassie, Margaret, and Gilbert. She will not be signing it Plain Jane just yet.

WOULD I EVER GET ANYTHING RIGHT? Barnwell just wrote our term paper deadline on the board. Not two Wednesdays from now, as I had wanted to believe, but next week. Crane Reese must have noticed the shock on my face because he leaned toward me with the topic list. He pointed to *The influence of Sir James Douglas' early life on his success as a leader.* He whispered, as Barnwell exited, "Only one left with references still in the library."

I whispered back unnecessarily. "Thanks." Sir James sounded as good or bad as the others, since I had not given much thought to any of them.

"I'm almost finished mine." Crane stood up. "Black immigration. I could give you my books tomorrow or the next day. Then again, maybe I wouldn't want the competition."

I rolled my eyes. "Believe me, you'd do well in competition with me."

I followed him out and thought he was going to suggest coffee again but he didn't. He said goodbye in the corridor that led to the library. I got the hint. A sick, empty feeling took over my stomach. Not from hunger, because I had remembered to bring a sandwich this time, but from my usual procrastination.

Everyone was leaving the library. Passing me, each carried an aura of superiority, of having mastered everything he or she had to learn. The only thing I was confident about at that moment was that I was the most inadequate student in the college. A familiar sensation that had played many roles recently. After Ray dumped me, I imagined everyone I encountered to be in a storybook-perfect relationship, and not long after that, I was sure everyone I looked at had a mother. Now they were all diligent students. With boyfriends and mothers.

The librarian informed me they were closing for the day. In a quavering voice that made me think of a punk at his first robbery of a 7-Eleven, I told her I had to have some books.

"Sure," she said obligingly. "What would you like?"

"Something on Sir James Douglas."

"You've got a lot to choose from," she said, typing his name into the computer without a hint of impatience. "Anything in particular about him?"

"His early life."

"B.C. Studies has some articles on his school days, and his mother and grandmother. Journals can't leave the library but I can give you a couple of good biographies. She led me through the shelves and picked off three books. "These should keep you going."

She signed them out and smiled as I left. I made a mental note to treat my felons with that kind of respect, because I was nothing more than that: a perjurer who had vowed to pass a course for credit and was about to give up on that vow.

I got into my car and took the club from the steering wheel. My forehead slumped against the cold hard plastic. I did not know how to write a term paper. I knew who did, but it would be losing my last shred of dignity to ask him.

Dad.

Dad? Just then I remembered we were to go to the island on Thursday. That was out of the question now with this paper sending a summons for my days off. If I cancelled, Dad would probably never suggest an outing again, sensitive as he was to my schedule. He treated me as if I was the hardest-working person at the most important job in the world, a joke if ever there was one right now. It was just after ten. I was in the area. He would still be up listening to comedy reruns.

He answered the door in his pyjamas. The surprise and concern on his face prompted my next-of-kin visit voice. "It's okay, Dad, I just finished class and thought I would stop by."

The entire house was dark and silent, even the kitchen where he normally kept company with his radio, grapefruit, and yogurt at this time of night. "Were you in bed?"

He smiled sheepishly, and my face went from worried white to shocked red. "Dad, have you got someone here with you?"

He added a flattered male smile to his embarrassment, then switched on the lights. I followed him into the living room. "No, actually... in other words, I was consulting my finger." He gestured for me to sit down.

I remained standing. "What?"

"Have you had anything to eat?"

"I'm not hungry. What about your finger?"

"I've been reading a lot since your mother died. Meditation, self-hypnosis, ideomotor responses. You contact your subconscious mind through deep meditation, then you ask it something that has you in a dilemma. It's nothing spooky," he added, seeing the look on my face.

"Nothing spooky?"

"Nothing outside your own experience, like, 'Will the Blue Jays win the pennant?' You're simply speaking to your subconscious where all data is stored and ready to be tapped."

"Of course. Fingertapping."

"You have to practise. I've been doing it awhile; I just haven't been caught at it before. You instruct your finger to act as the indicator of your subconscious, to cut through all the defences and conditioning that might be counterproductive to your best interests. Our conscious mind often sabotages our best interests, you know, and this is merely a means to open yourself to a new level."

"Your inner child?"

"Maybe, except I can't stand that term."

"Well, Sara's child then. You're taking over where she left off."

Exhaustion was moving in fast and I flopped on the old corduroy sofa, my head and feet braced against the padded arms that were thread-bare from years of my imprint. For once Dad had overruled a deco-rating decision of Mom's. He had insisted on keeping the old couch upstairs when Mom upgraded the living room with a saffron-coloured — real saffron is reddish not yellow, she pointed out — leather sectional. There was just enough room for it and Sara's Queen Anne chair in the passage between living room and eating area. Dad had lined the walls with shelves to hold Sara's books and a small TV: being surrounded by the library he had grown up with provided comfort, he insisted, and Mom had to concede to the little den between her modern front room and dining room. They kept most of their own books in the basement, but these served to remind us all of Sara's love of literature and knowledge. As a kid I learned the word "autodidact" from hearing my parents describe Sara to strangers. Then "unconventional and strange" took over in Mom's descriptions.

"No, I told you, I'm not trying to commune with spirits or see the future, I only want to make a decision from the clearest vantage point possible."

"And what were you asking your finger tonight? Or is that private?"

"I'm at an impasse with Sissipuss." He grinned shyly. "Should he team up with Cedric the Cockroach and help him redeem his despised insect image, then have Cedric and his family carry off the piece of sponge he pushes upstairs? You do know the myth, don't you?"

"Of course," I said, thanking Crane.

"But I wondered if I might be accused of borrowing from archy and mehitabel even though Cedric has been in my repertoire since you were a kid."

No way would he get me to ask who those two were. I had enough crow to eat ahead of me. "What's the alternative?"

"Two separate stories. The triumph of Sissipuss and the heroism of Cedric."

"Dad, these are supposed to be children's stories and I can't understand what you're talking about." Seeing his expression made me think fast. "Why don't you have Sissipuss ask his finger for the answer? I mean paw. No, better yet, ask his tail. It's more like a magic wand."

Dad's face lit up the living room. "His tail. That's brilliant. Especially since it's a bobbed tail and could suddenly become functional. Yes, make it funny — ask his tail whenever he needs guidance. Maybe Cedric could come to him, no, maybe..." Dad began mumbling to himself as if he himself were going into a trance. "This is exactly what I needed — a new idea, even if it doesn't work out." He bent down and gave me a rare hug before padding into the kitchen in his slippers and returning with two small containers of yogurt and two spoons, handing me one of each. The smooth liquid slid down my throat, easing my gnawing stomach a little.

"Dad," I said quietly, "I have something to tell you and to ask you."

"Anything."

I felt both treacherous and relieved to have my normally undemonstrative father in this state. "I don't know how to write a term paper. I need your help."

"History?"

"Sir James Douglas."

"Sir James has been a tenant in our basement for many years. He was a regular on the departmentals I drafted, so you'll find all you need downstairs. Which phase?"

"How his early life determined the leader he was to become."

"He was of mixed race, you know. His birth certificate was never found, but they established who his mother was from records of her will in British Guiana. He never mentioned his mother, but did name one of his daughters after her. Martha."

I set the empty yogurt container on the coffee table and fell back on the sofa as Dad's quiet voice repeated much of what Barnwell's booming one had said in class. Both washed over me, but this time I was soothed into assurance that everything would be taken care of. I was back home, after all, and everything always was. My eyes shut on the wish that I had brought a clean uniform for tomorrow. Mom left spare nightgowns and underwear in my old dresser for unexpected visits, and I doubt if Dad had moved any of it.

"He was a pioneer. I think it was the discipline of the Scottish schools, his physical stature and strength, and his ability to deal with all races that made him the natural leader he was," Dad continued. The last thing I heard was, "Then again, his brother was dismissed from the North West Company for incompetence and stupidity, so it wasn't all genetic..." until I felt Sara's afghan being gently spread over me.

"Dad," I protested feebly, lifting my head. "I have to get home. Do you think Janetta would forgive me if we postponed our visit until after my assignment is in?"

"I'm sure she'll understand with your busy schedule."

The rest of me raised itself to an upright position. "Thanks, Dad." I gave him a lazy hug. "I can always count on you."

"Ditto," he said, with a gleam in his eye that told me his night at the drawing table was just beginning.

My car got back home on automatic pilot. Ironing my shirt woke me up slightly, and I allowed myself a few minutes of bedtime reading after setting my alarm. Did I reach for the book on James Douglas? Of course not. Instead, I carefully unfolded the second last worn letter. The date and first line caught my attention. My great-grandmother and I were connected through more than just dripping noses. We were born on the same day.

December 8, 1894

Dear Brother and Sisters,

Today is my sixteenth birthday and I am not much
in the mood for a party. Mama wanted me to bake a
sponge cake with fluffy boiled icing for the occasion and
Tommy brought his friend Roland Hughes for a slice
after their shifts. We also celebrated Tommy's promotion
to timber foreman. He is too shy to bring Lizzie Carter
home and will still not admit she is his girlfriend.
Roland asked me what I wished for when I blew out
my candles and I said, only one thing — to see my sisters
and brother again soon.

    Mama tries to teach me to sew well enough that
I might take in sewing rather than wash clothes in
someone else's house. There is never any time left over
in my days. I cannot take much more of one customer,
but I would wash the other one's clothes for no pay.
Sisters and Brother, I wish you were here so I could tell
you about the dangerous things I hear from one about
the other.

I am tired now and must find my bed. Tommy and Roland have gone to the pub and Mama and Gomer are sleeping. It is cold and wet and dreary, and I hope my seventeenth year is made up of better days than the past one.

Please write to me often.

x x x x x x x x x Your loving sister, Jane x x x x x x x x x

"MERRY CHRISTMAS, THEN," says Stella.

Pulling her woollen cloak around her shoulders, Jane slips a small package from its inside pocket. "For Norman."

Stella smiles in surprise at the gift wrapped in red flannel and fastened with a green ribbon. "Why, thank you, Jane." She opens the fabric to reveal a pair of tiny blue mittens and matching helmet cap with button strap. "I'll bet you knit these yourself."

Jane nods. "You were supposed to keep it for Christmas."

"Oops," Stella giggles, closing up the package like a naughty girl.

Jane steps outside, the bite of frosty air pardoning her from the Cruikshank house until the new year. She welcomes the close of 1894, but does not greet its successor with the hope she mistakenly held at this time last year. After being forced to quit school, she had not believed her burdens would get worse.

"You sure you can't make it just once between Christmas and Old Year's Night," Stella's voice holds onto her. "I don't know how I'll manage the washing and little Norman with Lance's mother and sister coming over from Vancouver. They like things just so."

Jane turns back and says firmly, "Maybe they could help with Norman. I promised to give Mama a hand recovering an old chesterfield Thomas brought home, and there's all the Christmas baking yet to do."

Stella remains shivering on the threshold of the open door, no longer focussed on Jane, but on the path leading to the main road. Where her blue eyes once held anticipation of her husband's return, Jane now sees fear. The bruises circling her wrists disappear when she tugs the sleeves of her cardigan over her knuckles against the cold.

Jane also dreads meeting Lance on his way home. He is always drunk and quarrelsome after stopping off at the Whistle Stop tavern with other miners coming from the train. Abruptly she says to Stella, "I'll be off then. And you'd best go inside before you catch La Grippe."

She reaches the main road quickly and merges with the other traffic: wagons, horses, traps, miners on foot, a few on bicycles, women in service like herself, hurrying back to families where more cleaning and cooking await them. A light snowfall has filled in the deep ruts and covered horse droppings, lending the rough thoroughfare a purity not normally part of the scene. Since her sixteenth birthday earlier in the month, Jane considers herself to be a full-fledged adult, signified not by the supper and cake she made for herself at her family's urging, nor by the uncomfortable attentions of Roland Hughes, but by the realization that she no longer knows what it feels like to be a child. The carefree years in Wales are past. Running up the grassy mountain after church, hearing the breeze whisper in the currant bushes, minding Gomer as a plump youngster while her father sang and turned fresh-smelling earth to plant leeks, squash, swedes, parsnips, potatoes, and mint with her mother laughing nearby — all still exist in her mind's eye, but are gone from her bones and senses.

Up ahead at the company store, a crowd has gathered. Jane attempts to bypass it, fearing it might be a fight spilled out from the tavern next door. By the time she sees it is just miners and their friends starting the weekend, she is blindsided by a large woman backing out of the store. Lizzie Carter's face twists in irritation until she realizes it is Jane she has hit. They have never spoken before.

"Jane Owens."

"Hello."

"Where's that big brother of yours? Helping the family, I suppose." She speaks mockingly.

"I can't say. I've been at work all day."

"Maybe I'll have to visit his little sister to get an invitation to your home."

Jane flushes, not knowing how to respond, then is saved when Lizzie turns to stare at a sleek black coach drawn by two dappled horses.

A gold M emblazoned on the door causes the dispersing crowd to re-assemble. The curtained window makes it impossible to tell if it is Mr. Mackie or his son paying a visit from one of their mansions to their minions. The Scotsman never appears casually; he always has a good reason. The ponies prance on the spot, snorting aristocratically, as if they know they are transporting the most powerful man on Vancouver Island.

Jane takes advantage of the diversion to slip away through the rest of the onlookers, but not before noticing the passenger who emerges from the Mackie buggy. Butch Hargraves. Once outside, he leans back into the shrouded interior with a half salute, half bow, and a grin that suggests something secretive. At least, that is what Jane sees.

As Butch turns toward the tavern, the coach driver commands his horses to proceed. Butch's eyes have no need to sweep the crowd now that everyone has noticed his chauffeur. His gaze does touch Jane for a second and she believes her transparent thoughts cause the big, crude man to halt in his swagger. But without a further glance at her, he announces to the congregation of muckers, drillers, diggers, drivers, shakers, chunkers, haulers, and rope riders: "Let's have a drink. I'll stand you a round for now, and next time I promise drinks for the whole night." The miners cheer and shout, following Butch in to swill and swap crusty tales until one of them punches another in the face.

Spotting Gertie Salo coming from the store, Jane hurries off down the path home. The pokey girl would surely detain her with drawn-out stories of her aunts, uncles, and cousins, who are due to arrive soon from Finland and join those already here.

When she enters her back door, Tommy and Mama, both engrossed in their tasks, look up but say nothing. Mama has laid three chesterfield cushions onto a length of brown chintz to measure. Tommy planes the door frame of the opening he has just cut through the sitting room wall for the first new bedroom. It will be a small space when finished, barely enough for the bed and press he just bought from a miner leaving Wellington for San Francisco. But for the first time in her life, Jane will sleep alone. Thanks to Dr. MacRae, she has been assigned the room. On his last house call, Mama asked the doctor if she had consumption — almost hopefully, Jane thought, until she convinced herself she was mistaken — and he explained that her appearance was too healthy for tuberculosis. Her condition was still unidentifiable, he said, but it would be beneficial for her and Jane to sleep in separate beds. At these words Jane had to turn away to conceal her elation, taking special care not to look at her young brother, who thought he would be getting the new room. Until Tommy finishes the second room, the larger couch being recovered by Mama will accommodate Gomer's growing body more comfortably.

Jane often regrets that her older brother talks so little, but standing here now, peering through the gateway to freedom, she is proud of all the silent effort he has put into their home. All additions are made with dismantling in mind, but this impermanence has not caused her family to care less about their surroundings. Mama has even suggested hanging wallpaper when there is money enough after these improvements, and Jane has seen what she wants at the home of the fire boss when she delivered a peach pie Stella had forgotten: tiny interlocking chains of forget-me-nots. She is reminded how Mama liked beauty in the house back in Llantrisant — fresh flowers, wallpaper, and pastel-coloured walls. Whenever Papa called her house proud, he said it in a voice that showed he was Mama proud. Remembering what her mother has lost, Jane can sometimes understand her illness better.

"Mackie buggy was at the tavern," she says, slowly hanging up her cape and putting on a clean starched apron.

Tommy continues planing without turning his head and Mama sits back on her knees to say: "Owner checking up on his employees?"

Jane takes a pot of ham and leek soup from the cool pantry shelves and sets it on the stove before arranging a pan with sausages for the oven. "Henry Hargraves got out."

"Hargraves? Our meat man?" Tommy finally speaks.

"Louis Strong gives us our meat. He shares what he and Henry Hargraves hunt together." Jane glances at her brother to make sure he understands the distinction. "I don't trust that man."

Mama looks up sharply, leaving her finger to mark the spot she wants to cut. "For a young girl you have strong opinions. Has this man ever done anything to you?"

"It's Louis I worry about." She mixes flour, baking powder, and sugar into a bowl using experienced hands as measuring vessels.

Tommy sets down his plane and ladles some cool water from the pail into a cup. "You're too concerned about Louis. He manages fine." He stands next to his sister as she adds an egg and milk to the biscuit dough and plumps it up like a cushion before rolling it into balls.

"No one else seems to care about an old man living outside a community, away from his family."

Mama folds up the fabric for the day, straightens, and rises to her feet, wincing. "You store too much in your head, Jane. Most of it imagined."

"I'm not imagining. I hear things." She pauses. "At Cruikshanks." She slides the pan of biscuits into the oven, surprised at her own audacity.

Tommy sputters into his water cup. "Lance? Keep away from him. He's good at saying anything to get a rise out of people."

Mama takes the soiled plaid cloth from the table and replaces it with a clean blue one. "If you would pay attention to what I'm doing now, you could make better wages sewing and not get caught up in people's lives washing clothes. The lace you tatted yesterday on the hankie shows you've got a natural talent with your fingers. It could save you from gossip. Your father always said, 'Believing hearsay leads to disaster.'"

Jane wants to say, "Being honourable didn't keep him from disaster, now did it?" but instead she stands over the hottest part of the stove to camouflage the blood rising to her face. She had known it would be like this, so why is she surprised by her mother's and brother's refusal to listen? When her mother asks where Gomer is, she does not answer. Let one of them call outside for him. She is angry enough to suggest that he is as old as some of the little trappers who sit in cubbyholes in the mine wall, opening and closing stoppings to prevent buildup of poisonous damp. Let him do something useful for once.

Just then Gomer enters noisily. Sensing her daughter's vexation, Mary Owens speaks crossly to him. "And here's my towsy son at last. This family can't support guests for too long. When you're not helping to put food on the table, you can at least show respect by being on time for it."

The young boy opens his mouth to explain that he has been looking for Christmas trees, but knows any excuse without evidence will be too thin for this group who have all forgotten how to have fun.

Silence settles on the supper table, broken only when Gomer asks to be excused after gobbling the last crumb of Jane's custard pie. On his way to a chair in the corner where he has left the Boy's Almanac, he stokes the fire in the living room stove. A look of amusement at this novel occurrence passes among the three left at the table, prompting another rare event: Mama gets up to wash dishes. Spared for once, Jane puts away food, stirs the fruit soaking in brandy for their Christmas cake and pudding, and adds sausage grease to the tin of fat she will use to make soap tomorrow. For a change Mama's complaints of dishwater on her eczema, which has flared up from sizing in the chintz, serve to calm Jane in their familiarity.

Mama has just sat down with her knitting when a quiet knock is heard at the back door. Jane opens it to find Louis Strong standing on their stoop, holding onto something with an apologetic smile on his face.

"Miss Jane, ah don't aim to disturb your family circle, but ah spy a fine Christmas tree close to my cabin and having no use for it myself, ah'd be pleased if you could find a place for it." He holds up a Scotch pine, so perfectly shaped it might have been carved as a model for a Grimm fairy tale.

Louis hesitates at Jane's invitation to come in, insisting that he only wants to deliver the tree, but her smile soon has the old man standing awkwardly in the kitchen, bowing to the figures he can barely see in the next room.

"Good evening, Mr. Strong," says Mama from the couch, and Thomas offers his hand.

"Louis brought us a Christmas tree," says Jane, "a beautiful Scotch pine."

Louis shifts back and forth. "Good evening, good evening. Would you like me to carry it inside for you all?"

"I'll do it tomorrow," says Thomas, "when we've cleared a space for it and my sister has made the popcorn strings."

Jane nods. "It's just what we were looking for. Thank you, Louis."

"Maybe Mr. Strong would like a cup of tea before he heads back home," says Mama, advising Jane of the proper form of address in his presence.

"Of course," says Jane, so surprised by her mother's hospitality that she almost trips pulling a chair out for him. "Please sit down, Mr. Strong."

More and more embarrassed by the formality, Louis inches back toward the door. "Thank you, thank all o' you kind folks, but ah best be gettin' back home. My daughter Ruby say she might stop in to see her old man on her way from the teacherage before she goes to Salt Spring for the holiday."

"You're not going?"

"No, no, such celebrations ain't for me. Ah prefer the quiet. 'Specially now ah don't like to leave."

"Everything all right, Lou — Mr. Strong?" Jane follows him to the doorway, lowering her voice. "Is it what we talked about?" She blushes, "With your son?"

"You might say that. Getting harder and harder to trust anyone besides family and you, Miss Jane. Seems like your people a good set o' folk too."

"Tell me if I can do anything, Louis," she says beyond her mother's earshot. "But where's your laundry?"

Louis shakes his head. "No, no, Miss Jane. You need a holiday too. Ah'll be all right." Once outside, he breathes more freely, tipping his hat as he backs into the night.

"Merry Christmas, Louis," she calls. "And to your family," she adds to some muffled words coming from the darkness.

As Jane turns to go in, her eye catches the bright scarlet berries of their holly bush illuminated by kitchen light. All at once, the thought of the gleaming red and green proclaiming the season delights her. Carefully she breaks off a few of the prickly boughs for decoration in the house. In so doing, she is overtaken by a stronger, more unexpected sensation: a light heart. It ascends to a level it has not reached since her last Christmas in Wales. How had she believed just hours ago this place had been erased? Where did this ripple of joy come from? Is it mixed in with the thick, spongy Canadian air? Or is it that her family, fellow survivors of that faraway life, might just be listening to her after all? Perhaps Mama is right about her imaginings. Life does go on outside her head. Louis hinted at trouble again, but his face looked more peaceful than she has seen it for a while. Perhaps Ruby's visit has raised his hopes, as his has Jane's. Even more than hope, it is the realization that this moment and this place are where, who, why, and what Jane Owens is. They have everything to do with where, who, why, and what she has been, but the here and now is a leap from that collection of years. A flash of herself as a little girl in Wales comes to her. Writing the word "Jane" in big letters for the first time across her slate board, she remembers the strange, shy, and thrilling feeling that exploded within her. What was private suddenly became public — as if, in her young mind, she might have been a fluctuation of people and names until this one was recorded for everyone to view. She feels the same strength anchored to that name and that person again now. Remarkable as this vision seems, Jane knows how silly she would sound if she tried to explain it to Mama or Tommy. Maybe Cassie would understand if she could tell her in person, but she suspects what she feels at this moment can only be grasped beyond the realm of words.

Footsteps approaching on the path startle her back to the holly bush. They are followed by a low greeting. "Good evening, Jane."

"Hello, Roland. I didn't know Tommy was expecting you."

"How do you know I'm not here to see you?"

Jane flushes. "Come in, we've just had supper."

Roland pauses at the door. "Where did you get the tree?"

"Louis Strong brought it over."

Roland appears dismayed. "That's what I came for. There are nice ones not far from my place and I wanted to find out if you want one. Fir they are, nice size. Prettier than pine, my mother always said, when she was alive and we used to have Christmas."

Jane hears the music in Roland's soft voice for the first time. "A Welshman like us," her mother often says after his visits. She considers the Finns, the largest group of settlers in Chase River, too much unto themselves and their speech incomprehensible. When she says this, Jane wonders what the Finns think of Mary Owens, who never leaves her house?

"Thank you for asking, but the pine will do us fine. Maybe you could take a fir for yourself and your father. In memory of your mother."

Roland snorts. "Christmas at our house? The only way I know it's a holiday is that my old man will be passed out at home because they've closed the tavern. Our cookstove will be cold as a coffin, as usual."

"Then you must join us," says Jane, her hospitality quickly deflating as Roland's hand brushes her waist from behind on the way into the kitchen.

Mary Owens offers their guest a cup of tea, rising from the sofa to make it herself. Roland nods his thanks and makes himself comfortable on a kitchen chair, but Tommy has his jacket on. "We'll be going just now. Take a pint or two at the Whistle Stop, then maybe stop in at the Christmas dance."

Roland winks at Jane. "Your brother's in a hurry to get to the dance. Any idea why?"

Jane busies herself breaking the holly branches into smaller sprigs, not wanting to accept the possibility of Lizzie Carter in their lives. Clinging to the remaining shreds of her glow, she hopes to express her mood, if not the details, in a letter to Cassie soon. In the meantime, she will make the popcorn strings, then chase Gomer out of his chair where the light is brightest, and read *Jane Eyre*, which Mama found at a used book sale for her birthday on a rare train trip to Nanaimo.

"You're old enough now to join us, Jane," says Roland, interrupting her plans, "unless Mr. Louis Strong has you too busy washing his clothes."

Seeing that her mother is not going to answer for her this time, Jane replies, "There are too many decorations to be made for our beautiful tree." She sees a downward turn to the corners of Roland's mouth, imperceptible to the others.

"Maybe next time," he says, following Tommy out the door.

"Maybe," says Jane, without looking up from the holly.

A COP'S LIFE isn't all donuts and coffee, as some people seem to think. I've seen as many dead bodies as a nurse, watched more women strip than a peeping Tom, and been called more names than an umpire. I've also heard more tales of woe than a priest, but with fewer confessions, and I'm about as popular with my clientele as a dentist, but without his income. Today was one of the days I had to rely on a sense of humour to get through. Luckily, Sukhi was with me to aid and abet the giggles.

Our first call was an O.D. at 7 A M. The victim, Henry Lavoie, Caucasian male, was lying soaking wet and naked in the middle of his apartment's living room. The guests at the all-night party were his friends, all transvestites and also all soaking wet from having tried to revive him in the shower with their clothes on. Said clothes being negligees and nightgowns. When I started to take their statements, one 6'4" guy in a garter belt and stockings wrapped himself around me and declared, "You're the only cop I've ever met I can stand."

He was dripping on me like a dog and I shook him off just as the ambulance arrived. At that moment, Henry woke up, not in the least surprised to find himself wet and naked in a room full of strangers. While the paramedics got him onto a stretcher, my tall friend pulled a pair of hot pink spandex capri pants over his wet stockings, threw a shawl around his shoulders and volunteered to go with Henry in the ambulance. On the way out, he hugged me again as he grabbed a blow dryer from a table, promising to fix himself up at the hospital. Too late for another short guy in a woman's sheer wrapper, who shouted after him: "Leave that dryer, Nicki. How am I going to get ready for visiting hours?"

The most remarkable part of this scene was that it was no longer re-markable. In fact, Sukhi and I both agreed this file was less sordid than the domestic we attended yesterday where a man had tied his wife to the sofa and made her watch him have sex with a prostitute. A disgustingly fat, greasy, toothless drunk no one should have to have sex with, paid or not. Humiliation was usually the starting point in domestic calls, quickly accompanied by blows and screams. The transvestites, on the other hand, were not humiliating one another, and there was no vio-lence besides what the heroin and cocaine were doing to their systems.

I was in one of my moods where I didn't think it was right to be dis-cussing the price of gas over coffee so soon after dealing with these so-called misfits. But then Sukhi said, "How's your history class going?" and I was immediately aware of my own misfit status. If I could think of one more detail of ridicule — like the tampon in Henry's purse — I could stall this conversation, but all I could manage was "Okay."

"Okay? You like it, hate it, what?"

"My dad helped me with the term paper."

"You have the right to remain silent."

"He practically wrote the whole thing."

"Anything you say won't be used against you. I was only wonder-ing because Amara is thinking of taking some courses in the winter to finish her B.Sc. I told her I'd ask you how you like your instructor."

Sure. Amara would pull off 90s in whatever she took. Immigrants' children have all the luck with their parents making every decision for them. Easy for her to write her own essays when her father hardly knows the language. "My professor is great. Brings the material to life, if not me. Your wife will do brilliantly, as she always does."

Sukhi set his coffee cup down, put his hands on his seated hips, pushed his head into the back of the booth, and said: "What's up? You've been talking about taking courses for years and now you're sabotaging yourself. Why? Still caught up in the Ray business? Your mother? Work?"

I shook my head. "No, no, maybe. I don't know. As for the job, you know my doubts."

He resumed drinking his coffee, secure now, like a good cop, that he had me talking. And thinking. When we sat down, I was feeling queasy about tonight's history class. Not so much about what Barnwell would give Dad for his effort — that should be respectable — but he was to announce the topics for our final paper, and I would have to put myself through the shame of it all over again. What caught me off guard in the midst of this dread, however, was a warm wave of anticipation about the last of Jane Owens' letters waiting for me at home. She was doing this more often, passing through my thoughts like an old familiar song. As if we had once shared something intimate. But I had yet to discover what my great-grandmother was transmitting.

I had forgotten what we were talking about when Sukhi said, "I have bad days too."

"Bad days aren't years of wondering about your real calling. I worry when I stop thinking of these weirdoes as weirdoes, and worry just as much when I don't. Maybe I'm not sure of the difference between right and wrong, and that should be a must for cops and preachers. Only lawyers can get away with arguing either side."

"You add a human element to the job, whether or not it's deserved."

Accepting praise from someone always guaranteed to give it to me seemed a bit pathetic. Would I be this open with Nancy Grace?

"Ever think about transferring to another section?" Sukhi asked.

"Sure. Aren't we all sick of domestics? I think I'd like Serious Crimes."

"You? Someone as non-violent as you wants the gory cases?"

"Why not? We'd come in after the fact. I like asking questions."

"You're definitely good with witnesses. Look how Nicki couldn't tear himself away from you on that last call."

"What about you?"

"Same. I'd hate to break up the team of Ahluwalia and Dryvynsydes. It's hard to badmouth names like ours."

It sounded like a good idea, but I probably would never exert myself to apply. I downed the rest of my coffee and stood up to leave. Sukhi followed and we went through the motions of getting out our wallets until the waitress waved us away. At least we left tips.

My belt and all its accessories felt heavier than usual today. I straightened my shoulders to take the pressure off my back before getting into the passenger seat. Sukhi slid behind the wheel and I cleared us for calls. B&E in progress in Deer Lake area. Sukhi wheeled out of Denny's parking lot and was at the address before we could start the siren. It was your standard mushroom-coloured, two-storey, 2,500-square foot attempt at grandeur in a colony of almost-identical houses, all ten feet apart. A young man in an old sweatshirt and windpants beckoned us from the garage next door and we pulled into his driveway. He whispered excitedly to Sukhi, glancing at me as if I were a ride-along so keen I had borrowed a costume for the occasion.

"I called. They're still in there. Came out of the old van parked in the back lane. Got in through the patio door on the deck."

"Sure they're not tradesmen?"

"They're kids. With a crowbar."

"Stick around," Sukhi said. "We'll need a statement later." He had already flattened himself against the east side of the house, edging around toward the back. I followed, but not without a dismissive look at our witness: bead necklace, diamond stud in one ear, small hoop in another, a costume that was his way of declaring he didn't really belong in this neighbourhood when in fact, he simply hadn't shown any aptitude to leave it yet.

From the deck we could hear sounds of large objects being moved carelessly inside. Glass smashed. The patio door had been jimmied, and Sukhi drew his gun as he stepped quietly inside to the eating area. I pressed against the wall on the deck next to the open door and put my hand on my holster. Drawing my firearm always gave me a sick feeling, and this was no exception. I felt as if I were back on the basketball court, doing my best to stay occupied so I wouldn't have to catch the ball.

"Police," Sukhi called out, advancing through the arch to the living room. He didn't have to say "Drop it" because they did — a TV set, by the sound of the thud. With Sukhi in possible danger, the gun felt more comfortable in my hand. My feet were poised to run to the front of the house where any good thief would make his exit if he knew cops were at the back, but I could not set them in motion and leave my partner on his own.

Sukhi lunged toward the open passage with both hands outstretched on his gun. Two teenagers rushed through: the first eluded him, but he tackled the second and forced him to the floor. I yelled "Stop" at the first and chased him across the back lawn to where their van was parked in the lane. He ignored me and kept running.

"Stop or I'll shoot!" I called again, hoping he would drop to his knees without noticing I was aiming at his tires instead of him. He did stop. But it was to turn around at the door of the vehicle and face me with a gun of his own. He looked like a little boy with a Christmas toy, scared rather than menacing. "Drop it," I said, when a stab of fire hit my foot and I fell over.

With my ear to the ground, I heard another shot. My shooter fell and we lay together almost head to head for a few seconds before Sukhi reached us. He had not shot him, but the bullet whizzing past his head had caused him to collapse in fright and drop the gun. Thief Number One, handcuffed to the rail of the deck, looked on, ashen-faced and terrified. Faster than a magician, Sukhi cuffed hair-gelled, well-groomed Number Two, and locked him to the other end of the deck, at the same time calling for back-up and an ambulance. He then slid to where I was.

"You okay?"

I nodded as efficiently as I could with my cheek on the grass. My shoulder must have twisted in the fall and was throbbing. My boot was oozing blood, Sukhi said, and he tried to loosen the laces. He stopped short of pulling it off lest he cause further damage, and because of the yelps any movement provoked from me. When the paramedics arrived, he was holding my hand, his face as close to pale as I had ever seen it. At the same time, Rudder and Emile screeched into the back lane and Sukhi nodded in the direction of the prisoners. From my worm's-eye view, I could see tears on the face of my shooter and his accomplice as they were escorted into the P.C. I had a split-second twinge of sympathy, knowing what they would get in the back seat of the cruiser would be far from consolation.

The paramedics were the same ones who had picked up Henry at the transvestite party this morning. I noted the special consideration I was getting as they gave me a sedative; then again, Henry had not been in any pain. As soon as they began cutting away my size 10 boot with an instrument I couldn't imagine, all gratitude gave way to a flash of red heat, followed by white light, then darkness.

I awoke in the Vancouver General Hospital to find Dad sitting on a chair next to me. As consciousness seeped in, I became aware of a huge white slab of plaster rising from the end of the bed. I must have forgotten how long both my foot and my body were, because this came as a surprise.

"They brought you to Vancouver instead of Burnaby because of a specialist here," Dad said quietly. "Your ankle took quite a hit."

"Yeah?"

"The surgeons were working on it for two hours. We can be thankful you were wearing boots or you might not have a foot left." I could see Dad's hand shaking and I stretched mine across the sheet to clasp it. "Sukhwinder, Emile, Jake, and Dave have all been by to see how you were doing. Sukhwinder feels terrible that he didn't spot the young man's gun." Dad considered it presumptuous to use nicknames he had not given himself.

A glance around the room told me they had left their calling cards in beautiful flower arrangements. The only card close enough to read, however, was attached to a bushy azalea plant and was signed, "Smooth recovery. Ray." How quickly word got around in the halls of justice. I knew he wouldn't have the nerve to deliver them himself.

The crime scene was also coming back to me. I couldn't get beyond the scared face of the kid with the gun and his tears later. "Sukhi shouldn't feel bad. He was busy taking care of the other guy. I did see the gun. I was the one who should have shot, or disarmed him somehow."

"You weren't brought up that way."

"Have you forgotten my line of work?" I tried to roll over on my side toward him, but a sting from the intravenous needle in the other arm reminded me I wasn't free to do so. My shoulder also screamed at this motion. "What time is it?"

"Almost eight. Visiting hours are over."

"Day?"

"Wednesday."

"One way to get out of history class. We were to get our papers back. I should say your paper with my name on it."

"I didn't do that much. You put it all together."

"Yeah, I put the sheets from the printer in the right order."

Dad stood up to go. "I'll be back tomorrow. Anything you need?"

"My history books." I enjoyed the expression on his face: as if I had been hit in the head instead of the foot. "And one more thing: Jane's last letter is on my dresser. Please bring it too."

He stood next to me for a moment, pausing before he spoke. "You know, my first reaction when Sukhwinder phoned me was 'How will Bella get through this without her mother?' But my next thought was relief that she's spared the worry. And seeing you now, I know you'll be fine, if you do what they tell you in here."

I nodded as he rubbed the top of my head gently: it said more than a kiss would have from a more physically affectionate man.

After he left, a pretty little nurse came and explained in more detail what Dad had already outlined about my foot. I would have to be in here a few more days. While checking my functions and equipment, she remarked in a Caribbean accent: "You're brave to put your life on the line every day."

"I could say the same to you," I replied, feeling more negligent than brave. "You have a lot more than one life in your hands."

I was practically asleep when she left, and as usual lately, Jane Owens was in the twilight. At least her life of drudgery was a safe one.

✂ ✂ ✂ ✂
✂ ✂ ✂ ✂ ✂ ✂ ✂ ✂ ✂

DRYING DOES NOT HELP Jane's clammy hands. Like blood in a fresh wound, the cold film reappears as soon as she blots it and lifts the towel away. From the bedroom her mother's loud sighs are not enough to penetrate her thoughts until they become almost a shout.

"Jane!"

Mechanically, her legs carry her to the chamber of lavender and menthol they once shared.

"Can't you hear me? Or your brother coughing? You're in your head again."

When she concentrates, Jane does hear Gomer's raw rasps almost shaking the framework of Thomas' bedroom, but they have been background sounds for too long to distract her at the moment.

"Would you make him some hot lemon and honey? I don't have the strength for it right now."

"There are no lemons in the house."

"He'll have to hack away then. And fill Tommy's room with germs."

"I'll check with Salos. They might give us one or two until I can get to the store." Jane dries the last cup and sets it in the cupboard before wiping her hands again.

"You know I don't like to borrow. Gomer will get through this if you boil some water for vapours."

Her mother's words dispatch a bolt of resolve in Jane. She will go to Louis, after all. She cannot waste precious minutes babying her brother with a vapour tent when he gets as many colds as he can to keep from going to school. The numbness that seized her after hearing Lance Cruikshank on the road an hour ago is now transformed into determination of equal measure. In the early January darkness he did not notice her on the other side, but she could not miss his belligerent, drunken words to a fellow miner.

"Everybody's patience with that darkie has run out. We'll have a new coal seam soon, with or without the slave's permission."

A sharp crack of laughter followed Jane out of earshot. She had kept quiet the first time she heard Lance, but now she must warn Louis. What can an old man do? And what will be the consequences? At least Louis should know of this talk, if he doesn't already. His family might be able to help him. "I'll find a lemon for Gomer," she says abruptly, untying her apron and hanging it in the scullery. She notices her hands are dry.

"You shouldn't be out after dark. Cougars, you know." By her tone, Mary Owens concedes she is no match for the firmness in her daughter's.

"It's dark before supper now. I walk home in it every day." Jane has her cloak on before her mother can mention the vapour tent again. "I'll be careful."

She laces her boots, wraps a shawl around her head and shoulders, and steps into the damp night. Once outside, she digs her hands in the pockets of her long woollen cardigan, wishing she had brought her gloves. At least Thomas is working night shift, making her mission easier.

She looks toward the Salo house, envisioning Gertie and her oversized brothers sitting in their small kitchen filled with cabbage and turnip fumes. She has no intention of exchanging words with them over a lemon, while their mother demands in Finnish from the other room to know what they are saying. Hastening her step, she is soon heading in the opposite direction toward Louis Strong's log house. Traces of yesterday's snow cling to the base of trees and bushes, but the trail itself is clear. Her heart pounding with urgency, she is sure of her purpose, though not quite sure of what she will say.

Jane knows the route so well she could probably traverse it blindfolded without straying into too many thorns, but she welcomes the moon's accompaniment tonight. Its eerie light foils clouds and evergreens to guide her. She thinks of Hansel and Gretel, part of her lost childhood world in Wales. A rustle in the bush startles her until the hoot of an owl assures her it is not a cougar but some small prey running for cover. She moves so quickly she does not expect the shack of Butch Hargraves to appear as soon as it does.

Instinctively, she slows to listen for signs of life inside or out; if not, she always hurries past. Tonight muffled sounds issue from the cabin, indistinguishable until she gets closer. Voices. She stops short and crouches, finding a limited line of vision between the Oregon grape bushes and the window, lit by an oil lamp. Two figures move back and forth until one stops with his back to her. She recognizes the faded green shirt she has washed so often on the tall, stooped man. The bulkier one paces back and forth, the grimy windowpane muting words that convey frequent surges of tone. Louis turns to the side, and Jane sees he is holding his rifle. Have they just come back from hunting? When Butch stops to make a point, Louis turns away from him toward the window, half-cocking the rifle, then lifting it close to his bad eyes as if to inspect it. Butch backs away, reminding Jane of Louis' claim that he was a better shot and Butch knew it.

Jane pulls the shawl tighter around her head and throat, then re-clenches her cold fingers in the pockets of her cardigan. When she looks back to the window, neither man is in view. The creak of a wooden door at the side alerts her they are coming out. Jane quickly ducks from the trail behind a bush closer to the cabin. Louis emerges, black woollen toque on his head, tired feet trudging down the path.

"Ah got no time for this now. Ma son Maynard comin' home and he's what's on ma mind. Ma place want cleanin' up for him and that's whe' ah goin.'"

Normally Jane loves seeing the milky old eyes brighten when Louis speaks of his children, but tonight his words carry a harshness she has not heard before. Jane already knows of Maynard's return from a year of gold prospecting up north. She hopes to meet the older son by timing her laundry delivery while he is there, always trying in vain not to allow Adam's presence into this anticipation. Louis proceeds without looking back.

Butch has not ventured far from his hut. He hawks a wad of spittle into a bush next to his door. Jane does not see him reappear in the window light, nor does she hear the door scraping shut. Maybe he has gone to relieve himself in the trees, as Tommy does after a night at the pub. What else could he be doing at the back in the dark? Nothing there but two small butchering sheds. According to Louis, one contains hammers, knives, and axes for finishing off the slaughter and cutting up the carcass; the other is to hang the meat for curing. Both are without light.

Though she has an urge to make a break for it and catch up with Louis, Jane stays huddled behind the bush. She is afraid to reveal herself with a sound, in case Butch is closer than she thinks. The cold pinches her toes and, as usual, her nose has begun to drip. She fishes for a handkerchief in her cardigan, wishing it were gloves. A spell of silence encourages her to inch forward, peering for a better view of the door. It is still ajar. But there is no sign of Henry Hargraves. She thinks of Mama, hoping she has fallen asleep and will accept the explanation that the Salos did not have a lemon so she walked all the way to the store but it had just closed. She should not be away too long. From the sound of Louis' voice, he has had his own warning, making her mission unnecessary. She backs up slowly, convinced now to retrace her steps home as quietly and quickly as she can.

Just then, the light is extinguished in the cabin and the door slams shut. Butch stomps down the path and turns in the direction of Louis Strong's log cabin. The sudden transition back to darkness prevents her from being sure, but Jane believes she sees something in his hand.

She begins to tremble. Cold hands and feet forgotten, she feels her entire body shivering with fear. Longing to flee, she remains helplessly rooted to a square of moss behind an Oregon grape bush on the edge of the Hargraves property. Clouds have temporarily obscured the moon, and like the rest of the forest creatures, she must rely on her other senses for direction.

Butch's steps come to a standstill not far away. An abrupt halt followed by what she hears as a heavy sidestep into twigs and leaves. In the distance more steps, approaching from the opposite direction. Plodding feet at a rhythmic pace.

The next sound Jane hears will remain with her for the rest of her life. A clipped thud, occupying no more than a split second of time, less audible than a single tap on a door. Was it a hammer, the blunt edge of a poleaxe? Whatever the weapon, the blow was excruciating in its simplicity and ordinariness. Perfectly executed, an exact target cushioned by wool, by hair, by scalp, as if it were the soft spot on baby Norman's head. Not a grunt, a moan, or a scream. The vacuum of sound and light gives way to a putrid smell and a metallic taste in her mouth. A stew of the worst odours imaginable mingle in her nostrils: brackish water left standing in a vase, Butch's breath and stale clothes from the time he got close to her on the path, rotten eggs, spoiled chicken, the privy before she puts lye in. All conspire to choke her into a sputtering cough, but she catches herself. One of the men — but only one — has begun breathing again. Heavy panting as he drags his kill toward her.

Jane's mind hurtles through choices. She cannot turn back or the fickle moon, in full force on the path again, will give her away. She cannot stay crouched in the bush, so close to Butch's cabin. Her only recourse is to creep quietly behind the windowless end wall of the cabin until Butch goes inside. She matches her movements to his puffing breaths and reaches the backyard just as he turns down the path, manoeuvring the dead weight behind him. Hiding behind the smaller curing shed, she waits until he is at the side door of his cabin. Instead of going in, he continues in her direction.

Jane's terror is about to burst into something she cannot control. At the sight of the moonlit green shirt bobbing lifelessly past her just a few feet away, she swallows hard to stem dark bile oozing into her throat. She presses herself against the back wall, away from Butch pulling the corpse into the butchering shack like a deer carcass. Will he hack off a leg if it doesn't fit?

To steady herself, Jane grabs at a protrusion she makes out in the darkness. A hasp on the door of the curing shed. Sharp and ragged, it slices into two of her fingers. She touches it with the other hand and a rough finish tells her it is rusty. She squats, doubling over. The delayed pain spreading through her fingers from the cut barely registers against growing nausea that threatens to empty her insides. "I must not faint," she repeats, now past prayer and into an animal fight to survive.

At last, Butch slams the door of the other shed and thumps back into his cabin. Soon the lamp makes visible a wedge of the area just beyond her hiding spot. She resists an urge to look through the window. To see what a murderer looks like. Have Henry Hargraves' features rearranged themselves like a werewolf in order to perform such an act? Would he have gone all the way to Louis' cabin if Louis had not come back down the path? His repulsive face and manner had not prepared her for a possibility like this. Even more, she wants to slip into the butchering shed to touch the face of her old friend lying crumpled there. Perhaps there is still a pulse and she can revive him. And have her noisy efforts rewarded with a sledgehammer to both their skulls?

Jane knows Louis is beyond hope and that she must reach the main trail quickly before throwing up or passing out. Lifting her long skirt, she ducks under the window and, once behind the solid wall, makes haste to the main road. Instead of turning left to home and safety, she pauses. The same moonlight threatening her with exposure now illuminates something else. A faded red plaid bundle contrasted against a snow clump lures her eyes to the right. As if flung, it lies in a direct line from where she imagines the deadly blow to have taken place. She looks toward Butch's cabin and, seeing the door shut, tiptoes toward the parcel, now recognizable. Is this what brought Louis out again from home so soon after leaving Butch's cabin? Bringing clothes and sheets for her to wash in preparation for Maynard's visit?

Jane chokes back the thought that she was his final destination on earth. In reaching for the package, her light-headedness distils into clarity. She must think fast, wrench her fears from the present to the future. If she ends up with Louis' clothes instead of a lemon, she will have some explaining to do to her mother — and all the community. If she leaves it here, it will bear witness to the place Louis was felled. Butch would not have noticed the clue Louis left behind. Her hand wet with blood from the rusty hasp makes her decision. Gently she pushes the bundle under cover of a bush, beyond Butch's detection but evidence for anyone looking. Her own blood will provide proof of a struggle.

A burst of adrenalin then spins her into a full run along the trail back home. Only at a safe distance does she stop to catch her breath. Dripping from her eyes, nose, and fingers, she lifts her skirt to wipe all three. She advances more slowly, willing away tears that could betray the story she must concoct before facing her mother.

Mary Owens is right: Jane lives too much in her head. Should she tell everything she knows, as Stella or Gertie Salo would, with words that spring straight from their eyes to their mouths without passing through their brains? She thinks too much of expectations and consequences. Her mother and Tommy would never understand how she had ended up at the site of a murder through not minding her own business. The questions would put them all on public display. Mama's health would fail even more, Tommy's position at the mine could be in danger, if she was thought to be helping the one person holding back a livelihood for so many.

But Louis? Where was her loyalty to him? If she was his only friend, should she not stand up for him, dead or alive?

No smoke from the chimney means Mama must have fallen asleep and let the coal stove die. Jane lifts the latch of the back door quietly and steps inside. She reaches for a rag to wrap around her bloody hand before unlacing her boots and hanging up her shawl. Using her bandaged hand for a final swipe over her tear-stained face, she moves toward the stove. Her mother is at the bedroom door, sleep in her eyes.

"Why is it so cold?"

"The fire got low." Jane raises the coal bucket to the mouth of the stove, her back to her mother.

Mary Owens yawns. "What time is it anyway? Did you get lemons?"

"No." She does not explain.

"You shouldn't have been out in this darkness." Her mother sets the cold kettle on the heating stove. "Maybe I'll make a pot of tea to warm us up." Back in the kitchen she turns up the wick of the oil lamp and sees Jane clearly for the first time. Her hands clamp over her heart. "O 'm Celi! What happened to you? You've bled all over yourself. Your face is so smeared you might have come from the mine."

"A cougar," Jane says weakly.

"A cougar attacked you? Didn't I warn you?" Her mother's alarm has prompted an agility Jane has not seen since Wales. Also a dialect. "Look you, there is terrible indeed." She takes off the bloody rag and holds her daughter's hands in the basin, running cool, clean water from the pail over them. Jane remembers how comforting this ritual was as a child, her mother scouring their hands at the sink after a day of playing outside.

Gomer has wakened, slouching into the kitchen with a blanket over his shoulders, nose caked with mucous, breathing thick and congested.

"Go you back to bed, Gomer," his mother directs, helping Jane off with her cardigan sweater and skirt, leaving her in her petticoat and shimmy.

He whines for water and Mary Owens hands him a glass as she ushers him back to the bedroom.

Jane's voice has become weaker. "A cougar didn't attack me, but I thought I heard one in the bushes. I ran for shelter to a shed and cut my hand on a hasp."

"Your hand is swelling," her mother says, freshening the water in the basin. "Soak it while I get the iodine. There is careless you are, cariad." Shaking her head, she applies the brown tincture to the cut, waiting for its sting to subside before wiping her daughter's streaky face. Jane has not experienced such tenderness for a long time.

"It was rusty."

"I thought as much. We must work fast to save you from blood poisoning. I fear it might have set in. Sit you still."

Jane's clean face, growing more and more pale, turns to her mother to say, "Thank you, Mama," before she collapses on the kitchen floor.

"I'M SORRY TO WAKEN YOU, DEAR," said Janetta, standing next to my bed.

"No, no," I said, wiping drool from my face with a tissue still clenched in my hand. "I wasn't asleep." I tried to sit up and face forward, forgetting that the big white log of a leg had to be coaxed into position and, if possible, not at the expense of the shoulder. Uncle Lawrence stood in the doorway, cap in hand, as if waiting for permission to enter. I motioned them both to the two chairs in my private room.

"We've exchanged places since we last saw each other," Janetta smiled, sitting down. "Except you've become a celebrity. We saw the incident on TV."

"You must have given him quite a kick." Lawrence nodded at my foot with his usual blast of laughter.

"Yeah." I played along. "But he asked for it."

Janetta held a tapestry tote bag, which she was now opening. "We had lunch with your dad and he thought you would be up for a visit. He'll come later, so you won't be too crowded."

"Typical Dad. How are you feeling?"

"Better than ever, thanks. These are washed," she said, pulling out a bag of plums. "And I thought you should have the letters, since it could be awhile before you're back on the island." She took out a Ziploc plastic bag containing a slim paper packet tied with a ribbon. "Special delivery from Jane Hughes."

My wits were slowly returning after my nap, and I remembered the last letter. "Don't you mean Jane Owens?"

"She's Hughes in these. There are only five of them and I wish I had looked at them earlier. I would have preserved them in an acid-free album."

"I'll be careful." I pulled the plastic grooves apart and slipped the slim bundle out of the ribbon. The stationery was more like ordinary bond paper than the creamy vellum she used for her other letters. I opened the first one, dated December 17, 1895.

Dear Sisters and Brother,

I want to thank Catherine for all her letters over the past year and beg forgiveness for my silence. There have been many changes, as you probably know by now. Mama says she has written to you. Blood poisoning last February almost killed me. I was confined to bed for a month.

On May 2 I married Roland Hughes and we are living in his home following the sudden death of his father in April. Next year we will be moving to the new mine site of Extension, which is being built on a rich seam of coal that was discovered not far from our property in Chase River. I am still close enough to Mama to help her with housework. I no longer take in laundry, because one customer died and the other left her husband and took her baby to live with her mother at Departure Bay.

On December 4 I had a baby boy. He was big for being early and I thought he was strong, but he died that same day. We named him Owen and buried him in the Chase River cemetery.

Thank you for the birthday wishes. I am now 17 and feel twice that age. Merry Christmas to you all. I will let you know my new address, when I have one.

Your loving sister, Jane

My eyes locked on the letter, I reminded myself I was ignoring visitors who had come all the way from the island to see me. Lawrence had already stood up and sauntered out of the room. Janetta, however, appeared fixed on my reaction.

"Are you sure this is the earliest?" I asked her, confused after reading the one Dad brought me yesterday.

"Yes, they're in order."

"This is much more formal than the last one we have. No kisses at the bottom, for one thing." I retrieved mine, left in an envelope in the drawer of the swinging table. I handed it to my aunt. "Read this and see what you think."

Janetta pulled her reading glasses up from their chain and read aloud:

January 4, 1895

Dear Sisters and Brother,

The Christmas season has come and gone and we are now into a new year. I hope it will bring blessings for us all.

I cooked a grouse and plum pudding for Mama, Gomer, Tommy, and his friend Roland Hughes, who doesn't have a mother. Everyone was in good health and Mama and the two men sang carols while I put the meal on the table. Even Gomer joined in. To me there was still a sad feeling that you are so far away from us. I will never get used to that.

With the holiday over I start back to my laundry work tomorrow. As unhappy as I am at one house, I do it gladly in the hope that we will soon have the passage for you all. Cassie could come first until the others can travel together. I see joy in the face of my other customer who is expecting his son after a year of gold prospecting in the north. He needs hope to help him through his other problems. I wish I could do more for him.

Please write often. I miss you more than ever. Tommy sends $10.

x x x x x x x x x Your loving sister, Jane x x x x x x x x x

"Hmm," said Janetta thoughtfully, rereading the earlier one. "Yes, this is more intimate than the ones I've given you. You'll see for yourself. What I don't understand is how Mother ended up with these letters. They were sent to Wales, after all. And we don't have any of Jane's sisters' letters here. Shouldn't it be the other way around? From the sound of these — they end in 1915 — Catherine never does make it over. Unless it's in the last three years of Jane's life."

"Please don't ruin the suspense. I didn't think I would become as hooked on my great-grandmother as I have." My mind was still stuck at Janetta's first letter. Blood poisoning from what? Jane's marriage to Roland Hughes so fast without any warning? Obviously she got pregnant right after she got well. And the fates of her customers? But most of all, the tragedy of Jane's baby — would she not have said more about this heartbreak to her sisters? "Did you know about baby Owen? I don't remember Sara mentioning him. As far as I knew, Janet and Llewyllyn were her only siblings."

Janetta turned, a flash of annoyance giving way to resignation, as she noticed Lawrence pacing back and forth in the corridor, obviously a signal that she had been here long enough. "No, I didn't know of that baby either. Mother must have, since she had these letters first, but I don't remember her mentioning him."

"Oh, to have Sara here again."

Janetta stood up and smiled, resembling her mother so much in that instant I felt as if my wish had been granted. Maybe the heart attack had dissolved a few layers of reserve. "We'll have to fill in the gaps ourselves." She kissed my forehead and joined her husband standing in the doorway. "Don't try chasing anybody now," he called as they left, his laugh trailing through the corridor.

Squirming into a better position, I unfolded the next letter. Before I could read a word, a nurse came in carrying a pair of aluminum crutches.

"I'm going to take you for a short walk. We'll see how you navigate on these."

This should be interesting. I had limped as far as the bathroom, but that required only two or three hops. I was not looking forward to bracing the crutch with my shoulder, but I would do as I was told, as Dad said. Even slipping on the left sleeve of the hospital gown was more painful than I expected; that done, I stepped down on my cast and prepared for a stroll along the hall.

"Take it easy," the nurse said, seeing my mouth clenched in more than determination.

The rests lasted twice as long as the steps, and I felt I should apologize. "The trouble is, it's my right leg and my left shoulder. I have to give them equal chances to hurt."

"I know," she said, not unkindly. "That's why you have to practise. It will get easier as both heal."

"I'll work on it." I hoped to suggest she needn't waste any more of her time, but really I didn't want to be rushed through my pauses.

She reached up and gave me a pat on my good shoulder. "I'll check on you later."

Unaccustomed to pain, I could not believe how difficult it was to keep from acting like what I would call a wimp in anyone else. As I stopped to rest for the tenth time in five metres, a man emerged from a room across and down the hall. He too was propped on crutches with a cast just like mine, but on the left leg.

"Care for a three-legged race?" He smiled.

In returning the smile, I momentarily forgot the pain. He was attractive in an unassuming way. Soon he was next to me, negotiating his crutches like limbs. He waited for me to advance down the corridor in unison, so I listened to my inner voice saying "Suck it up." The shoulder would have to suffer for the mobility of the legs, I decided, swallowing a spray of stars that came from the choice.

His next question threw me off guard: "So, how did you do it?"

I had not thought up a response yet for strangers. I was not about to admit to being shot because of all the drama that would involve; nor could I say I was a nurse this time, in case he asked me a technical question about our injuries. To my own surprise I blurted out: "Doing a pirouette." For some reason, a memory of Gail's sprained ankle from our RAD classes in junior high came back to me. "And I should have known better. I'm a dance teacher." I then added hastily: "What about you?"

He stared at me as if he didn't believe me. Weren't dance teachers this tall?

"The Grouse Grind. A clumsy step for me too. It's not as if I haven't done it before."

I had climbed the brutal eight hundred metres of Grouse Mountain myself. Three times. It was always Ray's idea and I vowed each gruelling ascent would be the last. "I guess we'll both have to learn to be more careful." The punishment for my lie was a ripple of pain in the shoulder that added to the flush on my face.

"Maybe we should sit for a while. You look as if you need a breather." He lifted a crutch and pointed to an open door. "The lounge is in there."

"You seem to know your way around here," I said, dragging after him. The lounge was empty other than a pale old man watching TV with his intravenous stand.

"Yeah, I've been up and down a few times. Maybe I didn't have as many visitors as you."

I settled myself carefully in a chair, extending my leg and accidentally touching his, which was stretched out across from me. What did he mean by that? Had he been watching my room? "Or maybe I'm just lazy about therapy."

"You won't be doing too much dancing for a while." He gave me a crooked smile, unfortunately the kind I must beware of, for Ray Kelsey had one too. Height, thick, dark hair — all the warning signs were there. I glanced at his bare hands. The wedding ring was no doubt with his watch in an envelope in a locker.

"No, I guess not." My cheeks were hot. "I'll have to find some other means of amusement."

Then he blushed, acknowledging the innuendo I had not intended. In the midst of all our blushing, the old man raised himself creakily from his chair and did a two-step out of the room with his stainless steel partner.

"How long are you in for?" I tried to change the subject.

"You make it sound like a prison sentence. But I suppose you would be familiar with that, Constable Dryvynsydes."

I stared at him. So he had been watching my room and seen all the uniforms going in and out. But my name? Maybe he had seen the TV account. Nurses talk too.

"You're showing me up in detective work."

"At least in powers of observation. You don't remember me, do you?"

"Should I?"

"You should. You arrested me."

MY MOUTH HAD NOT YET CLOSED when a familiar voice quacked outside the door to the lounge. Megan bounced in followed by Lonnie. She wore hipster jeans that showed off her tight little midriff.

"The nurse told us you might be here." She gave me a hug that was arm's length by necessity. "So how you doing, girlfriend? Taking a fall for the force — that should earn you some brownie points."

Other than detecting a whiff of envy in her voice, Megan's irritating buddy talk went over my head. I was still fixed on my wardmate sitting across from me. I could not place him at all. Had he been in a grow-op raid? Surely he was not part of the biker scene, and I didn't recognize him without a helmet or bandana. As Megan gushed, he raised himself onto his crutches. Smugly, I thought, knowing he was one up on me. Then he nodded farewell with another smile and left before I could introduce Megan and Lonnie to him, thereby learning his name.

"There's a fruit basket from our team in your room."

I pulled myself to a standing position, trying my best not to wince in front of Megan, but she spotted the cover.

"Lonnie, see if there's a wheelchair around."

Defeated, I was soon being wheeled back to my room where a mammoth hamper awaited me. Fruit was incidental to all the other delicacies like tapenades, pâtés, crisp water biscuits, canned brie, sugared almonds — and those were only on the outside.

Megan demanded I give a detailed account of the shooting, and I did. She said she would have done exactly the same thing in my position, but I knew she believed she would have spotted the kid's gun in time to take him down one way or the other. It's a good thing — or maybe a bad one — that every set of circumstances is unique and it's impossible to know how we would really react, if given the chance. We like to glorify ourselves in judging the actions of others. We all do it, not just Megan.

Megan was doing her best to console me with shop talk — how both our teams were getting restless and talking transfers — but I was beginning to flag again. I was thankful when another nurse appeared with a trolley of pills. Megan and Lonnie stood up, signed my cast, and left. One of the pills calmed my shoulder and made me drift off again. I'm not sure how long my eyes were closed, but when I opened them, Dad was sitting quietly in the chair vacated by Lonnie. He didn't say a word until he was sure I would not go back to sleep.

"How're you doing?" He had brought some cashews and oranges, which he now tucked shyly behind the miniature deli and Janetta's plums.

"Better after the painkiller."

"I see you have some new signatures."

"What do they say?"

"'Chin up, Lonnie.' and 'LYLASBAWLM, Megan.'" He spelled it out and waited for an explanation.

I rolled my eyes. "Love you like a sister but a whole lot more. It's a high school thing."

"Isn't it a compliment?"

"Sure, if you mean it."

"How can you be sure she doesn't?"

I knew I was too hard on Megan and conceded, "You're right, she probably did."

Dad got nervous over my strong opinions about people. He didn't suspect hypocrisy or trickery in others because he had none himself. Sara had brainwashed Dad and Janetta with a theory she based on Grandpa's lush lawn wherever they lived. If the best remedy for weeds was healthy grass, the surest way to block resentment was with thick and impenetrable gratitude for what you had. Both Dad and Janetta had aced this exercise like star pupils, but despite repeating it so often, Sara never did master it herself. Neither would I. Indulging my irritation with the Megans of the world was like a guiltily satisfying second piece of cheesecake. Sara would have understood; I missed her for the second time today. "Janetta brought more letters, but I've only had a chance to read one."

At the hint of imposing, Dad stood up until I said firmly, "It's your family too. We can read them together." I picked up the second one, noting that April 16, 1900 was five years after the last. I read aloud:

Dear Sisters and Brother,

You have a new nephew Llewyllyn Thomas Hughes born March 4, 1900. At six weeks he is plump and healthy and brings me much happiness. I had given up hope for a baby after losing one before birth after Owen.

Thank you for your letters Catherine. Congratulations on your engagement. Clarence Williams is a lucky man. I hope he will stay clear of drink and treat you well. That is what matters for a woman in marriage.

The Extension mines are rich in coal but the town has grown up without planning. Stumps from timbers needed in the mine are everywhere, the water is poor and scarce in summer, drainage is bad, and we live in makeshift cottages that were moved from another used-up mine. The most lasting feature is the coal dust covering them. Our little house requires more space and many repairs, but Roland does not have an interest in such work as Tommy did.

I am reminded of Wales and of you whenever I look out upon the bluffs that surround this town, especially in spring when the oxeye daisies and delphiniums are in full colour. I also planted a lilac bush next to our front door and its blossoms, along with the white flowering dogwood tree in our yard, bring me much delight. We must look for beauty where we can.

Tommy and Lizzie and their two daughters live in the

new town of Ladysmith, where the loading wharves for the Extension coal are located. We are 12 miles apart and the mine train makes three trips a day between the two towns, but I do not see much of his family. Gomer stays with Mama in Chase River but for how long? He speaks of marriage to Thelma who cleans rooms in Mrs. Bailey's Temperance Hotel. Her family owns a dry goods store in Victoria and has a place for him in the business. Gomer has always hated the mines because the coal dust makes him cough and because it is hard work. He has never taken to work of any kind. I help Mama whenever I can. I have asked her to live with us but she says our house would be too crowded for so many souls. Tommy is building another room and she will probably move to Ladysmith.

Mama has taught me sewing skills like Margaret. There is more work than I need in this town, especially repairs for bachelor miners.

I would not have known Evan and Gwynyth from the photo you sent Mama. They are so grown-up. Please continue to write. I will try to do better than one letter every five years.

I remain your loving sister, Jane.

"At least we know we're not missing any letters," I said to Dad. "She doesn't write because her life is so dismal with Roland Hughes and she's not the type to complain."

"You solved that quickly." Dad examined the letter, shaking his head. "My namesake. Over a hundred years ago. Note the second 'y' in Llewyllyn. I guess Sara didn't know about the spelling or I could have been tied with the train station in Wales."

"The new baby has made her chattier. No more kisses, though. Or Cassie."

At the sight of all the floral and edible tributes surrounding me, I felt overwhelmed by my coddled life when no one ever looked after my great-grandmother except herself. Metres away sat my supreme guardian, who seemed to be reading my mind.

"I think you should come home with me when you're discharged. You won't be up to much for a while. I can check on your apartment and bring your mail for you every few days.

"Thanks, Dad. I might take you up on it."

No excuses for a weed in my lawn of gratitude. The prospect of cooking and doing laundry on crutches was more than I could face, especially when I wasn't big on either in my able-bodied state. It also crossed my mind—deviously—that Dad and his books would be there to consult when I did my final paper. The library texts he had brought from my place sat unopened on the night table, the fault of visitors, nurses, and sedatives, I rationalized. The cost of a couple of months rent on an empty apartment would probably be equivalent to home care and taxis if I stayed in it. And the force was good about compensation.

Dad stood up. "Smells like the food wagon outside. I'll leave you to eat your supper."

As soon as he was gone, a nurse arrived with a bouquet of daisies. Before I had a chance to see the card, the phone next to my bed rang and I knew both were from the same person. Gail had carried daisies at her wedding and sent them for Mom's funeral.

Hearing her voice made me realize how much I missed her, again followed by the thought that Jane Hughes would probably not have had such friends. When Gail asked how I was, I surprised myself completely by announcing, "I'm going to apply for Serious Crimes."

"Wow!" she replied. "So the shot in the foot has been a shot in the arm. How's that for a caption?"

I felt the same way. Maybe all the recent talk had made up my mind and, of course, Gail should be first to know. I couldn't explain that my great-grandmother had also played a part. How could I be so wishy-washy about taking a risk when her life was full of challenges?

"Wait 'til I tell Monty."

"He might be inspector before it happens."

She said she would see me at Christmas. It was their turn to spend it with her parents in Vancouver.

"Love you like a sister but a whole lot more," I said.

She laughed. "I haven't heard that since high school, but ditto."

"And one more thing." An idea had popped into my head. "Could you do me a favour and find out where that picture came from? The one of Sara and her sister that I bought at the garage sale? It's a duplicate of mine and I can't figure out how it would get to Willow Point. See if any of the family members can give you some background? Would it be a huge pain?"

"Not for a budding journalist."

I hung up just as my supper tray was set in front of me. White fish, mashed potatoes, cauliflower in cream sauce, white roll, vanilla pudding. Was the dietitian colour blind? I thought about putting the lid back on and nibbling from my gift goodies, but decided I should probably eat the fish. Soon the whole plate was clean. The painkiller had numbed my shoulder, now I had only to concentrate on getting on the crutches and out the door. When I reached the room two down and across the hall, I stopped and adjusted my crutch. Out of the corner of my eye, I saw a care aide standing over the bed with linen in her hand. I looked unabashedly now. The old sheets and blankets were in a pile on the floor and no one was in the room.

"Where's the patient?" I hopped to the doorway.

"Discharged." The aide smoothed the sheet to a boardlike surface, as I once did in Depot but never since.

"So soon?"

She shrugged. "He must have been ready."

"What was his name?"

"You can ask a nurse. All I know is someone is waiting for this bed."

Moving aside to let her pass, I continued down the hall toward the lounge to make sure he wasn't in there. Empty, of course, so I propelled myself back to my room. Rather smoothly, I discovered. Just as I sat down on the bed, a nurse I had never seen showed up with equipment. I waited for her to take my blood pressure before asking: "Do you happen to know the name of the fellow across the hall with the cast on his leg?"

"He's gone."

"I know, but do you know his name?"

"The tall man?" She was making it difficult.

I nodded, and she looked at me curiously until I added, "We've met before and I was embarrassed not to remember his name. You know the situation — we probably went to school together and I should know who he is."

"Warren Wright." She was so stingy with the information that I wondered if she was jealous. Hospital names aren't confidential and she should know I'd be able to get it if I had to.

"Was that Warren? He's grown a foot since I last saw him." I marvelled at the ease with which I could lie recently. Maybe I was ready for the undercover unit in spite of my conspicuous height.

With an eye roll at my blood pressure reading — as if it were a polygraph — she left.

Warren Wright. His history lay at my fingertips, but how soon would I get to the cpic computer again? He would be in my files, so it wasn't unethical, but it was not the kind of check I would ask someone to do for me.

Suddenly I wanted to get out of here — not only for cpic access, but to put in a transfer application from Dad's computer before I changed my mind. I flopped backward on the bed and lifted the cast manually to the other side. This and the walk down the hall cost more energy than I expected. I sighed, sank back against elevated pillows and picked up a letter.

September 25, 1905

Dear Sisters and Brother,

Our mother was laid to rest in the Nanaimo cemetery
on Saturday, September 23. Thank you for your telegraph
messages. We too were sorry you could not be here to say
goodbye. She went peacefully of pneumonia in Thomas's
home. Her twelve years in Canada were filled with illness
and I wonder if she would be alive and healthy, if she

had stayed in Wales. She would tell me such a thought is foolish because we will never know.

Thomas took care of funeral arrangements and Gomer and family attended from Victoria. My little Llewyllyn was disappointed that his older cousins Myrtle and Edna would not play with him, and he was kept from playing with his two-year-old cousin Ethan. His Aunt Thelma was afraid he would harm her son. She does not know what a gentle little boy he is at five and a half. Sometimes I fear he has grown up too fast in our home.

Thank you Catherine for your letters. I am glad that you enjoy married life. It is a blessing your husband is a bookkeeper and not a miner.

With coal dust everywhere I am thankful I no longer have to take in laundry for wages and hang clothes on the line. At least it has not hurt my garden where I grow almost everything we need — potatoes, carrots, turnips, leeks, swedes, parsnips, cress, peas, beans, tomatoes, and onions.

You will not believe me anymore when I promise to be a good correspondent. If we ever meet again, I will tell you all that has happened in the last ten years. I hope you will still write now that Mama is gone.

I remain your loving sister, Jane

How I wanted to know what Jane Hughes was leaving out of her letters. She had reeled me into her world and I yearned to discover more about this woman who started our family in Canada. Besides the absence of kisses I felt sad about the line "If we ever meet again..." A new, resigned voice had taken over the young girl who had agonized over her family being so far away. I did not believe she missed them any less; rather, that she now kept all her feelings to herself. Carefully I unfolded the second-to-last letter.

March 8, 1910

Dear Sisters and Brother,

It is with great joy I announce the birth of twin daughters
Sara and Janet on February 16. They are a blessing to our
family. Roland wept when he saw them and wanted to call
one Jane, but I agreed to Janet. Llewyllyn says they were the
best gift ever for his 10th birthday four days ago. He loves
them dearly and holds one while I feed the other. So far Sara
seems more spirited than Janet. Janet sleeps a lot and gives
me a chance to do housework and even a little sewing.

I am sorry to hear of Gilbert's illness. The mine takes
the health or the lives of its workers one way or another,
whether through accident, lung disease, or alcohol. I am
glad to hear Evan and Gwynyth and Gilbert's children
have all moved to Cardiff to seek their fortunes.

Margaret is not too old to find happiness in a second
marriage at 42, if she is worried as you say. Please pass
along my best wishes for the upcoming wedding. I will send
a gift as soon as I have the time and strength to take in
more sewing. I will buy something special at the Hudson's
Bay Company in Nanaimo.

If Roland did not see Tommy at the mine I would
not know anything of our older brother. Lizzie keeps him
to herself and her family. We hear even less of Gomer in
Victoria.

Catherine, your letters are precious to me, even when
I do not often reply.

Your loving sister Jane

This letter inspired a peculiar combination of possessiveness and awe.
It was the first mention of a person I actually knew. To think of my
Sara bringing the same joy as a baby to someone I didn't know caused
an unexpected twinge of envy. Did Jane know Sara better than I did?

I felt strangely left out of the magic moment between these two women, or one woman and two babies, one of whom was my grandmother.
I visualized Janet as Janetta, calm and practical.

Gradually the power of the letter became greater than my petty jealousy. How could I feel left out of a scene in which I did not even figure?
It was merely a piece of brittle paper I held in my hands, though not so
merely when I considered the timeline and contents. The part about
Roland Hughes weeping and wanting to name the baby after his wife
grabbed me, both for Jane's sake and because it was the first favourable
mention of my great-grandfather.

Just then, a nurse poked her head in the door. I refocused suffi-
ciently to tell her I was okay before picking up Jane Hughes' last letter.

March 4, 1915

Dear Sisters,

I am sorry to hear about our brother Gilbert's passing.
At least he does not have to suffer any more. Please pass
along my condolences to Constance who took care of him
so well through good times and bad. I am glad she will
be moving to Cardiff closer to her children.

At such times I must give thanks for my strong constitution. It would never do for me to be sick and fortunately,
other than hay fever and catarrh I seldom am.

Today is Llewyllyn's fifteenth birthday. He would not
have a cake but his sisters cried until I made one. He has
become quiet and moody in the last two years. He says he
will lie about his age to join the army so he can get away
from home and out of Extension. He would rather die in
battle than work in the mine. Many younger boys already
work there and I do not know how much longer I can fight
for him to stay in school. His grades are poor and I can
only bring in so much from sewing to feed an extra man
in the house. He is tall like Father.

The girls are very sweet. I am enclosing a picture
taken of them at Christmas in a studio. Roland had four
prints made and we will save one for each of them. Sara
has the floppy bow. She can never keep still, even in the
picture. I love them beyond measure.

Thank you Cassie for sharing my letters with Margaret.
I do not have the address of our sister Mrs. Lewis Prosser.
There are now five of Mama's children left. I wonder if my
beloved daughters will ever meet my beloved sisters. That
would be my fondest dream.

Now to bed for I am very tired.

x x x x x x x x x Your loving sister Jane x x x x x x x x x

The kisses brought a lump to my throat. Cassie was back with Jane. If
this was the end of my great-grandmother's story as recorded in her
own hand, at least it concluded on a happier note. It was coincidence
enough that I had two of the prints, but how did one of them end up
in Willow Point? Maybe Gail would turn up some clues.

I set the letters in the drawer of the night table and lay my head on
the pillow, whispering, "Now to bed for I am very tired."

✂ ✂ ✂ ✂ ✂ ✂ ✂
✂ ✂ ✂ ✂ ✂ ✂ ✂ ✂ ✂

WARREN WRIGHT. I could not get him off my mind. I checked Dad's phone book, but there were too many "W Wright"s to consider. I'm not sure what I was looking for, because I certainly didn't intend to call him. Maybe an address, so I could drive through his area and look the other way, as Gail and I had done with crushes in high school. Using memory of files, I came up empty. I ran through ten years of arrests without any clues. I hoped he wasn't a naked transvestite whose face I didn't bother to notice.

Dad, of course, was spoiling me. I hadn't even made a cup of tea for myself. Having two to cook for brought out skills he didn't know he had. The kitchen was one more domain where Mom triumphed, so neither of us had ever had a chance to experiment — at least that's my story. He made spaghetti, omelettes, breaded pork chops, and stir-fries, using packaged precut vegetables. I warned him Wendy's might go bankrupt as a result. With no escapes and all my needs taken care of, I had no alternative but to open the history books.

I had called Barnwell after the shooting; he was kind enough to relay notes and the final assignment by e-mail. I'd had my big plaster cast replaced with a lighter air cast — two hard plastic shells joined by Velcro straps — and although I still couldn't put any pressure on my leg, it was occasionally good exercise to hop down the stairs to the computer in the basement. When I looked at the list of essay subjects, the choice became easy: The influence of the Mackies on coal mining on Vancouver Island, focussing on Wellington, Nanaimo, Extension, or Cumberland. At the word Extension I felt for the first time in my life like the kid in the classroom who knows the answer. Would I be able to show off my letters in footnotes?

The index in my three texts led to whole sections on Extension, much to my surprise. The town was described by eyewitnesses as "the devil's gully," "a most undesirable place," and as one English writer from London put it, "All you see around you are a bunch of stumps and rocks and shacks; it's like the end of the world." The name came about, I learned, because it was an extension of the Wellington coal seam. Its accidental discovery was propitious because the Wellington pits were almost depleted and ready to close. William Mackie and his sons could not believe their good luck when Henry "Butcher" Hargraves reported finding a fallen tree with coal clinging to its roots on the southern slope of Mount Benson in the Chase River area.

Chase River? "...a rich seam of coal that was discovered not far from our property."

The seam was located on land belonging to a Negro pioneer, Louis Strong, who had established an orchard on the property and was not interested in selling. The 1975 publication date of the article accounted for the politically incorrect adjective. My grandmother's letter came to mind: "A Negro gentleman who lives in a cabin not far from us. He has an orchard...is a kind, hardworking man."

I read further. Not long after the seam was unearthed, the eighty-four-year-old body of Louis Strong was found dead at the foot of a bluff. February 1895.

Wasn't 1895 the mystery year for Jane Owens? Blood poisoning, marriage, baby, one of her customers died. She did not say how, but then she did not reveal much in that letter.

"This is too much," I said to my father, bent over his Sissipuss drawings. He hummed his interest without looking up.

I explained my suspicions about Louis Strong being Jane's gentleman customer.

"Did you check the other books?"

"Not yet. But you're a history teacher — have you heard of him?"

"Sorry. Poor fellow must have fallen through the cracks of my curriculum."

I could see he did not want to lift his eyes from the brushful of red paint he was carefully distributing within the black outline of a ball.

I picked up the second textbook and went straight to Louis Strong at the back. There he was again.

The circumstances surrounding Louis Strong's death were, in fact, suspicious. That his fall from the cliff was far from his cabin through terrain the old man knew well was questioned by his family. His body was found three days after Henry "Butch" Hargraves last saw him, claiming they had been hunting together; Hargraves invited him to stay for tea in his cabin, but it was dark and Strong wanted to get home to prepare for the arrival of his son Maynard. They were to go hunting again the next day, and when he did not appear, Hargraves checked on him, only to find the cabin empty and the fire cold. This was two days before the body was found. Furthermore, the man who discovered the corpse while walking his dog maintained it had not been at the foot of the bluff the day before.

Strong's son Maynard hired a detective and eventually found enough on Henry Hargraves to arrest him. An autopsy showed the remains in Strong's stomach were three days old, and the injuries — a single concussion to the head and a broken ankle but no bruises — were inconsistent with a fall from a high cliff. In the preliminary hearing, the Crown also relied on a bundle of clothes found a few feet away from the path to Hargraves' cabin. It argued that Strong was taking his laundry to be washed when he was struck down by Hargraves. Combined with this evidence, Mackie's announcement of a new mining development in the same area, as well as a sudden financial windfall for Hargraves, seemed enough for an indictment.

But there were not enough credible witnesses and no trial. According to the family, two men who had told Maynard Strong they had incriminating information died under mysterious circumstances: one drowned and the other was murdered on his way to Nanaimo. With no proven tie to Hargraves for the murder, he was free to enjoy his new wealth.

Something close to an electric shock passed through me. Laundry bundle? Was Louis Strong on his way to my great-grandmother's house when he was murdered?

What a cold case this was. I had watched defence lawyers do snow jobs on witnesses for the prosecution, but on the other hand, I had taken enough testimony to know that people really could believe something, and their imagination would provide the details. From experience, I knew I should not make assumptions without knowing all the evidence, but at the moment I was gagging on the injustice handed down to an old black man and his family for a fortune in coal. Jane had dropped several hints about worries on her customer's behalf. She also mentioned that he had two sons — a young one she had met and an older one on his way home from prospecting for gold. That might have been Maynard.

This personal link with history gave me the sense of having discovered penicillin or something else big and accidental. I couldn't be sure Louis Strong was the man Jane referred to, but if so, what a revelation. And yet, what was the revelation? That my great-grandmother might have known someone referred to in a history book? She does not offer clues to the crime, the statute of limitations long past anyway. I looked over at Dad drawing, oblivious to my excitement. It was the kind of moment I would never have understood if someone tried to describe it — just as I didn't understand shoulder pain before this. I felt like a spark igniting two files, unconnected until I found them.

Dad finally looked up. "Learning lots?"

"Lots."

"Maybe I should think about supper." He got up and stretched.

"I can help."

"Sit while you can. Someday you might be feeding me in a wheelchair."

"Hope I learn to cook by then."

"It's an easy meal tonight. Fish and chips."

Dad took a box from the freezer and spread the contents on a cookie sheet. He was more attentive now as I explained the coincidence of the laundry packet in the murder case of Louis Strong. What a thrill to have cracked the case with my star witness, Jane Owens. It would mean at least a round of drinks at the Shark Club. But I was ahead of myself. The dropped laundry did not implicate Jane.

As I was talking, Dad quietly put place mats, cutlery, and napkins on two TV tables, his in front of the Queen Anne chair, and mine in front of the couch. I swung my outstretched leg ninety degrees toward the little TV nestled on the shelves of the book-lined passage. As usual, the steaming plates of food arrived on the place mats just as the *Jeopardy!* theme started. Half an hour later, Dad stood with our empty dishes in his hand, waiting for the final clue. Tonight's was: "These people established a kingdom around the city of Pamplona in the 700s." None of the three contestants knew it, but Dad was right: "Who are the Basques?"

With another victory to his credit, he returned to his drawings on his island kingdom of dining table and I swung my leg around again, raising it carefully onto my island kingdom of couch. At that moment, the portable phone rang from between the cushions.

"Say goodbye to your uniform," said Sukhi.

"I'm suspended for negligence?"

"Don't you check your e-mail? You've been transferred to Serious Crimes."

My insides swooshed. I hadn't been downstairs at the computer today. "They must want to keep me off the streets to prevent further damage. What about you?"

"Me too."

An upward swoosh. "When do we start?"

"First of December."

"I'll be giving up thirty pounds of belt and this miserable cast at about the same time."

"And no more heavy boots. You'll need weights on your knees to keep you from lifting off."

We discussed the other changes in a plainclothes unit. No more four day on/four day off blocks, eliminating the deadly night shift. Instead we would work a regular Monday-to-Thursday ten-hour day shift, but we would be on call. IHIT — the Integrated Homicide Investigation Team — took over homicides in the lower mainland, but abductions, hostages, and any other serious crimes were ours, and it could mean working 24/7 for as long as it took to close them, weekend or not. We would also have the satisfaction of seeing a charge through to a conviction rather than attending a new file every half hour. He said there had been a major shuffle: Dave to Burglary, Emile to Fraud, and Jake had heard a rumour he'd made it to Special O, a surveillance assistance team that provides reports on a target to a requesting agency like IHIT, or any detachment.

I must have sighed, because Sukhi said emphatically, "Change is good." Then he remembered his other bit of news. "You might be interested to know that Ray will be prosecuting the case of the boys who shot you. Probably not for a while."

Downward swoosh. The thought of sitting in the courtroom as Ray's client was appalling. "No sweat."

Sukhi concluded the conversation with reports of his wife's high marks and, as usual, left me laughing from a call he had made that morning. I knew the place, a few doors down from Wanda and Terry. A woman had climbed into a basement window of the house next door to sneak up on her neighbour, a young widow she believed was in bed with her husband. Unfortunately, the window wasn't big enough and she got stuck halfway through. The neighbour, alone in the house and apparently innocent, heard her hollering and charged her with trespassing.

I shared Sukhi's news with Dad; he put down his brush and listened carefully. He was pleased with the prospect of plainclothes for me.

"Just about every cop killing has been someone in uniform. You need look no further than your foot to be aware of the dangers of patrolling."

I hadn't given my injured foot a thought during the conversation with Sukhi. When I did, it felt surprisingly stronger, lighter, no more throbbing. Strong enough to drive to the detachment. And before moving to a different unit, I would have to sort through my files to see what should be taken and what left behind. No personal motives.

✂ ✂ ✂ ✂ ✂ ✂ ✂ ✂
✂ ✂ ✂ ✂ ✂ ✂ ✂ ✂ ✂

OBSTRUCTION OF JUSTICE, APRIL 28, 2002, SQUIRES BAR AND GRILL, BURNABY.
WARREN EDWARD WRIGHT, BORN DECEMBER 17, 1975
RESIDENCE: #642 1804 DAVIE STREET
OCCUPATION: STUDENT/CAB DRIVER.

That's all CPIC gave me, so I went into the file. Warren WRIGHT was arrested for interfering with the arrest of his friend Tim LEWCHUK for disturbing the peace on the premises of Squires Bar and Grill, Burnaby. Upon consultation with arresting officer Cst. Arabella DRYVYNSYDES, charges against WRIGHT were stayed by Crown Counsel.

The only case I hadn't thought of. Now I remembered the scene well, except that the Warren Wright I arrested bore no resemblance to the one in the hospital other than height. He had shoulder-length wavy hair, a beard, and he wasn't wearing a dressing gown. Maybe I blotted the file out because I had not felt right about it at the time and still didn't.

A call had come in from a female patron about disorderly conduct at the bar. I had a new recruit with me, a strong young farm boy from Saskatchewan fresh out of Depot. I was in teaching mode, which meant I had to pretend to know what I was doing. Tim Lewchuk was drunk, and at the sight of us, he became more rowdy. He began shouting across the room at his ex-girlfriend, realizing she was the one who had made the call. He picked up a chair and proceeded to bash the wall with it, at which point my recruit and I attempted to restrain him. At the same time, Warren Wright stepped forward and tried to stop us. He'd also had too much to drink and said sloppily, "I'll take him home. He's up-set, please give him a chance."

In playing the human shield, he ended up pushing me down to the floor. I knew it was an accident because his was the first hand to help me up. But by then, other patrons had surrounded us, some gasping, one laughing, one calling, "Officer down."

The queasy feeling came back to me when I thought of it now. We had to take the wall-banger in, but I had not considered arresting his friend until I looked in the face of my recruit. Second night on the job: keen, dutiful, trusting my judgment. And it *was* embarrass-ing to be knocked down. Technically, the friend was obstructing jus-tice by intervening, so I made the call. Alone, I might have let it go, knowing how much else was really worth an arrest. We led them out to the car and I let the recruit handcuff Lewchuk and put him in the back seat. I wrote out a promise to appear for Warren Wright and ex-plained his friend would be let go tomorrow with the same thing af-ter he sobered up.

I remembered his shaggy head pausing to read my nametag in the glare of the neon lights from Squires. "You're only doing your job, Con-stable Dryvynsydes." He pronounced it easily in a tone that was flirty, mocking, and respectful all at once. The same tone he had used in the hospital lounge with the crooked smile. He walked away that time too — down the street, not back into the bar.

Later I explained the circumstances to Crown Counsel and had the charges stayed.

It might have been flattering that Warren Wright remembered me, unless he was a psychopathic cop stalker. Such types did exist, vowing revenge at any cost. I checked the Davie Street address against all the W Wrights, and of course, he wasn't still there. He had probably grad-uated, and I guessed it wasn't from cab driving school.

My session at the computer ended when Emile, Jake, and Dave ap-peared with coffee and congratulations, both on my transfer and being back on my foot. Jake had just received confirmation about Special O and was cockier than usual.

"Good thing it's not you in surveillance," he said to me, provoking a collective roar among the three of them over an incident I would give anything to forget. And be forgotten.

It was an impromptu plainclothes exercise on one of our night shifts. The four of us were watching an apartment house in two unmarked vehicles, waiting for the brother of a suspected dope-dealer to emerge so we could follow him. I was in a caravan down the street with Dave; Jake and Emile were in a car on the other side closer to the entrance of the building. After a few wasted hours, we decided to pack it in. I reached into the back of the caravan to get my wallet, accidentally flipping on the siren switch between the seats. When Dave turned on the ignition, the siren screamed through the neighbourhood, one already nervous about cops. I jumped on the switch as soon as it sounded, hoping anyone listening would think it was a fancy car alarm. Had our target been home, it might have been serious, but no real damage was done except to my pride. I would never be able to live down the look of horror mixed with glee on the faces of Emile and Jake as we pulled out past them.

"Have your fun while you can." As they doubled over in laughter, I wondered if I would feel as much rapport with the guys in Serious Crimes.

But I felt strangely hopeful. Strange, because so many of my professional blunders were rising to the surface on the brink of work that would require even more alertness. Sara might have said I was purging myself of psychic toxins. Next week — dreary mid-November — would mark a year since I broke up with Ray. I figured if bad things came in threes, Mom's death and the shooting should have set me free.

On the way out of the detachment, Megan gave me a hug. I promised myself to think more kindly about her from now on, at the same time wondering how long it would take her to apply to Serious Crimes herself.

My next stop was the doctor's office for what I hoped would be my second last appointment. He was pleased with my progress when he took off the air cast and examined my leg. The fractured bones were mending well. He said he was going to make me and my x-rays famous in a lecture he was preparing for a conference in the U.S. In three weeks I was to return and he would refer me to a physiotherapist, the cast from then on being at my discretion.

Back home, I felt restless but once on my favourite couch, I fell asleep. I must have been having one of my frequent coal mining dreams, because Dad's portable phone ringing under my pillow became the bell for the mine cage going up the shaft. I suddenly had a new purpose for my belt: phone, remote control, pens, replacing gun, baton, flashlight for easy reach.

Unknown number.

"Hello."

No answer.

"Hello?"

Low laugh of surprise. "Constable Dryvynsydes?"

"Yes." Was I hearing right? Hearing Wright?

"You might not remember me again, since you didn't the first time. We were in the hospital together with broken legs."

"I remember you."

"As a concerned citizen, I just wanted to know how one of Canada's finest is doing now. You were having a tough time with those crutches the last time I saw you."

"Better since then, but I'm getting sick of it. Walking cast should be off in three weeks. How about you?"

"Mine's been gone for a while. A simpler break, no doubt."

"So you're back at work?"

"I never left."

Mysterious as ever. Making me dig for it. "What do you do?"

"Web design. Graphics. Some book cover design. Whatever comes my way. From home."

I paused to let him talk more. How could I be sure he wasn't still stalking me? Was it a coincidence he phoned just after I had come in from my first outing? Was he calling from his cellphone across the street?

Who was I kidding?

"So you'll be back doing pirouettes by Christmas?"

"I hope so."

"Maybe we could meet for coffee when you're on your feet again."

"Maybe we could."

"From the listing, you're in the Cambie area, not too far from me. I'm in False Creek."

I was about to tell him I was at my father's, but my professional instincts kicked in for once and prevented me from giving out my unlisted number. Besides, I knew I would be here for a while. "Why don't you give me a call?"

"I will. My name is Warren Wright, by the way. Just so you'll know who's calling next time. And you can check me on your computer to make sure I'm not a dangerous offender."

"I might just do that." Was my laugh too forceful?

"What am I to call you?"

"Arabella."

"Interesting. Not a name you hear a lot."

I thanked him for his concern and when I hung up, realized the only thing not tingling was my leg. How could this have happened on the very day I identified him? Any earlier and I would have been much more suspicious. I probably owed him a cup of coffee to make up for his wrongful arrest. Uh huh, that was the reason.

Dad was just coming up from downstairs. "Was that the phone?"

"Someone I met in the hospital wondering how I was."

"That's nice of her."

"Him."

"Him then. I searched Louis Strong on the computer and there are a few entries. Thought you might be interested, so I left them on."

I got to my feet in what felt like a spring. "What would I do without you?"

The basement stairs still required caution, but the events of today had me feeling I was back in the game. The references to Louis Strong repeated a lot of what I had learned from my history books. Conflicting reports about his age — ranging from late seventies to eighty-five at the time of his death — didn't surprise me. I had dealt with enough witnesses to know everybody has his own story. Some accounts came from family members, some from diaries kept by other settlers, some from newspapers. One report claimed he didn't know his own age, born to a slave woman and her white master when such things were not always recorded. Despite the hardships of his early life, he grew into a strong, hardworking man who succeeded better than most in the challenges facing him both as a slave and as a pioneer in a new colony. The more I read about him — robust, hardworking, fearless toward human and wild life, with looks like a Spaniard — the more I thought of someone else I had just studied: Sir James Douglas. Did people of mixed race possess special powers? Like Barack Obama? And Tiger Woods once? I thought about Crane Reese in my history class, who said his people came from Salt Spring Island. Physically, he seemed a fine young specimen. I hoped he wasn't still taking notes for me.

I tried the last relevant website: the 1891 census of Vancouver Island. Louis Strong was registered in the Cedar, Cranberry, Oyster district which encompassed Chase River. Age seventy-five, head of household, self-employed farmer, born in the USA. That would make him seventy-nine in 1895. Did he give a younger age to the census taker? A few clicks later, I found Thomas Owens, also of the Cedar, Cranberry, Oyster district, age thirty-four, same enumeration numbers, head of household, miner, born in Wales.

How much more proof did I need?

Somehow I had to organize all this captivating information into an essay on the Mackies' influence. The connection between Mackie and Henry Hargraves was vague, despite Hargraves' claim that he had been paid for some technical advantage he had shown the owner. But Mackie was never accused, so Hargraves might well have been a free agent rather than a hitman. Assuming it was all true, that is. How Mackie got the land for the Extension mine was not the focus of the paper, and how much the Owens family knew was also not relevant, but I couldn't help wondering about it. Maybe a member of Serious Crimes would have a better chance of getting to the bottom of it.

X X X X X X X X X
X X X X X X X X X

IF SARA WAS RIGHT about birthdays being a harbinger of what the rest of the year will bring, I was in for an interesting twelve months. She also believed we should sit quietly and meditate on our goals and dreams with a candle, but so far this day wasn't giving me a quiet moment.

At 7 AM, I was surprised with a birthday cake at the office. A boost after a week on my new job and my new mended leg, still shaky on both scores. I knew Sukhi was the instigator, but when the other three members sang "Happy Birthday," it felt like an initiation into the team. I liked Tessa from the moment I met her. Big relief, since it's expected that females will get along and that isn't always the case. She was born in Guyana, was raised in Saskatchewan, and had a smile as big as the prairies and tropics combined. Another entry for my new theory of mixed race people possessing strength and beauty. She had come to Serious Crimes only a month before me and made sure I quickly learned anything that had confused her. Our sergeant Wayne was a cool guy; he did more watching than telling, and you knew you were in good hands with him. The fifth member, Dex, originally from New Brunswick, was a character. Okay in small doses.

When I checked my e-mail, I found a few Happy Birthdays. The first read:

You've had a tough year and I hope the next one will be better. Maybe we could meet for coffee sometime and discuss the case against the boys. Cheers, Ray.

Well, well, well.

The others were from Monty (from work), Gail (from home), Jake,

Emil, Dave, and Megan, all from their separate stations. Enough to warm the heart.

Our team was on call for the next case; in the meantime, I was finding out about the duration of Serious Crimes files. They could be wrapped up in a weekend or might drag on for years. So much depended on the availability and willingness of witnesses to testify, and of course, every case was at the mercy of the justice system with all its deferrals and loopholes. Today we learned that a case pending for over two years had been postponed again until next spring. Two Hell's Angels members were charged with a brutal homicide and second assault, and the key witness was under protection on Vancouver Island. To make sure we could count on him, two of us were to pay him a visit in the new year, and Wayne asked if my leg would be up to a trip. He said he had heard good things about my interviewing skills, at which I blushed and shrugged.

Sukhi and I used our lunch hour to work out in the detachment gym. The physiotherapist had prescribed gentle but disciplined exercises for my ankle. The rest of my body, immobilized for so long, cried out for a not-so-gentle workout. Then it cried out again when it got one.

At the end of the session, the sweat began flowing down my cheeks. Finally I had to acknowledge the tears I'd been fighting all morning. This was my first birthday without my mother. I'd been keeping her at a distance, mixing my anger at her dying with her perfectionist ways — as if that's all she was. Suddenly the full measure of the woman and how much I missed her flooded my mind and my eyes. Sukhi, ever sensitive, guessed what was happening, gave me a hug and left quietly, as I slipped into a cubicle in the bathroom, away from curious eyes.

A year ago today I was a mess. With the breakup wound still raw, I was spending work hours in a daze, then hiding under a quilt in my apartment until it was time to go to work again. My birthday happened to be a day off and Mom picked me up in the afternoon and took us both for a full treatment at a spa — facial, manicure, massage — after which we met Dad for a drink and supper at the Sylvia Hotel, followed by a movie at the Park Theatre on Cambie. Of course, doing all this with your parents instead of your boyfriend was an even worse reminder than if I had stayed home alone, out of public view. But Mom knew that with enough diversions, my attention would have to stray for a few moments from Ray, which they wouldn't do at home; every thought not of him was a healing step. The next day, she insisted I come to their place for my traditional birthday supper of favourites: cheese soufflé, curried chicken, calico bean pot, Greek salad, and cheesecake for dessert, prepared with Mom's usual excellence. Two more days down. Yesterday, when Dad asked me what time I would be finished my class tonight, I knew he had something similar planned, and that filled my tear ducts again. How he must miss her. How he never unloaded his loss on me. I tried to collect myself before emerging from the toilet stall. I splashed water on my red face and hoped the rest of the team would assume I'd had a rigourous session. Sukhi could be trusted.

After work I drove to my history class, the last of the term. For the first time ever, I was eager to hand in something I had written. The essay had practically fallen into place on its own. I asked Dad if I should cite Jane's descriptions of Extension and he said they were more historical than any other reference I was using. I scanned the pages I needed, trimmed them, blacked out personal bits, then copied and pasted them into the paper itself. I could not resist opening with the timely discovery of the Extension coal seam by Henry Hargraves on the property of Louis Strong, one of many black settlers from California invited by Sir James Douglas to the new Crown Colony. I went on to discuss how Mackie snatched it up and quickly developed the productive new mine, around which the townsite grew too fast and too shabbily. ("The Extension mines are rich in coal but the town has grown up without planning, since the water is poor and scarce in summer, drainage is bad, and we live in makeshift cottages that were moved from another used-up mine. The most lasting feature is the coal dust covering them." and "...coal dust everywhere...at least it has not hurt my garden where I grow potatoes, carrots, turnips, leeks, swedes, parsnips, cress, peas, beans, tomatoes, and onions.") How he had to relocate his shipping wharf from Departure Bay to Ladysmith/Oyster Bay because of a property conflict for his railroad; how he encouraged Extension miners to live in Ladysmith ("...live in Ladysmith where the loading wharves for the Extension coal are located. We are 12 miles apart and the mine trip makes three trips a day between the two towns...") but many re-fused to move; how he dealt with two big explosions; and how dissent over low wages led to regular strikes and lockouts under his ownership. How his sale of the Extension mine was as expedient as his acquisition, selling to a larger conglomerate just before the big strike of 1912–14, which resulted in so much violence and destruction that the militia had to be called in. This was the unanimous version of history I had gathered from my research. I saved the murder of Louis Strong for the end: the smeared price tag of Extension's existence. Even without a con-viction, I wanted it to be the last thing in the reader's mind.

Dad's only input was a final proofreading for typos and any glaring flaws in construction. Despite my lukewarm approach to schoolwork, the importance of grammar had been instilled in me by Mom, Dad, and especially Sara. A Grade Eight dropout by necessity, she had be-come a snob about educated people who still said "for him and I" and other grammatically incorrect phrases. She warned me not to marry anyone who didn't know the difference between "lie" and "lay" and if that was asking too much, at least to make sure he was open to learn-ing it. Ray qualified, so it wasn't the only determining factor.

Ray. What was going on with him?

His e-mail was deleted from my thoughts when I walked into Barn-well's classroom to an unexpected reception. All the students — twelve of us had stayed the course — and Barnwell himself clapped. "Welcome back, Constable Dryvynsydes. We're happy you can be with us for the last class. Today I'm just here to collect your papers and then we're go-ing out for beer."

Speechless and blushing, I finally mumbled my thanks before drop-ping my paper on Barnwell's desk and proceeding to my old seat next to Crane Reese. He was smiling wider than anyone and that embarrassed me even more. "I guess I owe you an apology for my alias."

He kept on grinning. "That's okay. Nurse, cop, what's the difference? You're both in emergency."

Barnwell's loud voice cut in to say the final exam would be held in this room next week. It would consist of three parts: thirty-five multi-ple choice questions covering early B.C. history from the Haidas to the

Second World War, and two short essay questions, both with choices. "We'll meet at Squires in half an hour. First round is on me."

Squires. How much of my past was coming back to haunt me today, when I was supposed to be meditating on the future. I didn't want to be too late for Dad's surprise supper, but did not want to ditch this group after their warm welcome. Crane Reese stood up and walked out with me. He had no car, so I offered him a ride to the bar. It was raining heavily when we got to the parking lot and we hurried into my Mazda.

"I missed you in class," he said, once we were on our way.

"Thanks. I hope you weren't taking notes all this time."

"Barnwell told us what happened and most of us saw it on TV."

He kept staring at me as if we were reunited pen pals, but I had to keep my eyes on the road. I had driven through car washes with more visibility. Back in Burnaby, I normally checked passing cruisers to see who was on duty, but tonight I couldn't see them. Maybe I needed the first rainy day to make me completely thankful not to be out on patrol any more. Barnwell was already inside at Squires pushing tables together; I took the opportunity to thank him for setting up my own personal correspondence course.

"Happy to be of service. Have they retired you to a desk job?"

Up close, his face looked older, lightly pockmarked, yet more attractive. Maybe I was a sucker for an expression always on the verge of sarcasm. "Not quite, but they've taken me off the streets. I'm in Serious Crimes now."

He raised an eyebrow and smiled. "You take good care of yourself."

Crane had stepped in to set chairs around tables and I stood for a moment, noting the upgrades since my famous arrests here. The old scuffed wooden colonial chairs and round tables had been replaced by high square tables and upholstered black leather bar stools with backs. I looked to the corner where Tim Lewchuk had flung the chair, the walls a fresh caramel colour. I thought I could smell new carpet — a possibility with smoking now banned in B.C. Squires was a popular hangout, yet some owners might have let it go, mistaking shabbiness for atmosphere.

Once everyone was assembled, we drank a toast to our professor and he drank one to our futures, academic and otherwise. Crane took the stool to my left and almost immediately Marla, on my right, began asking me questions with her eyes on Crane. She was a small, intense woman who had married early, divorced recently, and was raising children while working in a school library. This course was a step toward a library technician diploma. Eventually I sat back and let them talk across me, sipping a light beer that was making me sleepy.

After an hour of this odd conversation, I said I had to be somewhere. Crane, who clearly would not be driving, had just started his third beer and pushed his chair back when I did. His gallantry was becoming too much: one coffee and one ride didn't make us a couple. I gave a collective wave to all the tables and on my way out, noted Marla taking over my stool next to Crane, climbing its rungs like a stepladder.

The rain had lessened by the time I hobbled up Dad's front steps. My leg felt heavy and sore by the end of each workday, even with the cast I usually wore when I knew I would be on my feet all day. I'd found some almost stylish orthopedic-type shoes to accommodate it, and my limp was hardly noticeable unless I was really tired.

Dad had taken his drawing supplies from the dining table and set the placemats there instead of in front of the TV. I washed my hands and sat down with my leg outstretched on another chair as he took two warmed plates from the oven. Porcupine meatballs in mushroom soup, mashed potatoes, canned mixed beans. A Greek salad picked up from Max's Deli was in a bowl on the table. We were both thinking the same thing, both trying not to give into it.

"A few substitutions, you'll notice. I didn't know where to start with cheese soufflé and didn't want to ruin curried chicken for you forever."

I swallowed the lump in my throat for his sake. "Looks delicious, Dad. Porcupines are my co-favourites."

While we were eating, I recounted the events of the day, from the birthday cake, through the e-mails to the standing ovation. Dad's face shone as if it was his birthday and in a way it was. His first milestone without her. For dessert he had bought a cheesecake from the same deli, and we both wolfed down a slab. Then he handed me two envelopes, one with a bulge. His contained a heartfelt Daughter card and a gift certificate for the works at the spa where Mom and I had gone last year. The other was a Niece card from Janetta with a smaller envelope folded up inside. On it, Sara's unmistakable strong handwriting read: "Mother's handiwork and her gift for confirmation in the Methodist Church in Wales at age 12." Inside was a small silver bangle wrapped in a creamy lace-trimmed handkerchief. It was old hammered sterling, a genuine antique. I was already weepy thinking about Mom; now I felt dumbstruck.

"Those belonged to your great-grandmother," Dad said softly. "Janetta was digging again in the old trunk and found them. She called last week and I told her your birthday was coming up. She feels bad she didn't find them among Mother's things earlier. In fact, she doesn't remember Mother ever mentioning it."

I managed a low "Wow" as I stroked the fine lace border Jane Owens' hands had tatted so delicately. "The gift that keeps on giving. From Jane to Sara to Janetta and now to me. This little piece of linen has outlasted two lifetimes."

"Three," said Dad. "Don't forget your mother."

At the sight of his face now collapsed in sorrow, I threw my arms around him and we indulged in long-overdue sobs. "How could I?" I snuffled. "She's been on my mind all day."

Dad was first to recover, remembering that we hadn't drunk a toast yet. While he poured his favourite sherry, I went through the futile motions of trying to slip the small bracelet onto my big hand. I imagined it sliding up and down Jane's young, thin wrist as she ran laughing up a hill — wasn't Wales all hills? — after Sunday school on the day she received it.

Dad handed me my glass and clinking them both, he crooned: "To all the girls I've loved before. And still do."

"Did you know it was Jane Owens' birthday today too?"

"She would qualify for that select group."

"She's given me a present; what can I give her?"

"A moment of silence? A prayer of thanks? A word of homage."

"For starters, maybe. But I'd like to do more, except I haven't figured out what yet."

After we drained our glasses, Dad gathered up the dishes. I wanted to help, but he insisted I stretch out on the couch after my busy day. As the old corduroy absorbed my weariness, I tried to call up Sara's account of that last scene with her mother. Had she given anything else to her eight-year-old twin daughters besides photos? I knew the tricks memory played; the best thing you can do when trying to remember something is to forget it. And maybe my teenage indifference never did register more than half of what my talkative grandmother was saying.

I thought about the final exam next week. Why was the prospect of studying not filling me with the usual dread? My brain was too tired to start tonight, so I switched on the TV to a Christmas skating show. Figure skating always made me think of Gail and how she would look on the ice, had she persisted. When the phone rang, I was ready to say her name until I saw it was an unknown number.

"Arabella?"

"Yes?"

"It's Warren. How are you?"

"Better, thanks. I'm still using my cast off and on."

"Giving it up completely takes some time."

"That's for sure. I'm back at work, dragging my feet, you might say."

"I can't imagine you not doing your duty," he said ironically.

"You'd be surprised." I could feel my cheeks heating up.

"Did you ever find out why you arrested me?"

"I did."

"So I hope you know I'm not too dangerous to have coffee with."

"I do."

"I'd like to apologize, however, for knocking you down. And it would be more sincere to do it in person. Care to meet sometime in the next few days? You say when."

Fully intending to name an afternoon on the weekend, I blurted out: "Tomorrow — after work?"

"When do you get off?"

"Six."

"Shall we say The Cactus Club on Broadway and Ash at seven? And make it supper?"

"Sounds good."

My head was spinning when I hung up. The whole day had been so unpredictable that I almost expected him to say "Happy Birthday," but that would have been too weird. Gail had left a message while I was talking, so my intuition was working. I would e-mail her from work tomorrow and call her on the weekend. Now I needed rest. Dad was getting his grapefruit and yogurt ready and had turned on the radio for his golden oldies. I thanked him for a memorable birthday.

In my bedroom I kicked off my clothes, pulled on an oversized T-shirt, and slid under the quilt. For a moment I thought of sitting up and meditating, but decided it would be just as effective lying down. What were my goals for the coming year? To do well in my new job. To be rid of the sadness and doubts from the past year. To find happiness with...? I stopped short at that petition, since it was too big for me to decide so soon. I remember Sara once saying, "When you look at your love partner, you're seeing yourself and the exact stage of your own evolution. If you want to improve the calibre of your choice, you must elevate your own soul qualities." She had added her two pet sayings that "Ignorance is the only sin" and "Nothing is permanent," but figuring out what they all meant was beyond me right now. I finished with a word of thanks for my new acquaintanceship with my great-grandmother and especially for the family who had always been in my life: Sara, Dad, Mom, and Janetta.

As I did so, the scene of Sara recounting her mother's last days came back to me. Still no recollection of Sara mentioning a bangle, but when Jane was dying of influenza, she had asked for her pen and writing paper. Roland became angry at her for wasting precious energy, and Sara had to take them to her when he was out of the house. Jane had propped herself on her elbow on the cot, breathing heavily, but writing quickly and urgently. Just before she died, she gave Sara an envelope to mail that day. Sara was too anxious about her mother to think much more about it except that it was addressed to her Aunt Catherine in Wales. Who had that letter if Janetta and Dad ended up with the rest? Before falling asleep, I added another mission to the year ahead.

JANE SETS THE REST OF THE CAKE on a shelf in the cold scullery, noting fresh snow in the gaping space under the back door. In the crisp December air, its cover of white could almost delude an onlooker that Extension, cradled by bluffs, possessed the charm of a miniature mountain village. She shakes her head at the reality, and covers the plate with a large mixing bowl to keep the boiled icing from drying out. In all her thirty-five years, nothing but a lofty sponge layer cake frosted with swirls and peaks would do for a birthday. Today she added raspberry juice when Sara insisted on pink for her mother. Once Llewyllyn had chosen the colour of the icing — yellow or orange or bright blue — but at almost fourteen, her son no longer cares about such trimmings. Or about much of anything at all.

Supper over, he holds the thick tapestry curtain aside and waits until his mother steps back into the kitchen before entering the porch. He takes an old jacket from a hook, pulling it on carelessly outside in the cold. In the last year, he has found more and more excuses to avoid being in the same space as his father. Already taller than both parents, Llewyllyn makes Jane think of some Jane Austen characters — dark wavy hair, long lashes, and aquiline features. Oh, how she loved to read before her days were stretched to bursting with sewing. A cracking voice and sparse whiskers on his upper lip and chin have turned her gentle boy into a darker, brooding version of his younger self. Was this the same son who once assisted her so eagerly — in the garden, delivering mended garments, and hauling the water that was always so scarce in summer — now having to be coaxed to crank the ice cream maker two hours earlier?

At the sound of clean blows on billets of firewood, she breathes a sigh of relief; at least he has not wandered over to the pithead where the strike still offers too many harmful temptations for young men. She wonders if Gomer ever did learn to chop wood. Then she wonders when she will ever see her younger brother and his family again. Victoria might as well be Wales.

In the front room an unusual scene awaits her: Sara sits on her father's knee pretending to read "Snow White and Rose Red" — a story she knows by heart — while Janet plays with a doll on the rag rug at his feet. Jane sinks into her worn armchair and before she can pick up her knitting, Janet lands on her lap with the doll. Sara's dark eyes flash in their direction, but she resists the urge to join them and continues reading to her father. Jane believes it is her only birthday supper Roland has attended since she turned sixteen in her brother's home, almost twenty years ago. Not only is he present but unintoxicated, as he was back then.

During the early years of their marriage, she regarded the sober time he spent with her and Llewyllyn as something fragile, like watching a butterfly on a flower — knowing it will lift off and at the same time dreading its departure. Soon enough she came to dread his presence more than his absence, wishing to hasten the transition back into the world she has created for herself and her children. But after years of being able to anticipate his exit from the degree of trembling in his hands or from a slight upturn in his moody withdrawal, she had to admit today that her husband is not as predictable as she thought. Instead of rising late — as he has done since the strike started — drinking a shaky cup of coffee without a word or bite to eat, and leaving the house in dishevelled clothes, Roland had emerged from the bedroom in his best plaid flannel shirt and dark trousers, hair slicked down. His thin neck barely grazed the collar of his buttoned shirt. When he joined his children eating porridge at the table, Llewyllyn got up and left early for school, oatmeal half finished. Jane no longer asks Roland where he is going or when he will return, so his declaration came as a surprise.

"Takin' the train to Nanaimo. Be back for supper." Her quick glance caused him to add: "Going to see about work at Jingle Pot. Heard they're hiring diggers and drillers."

The twins raised their heads in unison, waiting for a reply from their mother in this rare morning exchange. None came.

Outings in good clothes have not been common in many mining households since the beginning of the big strike a year and a half ago. Beset by poverty, hardship, violence and even death, Vancouver Island's mining communities continued the standoff between striking mine workers and owners. Always shrewd, the Mackie family made a timely sale of its stakes in Extension and Cumberland to a conglomerate just before the big one began.

Despite his sympathies with the union, Roland has not joined. Brawls break out daily in beer parlours and Jane has gained new insight into her husband's character for withstanding threats and accusations of mugwump from union members. Though he suffers the same unemployment because he will never work as a scab, he claims he cannot ignore the blacklisting against union agitators when it comes to rehiring.

Jane's own emotions have been whipped and tangled by the hatred, like sheets in a wind. She knows good people in every group, including the strikebreakers, and understands that each only wants the most for his family. For her, the biggest shock has been the savagery of the women. Neighbours she has known for years turning on one another and on family members: shrieking, cursing, even pulling one another through the sooty mud that is the natural terrain of Extension. In her estimation, Roland's fencesitting stance has shifted from doubt through blame to where it now rests since the riot of last summer: a grudging approval.

Perhaps because of his neutral position, their little company cottage has survived two assaults. The first was of eviction, then of plunder. As part of a cluster on the edge of the village away from the pithead, it was left untouched when management decided to install its own workers in both the mines and in the company homes of the strikers. Strikebreakers were taken to live in the bullpen, an area close to the pithead protected by special constables. And it was here, near the entrance to the mine, that the violence and destruction reached its peak last August: a mob of angry strikers from Nanaimo, South Wellington, and Ladysmith, armed with picks, shovels, sticks, and guns, marched on the scabs in Extension who had acquired guns themselves and were waiting for them. For a few desperate hours, their valley community of three hundred swelled to fifteen hundred. Tipple area, trestlework, and weigh house were all burned, strikebreakers' families hauled out of their homes before eleven structures were burned and many others ransacked. Chinatown, its dwellings even more squalid than the rest of the rough town, was especially hard hit, due to the men's prejudice toward foreigners — as if the Chinese workers did not have enough against them, what with lower wages, a head tax, and a law prohibiting them from working underground until they were forced back to work by the company or sent home to China.

Jane will never forget the smell of fear and smoke, the shouts of the men, squeals of horses and pigs let loose, cries of women and children fleeing to the woods where they lived in tents for weeks. Roland marched with the strikers, but after the devastation she no longer considers her husband's position on the edge of the mob as cowardice. Especially when soldiers were dispatched from Nanaimo and many strikers put in jail.

And now with the Jingle Pot mine north of Nanaimo settling with the union, he had said "I'll be going then" to the back of Jane's head when he left to seek work.

Once she was sure he was on the road, she had checked the tobacco tin in the kitchen cupboard. She expected more than seventy-five cents to be gone. After the fifty-cent train ride, he would have only twenty-five cents, enough for five beers — just a warm-up for Roland. At least the hotels provided free sandwiches — if he would eat, which he often didn't.

The tin containing both their wages is used for household money. Before the strike, Roland contributed what was left from his pay after stopping at the bar; to this Jane added her seamstress fees. At the age of sixteen, she realized she would always be taking care of herself, and knows enough to keep what she can in reserve. The pouch in her dresser drawer contains as many pennies, nickels, and dimes as she can spare from household necessities, along with a lavender sachet and her two silver confirmation bangles. These are for emergencies, small gifts for the children, and neighbours in need. The sachet fund also buys school supplies for Llewyllyn, lately showing himself to be more and more undeserving of them. Fortunately there is a school in Extension or she would have an even bigger battle forcing him to walk a distance, as they'd had with Gomer. The strike has bought time for her growing son, who by now might otherwise be working at the picking tables or caring for mules.

From the start, the union has offered miner's relief even to non-member strikers who do not scab. Like wages, many relief pay packets did not make it past the beer parlours until the union arranged credit with local businesses in the same amount. Roland's allotment is $9 per week — $4 for himself, $2 for his wife, and $1 for each child.

Since then, Jane alone puts money in the tobacco tin. But she earns less now. Money is scarce among strikers, and she would be made to feel a traitor taking in work from strikebreakers' families. Those who are friends know enough not to ask. A clientele of lumbermen, merchants, and teachers from a wider area allows her to sustain her family. That and an outside root cellar of potatoes, turnips, carrots, and onions, along with a canner from which not a plum, cucumber, bean, peach, crabapple, beet, or tomato escapes being preserved, jellied, or pickled after the family have all eaten their fill of fresh ones. From her carefully managed bounty, Jane finds enough for small hampers for households with new babies or for those who run out of food between relief. Poor Mrs. Harper, with a milk leg resulting from her seventh birth, was the latest recipient of Jane's soup, pies, and fresh buns. At each new delivery, she says a prayer of thanks for her own strong constitution. She could not bear the thought of forsaking her children in any of their needs or care.

Jane always knows how much is in the tobacco tin. Roland is taking less, and she figures he must have stopped buying drinks for everyone, because his own inebriation level has not diminished. She consoles herself that he never drinks at home, even when his slurred maudlin words or raucous self-pity come back with him from the pub.

But when he had returned from Nanaimo late this afternoon, he had had just enough to keep his tremors in check. His voice was raspy but lucid.

"Nothing for us at Jingle Pot."

"I'm sorry." Jane looked up from the chicken stew she was stirring. The tantalizing, frothy pink cake already stood in the middle of the table for supper.

"Happy Birthday anyway." He tossed a flat paper bag next to it. When Jane made no immediate move, he said: "Open it."

Sara and Janet scampered in eagerly from the front room, resting their chins on the edge of the table; Llewyllyn retreated to Jane's sewing room. From the bag she pulled out something light and soft folded in tissue paper. Held up, a long-sleeved lilac silk blouse fell into shape: pearl buttons down the back, modish tucks on the bodice. Jane displayed it like a banner with outstretched arms, then up against herself over the starched white apron she uses for special occasions. The twins gasped at the delicate shimmering colour and material. She has had only a few store-bought garments in her life, and this is without a doubt the finest.

"Your favourite colour, Mama," Janet said.

"That's because lilac is her favourite flower," Sara added bossily.

Roland's nod indicated he had known this, his face expressing more than any words could. She thought of the Methodist church back in Wales, when the minister spoke of supplicants. Her husband's watery eyes were filled with supplication, beseeching her to judge him for this blouse and this moment and not eighteen years of disappointment. She smiled, then reached for him in a rare embrace. He began to weep. She held his bony chest tight against her, as she once had their young son when he cried. Locked in the clasp, Jane swallowed her own tears. They disappeared with all the others into a compartment hidden even to her: a trapdoor to the past, its valve-like aperture permitting only one-way passage. Her gratitude toward him encompasses much more than he or anyone will ever know. She herself cannot face the scope of it yet.

When his sniffling subsided, she released him and said quietly, "Thank you. It's beautiful."

And because he knew the question in her mind, he said: "I sold my father's watch. It's the only thing he ever gave me and this should go to you." Another surprise from Roland because Jane had not known he still had it after all these years.

Now, after sizeable helpings of stew and dumplings, cake and home-made ice cream, Jane looks upon her husband and their daughters. Unlike Llewyllyn and herself, both weakened by experience, the young twins lap up attention uncritically like puppies. In the forty-one-year-old face that looks closer to sixty, they see only pride in Sara's careful recitation.

At the sight of them, Jane feels a heart surge, a pang of joy. This has become a familiar sensation in the last three and three quarter years. She craves a new dimension to embrace it — or even a new word to express its intensity. Not one, but two perfect little girls. Two identical packages of life holding two such different personalities. Janet, her Snow White, speaks so little Jane worried about her development. Now she sees in the quiet twin the same strain from which her brother Thomas and sister Margaret are made, each happiest when engaged wordlessly in purposeful activity. Ever since she was a toddler, Janet would rather arrange dolls and help Jane bake or set the table than look at the books Sara loves so much. Already Janet sorts threads and buttons according to colour and soon she will be ready to learn the rudiments of the sewing machine. Sara shows no interest in domestic work, leaving Janet to pull the quilt up over their bed in the morning. But Sara is Jane's Rose Red, her beloved Cassie, full of curiosity, questions, and laughter. Such a magical child she never thought could exist, let alone belong to her. She too lightens Jane's long hours in the sewing room, singing and chattering to pretend friends, acting out all parts. How has her life of mistakes and ordeals been redeemed with these three blessings of children? She catches her breath, always afraid to break whatever spell has reshaped all previous trials into steps to this reward.

"Lance Cruikshank got killed," Roland says when Sara drops the book and crowds in against her sister on Jane's lap.

"How?"

"Drowned. Not an accident, they say. Scabbing at the same time he was collecting relief. Someone got him drunk and took him out fishing in Driver Lake in the middle of the night."

Jane digests the news. The year she spent working with Stella and Lance is now hazy. Before the twins were born, she ran into Stella in Nanaimo, fat and matronly, but with the same girlish giggle. She was working at the Black Powder Factory and still living with her mother in Departure Bay. Norman would be twenty by now and Jane wonders if she has ever passed him without recognition. Through Roland she knows Lance had married again, treated that wife badly as well, and was left on his own to drink and rant to anyone who would listen. Friends became fewer and fewer.

"You can't have it both ways. Miners don't forget that." Roland's voice implies neutrality about Lance's fate. He gets up to put coal in the stove; Jane's faded bluebell wallpaper affords no protection against draughts through the cracks in the walls. His hands on the scuttle wobble so much she fears the small lumps will fall out. Being helpful usually precedes his exit for the pub, but he sits back down.

"Also heard a man was left for dead in coontown."

Jane's body stiffens, causing Sara and Janet to look around at her face. "Must you?"

Roland shrugs and says with a sly glance, "Keep forgettin' your soft spots."

"Why is it so easy for everyone to degrade Negro people?" She catches her breath. "And the Chinese? To list them in the mines by numbers instead of names, for heaven's sake."

Roland knows his wife has included the Chinese in her retort to sidetrack any personal connection with the other race. He remembers how attached she was to old man Strong when she washed his clothes, but then after he died or was murdered or whatever happened to him, she hasn't mentioned his name. Had he been more fortified with drink he would have blustered at length about such terms just being casual talk and not meant to hurt anybody. "As I was sayin,' a fella left for dead was rescued by Jim Hamilton. A Negro scab he was," he says defiantly, "brought up from the States by the company. Shows the strikers have the big hearts."

Jane wishes to ask "Who beat him up, then?" but lets the story die.

"Tommy was on the train back. He'd been to Nanaimo for provisions."

"How is he?

Jane has not seen her older brother for a few months. With both men out of work, Roland brings no news of him from the mine, and since his marriage to Lizzie, he no longer frequents taverns. Tommy was one of the many Extension miners who followed company orders and moved his family to the port of Ladysmith because of the cleaner water and more agreeable setting. Stubborn ones like Roland refused to budge, choosing the constant clatter of machinery around the pit-head, the sulphury smell of the smouldering slag heap and soot everywhere, over a twelve-mile train ride to and from every shift. Eventually the Mackies had to give in and leave them where they were.

"Wonders if we need anything done."

"The back door lets in snow and the stairs are coming loose."

Both houses started out the same: square boxes from abandoned mines cut in half and brought on flatcars for reassembly in their new communities. Comparing Tommy's with Jane's, it would seem he and Lizzie were much more prosperous, as in truth they were before the strike. Not that Tommy earned more than Roland. As a digger, Roland could make more than anyone in the mine, depending how fast and how many coal cars he could fill. Being strong and steady rather than quick and energetic, Tommy was content to remain timber foreman in Extension after he moved from No. 1. But wages untouched by liquour left money for home improvements, and Tommy's cottage in Ladysmith, like the one in Chase River, stood out among the others around it. Fenced yard, orderly flowerbeds, painted blue wooden siding outside, and three bedrooms inside, one of which their mother had occupied until her death eight years ago. Myrtle, age seventeen, and Edna, fifteen, have their own rooms — a luxury, to be sure, when some families crowd seven or eight children into the same space. Tommy has also built a verandah around the house, enclosing the area near the back door to serve as a scullery and to house Lizzie's precious icebox.

Now the strike has levelled the fates of those with savings to those without. Lizzie brings in nothing, exerting herself as little as possible even in the home, so whatever Jane makes sewing seems like wealth by contrast. To supplement his relief credit, Tommy takes on the few carpentry jobs miners don't do themselves. Last spring Jane hired him to add a sewing room to their cramped cottage. He used free lumber from an abandoned building and she paid him with a sealer of pennies she had been saving for years. So that Roland would not wonder where she found the extra money during the strike, she and Tommy conspired in fixing three different prices. The lowest for Roland, the highest for Lizzie, who thinks her sister-in-law deserves no favours with everyone struggling, and the actual amount Jane gladly turned over to her brother instead of a stranger.

Just off the kitchen, Jane's new room uses warmth from the stove; at night a curtain isolates the whirring of her machine from the sleeping household. It has filled up so quickly with bolts of material and piles of clothes for repair that she cannot believe these heaps once occupied most surfaces of the house. All but the settee, which she always kept clear for Roland to land drunk in the night and leave her alone in the bedroom.

"Tommy says their icebox is for sale."

"What?" Jane stands up, carefully spilling her daughters from her lap onto the floor. They have become fidgety and scatter into separate corners. "That's Lizzie's pride."

"That's what he says. He thought if we wanted it, they could buy it back once the strike is over."

"And what if I grow to like it in the meantime?" Jane has wanted an icebox almost as much as a sewing room, but her special savings sealer is empty. "He doesn't know his own wife. She would never agree to it being in this house."

Lizzie has always begrudged Tommy's concern for his family. Mama's years of care in their home were not easy for any of them, care Jane would have willingly provided, had there been an extra room of retreat from Roland's drinking. She cannot guess the reason for her sister-in-law's jealousy of her. Lizzie has always had more of everything except a drunken husband. She prays she and her children will never have to depend on her sister-in-law for anything.

"There's another icebox for sale in Hamiltons' yard. Wardrobe too."

"I felt like a vulture buying my sewing cabinet from Mrs. Lewis when I knew she was selling furniture in order to eat. I won't be doing it again." Jane is in the kitchen putting the kettle on to boil. "And where would the money come from? Does Tommy think I grow it in with the leeks?"

"And I seen someone else."

Jane endures Roland's grammar in silence.

"Went to the Five Acres people about getting us a place there."

"You did?"

"A couple of lots are vacant. Two families couldn't wait out the strike and moved to Vancouver. They're going cheap as a company house. Seven dollars a month."

Twenty years ago, the Five Acres project was developed on Harewood Estates, on the southwest edge of Nanaimo, to give miners a chance to lease a parcel of land in that amount with an option to buy. The original condition was that they were to be fenced and cultivated, one Roland would never have fulfilled. But that work was done years ago, along with subdivision of the original plots, and houses stood on them all. Jane had never allowed herself to hope they might live in Five Acres.

"Did you sign up?"

"Thought you might like to go see for yourself tomorrow. The boy could miss school and watch the twins. He's wasting his time there anyway. Should be helping put food on the table. I was, at his age."

Jane saves her words, knowing she will send Llewyllyn off to school and then take Sara and Janet over to Maude Hamilton before Roland gets up. Maude will mind the girls gladly and the pie and potatoes Jane takes over when she picks them up will be appreciated. "I'd like that."

Roland stands up. Jane sees from his hands that it's time. Not for many years has she tried to stall him. "Would you like a cup o' tea?"

He shakes his head. "I'll be goin' out for a bit."

He steps into the bedroom, emerging in his rumpled everyday clothes. He hesitates. She feels the old irritation at his prolonged leave-taking. She has poured herself a cup of tea and is on her way back to the front room when he turns from the scullery, the open curtain letting in chilly air.

"Happy Birthday, then."

The blouse, draped gracefully over the back of her chair, tells her why he's lingering. "Thank you. It's the loveliest birthday I've ever had."

He steps outside, leaving his soft voice in her head for a moment, reminding her of Mama saying, "He's a Welshman like us."

Janet is already in her long flannel nightgown and Sara is retelling "Thumbelina" aloud to herself.

"Time for bed, girls. Sara, get into your nightgown." Jane hears Llewyllyn's footsteps in the porch, again thankful he is safe under their roof for another night. "Do you think you could read your sisters a bedtime story?"

His mother's request takes him by surprise. The twins squeal and jump under their comforter at the prospect.

In the kitchen, Jane stops to pour herself a second cup of tea. An old yearning stirs within her: to write to Cassie about this birthday. She pushes back the curtain of the cupboard and checks under the tea towels, where she keeps her paper. She forgot there is none. The strike has made stationery a frivolous expenditure. Besides, she does not know how to write a proper letter anymore. The landslide of years in Extension has trapped all the words and feelings that once flowed so freely. Letters from Cassie are infrequent now, and who can blame her? Long ago she relinquished her dream that Cassie might move to Vancouver Island, but she has not given up hope of a visit someday. Both sisters are married to men of means who might make it possible.

Jane adds enough coal to the cookstove for a few hours of work; she pushes aside the chintz curtain to allow heat to circulate. She sets the oil lamp on the sewing cabinet and teacup on the machine, then bends to sort through layers of cloth. She must finish a few things to replenish the tobacco tin after emptying it for the train trip tomorrow. She starts with the most welcome rather than the most urgent job: a white baby layette for a doctor's wife in Ladysmith — three smocked nightgowns of batiste cotton, a thick satin bunting bag lined with flannel, and a christening dress and bonnet out of organdie and lace. Rising from her chair, she catches sight of herself in the mirror she uses for fittings. Though her doe-brown hair has not changed colour since she left Wales, wisps escaping her upsweep look gold against the lamplight. The long Owens chin she has always regarded as unbecoming on a woman seems proud and full of resolve in semi-silhouette. Her figure has become more rounded in the bust and hips since the birth of her children, but she still has a waist; her extra pounds are not out of control like some miners' wives her age who have eaten too much starch during the strike. For a few moments she considers the reflection of this mysterious backlit woman who by day is plain Jane. If she is attractive enough for a fine silk blouse, could she still be a fantasy someone dreams of? Where would he be now?

SARA ALWAYS SAID THAT ANTICIPATION — both dread and longing — was more powerful than the experience itself. I was still trying to figure out if my first date with Mr. Wright exceeded or fell short of those wild and changeable expectations of my convalescence.

The evening after my birthday, I dragged myself into The Cactus Club. Mid-afternoon, while delivering subpoenas, I realized that my mending limb was still calling the shots. Warren, already seated with a view to the entrance, sprang up and ushered me back to the booth. We both wore bashful smiles seeing each other for the first time in arranged circumstances. At least our mutual injuries made opening conversation easy.

I was too edgy to concentrate on the menu, so I followed his lead in ordering a glass of red wine and pasta arrabiata. His hair was between the long bushman style from Squires and the remains of the summer brushcut he wore in the hospital. Unruly waves curled at his neck and forehead, his complexion rosy from having run — as he informed me — to the restaurant from his condo. An inspiration from one healed leg to one still in progress. This was my third variation of Warren Wright and I had to remind myself his multiple personality was my problem, that he was one and the same to himself.

He had grown up in Calgary, where his parents and married sister still lived. After earning a degree in graphic arts from the Alberta College of Art and Design, he had moved to Vancouver to take a job with an advertising company. When he discovered he wanted more creative independence, he gave himself options by enrolling in digital visual arts at the Emily Carr Institute and drove a cab to finance his studies.

That's when he got arrested.

"Were you scared?" I asked him.

"Of you?"

"Of me or the system?"

"I didn't think I'd go to jail, if that's what you mean. And I hate to tell you, but I didn't feel threatened by you. Your smile is irresistible and you have such an endearing way of blushing."

"You mean I smiled?"

"Not at me. Maybe at the restaurant owner, I don't know who. But I remember you blushing. You weren't wielding your power."

"Please don't let that get around."

"You were very professional, but the vibes I picked up said 'Maybe I should take this guy in with his friend' for the sake of the keen recruit with you. I could tell he was new to the job and eager for some action. He's the kind who likes power."

So he can read my mind. Dangerous. And he had the recruit pegged. Recently I heard the guy had been called in for using excessive force. I kept this to myself, however. I wasn't about to admit his judgment was better than mine.

He gave me an update on Tim Lewchuk: moved to Toronto less than a year after the arrest, now married with a son and working in a bank. That night was probably the worst of his life. He was nursing deep wounds from the break-up with his girlfriend and when she called the cops on him, he went over the edge. He hadn't had a parking ticket since.

The chatter went on so easily I hardly noticed we were eating. I could not help myself, however, from going through the checklist. Since Gail and I first became aware of boys as possible attachments, we kept adding eligibility requirements. And if this sounds shocking, I invite anyone to spend five minutes with a group of male cops to see how they rate our gender.

Family body types played a role with both Gail and me. Her dad was short and stocky with stubby fingers and she could never go out with anyone who wasn't solid or who had long, thin fingers. Men didn't come much stronger than Monty, so he was a shoo-in once he got her attention. My height left me fewer choices than Gail, unless I wanted to be looking down on a boyfriend's head; for some short guys, tall women are a turn-on. Dad had imprinted me with a liking for tall thin men and I felt the same way about long fingers as she did about sausage ones.

Gail and I were also divided on the smooth-versus-hairy question, and lucky for Mr. Wright, I was — that is, he should be — on the hairy side. Not gorilla hairy but a few tufts certainly didn't hurt. As I watched his long tufted fingers holding his glass of red wine, I wondered about my final physical stipulation: feet. Because of the size of my own, I could never consider even a tall man with small feet. Surprising that I hadn't already noticed the one without the cast in the hospital. Shoes were also important in my demanding little world, lace-ups winning out over loafers. At the moment, Warren's were safely under the table.

Of course, these qualifications were purely hypothetical if I didn't pass the guy's checklist. Again, Gail always had plenty to choose from and that gave her a confidence that attracted even more. No one ever thought I was cute, though Ray told me often that I was beautiful in a striking, original way. That a strong chin hadn't hurt Reese Wither-spoon. Hah! I should have known then where such language from a lawyer would lead.

Two hours passed effortlessly before I finally made a move to call it a night. He mentioned getting together again soon and I surprised myself by saying not until after next Wednesday, because I would be studying for my final exam until then. He was leaving for Hawaii for three weeks the day after. A travel agency he'd done work for had given him the trip in partial payment and he had friends with a timeshare there. He quietly paid the bill and helped me slide out of the booth, es-corting me to the door. Outside, I asked him if he wanted a ride home, but he was going to a bookstore after he walked me to my car on a side street. We wished each other a happy holiday, and as he started to leave, I stole a peek at the acceptable scuffed runners on his feet. Then he turned back — as I quickly shifted my eyes upward — and pulled a card out of the pocket of his leather jacket.

WWW

WARRENWRIGHTWEBWORKS

No graphics, just addresses and phone numbers. "In case you get the urge." He walked off with a jagged smile.

Inside the car, my impression of him as easy company reverted immediately to an elusive, complex infatuation. If Sara said anticipation was powerful, how about retrospection? Would I ever get a true picture?

The history final arrived soon enough. The night before, Warren phoned to wish me luck and to say he had been thinking of me. I had been thinking of him too — almost constantly — but as soon as I heard his voice, reality put up a shield of detachment. When I told him to remember his sunscreen, he replied, "I don't plan on lying around the beach all the time. I want to do some hiking." One for Sara on the lie/lay question. We promised to see each other when he got back.

A first for me to be excited about an exam; I had gone through Barnwell's notes three times and supplemented them with Dad's history texts when I needed more. I had even lain awake most of the night like a kid at Christmas pumped up for the occasion to start. Luckily, it was quiet at work all day or I might have used up my concentration.

Barnwell said he didn't know whether to hand back our papers before or after, weighing the possible psychological advantages and disadvantages for the exam. Someone argued we would try harder if our mark was low, and if it was high, it would act as an inspiration. Barnwell didn't need much convincing.

My mark of 90 per cent was a number I had not seen on an exam since my elementary school spelling tests. "*Inventive treatment of topic, using letters as historical documents. The Strong murder is worth a paper of its own. House arrest served you well. Congratulations.*"

It was enough to propel me through the exam like a howitzer. I was prepared for every question and had a chance to go through them all again, still high on the trajectory when he called time. But academic adrenalin was new to my system and when I stood up, my energy no longer reached my head. I felt myself swaying with giddiness, the kind that comes before a migraine.

We all said thanks to Barnwell and exchanged invitations to stay in touch. Crane waited for me and we walked out together. I asked him if he needed another ride, but he said he and Marla were going for a drink across the street. Would I like to join them?

I declined the offer, my thoughts already on the corduroy couch and an Advil to ward off the head monster. He handed me his phone number and address on a scrap of paper, waiting for me to reciprocate. I knew better. "Thanks, I'm between numbers at the moment, but I might track you down for a cup of coffee sometime." Had I reached the stage where I only considered men with business cards? Or had I ever had a choice before?

Driving out of the parking lot, I considered the excuse I had given Crane. It probably was time for me to move back to my apartment, and yet I was dragging my feet in every sense of the phrase. Maybe I would be stronger if everything weren't done for me. I couldn't deny I was comfortable at Dad's and knew it would be hard for him no matter when I moved out. But living in my parents' home much longer didn't seem right, especially when I was paying rent on my own place. Before I knew it, I had turned onto the street that would take me there. Approaching, I saw a young couple, followed by two women coming through the entrance. All were laughing. This was a positive sign, because at Dad's I tended to think of my apartment building as dark and forlorn without me in it. Now my mind swung to the other extreme, imagining the place taken over by Club Med types, as if all traces of my former existence had been erased.

I parked on the street and walked back. In the foyer I was relieved to see Mrs. Read sitting in one of the easy chairs waiting for her friend to pick her up for their weekly bridge game. Some things hadn't changed. She said she hoped I was coming back soon.

My mailbox was stuffed, since neither Dad nor I had been here for a week or so. Hydro bill, fundraising address labels, pizza coupons, early Christmas and late birthday cards. I opened the one with familiar handwriting. "Happy Holidays to you and your dad. Ray." What was he up to? Had he broken up with Blondie? I hadn't answered his coffee invitation and had not bothered to ask anyone at work if there were changes in the Crown Counsel office. I pressed the elevator button. The door opened on another friendly face coming up from the basement. The manager, Nick Shotenski, obviously held no grudges about my many calls over minor things, his favourite being the stuck bulb in the oven and the broken base left in the socket of the bathroom fixture. It gave him a chance to repeat his favourite line: How many cops does it take to change a light bulb? One, but only if she knows a Ukrainian.

I got off at the seventh floor while he proceeded to the penthouse with his toolbox. When I turned the key and pushed my apartment door open, I expected a breath of stale, stuffy air but was surprised by a pleasant, almost fragrant inhalation. It smelled like a mixture of Sara's satiny Noxzema cream and her favourite perfume, Je Reviens. I knew it was neither, but I also knew — thanks to Lonnie's brother Hank — that unaccountable currents somehow rearranged air particles and maybe this was one of those occurrences. I walked through my three rooms, none as dismal as I had imagined. Under the sink I found a plastic bag for my letters and left with the feeling that I still did have a life at this address.

Back in the car, I looked at my watch. Dad would have skipped his supper hour and be waiting to eat with me and hear about my exam. Sure enough, he had a deli lasagna warming in the oven, and when he saw my paper, he brought out the sherry and two glasses.

"If I do as well as I think on the exam and with the mark from your paper and this one, I might end up with a decent grade. These courses could get to be a habit."

"Why not?" said Dad, prouder than proud, lifting his glass in a toast. "By the way, Janetta called and would like us to go to Nanaimo for Christmas. I told her we had made reservations at the Sylvia for Christmas dinner. That we wanted to keep it quiet this year. And Gail called. She wants you to phone her."

Gail and I had been playing phone tag since my birthday. "It's too late now for Saskatchewan."

"She said she would be up late — at a meeting. You're to call whenever you get in."

I flopped on the sofa with the phone and dialled her number. She sounded out of breath. "Just got in from a long-winded committee.

But I've got interesting news for you about that photo from the Mingus family."

"What is it?"

"I spoke to Howard Mingus and he said his father is the one you should talk to. He lives in Medicine Hat in seniors housing close to his daughter, Howard's sister. Here's his phone number — his name is Wendell Mingus."

I wrote it down as we spoke. "So what's the interesting part?"

"You'll find out. Call him tomorrow."

"Not even a hint? Torturer."

"I'm too tired at the moment. But as I mentioned to your dad, we want you both to come for Christmas dinner at my parents' place."

"Thanks, but we've made a date at the Sylvia." People were kind, but I was not up to being part of someone else's Christmas. Mom always made a stylish production out of the holiday and Dad and I agreed not even to put up a tree for ourselves, let alone be reminded somewhere else.

"Okay, but the offer still stands. And it's not an offer, but a command for you to spend New Year's Eve with Monty and me, whatever we end up doing. Unless you have a heavy date, that is."

I gave an "as if" snort. "That's a deal."

"It's minus forty with the wind chill here. I can't tell you how much I'm looking forward to everything about Vancouver."

"Have a good sleep. And thanks for the non-information." We hung up.

Dad was singing along to "Memories Are Made Of This" on the radio when I told him of a possible clue to the photo. He shrugged.

My eyes were closing even before I got into bed. The pillow under my head felt like a cloud carrying me away to a sunny university campus lined with good-looking men holding out their cards.

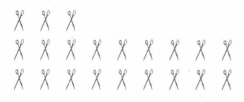

"MR. WENDELL MINGUS? This is Arabella Dryvynsydes calling from Vancouver. My friend Gail Pelletier in Willow Point spoke to your son Howard and he told her you might be able to give me some information. About a photo I bought from your family at a garage sale."

Wendell Mingus' voice held warmth but not age. "Yes, Howard called and told me of your interest. I believe the picture you have is one of my mother and her twin sister as little girls."

"Your mother?"

"My mother Janet."

"What was her sister's name?"

"It was Sara. But she died very young."

The blood left my head and began racing through my body. "Sara didn't die, Mr. Mingus. She was my grandmother. She believed Janet had died as a little girl."

From the pause at the other end, I guessed Gail had found out the revelation from Howard, but had not told him any more than she told me. "Mercy, what a piece of news you're giving me."

"Likewise." Just then I heard someone call "hello" in the background.

"My daughter Gloria has just come in to help me pack. How I'd like to talk more about this. Wait a minute — you're in Vancouver?"

"Yes."

"Tomorrow I'm flying to Victoria to spend Christmas with another daughter and I have an hour stopover in Abbotsford. You anywhere close to that airport?"

"Just tell me when."

"Gloria is driving me to Calgary for the 5 PM flight and I arrive in Abbotsford at the same time. Time change, you know."

"We'll be there. Dad and I will be the two tallest in the terminal."

"And I'll be wearing a brown leather jacket. A bit fancy for an old farmer like me, but my kids bought it for me to travel. See you tomorrow."

The Abbotsford airport was small enough to find Wendell Mingus easily, both from his description and from the process of elimination. The bulk of the passengers departed quickly, leaving only about ten for the connecting flight to Victoria. Dad was first to spot his cousin. I was struck by a resemblance as they offered their hands to each other. Same headshape — elongated at the back — and body language as they bowed slightly when shaking hands in a cordial, almost shy manner. There was also a similar softness in their grey eyes. Dad had a definite edge in height from the Dryvynsydes, but he could finally relinquish his title of biggest ears in the family. And Wendell dominated in hand size: two big rough paws — Gail would have liked them — one sporting only three fingers and a thumb. His face was sun-lined from a life in the field against Dad's white studious one. I gave Wendell Mingus a hug.

We took a cluster of four seats, one for Wendell's carry-on. "Where do we start?" he asked.

"How about the end?" I suggested. "When did Janet die?"

"2000. She was ninety."

"Same as Sara," I said in disbelief. "Date?"

"September 8. She had been failing for a few years with a heart condition and just got weaker and weaker. Mother died in hospital and it was a relief in the end."

"Mother hung on until October 2," Dad said, correcting himself to Sara in case Wendell mixed up their mothers, "but I think it was early September that we took her in with pneumonia. Do you remember, Bella?"

"I do. In fact, it was September 8, because I remember phoning Gail for her birthday from the hospital. I told Gail we were afraid she wouldn't make it," adding for Wendell's benefit, "Gail's my friend in

Willow Point who called your son." How Sara would have loved this cosmic connection in death with her sister.

Dad carried on, "But Mother recovered enough to go back home and she died peacefully of a heart attack a couple of weeks later. Sitting in her favourite chair with her cat and a book on her lap. The perfect exit."

Even my big frame didn't offer enough skin surface to produce the goosebumps necessary for this picture. Two complete strangers referring to Mother so casually when these women had shared the same womb. The only encounter more moving would have been watching Sara and Janet find each other. If life cheated those two out of such a meeting, it was now connecting these men before all memories of them were erased. As Wendell began to share his, I had a brief flare-up of possessiveness when he mentioned Jane, the same as I'd had when Jane mentioned baby Sara in her letter. My great-grandmother belonged to me.

"So I guess you know their mother Jane died of influenza when the girls were eight. Mother was sent to Victoria to live with her Uncle Gomer and Aunt Thelma, and her sister was given to another aunt and uncle in Ladysmith — I can't think of their names..."

"Uncle Thomas and Aunt Lizzie," Dad provided as Wendell resumed: "Well, Mother said Sara had died a year later."

Dad slapped his forehead. "How could that have happened? Sara believed the same thing about Janet."

"Mother — Janet — must have heard it from her uncle or aunt. She had no cause for doubt, so we never discussed it much. She wasn't one to question things anyway."

"Sara told us Aunt Lizzie ran into Thelma somewhere and she gave her the news that Janet had died of another wave of influenza a year later."

"Well, Mother wasn't much of a talker," Wendell went on, "but she did tell me once that she never got over her mother's death. Even worse was being separated from her twin sister right after. She said her mother Jane was a saintly woman, hardworking, gentle, and kind. Even when their father was drunk, she never screamed and yelled at him like some miners' wives. She would just take her girls into the sewing room and pull the curtain. Mother said her sister Sara was the lively one, always bouncing and chattering, but they were never more than a room away from each other until after their mother died. She spoke only once about that scene and it was right after my father died. She said as hard as it was to lose such a good husband, nothing could ever come close to the shock of losing her mother and sister at the same time."

My arms tingled again from hearing Sara's identical words in my head — "an inoculation against all future suffering."

"When my daughter Gloria asked Mother about it later, she told her that some things are best left alone. She never brought it up again. I guess I was the only one who heard about her mother's last days — unless she told Mona when they were together, but Mona isn't the type to show any interest."

"Mona?"

"Mona's my younger sister." He raised his eyebrows. "Now that I think of it, her full name is Sara Monica, but Dad came up with Mona. Anyways, Mona took Mother to live with her in Calgary after Dad died. She's a nurse and lives on her own."

Dad, the historian, wanted to put things in order. "I think we need some background. Where did your parents meet?"

"When farming got bad in the late twenties, my dad — Matt Mingus — left Willow Point to look for work on Vancouver Island. Found a job outside Victoria at the Bamberton cement plant. Took Mona and me there once to show us where it used to be — across the inlet from Butchart Gardens. Not too far away Mother was working as a chambermaid at the Goldstream Hotel. She was only sixteen, but she'd had three years' work experience at a dry goods store that belonged to her Aunt Thelma's family. Funny, how it was my dad told me all this stuff. Mother never liked to talk about those days, maybe because courting seemed too personal. Or maybe because she just didn't like to talk.

"Anyways, Dad couldn't understand a young girl never taking a day off from cleaning because she didn't want to go back home. When he asked her Uncle Gomer for her hand, he found out why. Constant bickering went on between him and his wife, mainly on account of

Uncle Gomer's laziness. He always had some health reason why he couldn't work. Dad said if you wanted someone more opposite to Uncle Gomer it was Mother. You couldn't get her to stop working; she was always cooking, cleaning or sewing. After Mother and Dad got married the cement dust got too much for him and he tried logging in a place called Little Saskatchewan. Men who couldn't make a go of it on the prairies ended up out there. Mona and I were both born there on the island. But that too dried up and his dad needed his help back home in Willow Point. It was just before the war and he escaped conscription by providing essential foodstuffs."

Dad interrupted with a laugh. "My dad got out of it because of his flat feet," he said quickly so Wendell could continue.

"So Mother and Dad took over the family farm from his father and stayed on it until 1970, when I took it over — I'd been helping up to that point, living in town, but by then Ella and I had three kids and Howard on the way. Ella was a farm girl and was glad to get back to the land. Mother and Dad moved into town, but he still liked to come out every summer and supervise." Wendell's chuckle indicated it was more than supervision. "That's why I decided to move right out of the community when I turned the farm over to my son Howard in 1999 — just so's I wouldn't be tempted to interfere. And his wife Cindy would have never put up with me; she's not the welcoming kind my wife was. Cindy's the one got sick of all the family clutter in the basement and put it in the garage sale. Some things dated back a hundred years, so I can't say I blame her. But when I heard about it, I thought it strange she'd sell everything after convincing Howard to move back into town. Claimed she couldn't stand the isolation from her friends and family eight miles away." Wendell shrugged, shaking off a remark he probably wanted to make about his daughter-in-law. "First time the Mingus homestead has stood empty in over a century. Howard's hanging onto it for the time being. My other son David comes from Swift Current in the summer to help on the farm and he stays there. Works on the rigs in winter."

I needed a review. "You have two sons and two daughters?"

"Girls came first: Carol, the oldest in Victoria, Gloria in Medicine

Hat, David in Swift Current, and Howard back home. David's the only one not married."

I counted them off on my fingers and had my thumb left for Mona. "Mona's your only sibling?"

"Just the two of us. Mona never married and insisted on taking Mother back to Calgary with her after Dad died, even though Ella and I wanted to take her in. Mona's a queer duck, not very talkative — a lot like Mother, in fact. But you couldn't get Mother out of the kitchen and you can't get Mona into it. My wife and I joked that she took Mother to cook for her. Dad and I were the nosy, gabby ones — maybe you've noticed." Wendell chuckled again. It was easy to imagine his family ignoring his chatter.

I sensed he was about to ask us some questions, but a glance at the clock told me to keep firing away while we had the momentum. "Tell us more about what your mother told you of her mother."

Wendell cleared his throat. "It was mainly that last part. She told me she and her sister did their best to help their sick mother lying on a cot behind a curtain in the kitchen. Sara kept cold cloths on her forehead and my mother kept the kitchen going — frying onions to put in a poultice for her chest to draw out the fever. She also mixed liniment with water for her to drink — I guess they used what they could back then. She said they were afraid of their father raging around the house and were glad when he finally stormed off. Said he was going for some medicine in Nanaimo for his dear wife, but it turned out he didn't make it past the bar.

"One thing always bothered Mother. Sara kept taking paper and pen to their mother on the cot. The first time, their father snatched it out of her hand. He shouted that their mother was too sick for writing and put it in the fire. As soon as he left and Janet went outside for water, Sara again brought their mother a notebook. They were doing lessons at home on account of the school being used as a hospital. This time Moth — Janet — screamed at Sara to let their mother rest. She said it was the only time her sister ever turned on her. 'Mama wants this,' she cried, 'You don't understand. You don't love words the way we do.'"

Recalling this, Wendell Mingus' eyes welled up. His untalkative mother was stung by her sister's remark and clearly passed on the hurt to her son. I wondered if my face looked as dumbstruck as Dad's. My mind kept detaching itself from this bizarre situation for a reality check: was the incident of the writing paper I had just recalled myself now being confirmed in the Abbotsford air terminal? Had I blotted out the argument with Sara and Janet from Sara's version? No, it was more likely Sara had not wanted to bring the pain of it back to mind, hers or mine.

Wendell spoke more slowly now. "The only other memory Mother shared that day of Dad's funeral was what happened not long after her mother died. Their father had not sobered up since his wife's death, then he heard his son had been killed in France — and uselessly, at that, because it was days before the armistice. His little daughters thought he would drink himself to death. For a while, a neighbour lady cooked for them, but then she got the flu. Mother herself baked muffins and bread until they ran out of flour. Mother remembered lying huddled with Sara under quilts to keep warm and to forget how hungry they were. She said Sara talked and talked to keep their minds occupied."

Wendell's cheeks had gained colour in the telling. "Hope I'm not going on too much," he said to the two faces he held captive. "Well, Mother didn't care much for games, but Sara forced her to play pretend people with her. They pretended to be at feasts put on by teachers, mothers, and brides, all kind and devoted women. Strange how these details still stick in my mind, maybe because there weren't too many from Mother to remember. She said they were under the quilt when Sara told her about their mother Jane's last words. Sara acted as if it was a secret and was only telling her because they had run out of games to play. She said their mother had asked her to name her son Lew after their brother Llewyllyn because he was a gentle man and had no one to help him. She musta meant when he died in battle." Wendell nodded at Dad, who had let his chin drop in his cupped hands. "And I see that she did." He paused. "This is amazing."

"But anyways, that's not the saddest part. Mother said she would never forget how hopeful they felt when their uncles — Thomas and

Gomer — and their wives entered the cold house with no fire and their father passed out in the front room. That is, until Aunt Thelma said they could only afford to take one girl each. Mother said the shriek that went up from her twin sister lived on in nightmares for the rest of her life. Mother wasn't the kind to make a fuss, but Sara screamed and kicked as Uncle Thomas packed up her few clothes. The last thing Mother remembered was Aunt Lizzie shaking Sara and telling her to hush up, that she should be thankful anyone would take her when no one wanted her. That was the last time she saw her sister."

None of us could speak. Finally, Wendell looked at his watch and stood up. He still had plenty of time to check in, but I knew from experience with Dad there was no point in trying to persuade someone his age that he didn't have to be early for everything. "We just got to my story. I haven't heard a world of yours yet."

"We'll have another chance soon, I hope."

He picked up his carry-on and we walked with him to security. Dad suddenly remembered the picture; we had almost been late trying to find a recent photo of Sara, now forgotten in my wallet. Wendell brought out one of his mother.

We looked upon Sara's double eighty years after that first picture. Except they were no longer doubles. Janet's hair was pure white, the permed shower-cap style many older women chose for thinning hair. She was sitting in a recliner — at Mona's, Wendell informed us — wearing a pale blue printed duster coat with no makeup. She had just opened a gift — a photo album from her grandchildren for her eighty-fourth birthday — and had a half-hearted smile on her face that she held down slightly, as if she had a stiff neck. Sara would never have been caught by a camera without lipstick or in a dressing gown, and I did not want to ask Wendell if this was normal for Janet, or merely a sign of her decline in later years. Surely a woman who worked as hard as she did wouldn't be in a housecoat much in healthy times. Dad commented that it could be Janetta in twenty years, explaining that his younger sister was the namesake of Wendell's mother.

The photo we offered Wendell showed Sara at eighty-six standing in front of the tea room at Ferguson Point in a hot pink blazer over a long black cotton dress. She wore knee-highs, even with sandals, and I smiled to think of her calling them "nylon condoms" because of the way they coiled up when removed. Her hair was grey rather than white and she insisted on keeping what was left of it in a short bob. Her face was also tilted down at an angle, as if she only agreed to the photo at the last minute with a sly, reluctant grin. The more I studied the two pictures, the more I could see a similarity in the general shape of their faces, the way their glasses sat an inch down on their noses, and even their coyness with the camera.

Too late we all wondered why we had not brought more pictures of Sara and Janet when they were younger. We exchanged addresses and promised to send some by mail, so that Wendell's family and Janetta might also get to know their new aunts. I asked him if there was anything else — more pictures, letters maybe — of Janet's early years left in the farmhouse. He shook his head: he was surprised the photo had still been there. He thought Mona had taken all their mother's personal belongings with her to Calgary. Speaking his sister's name prompted him to write down her phone number as well. I could check with her. Dad put his arm around his cousin's shoulder, and I had to persuade myself that the past hour had actually taken place.

THE YEAR WAS DOWN to its last four hours. After such a mixed bag of surprises, I had to be thankful the bad stuff preceded this bit of equilibrium and not the other way around. I shivered at the idea of Mom's death just happening and all that followed now being ahead of me. Our first Christmas without her was not as gloomy as we had imagined — Sara's theory of anticipation/dread again. The dazzling sun on English Bay from the Sylvia dining room left no room for dark thoughts. Later the glistening air and water inspired us to walk off our turkey dinner along the sea wall and back through Stanley Park. Even my foot felt the warmth and forgot to ache.

Gail and Monty would be here any minute. They wanted to put Clancy and Macy to bed before leaving them to their doting grandparents. We decided to gather at Dad's because none of us felt like fanfare and this way he would be included. I had turned down two other offers: Emile was having a party at his place for our old team and Tessa wanted the new team to get together in her loft in downtown Vancouver before going out to a club later. The year was ending on a promising note — ties to the past and future combined with my most timeless bonds.

In the living room, Dad's stack of Guy Lombardo records was playing on the console, so old it was now back in style as a retro piece. I had my pile of CDs in reserve to put on politely after his traditional New Year's Eve music welcomed our guests. I wiped the unused sleek leather sectional and lit Mom's big white three-wicked candle in the middle of her glass and marble coffee table. Bowls of chips and nuts and a tray of vegetables stood ready while Dad busied himself with glasses, bottles, and ice in the kitchen. If I could pass my first university course — I ended up with 88 as a final mark — maybe I could take a shot at cooking. But not until next year; I wasn't about to start with the elaborate fondues Mom always prepared on New Year's Eve. Instead, we had a shrimp ring and two deli quiches in the fridge for later.

Gail and I had not managed to see each other yet despite several phone calls. Her schedule was not her own with all the relatives here wanting to see them. I had also been working, other than Boxing Day when I made the mistake of hitting some sales on Robson. After half an hour, I decided to leave the bargains to the teenagers and to the immigrants whose experience with shortages gave them an edge at the bins.

As usual, when the doorbell rang I wasn't prepared for how big Monty was and Gail wasn't. Wouldn't I know by now? She looked sassy in a lacy cream poncho, black turtleneck, jeans, high-heeled boots and dangly earrings. After the hugs, Gail proclaimed her delight at being back in this childhood territory, then stopped short and swallowed, observing the absence of Retha. Dad hugged her again. Once we were all seated with drinks in our hands, Mom lingered as Gail brought up nostalgic incidents from our teenage years. Some I wished she had kept quiet. Like the time Mom and Dad were at a teacher's banquet and we started drinking Dad's Scotch, soon leading us to the bright idea of asking over Gail's latest admirer. When Mom came back unexpectedly to pick up a copy of the speech she was to give — the only time in her life she forgot anything — we hid him in the broom closet. Dad raised his eyebrows, and Monty sat looking amused by the story, the way he did whenever Gail said anything.

Before I could ask about her family, Gail said: "So how do you like your new cousin, Mr. Dryvynsydes?"

"Please call me Lew, Gail. And thank you so much for finding him for us. Hearing his story was a revelation — Bella must have told you."

"Actually, we haven't had a chance to talk and I'd like to hear it now. Don't forget I loved Sara too, so any twin of hers concerns me. I almost choked when Howard Mingus told me the picture was of his grandmother and her sister. I thought you two should share the revelation with Wendell Mingus."

"I figured as much."

Guided by their questions, Dad and I filled Monty and Gail in on everything Wendell had told us. About his parents meeting on Vancouver Island, their return to the family homestead in Saskatchewan, and his mother's final years in Calgary. Not intentionally, we saved the part about the little girls parting until the end. Dad had to bite his lip.

Gail's eyes misted too. "Sara never told you about it?"

"We all knew about her mother's dying request to name her son Lew, but not about the fight with Janet over the paper, or about the day of their separation."

"Shows how deep the wound went. What did Sara tell you of those years after the separation?" Gail asked Dad, assuming I wouldn't have been paying attention.

"She often spoke of her ordeal of living with Aunt Lizzie. She dealt with Lizzie's jealousy, stinginess, and laziness by working harder than ever, even though it made Lizzie and her older daughters resent her even more."

"How much older were they?"

"Edna and Myrtle were quite a bit older — maybe twelve years or so — and they had both married miners in Ladysmith and lived in their own homes not far away. But they were always around, according to Mother, and they made her life miserable. The one bright light was baby Laura, born to Lizzie in her forties."

"Sara was there for the birth," I added. "She told me she pretended Laura was her missing sister. She developed a bond with the little girl, who ended up frail and sheltered."

"Lizzie allowed it?" asked Gail.

"Seems she was so lazy she was happy to have the child taken care of. Mother said she would snatch her away only when she saw them getting too close."

"From Jane's letters, Uncle Thomas sounds like a decent, responsible guy — couldn't he do anything?" I turned the story back over to Dad.

"He probably tried, but from what Mother said, Lizzie was completely overbearing and he hated scenes. At least he fought for her to go to school until Grade Eight because he recognized her ability. Like

Janet, she left home as early as she could and found a job as a waitress at the Nanaimo Hotel."

"Wasn't that where she met your father?" asked Gail.

Dad nodded. "Miles Dryvynsydes was a miner too — a reluctant one — and she said they would always be grateful to the teacher who remembered his ability and recommended him for a job in a bank in Nanaimo."

I butted in, to show I did listen to my grandmother sometimes. "Sara often said that teacher changed the course of their lives. She loved dwelling on twists of fate. Didn't they elope just before he got transferred to Alberta so they could start their life as a couple?"

"It was to a little town called Milo, and from there they moved all over southern Alberta. I was born in Milo and Janetta in Medicine Hat."

Dad's pile of records had finished, so I slipped some Sarah McLachlan into the CD player while he was talking. "But that's probably enough of the Dryvynsydes family tree. We've monopolized the whole night."

Monty spoke up. "Not at all — it's fascinating. Remember, I was there for the first clue — the photo. And as a twin myself, I know how brutal that separation would be." Ignoring Gail's comment "That would be news to Wolfe," he asked, "How did both think the other was dead?"

"Sara said Aunt Lizzie told her Janet had died of the second wave of influenza the following year."

"And according to Wendell, Janet believed the same thing of Sara."

Dad, always fair-minded, said, "I hate to think either family made it up. They were both poor, and in those days, Victoria was a world away from Ladysmith if you didn't have the means to travel. Jane says in her letters the brothers did not go out of their way to see each other. Both families might have heard through a relative that the other sister was dead and did nothing to confirm it. Don't forget the wives weren't thrilled to have the girls in the first place."

"What about Laura?" Monty asked.

"When I was six, Mother had a telegram saying Uncle Thomas had died. I remember the date — September 18, 1936 — because Janetta was born the same day. Mother was quite upset that she couldn't take the train to his funeral, but with a new baby she wasn't allowed out of bed. She told me later she and Dad sent money to Lizzie for funeral expenses. And I know she sent money in Christmas cards after that. No word from that family until at least ten years later when Laura sent an announcement of her mother's death — very flowery about Lizzie being at home in the arms of Jesus. Lizzie had taken Laura into some fundamental religion. Come to think of it, that's when the bundle of letters might have arrived."

Dad straightened his shoulders, his face brightening at a released memory. "You know, that's right. We had just moved to Vancouver from Red Deer and there were still crates to be unpacked in the house. The package must have been forwarded from the Red Deer address. I was a moody seventeen-year-old, angry at leaving my friends behind to start a new school in this big city. The last thing I cared about was some unknown aunt or even a packet of letters, but I do remember Mother sitting down on her Queen Anne chair with her apron on in the middle of all the unpacking to inspect them. I'm afraid my interest didn't go any further than that — until this year."

"But how did Laura — or Lizzie — end up with them?"

Dad shrugged. "Can't say. As far as I know, there was just the death announcement with the letters. A few years later when Janetta married Lawrence and moved to Nanaimo, Mother asked her to look Laura up in Ladysmith; you'll have to ask Janetta for more details. I have a vague recollection of Mother saying the house was full of scriptures and crucifixes and Janetta wasn't welcome."

"Sara was generous to bother with them after those years of meanness," Gail commented.

On my way to the refrigerator for the shrimp ring, I called back, "The hardest thought for me is that Sara and Janet were both working in hotels a short train ride apart without knowing it. What a comfort they would have been to each other."

"That's not the worst of it," said Dad quietly. "If Janet and Matt Mingus went back to the family homestead before the war, that means the twin sisters were only an hour apart when we lived in Medicine Hat in the thirties. They might well have passed each other on the street, when the Minguses went there to shop."

"Think of it," said Gail. "Sara and Janet in the same store; Sara maybe even glancing her way as she leaves. You don't know your own face as others know it, especially if you're not looking." Her shoulders under her poncho shook a little.

"Dad and Wendell would have been playmates growing up," I said, returning with the food.

Just then the phone rang and Gail's mother asked to speak to Monty. Clancy wasn't settling down and wanted to say goodnight to his daddy. Monty took the phone and disappeared into the kitchen. I told Gail this was a good time to put a book mark in the saga of the sisters. We wanted to hear about her family. I pulled my little friend off the couch and hugged her tightly. "What a favour you've done for us, putting all this in motion."

"One phone call — what's that? I didn't know investigative reporting could be such a thrill. Maybe I'll use it as an assignment if I ever get around to journalism."

Monty returned and I steered the conversation to their lives in Willow Point: Gail's new positions as president of the Arts Council and Minor Hockey Association, Monty's act of bravery in rescuing a snowmobiler who had fallen through the ice on a nearby lake. At their urging, Dad brought out his illustrations in progress, promising the first autographed copy of Sissipuss to Clancy and Macy, should it ever find a publisher.

Of course, Dad had to bring up my history mark and I had to act embarrassed. He explained how I used Jane's letters as historical references until I gave him a warning glare. We were back in our family history again and I didn't want the year to end on this self-centred note. He got the message, promptly jumping up to set out champagne and glasses. Midnight was creeping up. I brought in the warmed quiches and sliced them as finger food.

Monty asked for New Year's resolutions.

I quoted Sara saying that a thought was the hardest thing in the world to change or be rid of — harder than any diets or exercises. Ray came to mind for so rarely coming to mind anymore.

"No more negative thoughts," said Gail, chanting it like an anthem.

I wasn't finished. "As a remedy against harmful thinking, I hereby store the spirit in this room at this moment in my Save file." With my thumb I pushed the centre of my forehead where Sara said our third eye perceived what the other two didn't. "I can call it up whenever I need consolation."

"This is getting weird," said Monty, "but why not, it's you, Bella."

Dad turned on the TV to make sure we were right on the stroke of midnight. When the crystal ball hit the ground in Times Square, we all hugged and toasted the new year with champagne.

A few seconds later, the phone rang. I expected it to be Gail's parents and answered without checking.

"Happy New Year from Hawaii," said Warren Wright.

My stomach gave a little flip as I walked into the bedroom, away from the curious eyes and ears. "You've still got a couple of hours to go. No big party going on?"

"There are a few people at the condo, but I'm taking a walk along the beach thinking of you."

"That's nice to hear."

A robust laugh from Monty in the next room changed his tone. "Sounds as if you're busy."

"My best friend and her husband are visiting from Saskatchewan."

"I won't keep you from them. I'll be home next week. Maybe we'll get together."

"Sure."

My blushing face gave everything away and Gail demanded details. I insisted there wasn't much to tell, but I knew Monty would never let me forget I was going out with one of my felons. "Soon you'll be forbidden from visiting prisoners in cells."

Gail started yawning and gave Monty a nudge. Morning came early for Macy and Clancy. Instead of responding, he asked for a pen and paper and began to write.

What we know so far: Source of photos. Janet's and Sara's whereabouts and lifespans from personal testimony and witnesses. Mother Jane's life from letters and witnesses.

What we need to know: How letters from Jane ended up where they did. Roland? What happened to him after being last seen lying drunk by his daughters at age eight? Rap sheet on Roland.

He tore out the page and handed it to me. I started feeling guilty again about the interest these two were taking in my investigation until the keen look in Monty's eye reminded me of why he was such a good cop. I could not let the team down and promised to phone Mona Mingus in Calgary. She was our only hope for any more clues. Gail suggested meeting tomorrow — this afternoon — at the Polar Bear Swim at English Bay. We both knew we would never find each other in the crush of spectators, but it made saying goodbye easier.

Dad looked tired so I shooed him to bed, assuring him I would clean up. Before he turned in, he said he had asked his finger about whether he should go to the Polar Bear swim and it told him no, for me to go ahead without him. I took this as a signal to bring up the possibility of moving back to my apartment, but not tonight. Alone in the kitchen, I had an absurd image of our family quirks. Would pressing foreheads and rising fingers eventually lead to communicating through a game of "head and shoulders, knees and toes" with no words at all? I giggled myself through the dishes.

JUST WHEN I WAS FEELING SMUG about leaving shift work behind, our team got called in. I was about to find out the trade-off involved in giving up regulated hours.

It was the morning after New Year's Day. Tessa was telling me about the party I missed when Wayne announced an infant abduction on Colleen Street. He grabbed his jacket and took off with Tessa in one vehicle while Dex and I followed in another. Sukhi was still on holiday visiting his wife's relatives in Kelowna. The two-storey house in question stood in a middle-class neighbourhood, but had been redone in grey stucco — the old-fashioned kind where tiny pebbles are thrown onto wet cement — black shutters and cream trim. Located at the curved end of Colleen Street, it gave the impression of not wishing to stand out in its good taste among the split-levels from the '70s, some freshly painted in taupe or celery, some left with their original orange or turquoise trim. The site was swarming with patrol cars and officers; one was cordoning off the yard, three more were in the back, and another was trying to calm a woman in her bathrobe at the front entrance.

"My baby, my baby," she cried in an accent. "I thought it was the paperboy." She stopped to sob against the constable's stiff vest and he patted her shoulder lightly. Male officers were cautioned against making this kind of physical contact. Women in distressed states could — and did — easily misinterpret such gestures. Without hesitation, Tessa gently took the woman's arm and guided her through the foyer toward the staircase.

"Come, Mrs. Kubik, I'll help you dress and we'll take you to the hospital to be with your baby."

Tessa impressed me more every day; she always seemed to do the right thing. I had been in these situations many times myself as a first responder and the procedure was second nature to me, but this was my first call with Serious Crimes, so I followed Wayne and Dex through the house, whose owners clearly had expensive tastes. I had shopped with Retha, after all, and knew high-quality leather sofas when I saw them. A stainless steel kitchen opened onto a back patio through French doors, and we used them to join the other members examining the fish pond and grass around it for clues. They told us what they knew so far.

At 7:30 AM, Selena Kubik, Caucasian female, thirty-nine years of age, native of the Czech Republic, answered the doorbell with her four-month-old son Anton in her arms. A Caucasian male, mid-to-late thirties, stood outside and without warning, snatched the baby from her and ran around the north side of the house. She took the shorter route through the house to beat him, grabbing the portable phone from the kitchen cupboard and dialling 911 to scream her address as she ran, but in the few seconds it took to reach the back patio, he had disappeared. She found her baby lying unconscious, face down in the murky winter water of the pond. He had a gash on his head. The emergency team arrived within minutes, but Mrs. Kubik's agitated state interfered with the swift measures necessary; she had to be restrained so the ambulance could take the baby to Burnaby General.

This was where we came in. Just as Wayne said Tessa and I would take Mrs. Kubik to the hospital in one of the cruisers, the two of them appeared from upstairs. Dressed and made up, Selena Kubik was more chic than pretty, in an angular, high-strung way. Her black hair was held back with a clip; her jeans had a perfect flare over mahogany leather boots. The grey turtleneck looked like cashmere and her espresso leather car coat was probably tanned from the same herd of exotic cattle as her furniture.

In the back seat of the cruiser, I noticed her face had gone from hysterical to stony; had she popped a tranquillizer in the bathroom? I took the wheel and Tessa began to share what she had learned, including Mrs. Kubik in the conversation.

"Her husband is out of the country on business. He called her yesterday to say he would be home late tonight."

"What business?" I asked.

"He is an engineer. He has been in Kosovo building bridges." Her voice was deep and throaty, like a European spy in a James Bond movie.

"No cellphone?"

"It is off. He is in transit."

"Blackberry?"

She shook her head. "I do not text."

I sensed her impatience with my questions at the same time as Tessa touched my leg gently to let me know they had been through this. Soon we were at the Burnaby General Hospital and pulled into an emergency slot. The car was in uniform, but Tessa and I were not, thus we were able to escort Mrs. Kubik to pediatric intensive care quickly and discreetly. A nurse took her to the baby's room where Cory, another member, stood guard outside. Sometimes an abductor tried again, especially if it was a husband. A flash of the inaccessible engineer re-entered my mind. Cory nodded toward the door and Tessa and I took turns peering through the glass. All we could see of the baby through the clear plastic crib were his black hair and tubes and wires extending from his motionless body. Moments later, two physicians — a young pretty woman and older man — came up from behind and went into the room. The four of them — Mrs. Kubik and the nurse on one side, and the two doctors on the side closest to us — stood clustered over the tiny boy. The older physician put his hand on Mrs. Kubik's shoulder and pulled up a chair for her next to the crib. Leaving her with her baby, the three then came out of the room together. When Tessa and I showed our badges, the lady doctor stepped away from the door and spoke.

"He's barely hanging on. The contusion on the side of his head came from a pretty hard blow. Bad enough, but then the water — a baby can hardly survive trauma like that. We're doing everything possible. Prayer might be all that's left."

The doctor patted my arm and walked back to the nursing station, giving Tessa and me another chance at the glass window. Selena Kubik sat stroking her child's black hair from the chair, the same vacant expression on her face. People dealt with crises in different ways and in various stages. Stupors were not uncommon — the mind's method of distancing itself from pain. I tiptoed in to tell her we would leave her here and be back later. Was there anything she needed?

"No," she said without looking up. "Thank you."

I stood next to her for a moment watching little Anton Kubik, who was unaware he was fighting for his life. Smiling in his mother's arms one minute, smashed against the side of a pool the next. I thought of Macy and Clancy at this age — or any age — and what Monty and Gail would be going through. Visions of Sara and Janet also pressed in, of the blows they took through death and separation. A sudden cramp gripped me in the area around my heart.

On the way back to Colleen Street Tessa filled me in on what she had learned from Selena upstairs between sobbing spasms. She had been in the kitchen feeding Anton when she heard scraping outside the front door. She thought at first it was a paper boy with flyers. But she heard it again and opened the door. A strange man was standing there. It was just getting light on an overcast morning and she could not see his expression clearly. She believed he was trying to rob the place when she surprised him. Alarmed, he said a few words in a foreign language, then grabbed the baby from her arms. He ran around the side of the house and she thinks when he heard her screaming inside, he got scared and threw the baby in the fish pond.

"Description?"

"Average height. Dark hair."

"Caucasian?"

"She thinks so. Could be central European like herself, though she didn't recognize the language."

"How many does she speak?"

"A lot more than we do. Czech, English, French, German at least. She wondered if it was Albanian — a Kosovar."

"What's the Kosovo connection? Isn't that where her husband is? Do you smell something fishy about that relationship? Wouldn't you think a husband that far away would leave a line of communication open to his wife and baby son?"

Tessa shrugged. "Sounds more like she doesn't want to use it. What can he do in the air?"

"Seems strange to me."

Tessa shrugged again, as she turned back onto Colleen Street. Next to our unmarked cars, we recognized the forensic identification team vehicle. The two members whose cruiser we had taken met us on the sidewalk to reclaim it. They would be back shortly for guard duty and alerted us that media vans were on their way. They often picked up news from police scanners; luckily they knew enough to wait for our publicity spokesman Tony and not to expect anything from us. Ident was already in the backyard with gloves, vials, and plastic bags, questioning Wayne.

"How's the baby?" Dex asked.

"Critical. We'll go back in a while."

The yard was enclosed on three sides by a five-foot cedar fence with a gate on the north side and a solid short stretch on the south. To reach the back, he would have had to open the gate with the baby in his arms. But if the latch were not secure at the time, it would have offered no more resistance than a swinging door. From the back, four escape routes were possible: over the fence into a neighbour's yard on the left or the right, into Charles Rummel Park bordering the back, or around the south side of the house and over that short joint of fence and onto Colleen Street.

The yard displayed the same understated good taste as the house. A sprawling oak tree to the left had a circular bench built around its trunk over a bed of fine white pebbles. Hydrangea bushes, not yet in bloom, hugged the back of the house, and a neat border of foliage I didn't recognize framed the large patio. A trellis thick with vines provided a half-roof and sides to the concrete area. A path of irregular stepping stones led from the patio to the pond. Two bent willow chairs stood facing the water on either side of the short walk.

Deep and craggy, the pond resembled a grotto inverted in the earth. A wave of ragged rock protruded on one side and more shrubbery circled the rest of it unevenly, a deliberate effect. Custom landscaping like this could cost as much as a house in Mission. The pond had likely not been cleaned since last fall; the stale water inside must have been rain-fall. Lilies or colourful fish might have brightened it in summer, but at the moment it held only a few leaves and twigs, and maybe a trace of Anton Kubik's blood. Ident had already taken a sample.

Dex was carefully examining the fence where a footprint or a scrap of mud or fibre might have been left behind, but complained that all he could find was raccoon shit. The abductor must have been agile enough to leap up to the fence rail and spring over the foot or so of slats at the top.

Hands on hips, Tessa stared at the adjoining yards and Wayne anticipated her question. "Yeah, we've spoken to the neighbours on both sides. No one saw him in one house and no one's home in the other. The park seems the obvious route to flee and will be harder to prove." Wayne stopped and looked down. Near the pond his foot had stepped on something: a clear plastic baby soother, easy for the eye to miss on first inspection. "Could be helpful," he said. "Makes you want to cry, doesn't it?"

Wayne called an ident member over and she photographed the soother before he picked it up carefully and slipped it into a plastic bag for the exhibit locker. One of our Serious Crimes members — today it was Wayne — collects and itemizes all exhibits to be examined later for fingerprints. The ident woman moved on to the stepping stones with her camera, shaking her head. "Not much to go on when the mother and emergency team have trampled over them."

I decided to take the inside route to check the front entrance. The kitchen was unnaturally clean and tidy for a house with a baby in it. Given that most of the houses I attended lay at the other end of the cleanliness range, I had still never seen one this immaculate. The only evidence of little Anton was a wooden box with toys and cloth books in one corner and an almost empty baby bottle on the cupboard; it was no doubt the one Selena Kubik was using to feed him when she heard the abductor at the front door.

An open bookcase made of pewter divided the living and dining areas. Books shared the shelves with a raku pot, three photos, and a cast iron candle holder containing a spray of narrow ivory tapers. The photos were all black and white. Baby Anton with a wide, toothless smile in a corduroy beret gave me another heart cramp. The good-looking man with Selena Kubik had to be her husband: older than I would have guessed, grey-haired, tall, a cosmopolitan face and stance in an open-necked white shirt and sports jacket. He might have been the poster boy for Hugo Boss Seniors. He was standing with his arms around Selena's waist and she had stepped forward, almost as if she were trying to get away. The third photo was of the husband holding the baby, both heads thrown back in pure joy and laughter. The close-up weathered skin suggested he was in his mid- to late fifties. Around the pictures stood a few art books, a couple of atlases, some history, and half a shelf of Czech titles nudging against — surprisingly — two Harry Potter books. Other than those two volumes, the bookcase had been arranged carefully, as if too many books would be regarded as clutter.

The putty-coloured walls were sparsely hung with original art. Again I thanked Retha for my recognition of quality. One was an enchanting restaurant scene by Keith Holmes, a Galiano artist Mom and I had met at an exhibition on Granville Street. In fact, Dad had wanted to surprise her with one of his paintings for Valentine's Day, had she stuck around.

But that was one of the few signs of colour. The poinsettia on the coffee table was creamy; the small artificial tree on the dining table was made of white feathers and decorated with silver baubles. I kept thinking of Gail and the other young mothers I knew; most would have been bouncing their babies to Christmas carols and bombarding them with the colours of the season. Maybe Selena Kubik did — the bouncing, that is.

Outside the front door, the sisal mat on the landing was caked with mud. While I was waiting for ident and Wayne to come from the back to photograph and seize it, the mailman walked up with letters in his hand. "What's going on?"

"You'll see it on the news." I pointed to two media vans discharging crews and equipment onto the property. "Do you want me to put that mail inside?"

He handed me two letters and some flyers and I looked around for a surface in the foyer or living room to set them. None seemed appropriate. No magazines or papers lay among the pottery and vases. I decided to leave the mail on a small built-in table under the phone in the kitchen, though even that held no pads and pens for jotting messages. To make sure this house wasn't just a movie set, I pulled open a little drawer underneath and found a notepad and a pen lined up inside. I set the mail neatly on top but not before looking at it. Both letters were for Jan Kubik — one from a solicitor Tomas Svoboda on Richards Street — and the other, the larger square shape of a greeting card from the Czech Republic.

In the backyard, Tony was taking notes from Wayne as the cameramen and reporters from various networks set up for his interview. They had already done a pan of the front of the house to give an idea of the neighbourhood. Tony would be an asset to any organization — good-looking, well-spoken, co-operative. Unfortunately, he didn't have much to share with the public today, other than a hazy description of a man with an accent and a baby near death in a hospital. We would eventually bring in a forensic artist once Selena was composed enough to give details.

Tessa appeared from the side of the house. She motioned Dex and me into the kitchen, out of camera range. "A young guy in the basement next door just woke up. His parents are away and he didn't hear us ring the first time. He was drinking all night and just after he fell asleep, he heard loud talking at the front, looked out to see a white Porsche speeding away in the hazy dawn, then heard screaming from the back. Or did he hear the screaming and then see the Porsche? He wasn't sure of the sequence of events because his hangover sucked him back into bed somewhere in the middle of it all.

Wayne escaped from the cameras to the kitchen just then and Tessa told him what she had learned. "Let's go back," he said to her. To me he said: "Could you go to the hospital to check on the baby and Mrs. Kubik again?"

I nodded.

On the way over in the car, I couldn't stop thinking about Jan Kubik and the shock awaiting him. The picture of him with the baby haunted me.

Cory was pacing back and forth in front of the hospital room when I went in. During the time I was away, Selena and the baby hadn't moved. A respirator was breathing for him and she didn't look up when I tiptoed in and stood next to her. Little Anton's skin was grey and translucent — almost pearlized — and I watched for a flicker of anything from him. Nothing.

"He is going to die," Selena whispered.

I put my hand on her shoulder. "Can I do anything? Has your husband been contacted?"

"No," she said flatly.

"Would you like me to help you get through to him?"

"No."

Her reluctance was clear. Why was I so eager to start the man's grieving process anyway? Contacting him through the airlines would simply ruin the rest of his flight, if in fact he was on his way. But if he were stranded in an airport, I believed he should be given the news to hasten his return. I'd learned about feng shui from Sara, who had even convinced Mom to set up her new furniture in tune with its principles of balancing energies. But having just come from Colleen Street, I sensed more of a chill in the house than blocked energy. According to home style magazines, its decor might win awards, yet I could not get past an emptiness that went beyond this tragedy. Why would she not want to share these life-threatening moments with her husband? Or was she clinging so close to the edge herself that an extra breath of response would send her over?

I slipped out of the room to find Cory talking to a cute nurse, so I sat down in his chair. I'd been in Cory's spot on several occasions, often spending my whole shift as a guard outside a hospital room. I'd seen murder victims die, accident victims both die and recover, suicide failures and successes. Most of the injuries and deaths we attended could have been prevented, unlike the rest of the patients in the hospital. That's why disgust and sadness choked my throat equally at the moment.

When I first joined the force, I believed the criminal mind might follow a pattern. That we could learn to recognize a certain type who committed brutal crimes. But I'd since discovered that cruel impulses can occur in both sexes, all ages, races, religions, and classes. Men definitely had the monopoly on instigating violence, and after a run of armed robberies you might generalize that poverty, lack of positive home influence, and drugs are also key factors in crime. But then we'd be called in to an Asian or East Indian revenge killing where the body is found in a Jaguar or Mercedes, or a man is stabbed on the doorstep of his million-dollar mansion. And when you started to presume certain visible minorities were more likely to commit the serious crimes, you would find someone the Hell's Angels had worked over — those tortures were unmatched. How many Caucasians associated themselves with Hell's Angels or the Mafia when they were so quick to suggest all Sikhs should be sent back to India, Asians to Hong Kong, and West Indians to Jamaica whenever they heard of a killing by one of them? I looked over at young blonde Cory openly flirting with the nurse and wondered if he felt any guilt by association when a white man murdered someone. Probably not. Yet I knew Sukhi did whenever we picked up a Sikh.

At the moment, I was down on the whole human race. Witnessing savagery was cumulative: it became worse, not easier, with every case. And the present one was about to prove the point, judging from the speed with which the two physicians now hurried past me and into the room. At first I resisted the impulse to see for myself through the window, but finally I stood up. I saw what I feared: the doctors each had an arm around Selena Kubik and were helping her out of her chair. They ushered her to the door, her face still frozen in a blank expression. Our abduction case had become a homicide.

"Any family we can contact for you?" the female physician asked as they brought her into the corridor.

She barely shook her head, looking at me as if I were the most familiar person in her world. "Please take me home."

I put my arms around her. "I can take you home to get some things, but we have to keep the house clean as a crime site." Remembering her house, I corrected "clean" to "untouched." "We can take you to a friend until your husband gets home."

When she didn't react, the doctor took me aside and said: "You'll get her help for the funeral with Victim Services? She seems impervious right now."

I assured her I knew the channels and walked Selena Kubik slowly to the elevator. Inside, I looked down on her, still in her trancelike state. Her dusky complexion had paled and appeared parched. No puffy eyes, red nose, or smeared mascara; no sign of moisture anywhere on her face. A media van parked at the entrance made me thankful to be in plainclothes and in an unmarked car, because they didn't notice us pulling away. Selena's silence unnerved me; all I could think to say was "I'm sorry" over and over. She nodded once.

Cory had called the team on Colleen Street, and Wayne, Dex, and Tessa were waiting with condolences when we entered the house. Mrs. Kubik said she would get her things and Tessa accompanied her upstairs again. While they were gone, Wayne filled me in on the visit to the boy next door. He was twenty-one, had the run of his parents' home while they were on a cruise, and was still celebrating New Year's Eve two days later. No more clues besides the talking and screaming and white Porsche, in no particular order and in reduced light. He said the Kubiks were courteous neighbours, but his parents didn't know them well. One of the neighbours across the street had also seen a white sports car drive away, but that was all.

"So there never was anything for Dex to find on that fence."

"Guess not."

"Strange she wouldn't have seen him take off in a car."

"It was parked down the street, according to the other neighbour. The perp could have run around the other side of the house after throwing the baby. Or even the same side he used to get there — she was inside, after all."

"He must have been awfully fast, and she slower than she thinks. She could have frozen for a few seconds. She's been that way all day."

Tessa brought Selena back down with a Louis Vuitton overnight bag. Wayne gestured her to a chair. "Mrs. Kubik, we're going to need your help in providing more details. Did you see a car?"

"No, I did not. It was misty and I only saw him at the front door before he snatched my baby. He was gone by the time I got to the back. I thought it was over the fence."

"Neighbours saw a white Porsche with a dark-haired man driving away at about that time."

"I never saw a car," she repeated.

"Do you feel up to talking to a forensic artist about a description?"

"No."

"In that case, we will take you to a friend or relative or hotel until tomorrow while we complete our investigation. Do you have one you can call?"

"I will take the hotel," said Selena Kubik, without answering. "And I want her to stay with me."

She pointed at me.

IT IS NOT UNCOMMON to guard a witness in a hotel room, but being a companion for Selena Kubik was definitely out of the ordinary. She was more a candidate for Victim Services than for us. Given her mental state, which seemed catatonic at the moment, Wayne decided she should have the attendant of her choice, namely me. He said an IHIT guy had just shown up, but there had been a run of homicides in the lower mainland recently, and they had no problem letting Burnaby Serious Crimes continue what we had started as an abduction.

Wind and rain had stepped up the January gloom a notch, and I put on the heater along with the wipers and lights on the way back to Dad's to get an overnight bag. He was working on his book at the dining table, when I dashed in from the downpour. After I'd thrown some underwear, pyjamas, and a toothbrush into my little carrying case, I began to outline the situation as quickly and simply as I could for him. Halfway through, I heard myself saying, "You shouldn't have to put up with these disruptions — the next one might be the middle of the night. It's probably time I moved back to my apartment to give you some peace and quiet."

Dad hid his flinch well. I could tell he had been thinking about it himself, and true to form, he would want to make everything as easy as possible for me. "I suppose," he started, "in other words…"

"In other words, Dad, I would be perfectly comfortable living here with you forever. No daughter has ever had better care in the history of daughterhood. But my place is sitting there empty and it doesn't seem right for me to be this dependent on my father."

"Maybe it doesn't *appear* normal, but you're always welcome here."

"You've proven that beyond a doubt — and who knows when I'll end up here again. But right now I have to get back to work." I reached over to give Dad a hug. "I can't say when I'll be back."

"Don't worry about it. I'll watch the news. Oh, by the way, Warren Wright phoned and said to call him." Was there a twinkle in Dad's eye at the foregoing conversation about having my own place?

"Thanks."

I ran quickly to the car to avoid getting wet. Before backing out, I took a couple of deep breaths to direct Dad, Selena Kubik, and Warren Wright to their respective corners in my head instead of jamming together behind my eyes in a growing ache. I was relieved to have spoken the difficult words to Dad. His accommodating nature made it easy, causing more guilt. Mom at least would question me on my decisions, making me earn them in a way. As for Warren Wright, the abduction had kept him at bay for a few hours, but now my eager/cautious thermostat started flipping again. I would return his call later.

The rain and late hour had removed all curious onlookers from the cordoned-off house on Colleen Street. I parked behind Wayne at the curb and leapt across the grass, using one hop to knock on the window of the cruiser in the driveway where Matt and Daya were eating sushi on guard duty. Selena sat primly in the foyer on a wrought iron chair, as if she were waiting in a bus depot and not her own house. She wore a gunmetal rubberized raincoat with a black umbrella across her knees. Her eyes noted my return, but nothing else moved.

Wayne walked with me to the kitchen. "Welcome to Serious Crimes. I learn something new in every case. We've booked a suite at the Holiday Inn Express at Metrotown for you. It's an odd request, but you might be able to get some forgotten details from her. They come out when people are relaxed or vulnerable."

"Yes, Sergeant."

Wayne shook his head. "Bloody bizarre is all I can say. Isn't her husband due home tonight? He'll arrive to a houseful of strangers and learn of a dead son. I wouldn't want it."

"She wouldn't give us anything on him."

"We've got our internal airport officer working on it — lots of flights to scan."

Wayne walked back to the foyer with me and promised Selena we would do everything possible to find the perpetrator of this horrible crime. She opened her umbrella on the landing and in what seemed to be her first human gesture of the day, tried to share it with me on the way to the car through the pounding rain. She underestimated my height and I nearly got a rib in my eye, but the thought counted.

Once in the car, she stared straight ahead again. At the hotel, she hung back while I registered, then followed me into the elevator and into the suite. I offered her the bedroom where she set her suitcase on the bed and hung up her rubber raincoat. I would take the pullout couch in the sitting room.

"Would you like anything to eat?"

"I am not hungry."

"I'm sure you're not, but you have to eat something. You need your strength." I sounded like Dad talking to me.

"I could not keep anything in my stomach." Her accent made her short sentences seem more formal than they were probably intended. Something about this woman appealed to me despite her reserve. I sensed a deflated spirit that had once been capable of wit and charm: like the cool girl at school whose shyness only adds to her allure on the rare occasions she breaks loose.

"How about a Jugo Juice smoothie? There's one nearby in the mall if I get there before they close. What flavour do you like?"

"It does not matter," she said, surprising me with a direct look. "You must be tired."

"It's okay," I said, then told her to put the chain on the lock while I was away.

Passing through the colourful lobby to the mall, I was seized by the wave of sleepiness Selena had just permitted me, but managed to blink it away. I found Jugo Juice and bought us each a tropical Proteinzone Super Smoothie. At a nearby Mediterranean takeout place, I got two orders of Greek salad and garlic toast. Anyone as worldly as Selena Kubik was sure to like black olives. If not, I'd eat both; I was that hungry.

Balancing two bags became tricky as I ransacked my purse for the key card, until I reminded myself I would have to knock because the chain was on. It turned out Selena had not locked the door and I warned her again as I slid it on. She had changed into light grey fleece pyjamas that passed nicely as a lounging suit. When I set the food on the coffee table, she immediately sat down and began drinking the smoothie and eating the salad.

"By the way," I asked, trying to make conversation. "Who reads Harry Potter in your house?"

"I do," she said without looking up. "I like to know what is sweeping the world. And I like fantasy." Then she looked at her watch. "Let us turn on the news."

It opened with a shot of her house, followed by Tony in the backyard announcing that a four-month-old baby had died in hospital after being thrown in a pond — close-up of pond — by an abductor. Burnaby Serious Crimes unit was working on clues to the identity of the man, as described by the baby's mother.

"They do not give my name," Selena commented in a neutral tone. I could not interpret whether it was relief or dismay.

"That's because your husband has not been notified." I persisted through her silence like a broken record on the topic. "It's his right as next of kin to be informed before the public is. Don't you think he should know before he drives up and finds his home filled with cops? Are you two having problems?"

"No."

"Then maybe you will help us contact him."

"Constable, I have already stated that he phoned yesterday and is due back late tonight — it could be midnight. I do not keep track of his flights because he is away frequently. He flies all over the world building bridges. I did not want to worry him before it was necessary."

"How long has he been gone?"

"Two weeks this time."

"Does he often work over Christmas?"

"They had problems in Kosovo and called him back. He did not want to be away from us for the holiday, but it was an emergency that required his expertise." She pushed her smoothie and salad across the table, half-finished. I still wasn't full after eating all of mine and asked for her untouched garlic bread in its paper envelope. I didn't expect to be in breathing distance of her, or anyone else, for a few hours.

We sat for a while watching the rest of the news. Just before the weather forecast she asked abruptly, "Have you ever been betrayed?"

"Yes," I said quickly, thinking of Ray, and then irrationally of Retha. "Have you?"

"Yes."

"Your husband?"

"No."

"You want to talk about it?"

"No."

A flash of the white Porsche came into my head, unbidden. "The dark man in the white Porsche — do you think of him as your betrayer?"

She looked up and held my gaze without speaking. Was she accusing me for asking such a silly question? I tried to explain myself: "That's the only clue we have to this whole tragedy and what happened to you today must seem like the ultimate betrayal — of fate, of life, of God, whatever you want to call it."

She lowered her eyes. "I am not a superstitious person."

Something had just slipped from my grasp and I wasn't sure if it was Selena Kubik or the case itself. The hollow in my stomach signalled negligence on my part — but whether it was a sin of commission or omission, I couldn't be sure. Sara claimed regrets of omission were much worse, but this was the same feeling I had when I'd turned on the siren by accident during surveillance, and that was definitely commission. I didn't believe Selena was taunting me with clues, but I did sense I had missed an opportunity for a deeper glimmer into her mysterious character. I should have listened silently instead of jumping the gun with something out of context. What did she plan to tell me? Had I blown my chance as her hand-picked confidante? I tried again, feebly — and of course, unimaginatively for a sophisticated customer like her. "Sometimes it helps to talk."

"About what?" she asked curtly, as if nothing had been said.

"About such things as — oh — treachery, grief, outrage, love." I collected the remains of our meal and set them in the wastebasket as I spoke. "My grandmother used to say that if thoughts were burning up your mind, the only way to extinguish them was to expose them to the air."

I could feel her unspoken words through my back, *Who said anything about burning thoughts?* Aloud, she said, "I think I will go to bed now."

"Will you be able to sleep? Did they give you anything at the hospital?"

"I have my own prescription." She got up and went into the bathroom.

In her absence, I put my feet up on the coffee table. My ankle was swelling and as soon as she turned in for the night, I would take off my socks. Some professional formalities seemed in order. As I leaned back into the couch, an urgent knock startled both me and Selena, who was just coming out of the bathroom. I jumped up and opened the door the width of the chain.

"My wife," said a tall man I knew from the photo was Jan Kubik. "I want to see my wife."

Selena nodded and I opened the door.

"Jan," she exclaimed softly at the sight of his stricken face, allowing him to take her in his arms. They spoke to each other quietly and desperately in Czech. Then they both began to sob. The unflappable Selena vibrated like a windup doll while Jan groaned, each locked in the other's embrace.

My presence at this display of intimacy felt indecent. I grabbed my shoes and purse and made my exit. After all, I was here at Selena's request for company; she was not under surveillance. I took the elevator down to the lounge and ordered a Coke. I deserved something stronger, but we weren't allowed to drink on duty. Collecting myself was a small feat compared to what the two upstairs were facing. First, I would call my team and give them hell for not preparing us for Jan Kubik's arrival. When I reached into my purse I discovered I had turned off my phone by mistake looking for the key card. A message from Wayne awaited me: "Where the hell are you? Jan Kubik is here at the house in a wild state.

We're sending him to the hotel. We think Mrs. Kubik should know."

Two missed opportunities in half an hour. Was Serious Crimes going to expose me for what I was? Maybe I should ask for a transfer to Traffic.

I called Wayne back to explain. In my defence, I told him the surprise was good for Selena because she didn't have a chance to steel herself and she needed those tears. "What's going on over there?"

"We're wrapping up here. Haven't found anything. Dex is working on the white Porsche but there are a lot more than you'd think in the lower mainland. The Kubiks are free to come home whenever they feel like it."

"Waste of federal dollars on a hotel room if they do. But I doubt it."

"Stay there yourself then."

"See you in the morning."

I wanted to give the Kubiks more time to themselves and toyed with the idea of a Labatt's Lite now that I was relieved of my assignment. But I ordered another Coke instead. The lounge was not full. A few couples sat at tables and three single guys at the bar. Next to me, two young women were engaged in lively conversation. Or at least one of them was; the other was letting her friend talk and occasionally dab her eyes with a tissue. Speaking of tissues, I needed one for my dripping nose and made use of the cocktail napkin.

My great-grandmother came to mind again. Wiping her nose was one characteristic I could actually visualize, along with the strong chin, hands, and feet Sara said she had. Why did I inherit her more ungainly tendencies when our go-between female gene carrier ended up so fine-featured and petite? Sara's delicacy ended there, however, and the more we discovered, the more admiration I had for the toughness she and her mother and sister had needed to endure what they did.

My eyes kept straying to the next table, accidentally meeting those of the woman who was listening. Her friend was becoming more emotional and I decided to focus my attention on my own situation. I dialled Warren Wright's number.

"It's Arabella. My dad gave me your message."

"Well, well, well."

"We got called in this morning on a case."

"The one in the news — the baby in the pond?"

"That's the one."

"How do you handle brutality like that up close?"

"Not easy. And I'm still at work. But I didn't want you to think my dad doesn't pass on messages."

"That's all? You didn't want to speak to me."

I laughed. "That too. How was Hawaii?"

"Too long, to be honest. I got homesick." He spoke in a provocative tone.

"How's work?"

"Enough of it, but I've got time to get together, if you do."

"A good idea. But I'll have to see where the case goes the next couple of days. Can you call me on the weekend?"

"You can call me again, you know. It was nice picking up to your voice."

"Whoever gets there first."

"Take it easy."

I'd always had an aversion to phoning men. On a personal level, that is. I had no problem calling the guys at work for any crazy reason. Maybe it was Sara who planted the idea that men should be the ones in pursuit, because Mom and Dad were pretty progressive. Sara said there was an old Persian (Indian? Chinese?) proverb that claimed the best marriages were those in which the men were more vulnerable or, roughly translated, loved a little bit more. Her own fifty years of Grandpa's devotion proved her point, and after all the domestics I'd seen, I had to agree. A less-than-doting husband usually had physical superiority, if he felt like using it. Not that women couldn't be equally formidable — think Aunt Lizzie — but they didn't usually break jaws or smash noses.

Sara's insistence that "a man chases a woman until she catches him" was basic to all species. Males are usually more colourful or show off more to attract females in the courting ritual. And although women now wore the plumage, it was still up to the man to instigate the mating ritual, she claimed — unless you were a praying mantis. I thought of her recently while watching a TV interview with the oldest woman in the world. The woman, a 116-year-old from some South American country, said the biggest change she had seen in her lifetime was not air travel or computers, but women pursuing men. In the end, it all came down to who was setting themselves up for rejection. And I'd had enough of that, thanks. I still hadn't settled the skittish feeling that came from actual contact, voice or otherwise, with Warren. He could call back.

The two women next to me had just paid their bill and were getting up to leave. One now had her arm around the other, who was openly crying. That didn't come from the safety of fantasies. Expectations, maybe, but not fantasies.

By now, the Kubiks might have spent themselves until the next flood of tears. I paid my bill and walked slowly to the elevator. I knocked quietly on the door, announcing who it was.

Jan opened the door and let me in. Pouches sagged under his red eyes and his skin was pale. "Come in, Constable," he said politely. "My wife is lying down."

"You must be exhausted yourself," I said. "To be greeted with this after an international flight."

"I am accustomed to exhaustion and even loss, but never one on this scale." He spoke even more formally than Selena and in a more measured tone.

"I'm so sorry for this tragedy." I took his two cold dry hands in mine. "Is there anything we can do for you and Mrs. Kubik?"

"Thank you, but no. Sleep will help her. She has borne too much by herself. A lifetime in a day."

"And you?"

"I am not ready to sleep yet. I am afraid of waking up later."

"Then I will leave you two alone. Your house is free again, whenever you want to go back."

"Thank you, Constable. We are better off here for tonight. We have a condo in Whistler and I might take my wife there tomorrow for a few days while the cleaning lady removes the baby things."

"Do you have any friends or relatives who can help her through this?"

"I will take care of her now," he said.

I picked up my overnight bag and handed him my card. "Please call if you need anything or if anything occurs to you or your wife that will help us solve this crime. Is there a chance the abductor was someone with a motive — or sent by someone?"

"No chance at all," he said firmly in the voice of a European count.

"We didn't think so, but we have to consider all angles, you understand."

"I understand, Constable. Thank you for staying with my wife."

"Take care of yourself, Mr. Kubik." I went out the door with my bag. "And don't forget to put the chain on."

As I stood in front of the elevator, I shivered. Jan Kubik seemed a civilized man, a product of European culture and attitudes. But the hotel room now held the same chill I had detected in the house on Colleen Street, one that was not noticeable when I was alone with Selena earlier, even as detached as she was. It must be generated by the combination of the two of them. What was the opposite of spontaneous combustion? Dry ice?

THE NEXT TWO DAYS DISSOLVED in a flurry of whipping rain, paperwork, more questioning of the neighbours, and a more thorough search for the Porsche. We decided to keep this lead from the media for now, in case the perp decided to paint or get rid of the evidence. Sukhi, now back in the office after missing the excitement, commented: "It's like finding the white Fiat that clipped Diana's Mercedes in the fatal crash."

"Peugeot," said Dex.

"The Peugeot was black, the one they swerved to avoid. White paint traces on the Mercedes came from a Fiat."

Wayne looked up from the sushi he was eating at his desk and said flatly, "First accounts described the Fiat as dark blue, later witnesses said it was black, red, and white. A recent inquest reported testimony of an erratically driven white Fiat emerging from the tunnel, but no evidence has ever been found. Our Porsche could end up the same way."

We agreed that young men usually knew their cars, but could we trust a hungover one on a misty morning? Maybe he was dreaming about a Porsche. The other neighbour simply said it looked like a white sports car, but every manufacturer had a few sporty models now. Sukhi and I joked about Jake's reaction if the murderer's vehicle turned out to be a Volvo.

"Selena said she thought it was someone delivering flyers on the front step," Tessa said. "Have we checked delivery people?"

"I've never known community freebies to be that early," said Sukhi.

"That's just what she thought it was," said Tessa. "The only sound that occurred to her."

"Did she give you any more when you took her to change, Tessa?"

"That was it. And then she withdrew completely."

"Speaking of upstairs, was there a nursery?" I asked.

"Khaki walls, lime green and aqua bedding. Everything spotless and in its place. I almost expected a pewter crib, but it looked like cherry wood."

My inside track with the Kubiks had left me with little information, but an overblown curiosity about the two of them. When and why did they come to Canada? What was Selena's profession, if any? If I hadn't silenced her with my awkward questions, I might have found out more. I couldn't get past the horror of what they were going through and had to fight the urge to call them — even in Whistler, if that's where they were. But what would I ask other than how they were doing? Sensing my nosiness, Wayne gently reminded us not to get too personally involved in these files. Victim Services was available and we should confine our interest to pertinent evidence; otherwise, some of it might be tainted.

After days like these, Dad's warm suppers were more than welcome. It was becoming clearer why men get married. Or used to. Today there were no guarantees of home-cooked meals from the woman of the house. Almost as soon as I finished eating, I fell asleep, either on the couch or after a page or two of reading in bed. I was providing all work and no company for Dad — a good time to prepare him and myself for the move back to my apartment on the weekend. I would take my stuff over in the afternoon and invite him to come for supper later. At least I could try to reciprocate a thousandth of what he had done for me.

On Saturday morning, as I was packing up my clothes, the phone rang.

"So you made the national news on your first file," said Monty. "We looked for you in the clips."

"I hid. But it's been quite a week."

After a few minutes of shop talk, he came to his next point. "What about the other case?"

I had to think.

"Jane — your great-grandmother. We've been waiting for a followup. Gail and I are having coffee and got talking about it. You were to call Wendell's sister, remember."

"Aren't you the tough corporal? It's only been a week — do you know how consuming this has all been?"

"No excuses." He gave his giant laugh. "Here's Gail."

Gail too was laughing, but did not let me off the hook about phoning Mona Mingus. "Don't forget I broke the Mingus connection, so you have to do your part. Maybe she knows how those letters got back to Canada from Wales."

"I always thought other people's genealogy was a bore."

"You're not other people."

"Okay, okay, I'll call." We chatted then about the kids, the weather in Saskatchewan, and the gruesome case. As a cop's wife, Gail knew I couldn't say much, and there wasn't much to say anyway.

Dad was passing as I hung up the phone and I relayed the conversation to him.

"Why don't we call Mona Mingus right now?"

I figured, as the contemporary cousin, he was volunteering, but he handed the number to me. Obediently, I dialled.

A low voice at the other end answered.

"Mona Mingus?"

"Yes." Also a slow voice.

"This is Arabella Dryvynsydes in Vancouver."

"Yes."

"My father and I met your brother Wendell recently and we've confirmed that we're cousins."

"Yes."

"Your mother and my grandmother were sisters."

"Wendell told me about you."

So why didn't you say so immediately? I wanted to reply, but contained myself. "Did Wendell mention any letters written by your grandmother?"

"Yes, he did." Pause. "He also told me you bought that picture of Mother and her twin sister at a garage sale. We never knew where that picture got to, Mother and me. When her mind started wandering, she forgot about it, but I never did. Cindy had no right to sell it."

"I wanted to match it with one I have from my grandmother. But the letters — do you still have them?"

"Yes."

The pause now came from me as I caught my breath. "Have you read them?"

"I don't think so."

Explain yourself, woman. "Uh, if you had, when might it have been?"

"I believe there's only one or two. I might have opened the envelope when I brought Mother to Calgary. To see if I should put them in the financial or personal pile."

"What did you decide?"

"Personal."

"And it's still there, you say."

"Must be, because I haven't touched that trunk for over thirty years."

"Would it be possible for you to send it to Dad and me? We'd pay the courier."

"No, I'm afraid it wouldn't be possible. I don't want to disturb Mother's things."

"Do you think we could have a look at it sometime in your presence? If we ever make it to Calgary?"

"I'm not so sure about that. All mother's papers are pretty old. They might crumble."

At an impasse, what to do with a balky witness? Offer a trade and leave them an out to save face. "We know how to handle them. We have a pack of our own. We'll bring the picture back to you, if we come."

Her stumped silence told me I had her. "Well, maybe if you were very careful with them."

"We would be. Do you know, by any chance, how the letters ended up in your mother's possession? I believe they were originally sent to Wales."

"Mother said they came from some Aunt Lizzie on Vancouver Island."

I was baffled. "Aunt Lizzie? Are you sure? She's the one Sara — my grandmother — lived with. They thought Janet — your mother — was dead."

"That's all Mother ever said. And I know it was Lizzie because when she told us, Dad made a joke about his old Tin Lizzie car. I remember that for a fact."

Mona's tone made clear that she had reached the end of her patience, especially after the concession. "It's been nice talking to you, Miss Mingus," I lied. "Mona" sounded too friendly for what was not a friendly exchange. "I hope to speak to you again in person soon."

"Goodbye."

I shook my head and said to Dad: "Wendell was right, she is a queer duck."

He was in the dining room arranging the pages of his labour of love. "Didn't Wendell say she took after their mother?"

"No sister of Sara could be that uncommunicative." I told him about the letters, how we had to go to Calgary to read them.

"You, maybe. I have no plans for a trip to Alberta." Tenderly he tapped the sheets into alignment: his rhyming story in a whimsical font, shown off by vivid illustrations. Market research had advised him that children's book publishers want plain text and prefer to find their own artists, but his little book was going out as a package. He could not resist sending his vision of the finished product.

"Did you hear the part about Aunt Lizzie? How could Aunt Lizzie have sent the letters to Janet? They all thought she was dead."

"You're the sleuth." He attached a cover letter and a folded self-addressed stamped envelope to the manuscript with a paper clip, then slid the bundle into another manila envelope.

This was his baby. His mission to keep himself from going under in the absence of his mate. Sissipuss had been a more loyal companion than I had been during the months of his bereavement. Now Sissipuss and I were both leaving him on the same day. What would the empty house hold for him now? "What's your next project?"

"You mean until I have to enlist lawyers to fight for film rights?"

"Yeah, until then."

"Not sure. Guess I'll think of something."

I watched him cross the kitchen and set the envelope on the counter next to the dish of keys, so he would not forget to take it to the post office on his next outing. As if he ever would. He seemed to have lost weight without my noticing; a thin face made his ears look larger than ever, the wattle of skin on his neck more pronounced. When he reached for a plate on the top shelf of the cupboard, his head extended horizontally like a turtle from the rigid shell of his shoulders, not vertically as a supple neck would carry it. Fighting to deny the thought of my father as an old man and what I might have done to delay it, I strained to think of something cheerful to say. "I can hardly wait for the book launch. I'll learn to make appetizers by then and we'll have it here."

Dad snorted gently. "All I'm aiming for is not to run out of publishers when it starts coming back."

I gave the envelope a good luck tap before loading my things into the car. On the way to the apartment, I stopped for groceries: fixings for chicken pasta and salad for tonight, along with the usual staples of bread, milk, eggs, cheese, and yogurt. If I made enough, I wouldn't have to think about food for tomorrow or for work on Monday.

January continued its wet imprint on the lower mainland, fogging over the mountains and often blurring the line between sky and sea, both the same aluminum grey. People complained about January blahs, but I still preferred the month to the gloominess of November. At least we were inching out of darkness rather than into it. And on days like this when the rainclouds parted in a sunny smile, we were reminded why the city is the most inviting on earth. The sudden afternoon light, a sharp glare in my rear-view mirror, accompanied me to the underground parking of my apartment and was still streaming through my patio doors from the little balcony when I carried up the first load. A bright note for my re-entry into independence from assisted living.

No whiffs of the fragrant currents that filled the place before Christmas, so I cracked the sliding doors for fresh air. I then lit a cinnamon candle and put on my Susan Crowe CD as I organized the food. I first heard "Fall Back Up Again" after my break-up with Ray, and it never failed to exhilarate me. My bare feet began to dance around my own little space and I poured the sole beer in the fridge to welcome myself home. From this stimulated state I heard the ivory walls cry for colour: a mustard or sage would do wonders until I decided what to do with the striped couch. Slipcovers, maybe? A bright throw co-ordinated with some squishy cushions? I craved relief from sombre interiors like the Kubiks.

Dad arrived right at five with a bottle of wine. "Warren Wright called again. Is he anyone I should know?"

"Too soon to tell. Maybe I'll bring him over to meet you." Eventually I would have to divulge my cellphone number. Dad couldn't be my answering service forever.

After supper, Dad watched the hockey game while I put clothes away. At nine, Wayne called to say he was sending Dex and me to the island on Monday to check on the witness under protection for the Hell's Angels trial. We were to deliver a subpoena, check on his earlier testimony, and assure him he would have a guard with him at all times. It made sense to send Dex because the guy knew him and trusted him, but I had been hoping unreasonably for a day with Tessa for this assignment. The thinking goes that a strategic shuffling can strengthen the team as a whole. Sukhi and Tessa would stay on the Kubik file; the longer the culprit to a high-profile baby murder was on the loose, the more incompetent we looked.

After the conversation, Dad jumped up. "I'll be off. You need your rest."

"He said Monday, Dad. Why don't you finish watching the game?" My words were futile because he would never get over feeling like an intruder on my turf, whereas the same feeling did not apply to me on his. "Our home was once yours and always will be," Mom had once said by way of explaining this double standard, "but yours was never ours." Maybe not in our culture, but aging parents were a permanent fixture of a lot of immigrant homes where I'd taken calls.

He edged toward the door, pausing to ask if I would be able to work in a visit with Janetta when I was there. Not that I should do it on company time, but in case there was a wait between ferries, he knew she'd love to see me. That thought had already occurred to me. After his quick exit, I breathed a sigh of gratitude. We had survived the transfer.

When I dialled Warren's number, I opened again with "My dad gave me your message." He responded with a low laugh and I pressed on. "I'm back in my apartment so I'll give you my cellphone number. I'm not going to bother with a land line."

"I'm ready."

"How've you been?"

"Okay. A friend is here and we're on our way to Torchy's for a drink. Care to join us?"

"Maybe next time. It's been a long week."

"How about coffee tomorrow? And a walk along English Bay if the weather holds. Even cops get some Sundays off, don't they?"

"Sure. What time?"

"Two? I can pick you up."

"Thanks, but I have an errand to do first." It was still too soon to give out my address. "How about meeting at the Sylvia at two? We can take it from there."

"Sounds good," he said; we hung up.

A few palpitations, as I imagined the two of us strolling along the sea wall in the bright brisk perfection of a day like today. Greedy, bossy seagulls swooping around us, mingling energies with joggers, walkers, and winter sun. Maybe my hopes and fears would quit their standoff and settle into a workable state.

But I didn't get the chance to test myself. As soon as I hung up, Wayne called again to say there had been a change of plans. The witness had a doctor's appointment Monday but was available Sunday afternoon, so we had to accommodate him. Dex and I were to leave on the 11 AM ferry. Two hotel rooms were booked for us in Nanaimo tomorrow night. We'd have the rest of Monday off. I called Warren back with apologies: "Welcome to a cop's world. Are you sure you have the patience for this?"

"I'm sure."

THE SUN'S SMILE had lasted only an afternoon. When Dex picked me up at nine-thirty the next morning in a work car, we were back to blinding rain. I felt some consolation knowing a stroll along the sea wall would have been out of the question. Coffee shops are normally dry, however, and I had a stab of longing about missing out on that. Why was the longing most intense in the no-contact zone?

Traffic moved slowly over the Lions Gate Bridge. We heard on the radio it had been closed for over an hour because of an accident. Involving vehicles, at least. Sometimes jumpers on bridges stalled traffic for hours while being coaxed off the high beams. The serious ones succeeded with no fanfare.

We arrived just in time to drive onto the Horseshoe Bay ferry and climb the metal stairs up to the cafeteria. No fresh air or scenic vistas today. Dex ordered a hamburger and fries and I had a bowl of clam chowder and a piece of cheesecake. After lunch, he pulled out a deck of cards and I figured rummy was as good a way as any to spend the rest of the trip with Dex. At work he had been called intolerable, a lovable fool, a nerd, and the keenest cop on the force — all of which carried a bit of truth. Rumour had it he slept with his badge. He had been in Serious Crimes for two years and eyewitnesses claimed that he whistled a happy tune whenever his pager went off. No matter when it was — the middle of the night, Christmas dinner, or even on what to him was a rare event: a date. Nearly everyone else I knew came up with a curse or two; some wives even cried when their husbands' pagers vibrated — no, not for the obvious disruptions, but in the middle of shopping malls when they finally had the guy's attention.

Amusement for Dex consisted of his collection of Fwds from the internet. At work he had a cabinet full of them, also copied and filed at home with those that came in on his own computer. Every joke, virus alert, and uplifting message got printed and stored. Those whose blessings would be invalidated if not sent to ten people, were. Someone on another team remarked that a spam-filtering service was as close as anyone could come to a restraining order on Dex.

But now across the bolted-down table with the ridge on it, all I could see was a thirty-three-year-old man concentrating on his cards. Sandy hair, decent body, a face too pasty for my liking but whose features were more or less in the right place. Dex was not unattractive to certain women, though his two short-lived relationships had given way to his preference for the job. He referred to girls as "gals," and I'd caught him once saying "a gal was swell."

He was no quirkier than any of us, really: Dave, Jake, and Emile came to mind, and I was known for my scatterbrained ways. So why was such a dedicated member the butt of so many jokes? Because he had no sense of humour. He was too naïve to hide his obsessions, or to refrain from announcing, say, that he used one of his cat's discarded whiskers as a toothpick. The guys were continually at him not to share these things with the outside world, but he didn't get it. According to Sara, it was a missing sense of the absurd that kept people from laughing at themselves and made others laugh at them. But today my partner was far from innocent and took great glee in whipping me soundly in every game of rummy. I finally called it quits and said we should go down and wait in the car for debarkation.

Dex's undistracted mind stored data more accurately than most, so when we lumbered off the steel grates and ramps of the ferry onto the highway again, he knew exactly the route to find our protected witness Andy Lambert in Lantzville. The door opened before we had a chance to knock.

I had read the file and spoken to Dex about Andy Lambert, so I knew his age — fifty-six — and about his drinking problem and poor health. Still, I was not prepared for the crumpled man who greeted us. Looking closer to ninety, he moved like a stooped invalid. He had obviously dressed for visitors, his thin grey hair slicked back with grease, a plaid quilted jacket over what was probably his cleanest T-shirt, and ancient faded grey dress pants cinched at the waist with a brown belt. An old black Lab, grizzled at the mouth, stood protectively next to his master and, at a calming gesture, wagged his tail. Dex shook Andy's hand and I sensed a rapport between the two men. When he extended it to me, he bowed slightly, as Dad and Wendell Mingus did.

We entered the dingy trailer and Andy motioned us to sit down. I chose the shabby recliner over the gritty blanketed sofa, which emitted a smell of stale dog farts. Andy eased himself down next to his loyal companion and Dex remained standing.

"How ya feelin'?" Dex asked in a trailer park voice I'd never heard him use.

"Good days, bad days. I take them as they comes."

"You up for the trial? They've rescheduled it for April 5. If it don't get cancelled again."

Enough, Dex, I said to myself of this attempt to speak Andy's language.

"Should be. If I live that long. Been four years already."

"We can come here and get you, or meet you at Horseshoe Bay, whatever's best. You'll have a guard with you the whole time — hotel, courthouse, everywhere." He opened his briefcase and handed him an envelope with a subpoena. "Just to make it official."

Andy set it on the arm of the sofa without looking at it.

Dex pulled over one of two kitchen chairs standing against an Arborite table that folded out of the wall. He sat down and removed a clipboard with pages from his briefcase. "Just want to go over some of your prelim testimony to make sure it's accurate. Freshen your memory."

Andy began shivering on the sofa next to the dog.

"Would you like a cup of coffee first?"

He shook his head. "Just get the shakes now and then. And I'm supposed to be asking youse that question."

Dex told him we didn't need anything and began reading. "You are prepared to testify in a court of law that Mitchell Pogue, an agent of William Hubbard, on trial for the murder of Harold Lorimer, threatened you with your life if you did not give Hubbard an alibi."

Andy nodded.

"That William Hubbard sent his cousin Mitchell Pogue, also known as Macho Mitch, to your motorcycle repair shop, Lifecycles, just before closing on May 9, 2003. Pogue told you that you were 'screwed' if you did not comply with Hubbard's wishes." Dex looked at Andy for confirmation before continuing.

"When you were questioned by Constable Patricia Luknowsky of the Burnaby RCMP detachment, you told her that William Hubbard had brought his bike in for repair on Friday, April 18, 2003 between 20 and 21 hours." From the transcript Dex then repeated Andy's own spoken words to the officer: "'I was working late that night. The bike had a short in the lighting system and Hubbard said he would wait while it was being fixed so I wouldn't waste time 'fartin' around.' The job took longer than I expected because I didn't have the exact part in stock and had to make do with what I had. Hubbard left just before 22 hours. I was alone on the premises.'"

Andy hung his head, remembering the lie.

Dex went on reading from the file. "After Hubbard was arrested, Pogue returned to the cycle shop. It was just before closing on Friday, May 9 and Pogue told Lambert's helper, Rodney Searles, to leave. When the two of them were alone, Pogue repeated to Lambert just how important his alibi testimony was for Hubbard. To make his point, he pulled out a knife, forced Lambert to kneel down, tied his arms behind his back, blindfolded him, and beat him on the face, abdomen, and legs with a tire iron. Before he left, Pogue untied Lambert and he collapsed bleeding on the floor. Pogue said: 'You'll heal in time for the trial. And if you don't say the right thing, you'll never talk again. We'll cut your tongue out. And your heart along with it.'"

Andy shivered more severely. Dex and I observed a moment of silence for this broken victim of Hell's Angels brutality, old beyond his years, trembling still as much in fear as from his other afflictions.

"You okay, Andy?" I asked.

"It'll pass," said Andy. "Until the next one. Doctor says my liver took the worst beating back then, besides what I done to it myself."

"We'll look after you," Dex repeated, and Andy relaxed a little into the couch, his big dog licking him as he brushed against his head.

"How were you brave enough to go to the police after a threat like that?" I asked.

"My sister. I dragged myself to the office and called her. She came and took me home to Abbotsford with her to mend. I told Rodney to take charge of the place and reversed the facts — that I had a sudden call to look after my sister who was in an accident. Didn't want to go to a hospital cause they ask too much.

"After I was back at work a couple o' months, I seen in the paper where Macho Mitch Pogue had been picked up as a suspect in the murder of a sex trade girl. Him and another piece of scum threw her in the Fraser River, hands and feet tied. Maybe I ain't so brave comin' forward, knowin' he was in jail. Not that I'm stupid enough to think they wouldn't send someone else after me if I talked. But my sister won out. She had been at me the whole time to tell what I knew. 'The police will protect you,'" he said in a woman's voice. "And you have."

"We couldn't leave you in the lower mainland."

"Could be a lot worse. Got another sister in Parksville looks out for me." Andy directed his remarks to me, the newcomer to his situation. "Your boys keep an eye on me too."

By that he meant the Parksville RCMP who included him in their patrol of the island highway. Dex stood up and put his hand on Andy's shoulder. "That's about it, then. We won't take up any more of your time."

"Time?" cackled Andy. "That's all I got. Though maybe not so much — I'll find out tomorrow at the doc's. My sister's takin' me in." He took a loose cigarette from his jacket pocket and lit it shakily. "Only my second one today, so don't get on my case. Hope it don't bother either of youse."

I couldn't say why, but this small wasted frame and slicked back hair produced in me an image of Roland Hughes. Is this what he looked like when he finally pulled himself off the floor after his wife and son died? Emaciated and shaking, but not without manners, as he addressed the new guardians of his twin daughters? Or did he scream drunkenly at them?

"We'll call you again before the trial and make arrangements for your transfer," said Dex. I joined him at the door, wondering what my role had been in this assignment. He could easily have handled it by himself.

"You're a pro," I said, once back in the vehicle.

He gave two quick farewell honks of the horn to Andy, still standing at the front window watching us. "You sound surprised."

I grinned, promising myself not to join in the groans and eye rolling next time he acted like a jerk. The rain had let up, but from the colour of the skies, we knew it was only a breather. It was almost suppertime when we pulled into Nanaimo. I didn't want to desert Dex, but I was eager to see Janetta. I was raised never to call on anyone at mealtime, so I waited to phone until Dex and I had stuffed ourselves on a seafood platter at a fish house on the harbour.

Janetta coaxed me to stay with them, but another of Retha's company rules was to consider the extra sheets to wash. I insisted my hotel room was booked, and I would come over in the evening and again for breakfast. We had Monday off for the return trip, so there was no sense in rushing back. Unless you were Dex, I discovered. He informed me he was going to take the first ferry back in the morning to be at work before ten. If I wanted the car, he could catch the express bus from Horseshoe Bay into Vancouver and the LRT to Burnaby. Of course, I refused the work vehicle for my personal use and assured him I could get home on my own. My new resolve about Dex was going to require a lot of discipline.

He delivered me to Janetta's house, where she hugged me so tight I thought she must have had a bionic heart transplant. Lawrence showed his pleasure at my presence less obviously by taking me back outside to the steps to see his latest creations. As if I could have missed them: three glowing white clusters of fluorescent bulbs — short, medium, and tall — topped with red flame bulbs. "I leave them on till Ukrainian New Year."

"Your family are German, aren't they?"

"Out of respect."

Janetta made tea and brought the pot into the living room. She was wearing a royal blue velour lounge suit and settled back on the recliner as I pulled my feet up under me on the sofa. I felt comfortable being back in this home laden with family connections, most prominently my aunt herself, bringing Sara back to earth in so many of her expressions. Something set them apart, however, and what it was gradually came to me. The shade of her outfit. Sara avoided primary colours and would never have worn royal blue. Hers would have been seafoam or indigo or slate. She liked colours that couldn't be easily named, and I realized how much she had influenced me when I bought my last blazer. The tag listed it as oregano, and I was undecided until three different shoppers, all strangers, stopped to say "That grey looks good on you," "I like that shade of green," and "What an interesting brown." I was sold. But Sara's daughter was less complicated than both of us and looked just fine in her choice of lounge wear.

I thanked her for the bangle and handkerchief for my birthday, and together we marvelled at the four pairs of hands that had possessed them over more than a hundred years.

"I'm embarrassed to say I didn't go through Mother's things any earlier, and would not have gotten to it now if you hadn't asked about the letters. She must have divided the treasures from her mother between your dad and me: photo for him, girl's things for me. She gave them to me when I got married, and they've been put away since then. Isn't that awful?"

Seeing the direction the conversation was taking, Lawrence, who had been hovering around the dining room waiting for his chance to show me something else, excused himself to the basement to watch TV. "Call me when Bella needs her ride to the hotel."

I told Janetta all the details of our visit with Wendell Mingus and of the difficult call to his sister in Calgary. How Mona said Aunt Lizzie had sent letters to her mother, which seemed strange to us because it was Lizzie who told Sara Janet was dead. And how Dad had had a flash of recollection about Sara receiving her packet along with Lizzie's death notice when they were unpacking in Vancouver.

Janetta lifted her feet to an ottoman, ankles swelling above fluffy pink slippers. "Lew always did have the better memory. I was only eleven at the time and was busy washing cutlery in the kitchen, but I do remember Mother sitting down for a couple of hours with those letters and then being quiet the rest of the day. I was feeling sorry for myself because Lew had been mad since he first found out we were moving, now Mother wasn't speaking, and Dad was at work. No one seemed to care I had to leave my friends in Red Deer behind too."

I helped myself to more tea. "Is Laura still alive? Would she know anything?"

Janetta made a face, looking even more like her mother on the verge of a critical opinion. "She's an oddball. Mother asked me to look her up when we first moved here, because she herself wasn't fussy about coming back to the island, even to visit us. I guess those early years left their mark."

"What was she like?"

"Unfriendly. Religious. Not exactly slow but not what you'd call normal. I told her my mother had remembered her fondly as a child and she listened — she even said she missed Sara when she left their home — but after fifteen minutes she had to go to a Bible study group. She showed no interest in getting in touch with Mother or seeing anything more of me."

"She and Mona Mingus would make a good pair. What's with this antisocial branch of our family?"

Janetta shrugged. "Laura must be more outgoing in her church. Or maybe they take her the way she is. When I gave Mother my report, she said she was thankful Laura belonged to a group who had her welfare at heart, even religious extremists."

"How old would she be now?"

"Late eighties, ninety, if she's still alive. Lawrence reads every obituary and we haven't seen one for her."

"I wonder..."

"Why not?" said Janet reading my mind. "Let's get the phone book to make sure she's still listed. Lawrence always wants an excuse to go to Duncan for German sausage. We could drop you off and pick you up on our way back. I doubt you'll want much time there."

"You won't come?"

"Been there, done that." She laughed.

"T Owens" was still listed. Keeping her father's initial for seventy years definitely said something about the woman. The trip was on. We chatted a bit about Doug and Lenny, Dad and his book, my move back to the apartment, and the Kubik baby case, which was on everyone's mind. Her drooping eyelids told me when it was time to leave. Again she regretted I wouldn't stay, but I insisted I would be tempted to keep her up too late talking. My chauffeur was already in the kitchen, past his bedtime.

"I've been weighing the pros and cons of phoning Laura," Janetta said when Lawrence brought me from the hotel for breakfast the next morning.

"And?" I asked, sitting down to the muffins, mini quiches, and fruit salad Janetta had laid out on the table.

"I think not," she said, pouring our coffee and taking the chair next to me. Lawrence did not join us in this spread, having explained to me on the ride over that he had already eaten his porridge and would now chart the best route to our target. "She's so suspicious of the outside world — or was back then — that she might find an excuse not to see you. If she's not home or won't let you in, we'll take you on a scenic tour to Duncan."

I nodded agreement and we ate quickly, both of us impatient to set out on this adventure. The skies were clear for a change, but the air was chilly and Janetta put on a fire engine red car coat (Sara's would have been brick or salmon), pulling the collar up around her thin neck.

Ladysmith carried elegance in its name. I always associated Paul Simon's song "Diamonds on the Soles of Her Shoes" with the word, because of the link between diamonds and a lady, and also the vocals by Ladysmith Black Mambazo. That was even before I learned in my history course of the African connection to our Ladysmith: that the former Oyster Bay settlement was renamed in 1900 in celebration of a British conquest over the Boers at Ladysmith in South Africa. Our British colonizers doing their best to rule their subjects with common ground.

Here I was in the back seat of Uncle Lawrence's car heading toward a destination I knew only from books and as Pamela Anderson's birthplace. Lawrence didn't miss a chance to rub it in. "Guess you city people don't find the island interesting enough to visit."

My nervous laugh was meant to deflect anything more personal. As a child, I never thought about why our two families didn't see more of each other, though Janetta herself explained last night that Sara wasn't keen on being back here. And Dad claimed Janetta was intimidated by Mom's superhuman energy. Mom never voiced any superiority; she just kept stacking up accomplishments. Maybe Janetta viewed our few visits to Nanaimo as acts of condescension — like a president flying into a war zone to have Christmas dinner with the troops.

But I was now pleased to be in the company of my aunt, more light-hearted than ever. Had her brush with death given her a new freedom, or had she finally come into her own as the only female survivor, no longer in the shadow of the other two dynamos? Maybe she had always laughed this much and no one had given her a chance to show it.

Ladysmith was closer to Nanaimo than I thought. And Chase River was merely a suburb we passed through to get there. Strange how these areas seemed like separate worlds from my research and Jane's letters, and on foot, they probably were. For me, the region was a commoner's version of Camelot, a realm that once existed through folklore and was now paved over with Tim Hortons and Rona, and architecture that could have been found anywhere else in North America. As we descended through the residential area, Ladysmith revealed itself as a delightful seaside resort, restored with pride of heritage: lantern streetlights, a traffic circle with an anchor fountain. "You want to see it in summer," Lawrence said, "with all the flowers. Voted one of the ten prettiest towns in Canada."

Single-minded pilots like Dex and Lawrence have their drawbacks; it might have been interesting to get lost for a few minutes on these quaint streets. Or even to slow down when Janetta pointed out landmarks of interest like the Temperance Hotel from 1900. We did agree to meet at a coffee shop bakery on the main street where I would walk and wait for them if the visit with Laura became tedious.

Laura Owens' little house stood on one of the side streets leading up a hill. I was surprised to see a number of miner-style bungalows, but the others had been refinished more recently and, in some cases, enlarged. Laura's sagging glassed-in verandah and flaking white siding with a few remaining slivers of blue trim spoke of neglect but not abandonment. The front yard was spread with small stones. "Less grass to cut," said Lawrence. "Someone did her a favour."

Janetta shook her head in wonder. "It didn't hit me on my last trip that this is the original mining cottage where Mother went to live after her mother died. It must have been repainted and reshingled — quite a while ago from the looks of it — but the structure is over a hundred years old."

Sliding out of the back seat, my curiosity gave way to apprehension. I almost hoped there would be no answer when I rapped lightly on the glass door of the cold, empty porch before letting myself through to the main entrance. Janetta and Lawrence stayed parked on the street, like parents seeing their daughter safely into a new school. I knocked gently again, three times, and was about to turn back when a little old lady in a loose black dress opened the door.

"Laura Owens?" I asked, feeling like Gretel at the gingerbread house.

When she nodded, I said in a rush: "I'm your cousin Arabella Dryvynsydes — second or third or fourth, who knows? Sara Hughes was my grandmother. She lived with your family as a child and spoke lovingly of you."

From a head and body that quavered uncontrollably, she regarded me with more shrewdness than suspicion. Finally she spoke in a voice that came in little puffs between tremors, as if someone was giving her the Heimlich manoeuvre after every word. Like Katharine Hepburn. Even her grey hair was pinned up at the back and rolled at the front in the same style, but that's where the similarity to the actress ended. Laura's face was round, her grey eyes wide. "You may come in."

I turned, waved Janetta and Lawrence on their way, and followed her into the house. Nose-clogging staleness attested to the years that were layered here. If I were to compare home odours of this trembling old lady and the trembling not-so-old man we had visited the day before, I'd say both could be traced to infrequent laundry and baths, but this place gave off a dry mustiness of mothballs and dust where Andy Lambert's trailer reeked of damp, smoky, mildewy, leaky dog smells.

Inside, the house was more spacious than it appeared. I'd taken calls to similar-sized bungalows that had not started out as miners' cottages. The living room opened onto a large kitchen at the back, and through an archway to a corridor on the left could be seen two small bedrooms and a bathroom. What distinguished it from my clients' residences in Burnaby was that it was crammed with religious mementoes. I was no stranger to Hindu and Sikh prayer rooms, but could not remember seeing Christian adornment on this scale. The Lord's Prayer carved out of lace hung on a feature wall; three-dimensional plaster plaques of hands praying, crosses, and the head of Jesus were mounted all over the remaining walls. Ceramic figurines of the Virgin Mary, Jesus holding a lamb, lambs by themselves, and Jesus by Himself stood on every table and shelf, underlaid by doilies. Yellowed doilies also covered the arms of an old brown velvet sofa and easy chair. Was the largest disintegrating piece of lace on the back of the sofa what Sara had in mind when she made jokes to me as a kid about not sitting on Auntie Mc-Cassar? Thinking of Sara in this very house caused me to catch the breath I was so cautiously inhaling. In my mind I morphed the little girl in the picture from a child through puberty to the young woman she was when she escaped, all without guidance or encouragement. Laura Owens now waited for me at the kitchen table, so I left this museum and sat down across from her.

"Where did Sara sleep?" I asked.

She pointed to a room off the kitchen, probably added on to the original house by Uncle Thomas — was that also where his mother ended her days? The door was open and I could see a faded yellow chenille bedspread. "In there. I slept there too. Still do."

The old lady seemed remarkably unfazed by a stranger twice her size firing questions at her. In my head was Sara's voice: "Be gracious, use your manners. She's frail." Laura Owens might be stooped and shrunken, but from what I could see, she was not delicate. Through her tremors she stared unblinkingly, almost like a war criminal who had been expecting me. Not surprised, not sorry.

"Thank you for letting me visit, Laura — or do you prefer Miss Owens?"

"Laura."

I complimented her on her independence and asked about her health. She said she had no complaints for a woman of almost ninety. Some stiff joints and failing eyesight, but with the grace of God, Meals on Wheels, and home care for cleaning and cutting the back grass, she still had the strength to look after herself.

"Would you mind if I looked in the bedroom? To imagine Sara in it." She nodded and tried to pull herself from the chair. "Don't bother to get up."

"Used to be two cots for us," she called in her helium voice, as I surveyed the double bed where she now slept. "When I had a bad dream, Sara would push them together, then back again in the morning before Mommy saw."

I spotted Mommy in a sepia photo on the wall. A large woman with a no-nonsense face looking out of place in a wedding dress. Next to her stood a shy-looking man even more out of place as a bridegroom. Jane's big brother Thomas. "Why did your mother not want you and Sara to be close?"

"She thought Daddy had to give too much to his family. His mother lived with them, and then they were forced to take in Sara, another mouth to feed."

From a second picture of Lizzie as an older woman, perhaps dressed for church in a colourful shawl, I guessed that if an extra mouth were to be added to their household she would want it transplanted in her own face.

Laura added, "Things were hard. Money was scarce." She identified the two other pictures in her room as Edna and Myrtle and their families, both older sisters long gone.

"Do you see much of your nieces and nephews?" I asked, rejoining her at the kitchen table. "No. They live their own lives."

"Did you know Sara sent money to your mother for a few years after your father died?"

"Yes, Mommy told me."

"But she never answered her."

"No."

"Why?"

The war criminal expression intensified. This was not a one-way conversation like the one I'd had with Mona Mingus. Laura Owens seemed ready to explode.

"Mommy felt bad."

"Why?"

"About Janet." Laura's movements had become so spastic I was afraid she might fall off her chair.

"Janet?"

"Sara's twin sister."

"What about her?"

"Mommy knew she wasn't dead and didn't tell Daddy or Sara."

The breath rushed out of me. "Why not?"

"Mommy went to Victoria to visit her sick brother and met Aunt Thelma. Aunt Thelma told Mommy she was fed up with Uncle Gomer. He didn't bring in any living, only more relatives to feed and clothe. Mommy feared Aunt Thelma might get so fed up she'd send Janet to us, because she knew Daddy and Sara would welcome her."

"So she told your father and Sara that Janet was dead."

Laura nodded.

"And Thelma must have told Janet the same thing. Maybe the two aunts made a pact."

Laura shrugged — I think. Her twitching was too random to be sure. "Mommy said she had the best intentions to tell Daddy but never got around to it. And then Daddy died and Mommy had a breakdown."

"How about telling Sara?"

She ignored my question, determined not to have her version of the story sidetracked. "Mommy took to her bed when Daddy died and couldn't move. Until Jesus pulled her up and saved her life. Praise be to God."

"So that's when she joined the church?"

"She was baptized and cleansed of all her sins. May her soul rest in peace."

"How old were you?"

"Seventeen. I missed Daddy something bad until Mommy explained I had to forget him. The church was our new family and God was my father. Daddy wanted me to take a stenographer's course, but Mommy needed me at home. Learning too much can take us away from the church, if we're not careful."

My heart was pounding with the power of three — mine, Sara's, and Janet's. "Did you understand what your mother's secret meant to those twin girls?"

"I felt sad when I heard it later because I remembered Sara telling me how much she missed her twin. Even though I liked being her new little sister."

"If your mother found forgiveness, why didn't she want to repair what she had done years earlier? Why didn't she write to Sara then, later in life, and tell her Janet wasn't dead?"

Laura bent her head as if in prayer, and for a moment I feared she was on the verge of a seizure. But when she looked up again, her head was steady. Like the hands she splayed firmly on the table in front of her. She spoke quietly. "Shame. Mommy carried the bitterroot of shame for what she did. Constant prayer and service to the church gave her strength to live each day. And God's grace would one day bring her strength to act without fear of retribution from Sara and Janet and their families."

"Do I look as if I'm about to strike anyone dead?"

The last words got caught in my dry, constricted throat. I asked for a glass to help myself to some water and she pointed to a cupboard. While the faucet ran, I thought of Sara washing dishes in this same spot, a pump likely installed by Uncle Thomas at the sink. Did she look upon this grassed-in yard, or was there a garden filled with vegetables she had to tend? I walked twice around the table before sitting down again to make sure my legs hadn't turned to mush.

"Then the letters came from Aunt Catherine in Wales," Laura continued. "She wanted her niece Sara to have their mother's letters, and the only address she had was Daddy's, here in Ladysmith. Like everyone else, she thought Janet was dead. Mommy said this was her sign from God to tell Sara and Janet the whole story. She divided the letters into two packets and wrote a letter to Aunt Thelma in Victoria to see if she had an address for Janet. Uncle Gomer had died and Aunt Thelma sent an old one in Saskatchewan."

"Did you or your mother read the letters?"

Laura shook her head. "Mommy and I weren't much for reading. Or writing. She had a time trying to compose the letters to Sara and Janet. Tried so hard she got fever doing it."

"And?"

"She died. Jesus called her home before she could write the letters. I had to put addresses on the packets myself and mail them to Sara and Janet. Along with Mommy's death notice. And they were never returned, so I have to think they reached them."

I needed more water. Now my legs and arms had begun to jerk. To all appearances, an energy transfer had taken place between this distant cousin and me. Were unscrubbable atoms of Sara's DNA still in the house making mischief with us? "They received them," I said, "but why didn't you write the letters to Sara and Janet?" I caught myself sounding harsh, realizing her writing skills might have been even less polished than her mother's. But she didn't flinch.

"When Jesus took Mommy home so sudden, I knew it was a sign to send the letters from Wales just like that, without explanations. Otherwise, He would have spared her long enough to write her own notes. The Lord's messages are clear through intimacy with Him." She paused and gave me a cunning smile. "But I did one naughty thing. I decided to send them all to Sara because she was good to me. At the last minute I realized my disobedience to Mommy and put one — the thickest — into the envelope for Janet along with the letter from Wales."

I stared at Laura Owens sitting unapologetic and resolute across the table from me. She was not slow or backward or however we had tried to describe what we knew of her. She was brainwashed. Indoctrinated. Programmed. Conditioned by classic cult tools. Deprived of a kind father, already isolated from other children by a domineering mother, she was ripe for a fundamentalist religion that provided simple answers for everything. No shifts in perspective, no fresh new views drifting in with the spring breezes. Laura took on the same beliefs without having to undergo the conversion of her mother. Certainty was the most dangerous weapon of all. I'd seen a teenage girl stabbed by a mini-cult of her peers, and the one who used the knife was the most decent of them; in a fragile stage because her parents were separating, she had drifted into this group where everyone agreed. Forgotten words from Sara passed through my head: Doubt should be the cornerstone of faith.

"Then the better question would be: Why are you telling me now?"

"Praise God, another sign. God speaks to us in deep sleep and I knew you would be coming. And because all prophecies say the end of the world is near, I was certain He wouldn't waste any time. He didn't tell me who or when, but when you stood at the door, I knew. I did not expect you to be as young and comely as you are. Years ago, Sara's daughter paid me a visit, but I had no sign then. Just before Christmas, I had a dream about Mommy and Daddy holding hands with twin girls and they were all smiling. I awoke knowing Jesus wanted me to receive you and tell the story."

If I was sitting across the table from a lunatic, I felt an odd kinship with her. The hermetically sealed spirit of the little girl who made life bearable for Sara had really not matured since then, and in a weird way, I now became the other end of that chain. Her old face was remarkably unlined by experience, doubts, curiosity, or hard-won wisdom. Stunted yet preserved by her mother's convictions, she retained her innocence. No breakdown needed for her salvation, it was hers by extension.

And what was I but an extension, through Dad, of Sara? Just as this elderly cousin coasted on what her mother had gone through and passed on, so were our comfortable lives determined by what Sara had borne, distilled, and set in motion for us. But forget the go-betweens — Laura and I both sat together at this table because of Jane. The Owens line got her here; the Hughes merger brought me along a different path to this juncture.

Just then, a synapse in my brain sparked an unplanned question. "Did you happen to know Roland Hughes?"

Laura had to think who I meant before her breaths began pumping out words — her reprieve had not lasted long. "Uncle Roland? Yes,

I met him when Daddy died. After the funeral, he came to the house. Mommy had taken to her bed from the strain of Daddy's death, so I sat with him there in the parlour."

I glanced backward to make sure the doily-encrusted room was the parlour she was talking about. My jitters continued.

"Uncle Roland wanted me to know that Daddy had been his best friend when he was young. Even before he became his brother-in-law. Funny, how I never forget anything about Daddy. I still miss him so. I can picture Uncle Roland sitting on the chesterfield telling how he went to work in the mines as a boy of thirteen because his mother was dead and his father was mean and drunk. He said that Daddy, being a few years older, looked out for him underground, and the Owens house was the only place he felt any kindness. Uncle Roland's parents came from the same part of Wales as Daddy did."

I swallowed, wishing I had a notebook to record this rap sheet on my great-grandfather for Monty. "Tell me more about him."

Despite her shaking body, the flush of revelation had taken years off Laura's face. Basking in her unique authority, she might have drawn energy from my own hot cheeks. It's possible she had never felt this powerful before in her long, cloistered life. "He was small and stooped and looked old. Lucky he had a strong wife with him."

"Wife?"

"Kay. They took the ferry over from Vancouver just for the day. He said he had to pay his respects to Daddy if it was the last thing he did. And then he touched Kay's shoulder and said if she hadn't saved him from the bottle, he wouldn't have lasted long enough to do it."

"What was she like, this Kay?"

"Seemed a nice lady. Younger than him. Bigger too. They didn't stay long because Mommy was moaning in the bedroom and Edna and Myrtle and their families were in and out. He apologized that they weren't close family, but it was important for him to talk about Daddy. I remember his soft voice."

"Did he ask about Sara?"

Laura's flush was fading and her words more laboured. She almost whispered: "He wondered where she was. I didn't know because

Mommy never talked about her and was in no condition to be questioned then. The next day we received a card from Sara with money in it and I could have given him her address. But it was too late."

Suddenly I'd had enough of missed opportunities. I stood up. Our family situation was no less absurd than many domestics I'd attended: a reminder that we are never as far removed from one another as we like to think. I walked around the table and bent down to kiss Laura's cheek. "Thank you. You don't know what this means to me."

Her eyes looked past me to a clock on the wall above the refrigerator. A film of indifference told me I was quickly becoming invisible. "Meals on Wheels will be here right away." She started to lift herself from the chair; I took her arm gently to help her to a standing position where she could ease the stiffness out of her old joints. "I can't miss them," she said, urgency growing in her voice.

Routine sustained her as much as the food — I knew that from Dad. I walked ahead of her through the front room and cold verandah, turning back at the door to say, "You've given life to my ancestors and you're the only one who could have done it."

Her bobbing head scanned the street, oblivious to me now, though she did look my way one last time to say: "Praise the Lord. May all their souls rest in peace."

"Amen."

When a car stopped, she became more agitated, but I had to disappoint her. "It's my ride, Laura," I said, waving as I walked to Uncle Lawrence's car. "I'm sure yours will be along soon." As we pulled away, I was thankful to see a minivan take our spot.

Janetta's eyes were bright. "Perfect timing. You must have something to tell, if you're still here."

I began my account, allowing my own flush and pulse to decrease as I did. Janetta's eagerness for details matched mine, from the tragedy of the twins' deliberate separation to news of a step-grandmother no one had known of. One of the stories I asked Mom to read to me over and over as a kid was "The Pied Piper of Hamelin." The darker elements of someone picking up first rats and then children and leading them through the streets into a mountain fascinated me. Looking at my aunt's rapt expression turned back from the front seat, and even Lawrence's ear half-cocked in my direction in spite of himself, I felt like the Pied Piper. The unravelling story had drawn in Gail and Monty, Dad, Janetta, Wendell Mingus, and now Laura Owens. Mona Mingus hardly qualified as being under the spell, but she was still part of it. Then as now, I wondered what was in the mountain.

"That's Mount Benson," said Lawrence, now back in Chase River. "You got time for a quick tour of Extension? That's where Mrs. Dry-vynsydes was born, after all."

It took me a second to realize he was talking about Sara. Most men did not refer to their mothers-in-law so formally. "By all means."

Turning north in Chase River onto Extension Road, I tried to picture Jane walking this distance when she left her mother to marry Roland Hughes and live at Extension. What would the area have looked like then? We soon dipped into the legendary mine site — the remains of it, that is.

A large slag heap, almost overgrown with brush and trees, was only noticeable if you were looking for it. The winding cinder roads through the little valley were thick with trees which Lawrence identified as arbutus, maple, alder, cedar, and often intermingled with rock walls that had split into crevasses or boulders. Miners' cabins still stood along the streets; some cedar shingle sidings were so discoloured they might have been relics from the Great Strike, but the old trucks and piles of firewood outside suggested they were still occupied. A few had been improved with newer vehicles in the yards, and even modern houses with landscaped lawns surprised us once or twice. There was no central core with services, though we did discover a boarded-up school and general store where a main corner must once have flourished. I was seeking a clear lookout from which we could see the whole little valley, but despite Lawrence's patience, we kept circling through the same few streets with no vantage point. A derelict wildness had taken over the craggy, wooded lots that my cop's instincts said could provide a convenient cover for criminals and drug dealers.

"I do remember spectacular dogwood and delphiniums one spring, years ago, when we took a drive out here," Janetta said brightly.

Maybe I should come back again in April.

Lawrence remarked that the bluffs seemed higher than before, maybe because the fir trees at the top had grown so tall. I thought of the Louis Strong case. Were those the same bluffs where his body was found?

In the midst of my father's history, territory, and relatives, a bittersweet flash of my mother caught me off-guard. She would have been as delighted as Sara to think a love of learning had finally rubbed off — from the Pied Piper of Hamelin to college textbooks. The stubborn daughter, whose curiosity she had tried so hard to inspire, was beginning to understand why she — and her mother-in-law — had driven herself to know more. And more.

Janetta's face, still half-turned toward me, held the same awe I felt at being here. But in the end, there was no more to see of this forgotten colony.

"We've got time for lunch before the ferry," said Lawrence, climbing the road out of Extension and swinging back onto the Trans-Canada Highway. "There's a good fish and chip shop in Departure Bay."

"Never thinks of cholesterol with all this sausage and fried food." Janetta winked at me.

As we indulged, she reviewed all our findings and promised a visit to the Nanaimo cemetery on my next trip to the island. Jane Hughes was buried there, but finding the grave would take some time. When they dropped me at the ferry, she squeezed in one more mission with her strong hug. "Mona Mingus has two more letters. Be sure to let me know what you can get from her."

Easy for the followers to say. The Pied Piper had roads to travel and work to do.

✂ ✂ ✂ ✂ ✂ ✂ ✂ ✂ ✂
✂ ✂ ✂ ✂ ✂ ✂ ✂ ✂ ✂
✂ ✂ ✂ ✂ ✂ ✂ ✂ ✂ ✂

"FIVE MORE DEATHS," says Roland, tossing a bag of sugar on the kitchen table.

Jane's elation at the sight of the scarce commodity is frozen by his words.

"Two in combat, three from flu."

Jane knows the wire would come directly to them if Llewellyn were among the casualties, but she holds her breath. "Any we know?"

"Not the soldiers. Young fella from Lantzville and a lumber man with a big family from Ladysmith. Tommy would know him."

"And the flu deaths?" She still does not exhale.

"Black, white, and purple."

"The black?" she whispers, impatient at Roland's stalling with the colours of sashes on doors to denote a dead adult, child, or senior citizen.

Roland nods and says softly. "Marjorie."

Jane's breath is expelled in a sob. Roland puts his spindly arms around her until she collects herself and wipes her eyes with her apron.

Her best friend. Just four mornings ago they were cleaning their adjoining cabbage patches when Malcolm Stockand, a snooty book-keeper, strutted down the street past them and tripped on a piece of horse manure. The look on Marjorie's face provoked a giggle from Jane, triggering such an explosion of laughter that Sara, Janet, and Marjorie's daughters stopped playing tag to stare at their mothers doubled over, holding their sides. Then, suddenly, Marjorie, still laughing, clutched the sides of her head and said, "I must have burst a blood vessel behind my eyes from all this laughing we do."

When the pain in Marjorie's head removed the smile from her face,

Jane's went with it. And when Marjorie's nose began oozing blood, Jane followed her through the gate they never shut between their properties and replaced her sopping handkerchief with her own clean one. Since then Jane's head has been filled with prayer.

"When?"

"Just now. Kids were at the store lined up for sugar with the rest of us when Milt came to get them. Saddest thing to see your camphor necklaces swinging on them all. Like inmates escaped from prison."

As a precaution against the rampant disease, Jane had wrapped camphor gum in flannel and tied it to cords to be worn around the necks of the Gilchrist family. She also made masks out of gingham muslin to elude the airborne virus — enough for her family and for Marjorie's mother, who came from Comox two days ago to help. The house was now in quarantine, much to the dismay of Sara and Janet, who spent every possible minute with Suzanne and June, including walking to school together. Jane wore gloves when she handed food and pans of ground onions for chest poultices across the threshold to Milt or Mrs. Osler, speaking through closed lips.

She thinks then of the white and purple deaths. "Who else?"

"Jack Gilmour's kid in Wellington and Minnie Ellis."

She winces at Minnie's name: a spinster just retired from a long career running a millinery shop in Nanaimo. "Where will it end? Both calamities — overseas and here at home? Did you check the post office?"

Roland shakes his head, as he has done every day since their last letter from Llewyllyn two months ago. He watches his wife nervously spinning around the kitchen, touching every surface aimlessly.

"The girls — where are they?"

Sara's wails from the end of the garden reveal their whereabouts. Soon they fill the house. "Suzanne and June's mother is gone. And she's never coming back."

Janet follows behind, tears in her eyes. She hugs Jane's waist. "I'm glad it's not you, Mommy."

"We must go to Uncle Milt and the girls to see what we can do for them."

"But not inside the house. It's full of germs," cries Sara. "June told us not to come in yet. Their grandma's washing Aunt Marjorie's bedding in carbolic acid."

"Food, food, what can I take?" Jane continues circling. "I've got onions ready in the icebox for her."

Roland hands his wife a cardigan from a hook in the porch. "They won't be needing onions, and food can wait. Let's just pay our respects to Milt for now." He slips on his jacket, one side hanging lower than the other, and guides her out the back door. The twins fix themselves to her arms, Sara snuffling loudly. At the bottom step, Jane stops and covers her eyes. The death wagon has stopped at the front of the Gilchrist house. Milt helps the driver carry a flat, blanketed form on a stretcher through the front door. They slide it onto the back of the wagon where two more bundles rest.

What's left of Marjorie is the very least of her. Jane did not know she had a funny bone until four years ago when they moved next to the Gilchrists in Five Acres. Marjorie made gardening, canning, quilting, knitting, and even drunken husbands amusing. And now she is gone, just like that: one of thousands of corpses piled up across the continent in this fashion, while funerals are stalled and wakes discouraged for fear of contagion.

The blonde heads of Suzanne, age nine, and June, age seven, huddle together at the side door, crying. Stopping to speak to them, their grandmother emerges onto the stoop with a basketful of wet sheets and towels, which she proceeds to hang on the line. Disinfectant fumes reach their nostrils through the crisp September air. Everywhere the strong smell has replaced the season's usual fragrant scent of fresh apples. When she sees the girls, Sara breaks away from her parents and runs across the two large garden lots. Save for some squashes and pumpkins and a few turnips left in the ground, both yards have been cleaned and readied for winter by Jane and Marjorie. Janet, still clinging to her mother, accompanies her parents to the front of the house, where Uncle Milt takes a black sash from the death wagon driver and nails it to the door.

At the sight of his neighbours, the new widower dissolves. The spectacle of massive Milt Gilchrist collapsing into her parents' less robust arms drives Janet to safety at the back with the other girls. Milt requires support from both Jane and Roland, whose own strength is only up to the task because of the relative sobriety inflicted upon him by Prohibition. Occasional binges at a blind pig in Nanaimo make him wilder than ever, but at this moment Jane regards the flask of moonshine he extracts from his jacket pocket as being worth the consequences.

"Milt, take a shot of this to calm your nerves."

Milt straightens up at the prospect. "At the woodshed, then." He nods in the direction of his teetotalling mother-in-law outside the side door.

Jane joins Mrs. Osler, a short, rotund woman, in a tearful embrace. With her longer arms, numb from the weight of Milt, she pins the last of the linens to the line. Fear of germs forgotten, the young girls bunch together on a swing Marjorie had installed from her favourite oak tree.

Marjorie's mother lowers her voice, still rippling with a Scottish burr after forty years in Canada. "And did ye know she was expectin'?"

Jane's face shows she did not.

"Nobody knew. Not something she would share until she was sure. And she would hae taken the secret with her, 'cept the baby came out last night. Blood all over my poor darlin',' from her nose, from her ears, and then —" Mrs. Osler's stiff upper lip begins to tremble.

Stunned by this report, Jane cannot help feeling let down that Marjorie didn't confide in her.

Or did she?

On that first evening when Jane took across stew, blueberry cobbler, and onions, Marjorie requested her cot be in view of the door. Removed at the back of the kitchen from drafts and from spreading infection, she still had the strength and will to communicate. Milt stepped aside for Jane to blow his wife a kiss from the stoop. Marjorie raised herself against a pillow. She pointed to her nose, which she was still blotting with the other hand, thrust a finger into her mouth to indicate vomiting, and finished by poking it into her ear, shrugging comically at all these orifices spewing forth. For once Jane couldn't manage a smile, especially since the ear finger came out red as well. Marjorie shrugged again, this time more seriously. Checking to make sure Milt and the girls were out of range, she pointed between her legs. The curse, Jane translated, to top everything off. And when Marjorie drew a bulge over her stomach with her hand, Jane assumed she meant the bloating that went along with the monthlies. Then a coughing fit threw her back against the pillow, ending the pantomime and sending Jane home through a tear-blurred dusk.

Why did people have to lie down to die? Or "lay down and die," as she had heard so often during this epidemic from people who hadn't found grammar class as interesting as she had. The indignity of Marjorie trapped helplessly on the cot put Jane in mind of a graceful prancing pony felled by a broken leg, then humiliated that it could not get up again. She should have stayed away after that, for her last delivery of food has left her haunted by Marjorie's face: trying to smile from the pillow, blue from pneumonia, coughing up blood-tinged froth that would finally clog her lungs and drown her.

"I'm so sorry," she says, putting her arm around Mrs. Osler.

"Milt might be too shy to talk to you about it. Or too upset. But she would want ye to know. She loved ye like a sister, Jane."

"And I loved her. She's the only one to fill the emptiness I felt from leaving my sisters behind so many years ago in Wales." Her heartache swells at the thought of Catherine and how they have not been in contact for so long.

"'Tis such a pity the demon Blitz Katarrh singles out pregnant women. A neighbour o' mine in Comox, four months gone, started coughing one day and was dead the next. Aye, why does it strike those in the prime o' their lives first? Why not take an old lady like me?"

"You're not so old, Mrs. Osler," says Jane, aware that the virus does hit those between twenty and forty most severely. Like many British, Marjorie's mother chooses the German word for the scourge, consolidating her loyal opposition to the two enemies being fought. Jane eschews that term, catarrh touching her too personally as the only physical weakness she has ever known. She has read in the newspapers its many labels: Flanders Grippe by British troops, Naples Soldier by the Spanish, and its most accepted name, Spanish influenza or Spanish Lady. Despite the occurrence of cases in China, France, the U.S., and

Britain before the first public report from neutral Spain, those countries, being at war, censored their press.

"Still, I'd gladly hae gi'en my remaining years to Marjorie, if I could. I hope ye're not wi' child, dearie."

Jane blushes. Until recently she could say no for certain. But two Saturdays ago, she and Roland had gone to a wedding dance at the Harewood Hall. Marjorie had insisted on it by inviting Sara and Janet to sleep over at their place. Wartime demand for coal made the Harewood mine operational again and Roland had left Extension to work there, closer to their home on Five Acres. A young miner he had taken under his wing was marrying a girl from Victoria and wanted him as best man.

"The kid makes me think of me with Tommy," he told Jane when she voiced her objections to being in a public place, "so I want to be there." Marjorie had backed him up, saying friendship was a gift not to be ignored; to console Jane, she would brew some preventative tonics for them when they brought the girls over. "Dr. Gilchrist's orders," she clowned, forcing her concoctions on them: oil of cinnamon gargle, salt water up the nose, washed down by a mixture of warm milk, ginger, sugar, pepper, and soda.

The potions served two purposes: to protect them from the virus and to free them for a few hours from the past and future. Home ownership, steady work, and Prohibition have given Roland a composure he cannot completely subvert with a few nasty benders at a speakeasy. Jane knows that unspoken fear intensifies his indulgence: a long silence from Llewyllyn or trouble at work adds to his underlying disappointment in himself. But that night, sipping on fruit punch, he was toasted by a host of young miners for his experience — he could still hold his own with the new diggers — and his wit in tight spots.

"That'll be news to my wife because I haven't got a smile out of her for twenty years," he said for Jane's benefit. But he did get a dance — several, in fact — reminding Jane of their own wedding and what an unhappy occasion it had been except for those few masterful spins with Roland. She thought of the many dance floors that had been deprived of his slight, graceful Welsh figure, so much more smooth and agile than the stolid men in her family. They glided and two-stepped to songs

Jane had only swayed to on the radio alone in the kitchen: "After You've Gone," "Hindustan," "Darktown Strutters' Ball," "Johnson Rag," "If You Were the Only Girl in the World." The dance finished with a medley of patriotic songs — "Over There," "Oh! It's a Lovely War," "Keep the Home Fires Burning," "Mademoiselle from Armentières" — and couples still clung together after the last chord of "Till We Meet Again," no one ready to go home. As if the harvest moon and local musicians had thwarted the world's dark elements to cast a spell of redemption on the celebrants in Harewood Hall.

The end of the evening flashes into her mind. In the darkness of their bedroom, the pulsing rhythms continued. Ardour, abandon, and opportunity combined and ignited for only the second time in Jane's life, reviving phantoms of the first.

She looks down when she answers Marjorie's mother: "No, ma'am, I'm not in the family way."

"Ye mind yerself nonetheless. Numbers aren't on yer side. Yer husband, on the other hand, seems to keep himself pickled against all disease."

Jane is taken aback by Ethel Osler's bluntness until she remembers her status on the Temperance League. Marjorie joked about her mother winning the presidency over two Finnish women, usually the Prohibition champions. She and Jane would shuffle their bottle or two of homemade blackberry wine from Jane's root cellar during her mother's visits back to her own, out of Roland's reach. Often at the end of the day, the two women met for a few sips, safely camouflaged in teacups. Such times produced in Jane a cautious admission that she might actually be experiencing bliss as it happens. Remembered bliss, like her childhood in Wales, does not hold the same power as a gasp of wonder at a sunset, or an enormous, misshapen beefsteak tomato. Or a shudder of joy from the shrieks of four little girls mingling with the delectable smoke of a wiener roast. Or the physical convulsions brought on by a preposterous comment from Marjorie. An awareness of sensations like these repeated over a stretch of days, months, and even years must surely define happiness, a state she had never claimed for herself before this.

"Ye know all the preventions, I hope."

Jane nods, but Mrs. Osler continues in her crusader's voice: "Personally, I swear by violet tea meself. It's kept Len and me safe. And onions, o'course. Heard of a mother who saved her family by burying them for three days in raw onions and forcing onion syrup down their gullets all the while."

She too has heard of these remedies, but listens politely as if it is new and helpful to her.

"And d'ye know about sprinklin' hot coals with sulphur? Smoke fills the house and kills the germs. A woman up in Saanich saved her family that way. That and a lot o' prayer."

But none of these measures could save our beloved Marjorie, Jane thinks to herself, and all were tried. Are we the failures then?

She knows the futility of contradicting a true believer like Ethel Osler. Opposing arguments slip into Ethel's mind like a stone into water: a quick splatter without any effect whatsoever on her thinking. Jane's sister-in-law Lizzie falls into that category, allowing no discussion about any of her opinions. If she were to get religion, she would be swallowed up entirely and take everyone else with her. All the more pity for Tommy. He will have it hard when their new baby arrives in the new year. As if his wife were not demanding enough through her first two confinements, she will now feel entitled to slavish service at her advanced age.

And what could be bringing on all these pregnancies later in life? Dear Marjorie was thirty-six, four years younger than Jane herself will be in two months, and Lizzie two years older at forty-two. Is it the Grippe driving couples to frantic, unprecedented clinches? She reddens again, considering herself eligible.

"What about the girls?" she asks Ethel Osler.

"Pray, how can a man underground take care of two wee girls? They'll be comin' back to Comox with me for now. Me daughter Josie in Vancouver has only one o' her own. She might be willin' to take them."

Jane's limbs go cold at this triple loss. Suzanne and June will have no more say in the shuffle than family pets. She has met Marjorie's sister

Josie: an exact replica of their mother in shape and attitude. Practical, hard-working, responsible, outspoken. And humourless. The girls' needs will be met without softness or gaiety; she cannot bear to think of their deprivation. Her own selfish loss of their mother fades beside the many years they must live without her. She cannot permit herself to imagine Sara and Janet being dispossessed this way.

"Can I help? Could I take them while Milt is at work?"

"Lord knows the wee lasses are like four sisters themselves. But ye've got enough to worry about, dearie, wi' him and all." She nods toward the front of the house where she last saw Roland, and Jane instinctively steps in that direction to prevent any view of him leading her son-in-law astray.

"Just for a short time. To get them accustomed to their mother's absence in a familiar place. It seems so drastic to lose everything you know all at once."

"No point dragging it out when they can't stay here."

Jane looks across at the girls and swallows her tears. As usual, Janet and June have been nudged off the swing, leaving Sara and Suzanne to chatter and rock together on the spot. The quiet twin and younger sister appear content to be counting ladybugs in dry oak leaves. "If you and Milt change your minds, the girls are always welcome in our home."

A chilly breeze brings a shiver to Jane through her cardigan. She touches Mrs. Osler's sturdy arm, now folded across her bosom shelf, and turns to run back home across the garden path where so many memories of Marjorie have been planted.

Inside, she hopes Sara and Janet will not follow right away. She needs a moment alone. Grief is gaining momentum, now gathering thoughts of her son, too long silent, and in constant peril. She opens the drawer of a desk she bought for the girls at an estate sale. It stands between kitchen and sitting room and Sara makes the most use of it doing lessons or drawing while Jane is cooking or sewing with Janet by her side. Carefully, she takes out a pile of seven letters. She rereads the one on top for the twentieth time. Sara is already a better speller than Llewyllyn will ever be.

July 2, 1918

Dear Mother,

Thank you for your letters to Belgium. I read them over
and over. We are in Flanders after a batle at Kemmel
Ridge. I am still in one piece and that is a mirakle.
Thousands of soldiers have been killed or mamed. And
now the Spanish flu is taking anyone left. Our officers
say this war will soon be over. How I hope so.

I hope you are all staying healthy. Say hello to Papa
and tell Sara and Janet I will bring them something
spesial from France. Our company moves to Pikardy
next. Please keep writing.

Your son,

Llewyllyn

Jane has sent several more letters to the military post office address
over the summer. Is he in one piece even now? Casualties from the Battle of Amiens were high — was he there? The bedroom he could hardly
wait to leave is Jane's sewing space, now used only for their own clothes
and special orders, thanks to Roland's regular hours. She wonders how
often her son longs for its comfort in the wet, bloody trenches.

She folds the letter up carefully and returns it to the drawer. A few
pieces of vellum paper remain in the pad she bought for letters to
Llewyllyn. Jane vows to write to Catherine before she loses everyone
she loves.

From the Gilchrist yard, a familiar inebriated voice disrupts the
quiet. The damage has been done. She thinks of Milt stumbling into
the house where his mother-in-law now rules. Will the queen of ab-
stention in good conscience deny a man the chance to numb such fresh
sorrow? She hears Marjorie whisper and giggle, "Now's the time to slip
a little gin into her violet tea. She won't notice the perfumey taste."

Jane almost smiles.

JAN KUBIK'S ACCENT was unmistakable. He had phoned to invite me to a small memorial gathering for their baby son. "It is not a funeral or a burial. We have had the cremation. And it is according to my wish, because my wife wants nothing. I am keeping it as small as possible, just to honour Anton. We would like you and Constable Holder to join us at 3 PM tomorrow for a short walk through the Van Dusen Gardens followed by a glass of wine inside."

I thanked him, hung up, and passed on the message to Tessa, who, her attention fixed on the computer, nodded her willingness to attend.

"If we're excused, that is," I said to Wayne, bent over the Criminal Code checking a section on sexual exploitation for a case that had just come in.

"All in the line of duty," he replied without looking up.

"Isn't the cremation a bit early? Do we have everything we need?" asked Dex, printing off a fresh virus alert for his collection.

"Autopsy was done when you were on the island. No surprises. We released the remains."

Still no headway in the Kubik case. Typically, IHIT would have taken it over by now, but because of my work with the family — or whatever you wanted to call it — they had told us to run with it. Pressure or what? No more leads from neighbours, from evidence, or from the Porsche — if that's what it was. I remembered Monty saying there were channels to follow in investigations but no clear patterns of criminal behaviour. That a conviction might come where and when you least expected it. Were we to sit and wait then until the perpetrator was revealed? Such a sensational homicide would not be forgotten by the public, and I hoped it would not turn into a cold case like the Louis Strong murder, still unproven a century later. At least they had a suspect—more than we had.

Sukhi had left minutes before and I caught up with him in the cold dark air of the parking lot. His wife had just called to tell him she was pregnant, exploding his breath in visible puffs of joy. I gave him a hug, then jumped in my car and turned on the heater full blast, wishing I had a deluxe model with seat warmers. Just before I reached home, my cellphone rang.

"You're a busy woman," said Warren Wright.

"It's been a busy year, all eight days of it. How are you?"

"Beginning to feel like a stalker. Wondering if I should quit calling."

"No, don't do that." I stopped to use my entry card to the underground parking lot and the steel door segments clattered noisily into the ceiling.

"So where are you now—patrolling cells?"

I laughed. "Just driving in. I'll be upstairs in a minute."

"And you don't want me to know where you live."

"Maybe soon." His soft voice was causing my caution gauge to dip out of its safety zone. "How about supper tomorrow night?"

Did I say that? He sounded as surprised as I was.

"Well, well, well. I think I'm available."

"The Mongolian Grill on Broadway and Cambie at six-thirty?" The Van Dusen Gardens weren't far from there and I would no doubt welcome a change of mood.

"I like this take-charge attitude. Like old times."

Just after lunch the next day, Tessa was assigned to interview the victim of the sexual exploitation charge: a fourteen-year-old girl who alleged her volleyball coach had touched her inappropriately. I was thankful Tessa was the primary on this because I didn't have much experience with sex crimes; she was patient and kind and would get the most out of the girl without upsetting her. That meant I would be our only representative at the memorial.

Turned out I was the only other person at all. I saw Jan and Selena getting out of their Mercedes near the entrance just as I found a space at the end of the crowded parking lot. Jan greeted me formally with a handshake as I explained Tessa's absence.

"Thank you for coming. It is just the three of us then. I had wanted to invite my wife's sister and my brother but she would not hear of it."

Selena, in a short tweed jacket, brown pinstriped pants, and low-heeled, blunt-toed boots, stroked my oregano blazer approvingly by way of a greeting. I was glad I had ironed my cream silk blouse and best black slacks to wear with it, and at the last minute stuck an antique brooch of Sara's on the lapel.

So I ranked above relatives again? As insiders to the case, Tessa and I required less energy on Selena's part — was that it? But what kind of family was this? At least there were more members than I thought, and the circle might even be larger, if I listened carefully.

All the decorations from the spectacular Van Dusen Gardens Christmas festival of lights had just been removed — Gail had gone with her family and reported it better than ever this year. Today the overcast sky and dormant foliage were less than alluring — unless you were a plant lover, which Selena apparently was. As we started through the groomed trails, I restrained my reckless curiosity and slipped in casual questions as one might offer tidbits to a wild cat you wanted to tame.

Unable to get past Selena's reticence, I spoke to Jan when she stopped to admire a shrub, thereby turning the nature walk into an opportunity to learn about more than just flora species. I learned that his younger brother was a bachelor accountant in North Vancouver. Selena's older sister in Coquitlam had been married briefly to a Canadian, had no children, and now managed a furniture store on United Way. They had all immigrated to Canada in 1990 just after the Velvet Revolution when Czechoslovakia was freeing itself from Communist rule. They were all Bohemians, Jan declared proudly, though he was from a wealthy background and Selena's father was a bricklayer. During the Communist crackdown in 1969, his parents, landowner professors, were sent to a work camp in Siberia, where they died. He was a student in Prague at the time and had no choice but to remain there, take care of his brother while they both studied, and later work for government firms. For years he would not consider creating a family under such a regime, until he met and was captivated by Selena. She was a window dresser in one of Prague's few fashion boutiques and was to him "like an orchid — beautiful, untouchable, and requiring just the right light and temperature."

Between these intriguing snippets, Selena would rejoin us after contemplating a Christmas cactus or a larch sapling, her eyes alight with wonder, before being dulled again by the sound of her husband's voice. When she lingered at another flower in waiting, I would gently remind Jan where he had left off. Not that he needed it, because there was a relentless quality about his sentences that did not leave a word hanging. He told me Selena took to Vancouver like a seagull and immediately found a job working for a professional theatre company in the costume department. She was happy there for a few years, but when their attempts to have children failed, he persuaded her it was due to the stress of deadlines and opening nights. He made a good living and she should be content to stay home.

"Was she?" I asked, knowing the answer.

"No, she was not," he sighed. "When this intended stress-free period also did not produce any children, she joined another community theatre group as a volunteer. I often wondered if I craved a family more, because I had lost my parents so young and finally felt safe enough in a country to bring a child into the world. My wife needed a creative outlet, and one or two productions a year kept her satisfied without the long hours. Eventually little Anton arrived, and she realized instantly what we had been missing. We are not young parents, Constable Dryvynsydes, especially me, and I had given up hope for such a gift."

Selena caught up for the end of her husband's words and his arm reached out toward her: "...the whole ordeal has been unbearable for my wife, and all I ask is strength to take care of her."

When she continued to walk on ahead of us without a pause, I wondered how he could be so blind not to see that his gestures, intended to comfort her, were having the opposite effect. It did seem strange that he always referred to her as "my wife," and never by name.

With Selena again out of range, I used the final stretch to ask, "What's your connection to Kosovo?"

"You mean, why was I over there? I work for an international engineering firm and they send us wherever infrastructure is a problem, often through war or poverty."

"So there is no one from Kosovo in your firm?"

He looked confused. "The only Kosovars of my acquaintance have never left their native land. Why do you ask?"

"Just wondering," I said, reaching the entrance to the building where sludge-grey clouds were threatening to spill their contents. Selena waited for us under a palm frond with her eyes downcast. Again I asked myself how a woman as desolate as Selena could come across as more natural than her husband, whose sense of duty and correctness took the place of spontaneity.

Inside, we took a booth in the airy garden-style restaurant with its floral tapestry. Because I was more or less on duty, I ordered cranberry juice and tonic water. Selena ordered a glass of ice wine — the most expensive item on the list — and Jan, Riesling. Glasses in hand, I waited for a toast. Little Anton had hardly been mentioned this afternoon and I was about to say something when his father clinked his glass against mine. "To Anton's short life and all the joy it brought us. May his beautiful spirit rest in peace."

"To Anton," I said, "I wish I had known him."

Selena raised her glass to be touched by her husband's and mine, but said nothing. Her dark eyes were restless and alert, like a cat when its ears go down. Then she pulled a pack of cigarettes from her purse. "Would anyone notice if I sneaked a puff or two?"

Jan's face grew red with embarrassment and anger. "You know it is not allowed. You are putting Constable Dryvynsydes in an awkward position by breaking the law in front of her."

I felt more awkward over this obvious power play than the smoking bylaw; the restaurant manager would tend to that.

"Since when did you start again?" Jan demanded, as if she were a small child.

"You don't think I have reason to smoke now?"

"Reasons don't make abominable habits right." A spray of spittle misfired and Jan excused himself politely, dabbing his mouth with a napkin.

Just then a waiter arrived with appetizers and Jan's curt but polite thank-you brought the skirmish to an end. Selena had clearly provoked her husband to demonstrate his condescending manner and toyed with her cigarette package a little longer, smiling at me as I scrambled for a neutral topic. Grateful for the Olympics, I threw out questions about favourite events, budgets, changes to the city. We were able to finish our drinks without incident, Jan taking the lead again as the most in-formed. It didn't occur to me until later that none of us mentioned the capture of the perpetrator, the reason after all that I had become part of our strange threesome. Nor did I ask what they had done with the cremated remains, a more deliberate omission on my part to respect their privacy.

Shortly before five, Jan stood up in his usual formal manner, as if a heel click and salute might follow. Selena dawdled putting on her coat, intentionally causing him annoyance he had to hide. I thanked them for including me in this tragic occasion, and promised to notify them of any progress in the case.

Outside it was pouring. The Kubiks jumped into their Mercedes close to the entrance, and I ran the full length of the parking lot to my Mazda. Two cars had hemmed me in and I swore a bit standing there in the rain — it wasn't as if my vehicle took up much space. Just as I started to wedge myself through the wider opening to the passenger door, the brake lights of the car on the driver's side went on. I stepped back and allowed it to pull out. That split-second decision to wait rather than seek immediate shelter in the car would make up for all the other delayed reactions I had been guilty of in my career.

How, through the steamy downpour, did my eyes happen to fall on the licence plate of the white car backing out, noting the small Porsche crest above it? Or would a plate with PIN IT stand out anywhere? By the time this data registered, the blip of a dark-haired male driver through a foggy window turning out of the parking lot was all that was left.

I jumped into my own car and let the possibilities blossom. Was it coincidence that a white Porsche with a dark-haired man was parked metres away from the Kubiks at a memorial service for their murdered baby? If I didn't want to check for myself at the office, I would have phoned the licence in; as it was, I had less than half an hour before meeting Warren. To calm my impatience, I decided to make a pit stop at Dad's on the way to the restaurant.

He had just finished a plate of sardines on toast and listened eagerly to all the details of Nanaimo, Ladysmith, and Extension. Family resemblance was a strange thing; Dad did not look at all like his sister, but his expression of shock and sorrow upon hearing of Lizzie's intentional separation of the twins was the same as Janetta's. At the end he said, "Shouldn't we tell Wendell?"

This time I wasn't going to be the "we" who got roped into calling the Mingus family. "Good idea. I'm sure he'd like a chat with you. I've got to get going — I'm meeting someone for supper."

"Anyone I know?"

"The same someone you might someday."

Five minutes to Broadway and Cambie doubled in the rain, and by the time I parked on Yukon Street, Warren and I reached the door of the Mongolian Grill at the same time. Again he had run from his place in False Creek, and his hair and Gore-Tex jacket were dripping like a wet dog. He pushed the door open for me.

"Never heard of cars?"

"Heavier than I expected. I can usually do it in eight minutes but underestimated the resistance." His scrubbed, fresh skin, ready grin, and heaving breaths contributed to my own quickening pulse as we hung our jackets over chairs and ordered a beer. We both knew the routine of the Mongolian Grill and loaded our plates from the many trays with an eye to guessing the exact weight of each and getting it free. It was strictly a game, as I rarely came close and embarrassed myself that night by being two hundred grams over my estimate, and even worse, over his. Who knew seafood, kebabs, and sautéed vegetables could weigh that much?

Conversation was easy — so easy I thought he must be putting me on. I couldn't get that old joke out of my head: Who would want to join a club that would have me as a member? In other words, I figured it was a set-up for future humiliation. No suggestive remarks or allusions to more dates, just a relaxed exchange with a lot of laughs. He'd gained a slew of new contracts through the Olympics and was stretched but not complaining about business. He seemed to realize I couldn't discuss my work and didn't probe.

The matter of the licence plate still niggling at me, I was first to stand up. When we stepped outside, the rain had stopped and he refused my offer of a ride home for a second time. "Who's the mysterious one now?" I asked when he mumbled something about fulfilling a running quota.

"I'll talk to you soon." He waved and broke into a jog across Cambie. Or did he say "again"? There was a difference. Whatever he was doing, I had to concede this guy was good. To keep me balanced on the edge of hope and fear without toppling into either wasn't easy.

Traffic was smooth; I reached the Burnaby detachment in no time. I entered PIN IT and came up with:

GREG MCGIMPSEY
3811 WALL STREET
VANCOUVER

The name didn't sound like a Kosovar. But if it turned out to be the Porsche in question, the kid next door had a keen eye, however bloodshot. Wall Street was down by the water, close to the Cannery Restaurant where Ray and I liked to go whenever he won a case.

Ray who?

Tomorrow I would pay Mr. McGimpsey a visit.

The next morning, Tessa was working on the sexual assault case, Sukhi was following up on a stabbing at a club the night before, and Wayne was on his way to receive an award for work he had done on a homicide of a teenage boy two years ago. It was Dex and me again. Follow-up calls could sometimes be made alone, but only if the potential for violence had been ruled out; in the lower mainland that could be narrowed to checking back to see if a stolen fishing rod had been returned. I filled him in on what I'd seen the day before.

A refreshing break from yesterday's rain, the sun sparkled on Burrard inlet between wharves and warehouses. Dex drove and I stopped scanning numbers at the sight of a white Porsche parked in a short driveway next to a two-storey house where renovations had started and stopped. The open verandah was painted ivory along with the trim on the downstairs windows, but the upstairs window frames were weatherbeaten brown against flaking blue siding. Wind chimes made from metal peace signs tinkled on the verandah as I pressed the buzzer. It took two rings before a young man, probably in his late twenties and dressed in sweatpants and a tight T-shirt, opened the door. We gave our names, showed our badges and asked if we could come in. Baffled, he gestured us into the living room. I got straight to the point.

"I'd like to ask you a few questions about the Kubik family, whose baby was murdered recently."

His eyes widened and the skin on his forehead stretched into his scalp like a mask being tugged from the back. "Yeah, I heard about that. Terrible thing."

"Do you know Jan or Selena Kubik?"

He took a deep breath. "Yeah, both of them."

I needed a deep breath. "How?"

"Selena and I worked together for a while in a theatre group." Our silence begged for more. "Community thing, non-profit. She was in charge of costumes. Had a real talent for it. Got the right look for every character. Hit all the vintage shops and flea markets. Never went over budget. Met Jan through her." What else did we want?

"Your capacity?" asked Dex, once again adopting the lingo of the interviewee. Or what he thought their lingo was — maybe he should join a theatre group to practise.

"Bit of everything. But I'll take dramaturge."

Greg McGimpsey was a good-looking guy in a bohemian way, and the opposite of Selena — the *real* Bohemian — in grooming. Uncombed hair not as dark as I'd thought through the blurry window, but an unshaven, swarthy look with features that suggested a poet who rides a motorcycle. Defined lips, hazel eyes that rolled expressively when he spoke, a fit, muscular body that might have been covered in tattoos, though none were visible. He was shorter than I was, and I had never got past my own defensiveness when dealing with men this size. I foolishly assumed they were resentful about their height, and therefore tried to minimize my own. If this was ego to believe he wished to be my size, my hunched shoulders felt more like a sign of submissiveness.

"When was this?"

"Oh, a year ago maybe. She quit when she got pregnant. And we've only done one show since. Arts, you know. Funding cuts."

"So you have a day job?"

"More acting whenever I can. TV, movies, commercials. Residuals go a long way. Temp jobs when all else fails."

Crane Reese's face came into my head and I imagined the two of them joking together at the buffet table on a movie set. "When did you last see Selena?"

He looked down, as if he were counting the months. "Hard to say. She came to our production last fall. And I ran into her once downtown. On the street, or was it a mall?"

"Was she alone at the play?"

"Yeah. Left the baby with her husband."

"Did you offer your condolences when you heard about the murder?" asked Dex.

"Yeah, I called as soon as I heard it on the news. Selena wasn't answering. Spoke to Jan, told him how sorry I was. What's this all about, anyway?"

"A white Porsche was seen leaving the street outside the Kubik house on the morning the baby was killed." I nodded toward the car in his driveway.

"You've got a big job if you're checking every white Porsche in the city."

"Your Porsche was seen yesterday at the Van Dusen Gardens."

"Last I heard, there was no law against that."

"Is it a coincidence that the Kubiks were inside commemorating the loss of their child?" asked Dex.

"Must be."

"You often take walks through Van Dusen in the rain?"

"My girlfriend — fiancée, actually — is into plants." He began pacing around the room dramatically, his face inflamed with a mixture of emotions I couldn't separate: anger, embarrassment, indignation. Guilt? I could picture him onstage captivating an audience with his dark, explosive energy and wondered how much of this was an act. "Ever heard of a season's pass? I was buying her one for her birthday."

"I see."

And I did. What was so incriminating about a car being next to another if it wasn't what we were looking for? But something didn't sit right. I surveyed the shabby-chic room: ochre-coloured walls, original unfinished wooden floors topped with two threadbare Persian rugs to mark the living and dining areas. A sagging, worn grey velvet sofa and chair trimmed with carved wood stood in front of a painted red brick fireplace minus a heat source. A bamboo papasan completed the seating arrangement and behind it lay a pile of floor cushions — presumably in case of a cast party.

At first glance, the room could not have been more dissimilar from the expensive, ultramodern interior of the Kubik home. Or was it? I'd learned from Sara and Retha about authenticity, and these drastically different styles were both authentic: nothing imitation, pretending to be other than it was, like fake wood or brick panelling, framed prints from furniture stores. And then I spotted a link. Among the theatre posters and masks dominating the walls hung an original painting by Keith Holmes, a framed restaurant scene similar to the one in Selena's living room.

"You and Selena have the same taste, I see."

His eyes flashed. "There's a gallery close to the theatre. Cast and crew often stop in there to check out exhibitions."

"Pricy purchases for struggling actors."

"We're an amateur group. Pharmacists, teachers, mechanics, undertakers, movie ushers, homeless people. We all went to that show together, and a few of us ended up with a Holmes painting. Do I have to explain what I use my money for? I happen to like real art and vintage cars. Which I got for a song from a cousin who was moving to Europe, by the way. Anything else you want to know?"

"Did Selena Kubik smoke when you knew her?"

"Heavily. Selena is an intense woman." Just then his cellphone rang. He answered in a controlled voice. "Not a good time, hon. Call you back."

"Your fiancée?"

When he nodded with a sigh, I realized my interrogation was slipping out of bounds. I felt awkwardly tall again, stooping to snooping.

"Are you finished with me?"

"Almost." Dex took over. "What were you doing at 7:30 AM on January 2?"

He sighed again and answered. "Sleeping. We had a festive New Year's. Celebrating our engagement."

"Any witnesses? Were you alone?"

"Yes. Tracy left early for work. She's a physiotherapist."

"One more thing." I made my way to the door. "Do you have any connection with Kosovo?"

"Is that a store or a dog?"

"Thank you, Mr. McGimpsey. We'll be in touch." We stepped out on the verandah and he pulled the door behind me with another sigh. Wind chimes serenaded us to the car.

"DOES HE SEEM LIKE A KILLER?" Wayne asked when we gave the others an account of the visit with Greg McGimpsey the following morning. We were all standing at our desks drinking coffee.

"How many do?" asked Sukhi.

"Not really," I said at the same time. Police questioning puts people on the defensive, guilty or not, and we had to allow for that.

"Was there more than he was telling you?" asked Wayne.

Dex and I both shrugged. "I can't get past all the coincidences: white Porsche being spotted twice around Selena Kubik and then he knows her. Yet his answers made sense."

"We can check his alibi with his fiancée, for what that's worth. We know what she'll say. In the meantime, there's not much we can do with him." Wayne reached for a book on a ledge.

"How about Selena?" suggested Tessa. "Asking her about Greg Mc-Gimpsey?"

"Just what I was thinking," I said. "Also talking to her sister at the furniture store. And Jan's brother. Maybe a clue to possible enemies. Are you in?"

"Sister and brother, sure. Selena, no. She's threatened by numbers and you now have the inside track. Whenever you're ready."

Just then my phone rang. "Constable Dryvynsydes?" A frantic woman's voice. "It's Wanda Dean, Terry's mother. You was at our place six months ago when he was threatening me with a knife."

Wanda and Terry. The house where I had my epiphany about victimhood. "Yes, Wanda, what can I do for you?"

"It's Terry again. He stab hisself."

"Did you call 911? Is he conscious?'

"He's awake but he's talking nonsense. You know him. You got through to him."

"Where's the wound?"

"In his shoulder."

"I'll call the ambulance and will meet you both at Burnaby General right away." As I was going out the door, ringing phones took the rest of my team down to their desks like volunteers at a telethon.

Terry Dean. Last fall while I was convalescing, Sukhi phoned to say they'd been called in to the same weird household with Terry going wild smashing things through the screams of his mother and two neighbours. Sukhi had to take him in because they couldn't get him to stop. He'd be fourteen now, I reckoned, pulling into the same space I had used a week ago for Anton Kubik's final hours. Life was a beeyotch.

I found Wanda Dean in Emergency howling behind a gurney. Six months had left their mark on her. Puffiness still enclosed her eyes but had deflated into creases on her cheeks. Signs of youth had become harder to find. Her wailing increased upon seeing me.

"He can't die!" she cried, pounding on my chest which was level with her chin. I took her two hands in mine and led her to a bench outside the door where Terry was taken. "My son, my son, my son," she chanted until her sobs quit, leaving only boozy breath in the air.

"Tell me what happened."

"Terry, he come home this morning about eight after being out all night. I knew he been into drugs soon as he walked in. His sisters were getting ready for school and he scared them with his language and threats and all. They're good girls."

I remembered Terry's whimper: She loves them to death. She wants to see me in jail. "What did you say to him?"

"I told him maybe he should lie down and rest hisself. I would fix him some breakfast, get some eggs into him. You're probably hungry, son, I said to him, trying to calm him down." Wanda used an overly sweet tone to quote herself, her small dark eyes sincere. She could probably have passed a polygraph test because she believed her own story.

She heard herself talking gently instead of in the hysterical, accusatory voice she always used with Terry.

"What did he do?"

"He went crazy, like. Least the girls were gone to school by then. He went running through the house with a knife, saying he was going to kill hisself."

From homicidal to suicidal since our last visit. "Did he say why?"

"Some rubbish about our family. Like he living in a sewer and walking around covered with slime." She shook her head in disbelief, then looked at me pleadingly. "I've been a loving mother, Officer, only Terry keeps going wrong. He don't appreciate what I'm trying to do for him."

"Did you ever contact the counsellor on the card I gave you?"

"Not as yet." She lowered her face, sheepish about this. "I meant to, but then I was sick, and Terry wouldn't listen anyways." Wanda grabbed my hands again and cried, "Please, please don't let my only son die. I couldn't live without him."

A gowned doctor pushed through the doors. "Mrs. Dean?"

"My baby boy, is he going to be all right, Doctor?"

Assessing her condition, he told us both, "He's resting now. And he's going to pull through. The knife missed his heart, but he severed a ligament in his shoulder. Maybe if you go home and have some coffee and come back later in the afternoon, he'll be awake."

Wanda understood doctor-speak for "Sober up." She had heard it before. "Can the officer go in?"

He nodded hesitantly, not wanting to be too obvious in his favouritism. "Just for a minute. He needs his rest."

I walked in quietly and saw an angelic face asleep on the pillow. The nurses had missed a tear-stained smudge on the same spot of his cheek as when I negotiated with him in his messy bedroom. His unwashed hair had been pushed off his forehead, smoothed now of its angry scowl. A dreamy expression on his mouth claimed he was oblivious to the thick bandage around his shoulder. And to his dismal world. Terry was surely a candidate for foster care despite the ruckus Wanda would put up about wanting to keep her son — if only he would change. And his forlornness would go with him to whatever bedroom he found himself. He could be made to pick up his socks, but the disorder would still be inside. I left the room, letting the image of him there overrule thoughts of his future prospects.

"He's asleep," I said to Wanda, who had nodded off herself in my short absence. "I'll take you home."

"Thank you, Officer."

Hangover and exhaustion reduced her to silence in the car. I gave her a phone number in front of her house. "Call the hospital in a few hours. You need a rest yourself. Do you have a way of getting back there?"

"My neighbour has a car."

I knew it would be Freddy's mother, since Wanda probably didn't have many friends. "Take it easy on Terry. He needs understanding."

She was too tired to protest about all she did for him, almost losing her footing getting out of the car. How soon would she pour her next drink — or would it be straight out of a bottle?

Heading back to the detachment, I decided I should not be so judgmental about Wanda's lack of friends. My social calendar was filled with my father, my aunt, regulated sessions with Warren, and the Kubiks. Who was I to talk? Maybe I'd suggest a drink with Tessa after work. Even Megan came to mind, which would mean Lonnie as well. Being a tight twosome was fine, provided you didn't split up, as Ray and I had. Friends fall away and are established in new orbits when you're single again. I had school friends all over the city, but after Mom died, everything seemed too much of an effort. And having Gail as a best friend, no matter where she lived, had made me lazy because she was usually as far as I needed to reach.

Tessa was the only one in the office when I got back. We decided it was a good time to visit Selena's sister Vlasta O'Brien at the Sofa Shop on United Boulevard. She had the same gypsy colouring as her sister, but she was taller and had a lushness about her that stood in marked contrast to Selena's angular bone structure. Large, half-lidded eyes gave the impression she would not be hurried or distracted. Only a guess, but I saw the bricklayer father in Vlasta and an unfulfilled mother in Selena.

"What can I do for you?" she asked warily at the sight of Tessa's badge. Being in sales, her intonation was more Canadian than Selena's.

"Routine questions," Tessa assured her. "We'd like to know if you have any ideas about a possible motive in the Kubik case. Maybe something your sister has blocked out or doesn't think is relevant. She's understandably traumatized."

"Selena and Jan had no enemies." Vlasta gestured us to one of the hundred sofas in her domain, a lime green brocade. From the flair with which she crossed her legs and flung her silk scarf over her shoulder, I got a picture of two young elegant Bohemian sisters in smoky basement bistros having their pick of political poets.

"Do you see much of your sister?"

"Not as much as I'd like. Or as we once did. When I was married, we did things together as couples, but when that split up I found myself with single friends. Both Jan and Selena made the effort to include me, but I felt like a spare tire — ?" She faltered.

"Fifth wheel?" Tessa filled in.

"Yes, that is the term." She laughed too long, but I'm sure this interview was making her uneasy.

"Did you know any of Selena's theatre friends?" I asked.

"A few. She was happy in that world. She did not like that Jan made her give it up."

"But she joined another."

"Yes, a smaller group. It wasn't the same. My sister is a perfectionist in all her projects. She has always needed more stimulation than the organization of a household, which she does quickly and naturally. Bigger challenges bring more satisfaction."

"Do you know Greg McGimpsey?" I watched in vain for telltale signs.

"Greg? Sure. I met him at the shows. They were good friends. But you don't think...? Nononono," she trilled, as only a European can.

"Have they seen each other recently?"

"I wouldn't know. My sister is not one to confide in anyone. Even as children, I told her my secrets but she kept hers. In flare-ups I spoke my mind, but she never did. I envied her for not speaking hurtful words she would later regret, because I always did. She would never deliberately offend anyone, she would retreat. I know her longer than anyone and still do not always know what she is thinking, but I do know she is compassionate. She keeps her kindness hidden; it is — what should I say — organic? because she does not give it in exchange for any thanks. When I went through my nasty divorce, she was my rock. She called me every day, not saying much, just letting me know her arms were open." She bit her lower lip. "And now she has refused all my attempts at comfort in this tragedy, and that hurts me deeply. The last time I saw her was for Christmas dinner at my place with some friends. Jan was overseas. She had Anton with her, such a beautiful, happy child." She wiped her eye with a knuckle.

"What was she like as a mother?" Tessa asked.

"She adored him. Could not take her eyes off him even when I was holding him. He brought a permanent smile to her face."

"And Jan?"

She made a soundless whistle. "Maybe more. He worshipped Anton. The baby brought them together; they needed no one."

"Were they apart?"

Vlasta looked across the showroom and waved at a well-dressed woman who had just come in the door. She answered before standing up, "Jan is European. Selena was North American long before we immigrated. He was crazy about her and swept her off her feet. At times his protectiveness was smothering, I believe, though she never complained of it. Anton removed any frustrations."

Which are back again, I thought to myself.

"That will be all," Tessa said. "Thank you."

In the car we discussed the conversation. All assessments of Selena were consistent: her sister's, Greg McGimpsey's, and ours. Intense, secretive, obsessive, to which Jan had added a delicate orchid quality she did her best to deny. As tempting as it was to imagine a woman like Selena was withholding something, her sister confirmed she had been this way all her life.

"How about the other Mr. Kubik?" asked Tessa, who was driving. "You up for it?"

"Why not?"

We took the Iron Workers' Memorial Bridge to North Van where the firm of Merrick, Fishman, Bell, Kubik, and Berger could easily have been missed on Marine Drive, set back as it was in a brick building behind a well-kept hedge. They clearly weren't out to attract drive-by business. The subdued atmosphere of the reception area changed upon Marek Kubik's entrance.

"Come in, please come in." He ushered us into his office with the manners of his brother magnified a hundred times. "Have a seat, ladies, or do you prefer 'Officers'? I do not like to be politically incorrect. Can I get you some coffee or tea?"

We shook our heads. Then we caught our breaths, for the oxygen in the room had been displaced by this dynamo. Marek Kubik was Caribbean-tanned, flamboyant, with a head of hair like Beethoven, and unless he was playing a role down to the smallest gesture, decidedly gay. When we told him the purpose of our visit, he exclaimed: "My poor darlings, Jan and Selena. They have endured more than anyone should have to in a lifetime."

"How often do you see them?"

"Not enough. I am indebted to my brother for my education — no, for my life. It's as simple as that. But we move in different circles. And the child brought another dimension to their lives, made them more insular. They both worshipped him, and I cannot bear to think of their loss."

Tessa asked the question about enemies and like Vlasta, he was adamant. "Never. It had to be random. A madman. A psychopath." He sat down behind his desk on a maroon leather swivel chair.

"Did you know Greg McGimpsey from the community theatre where Selena volunteered?"

"Greg? Yes. I attended all Selena's productions and met many of the others. What would you like to know about Greg? Surely you don't suspect him in this terrible crime. He and Selena were good friends."

We explained that we were following up on all our evidence. I did not add "meagre," but he was nevertheless quick to comment, in a tone just short of sarcasm: "So the police are stumped. I wish I could help."

"And none of Jan's colleagues would be jealous and go wacko?" Tessa said.

"They're engineers, not postal workers. My brother has an over-developed sense of responsibility, you may have noticed. He makes sure everyone is taken care of, so no one in his firm could have felt bitter or neglected. First-born syndrome, in case either of you suffers from it. Sometimes I think it's all my fault by being there for him to watch over when we were robbed of our parents by the Communists. He became prematurely staid and I, prematurely frivolous." He expelled the last word with a hiss. "If there ever is a ripe time for either."

"And Selena?"

"Enemies? No. Misunderstood? Always. I adore my sister-in-law probably for the same reason the world at large finds her inaccessible and taciturn. A half-laugh from Selena is worth a month of grins from someone who gushes all the time. Selena's humanity is rock solid and she doesn't have to broadcast it to the world. Besides, we share a love of theatre, so we have experienced many mutual delights."

"Does it bother Jan?" I asked. "Your ease with each other?"

Marek shrugged. "Down deep? I don't know. He jokes that I would have made a perfect mate for Selena, but he also knows I am not a threat."

Did he? I could see how Jan would envy his brother's vitality, which he himself lacked.

He leaned back in his chair, bending his knees against his desk. "And you two beautiful women are no doubt too young to be aware of the intricacies of partnerships that my brother and I have learned. Some women — and just as many men, for that matter — thrive on fantasy. When it becomes reality, they cannot bear it, even though they think they cannot bear it if it doesn't. Jan is Selena's reality and the theatre her fantasy."

I thought of Harry Potter on her bookshelf and her comment in the hotel room. Then I thought of Warren, wondering if I had the same problem. "We're older than you think."

"Selena came from humble origins and wanted more," he went on. "In choosing Jan, she bettered her opportunities in life. She is a woman who yearns to improve herself, fulfil her needs. Artistically, the urge was gratified by costume design."

"And personally?" asked Tessa.

"Ahh…" Marek paused. "If the baby had not come along — who knows? Though she never complains, she is not one to hide her dissatisfaction, if you know her at all. But she — and Jan — were rescued by parenthood. A lifetime of new challenges."

He stood up, apologizing. "But I digress, Officers, unless this is what you came to hear."

I was mesmerized, but I could see Tessa shifting from foot to foot.

Marek continued. "We are quick to condemn discontentment in today's society — they give courses in happiness now, for God's sake — but it is also the root of all progress. Often it becomes bleak and ugly and turns on itself and those around them, but without dissatisfaction and the urge for something better, we might still be chiselling our letters on stone tablets, except there wouldn't be any letters. And everyone would stay with the first person he or she kissed."

I wondered if he were talking about himself.

"Thank you, Mr. Kubik," Tessa said, handing him her card in case anything occurred to him later that might be relevant.

Back in the car she said to me, "You could have stayed there all day, couldn't you?"

I had to confess I missed talk like that. Sara was the philosopher in our family and served up analyses of people and life as naturally as peanut butter and banana sandwiches. Dad had inherited enough of his father's practicality not to indulge in any kind of navel-gazing. If a need for improvement was the gauge, Mom must have been as dissatisfied as Selena Kubik. And I questioned my own motive to take another course: was it to keep self-loathing at bay? Not out of the question.

"You're in the right job if you're fascinated by peculiar people."

"I guess I am. My mother had to drag me off buses when the crazies stood up and preached in the aisles."

Tessa laughed. "There's still time to visit Selena today, if you want more."

"I've had enough for now. And I have to figure out a way to see her without Jan."

We were on the bridge, heading back to Burnaby. Tessa looked at me skeptically. "You think you'll learn anything? There hasn't been much new insight today."

Ah, but there has, I wanted to say. I've had a refresher course in self-awareness from Wanda and reality checks from reality Czechs. Instead, I said, "Feel like going for a drink at Squires after work?"

"Sure."

By the time we changed, we had decided on the Shark Club; we felt more in the mood for its upstairs fireplace than crowded sociability. Both of us had prowled the bar scene in our day and neither felt like it tonight. Tessa had just met a guy who "didn't depress the hell out of me." After failed relationships we were both gingerly tiptoeing our way back into the realm of possibility, as if it were studded with landmines. Tessa said her father kept threatening to find a nice Guyanese boy for her — in Guyana. But she wanted no more blind dates. We debated the merits of arranged marriage and agreed that making our own romantic decisions might not guarantee any more lifelong fulfilment, but it was the principle of the thing.

"But I'm caving in on the no-cop rule, so why not everything?"

Her new prospect was in polygraph in North Van. Members married each other all the time, even gay ones, but I too had made a pledge to avoid dating them. There were advantages in co-ordinating shifts, understanding the pressures of extra hours and working with the criminal element, but to me it was too much of the same. Ray dealt with my clientele once we were finished with them, but we didn't sit in cars and offices together all day.

"Who knows where it's going?" Tessa couldn't conceal an adolescent smile that disclosed where she wanted it to go. "How about you?"

"Same. I feel I'm watching it unfold from the sidelines, wondering why our timing is always off. A warning?" My nose had started dripping, but I had tissues this time.

"Men," Tessa declared with a long drink of vodka cranberry, shaking her thick spray of curls pushed back in an orange headband. Like Vlasta

O'Brian, Tessa was a woman of lush textures and features: creamy mocha skin, teeth an advertisement for whitening strips, long lashes on dark, compassionate, but shrewd eyes. Even her nails were strong and well-shaped compared to my stubby, broken ones. With a mouthful of ice, she gurgled, "I'm not making any stupid compromises this time."

I nodded. "My mother always said, 'Never be with a man you have to make excuses for.' The thing is, I didn't have to for Ray, and it still didn't work."

Tessa shrugged. "In the meantime, I am actually going to Guyana with my dad. I've never been back to my birthplace and would like to see the island he came from in the Essequibo River. And my grandparents' graves. I want to know more about them. I've had a sudden burst of interest in my black heritage after living all these years on the white side. And Dad won't be around forever as a tour guide."

"That's cool."

"He says he's taking me for security purposes against all the killing and robbing going on down there. It's become a big-time drug stop from Colombia."

"You'll be ready for Whalley when you get back."

The mention of Tessa's unknown grandmother filled my mind with thoughts of Jane Hughes, but I was too tired to share them with Tessa at this hour. The mystery of human bonds and bondage had reached its fill for the day. I wiped my nose again. "And you might just meet someone to give your polygrapher a run for his money."

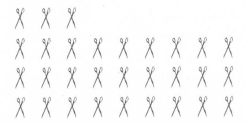

AT FIRST, Jane thinks it's her usual catarrh. She takes it as a reminder to wash more handkerchiefs, soon forgotten in an impatient crunch of the warped back door. Roland enters with a newspaper in one hand, a letter in the other. He nods and gives her the letter.

The childish handwriting prompts Jane to tear open the thin blue envelope recklessly. To see better, she stretches her arm out and reads aloud:

September 15, 1918

Dear Mother,

I have just been discharged from a medikal unit in Pikardy. I lost a thum from blood poisoning in the battle of Amiens and my comander says I must be lucky. Many others did not survive. This was a big viktory and the next one shood bring the Germans to their nees.

Sometimes I cry like a baby to be back home. It is not brave but I do it alone. All my close friends have died from bullets or bayonets or poison gas and now spanish flu. Pray for me to be back in Nanaimo by Chrismas. I have pressents for you and Sara and Janet and Papa. In the new year I will find a job in the building trade. Never in the mines. They are dark and dirty and damp like trenches.

I hope you and our family are going fine. I miss you.

Your son,

Llewyllyn

Jane presses the letter to her heart and closes her eyes, tears escaping down her cheeks. "September 15. That's five weeks ago. Where is he now? Oh, where is our poor boy now?"

"He's a man, wherever he is," says Roland, removing his jacket and revealing the camphor pendant he wears at his wife's insistence. "And the war's as good as over, if you can believe the papers and the talk. He should be home soon."

"Sure enough, he's been through more than many men, but he's still a lad of eighteen. How can he build houses without a thumb?" Jane thinks of her own infected thumb that almost killed her. Why was she spared hers and not her innocent son?

Night shift behind him, Roland settles back on the couch where he opens the Nanaimo Free Press with shaky hands. A two-bits bucket of near beer, the only legal beverage now, does not pack the punch of even a pint of what he needs to still his tremors. From the corner of his eye, he watches his wife reread the letter three or four times before relaying the news he brings daily from the mine and bar.

"Heard your old neighbour Gertie Salo died of flu in Chase River."

Jane shakes her head in dismay. She remembers young, slow Gertie, now the mother of five, who still cares for her mother because she speaks only Finnish. "That's a houseful of dependents who won't know where to start without her."

"And Milt's packing up."

Jane clears her throat with a dry cough and looks sadly toward the house next door. "When?"

"First of the month. Got a buyer for the property and says we should like our new neighbours. He works at Wakesiah but takes jobs in the bush when he can." Miners who owned their own homes were permitted to farm or work in the lumber industry when there was a slowdown in the mines, rare as such opportunities were during wartime demand for coal.

"Married?"

"Just. Milt said the wife seems shy, but he told them you'll make her welcome."

Oh did he now? Who says she has to welcome another woman living in Marjorie's house? She cannot look in that direction since her best friend died and her mother took the twins' favourite playmates back to Comox with her. She sends food for Milt with Roland because it is too heart-wrenching to pass the empty swing and hear the laughter again in her head. "Where's he going?"

"Vancouver. New Westminster, maybe. Marjorie's sister is likely to take the girls and he wants to be close. Might work on the wharves to start. Strong as he is, he won't have a problem. He can't take it here alone."

He's not the only one, Jane thinks. When Suzanne and June left with their grandmother, Sara and Janet were listless for so long Jane feared they had the flu. But they are playing quietly in their bedroom at the moment, both healthy. She looks in to find Sara reading Black Beauty aloud to her teddy bear and Janet crocheting a bracelet for her doll.

Their school has been converted to a hospital and she feels safer having them at home. She has already done lessons with them this morning, marvelling at how quickly Sara picks up all her studies, even numbers. Her curiosity reminds Jane of herself at that age, and she makes a pledge that Sara will get all the schooling she wants. Janet learns just enough not to disappoint her mother. At the end of lessons they sing songs: "Li'l Liza Jane," "Pack Up Your Troubles in Your Old Kit Bag," and "Oh! How I Hate to Get Up in the Morning," saving the silliest ones for last, like "Aba Daba Honeymoon," "K-K-K-Katy," and "Oh Johnny, Oh Johnny, Oh!" to finish with giggles. Since Llewyllyn's letter, "Roses are shining in Picardy..." is now running through Jane's head, her twins always coming to mind as the roses in any song. Longer now, their dark hair tied back in a ribbon is silkier than ever; Jane has never seen such beauty before. Her gasp of gratitude gets caught in her throat as a rasping cough.

Janet looks up from her bracelet. "Mama, drink some milk and ginger."

"Not now, it's suppertime." Jane shivers, pulling her woollen cardigan around her. "It's cold in here." She turns to Roland, who puts down the paper and adds a half-scuttle of coal to the burning embers in the stove, shrugging. She files her son's letter with the others in the desk drawer, then stands in the kitchen, rubbing her hands in front of the warm oven until Janet comes out to set the table for supper. Sara remains reading in the bedroom.

Jane hands Janet a knife and two tomatoes to slice on a plate. "Mind your fingers," she says, more from habit than real concern. With the war dragging on and the flu raging, she feeds her family frugally from provisions she herself has put up. She takes a barley, mushroom, and bacon casserole from the oven along with a fresh loaf of bread. A sealer of pickled green beans completes the first course and will be rewarded by pumpkin pie.

The calmness of the scene also prompts Jane to give thanks for a healthy family with enough to eat, adding silently, "and no drunken ravings," once commonplace before Prohibition. She regrets her son cannot see his father this way, just once. "Let us pray Llewyllyn is also well-fed, warm, and whole at this moment and will be back with us soon."

She dishes out portions onto three plates, knowing how much each will eat. She puts a spoonful of barley and a tomato slice on her own, hoping no one will notice she doesn't touch it. Her appetite is rapidly being replaced by nausea. It spreads from her stomach through her chest to her throat, where it mingles with congestion in her nose. She coughs again, using an overused hankie from her apron pocket to cover her mouth. She asks Sara about *Black Beauty* as a distraction from the aversion she feels to the food. She has not experienced such queasiness for — for nine years.

Could she be pregnant?

She looks across at Roland, intent on his food, and blushes. In six weeks, she will be forty years old and the prospect of a latecomer like Gomer had never occurred to her. If it is to be, she must stay strong to spare her daughters from raising a sibling as she was forced to do. And now her younger brother in Victoria might as well be dead to her, if indeed he is still married to Thelma and working in the family business there. Even Ladysmith seems a world away when it comes to travel and inclination, but at least Roland brings occasional news of Tommy through the mine circuit.

Janet jumps up from the table to ladle more water into their drinking glasses, taking the last from the pail. The pump at the sink is jammed and Milt has made his outside well available to them. Will Milt repair theirs before he leaves, as he promised? Jane hopes so, because Roland is oblivious to such inconveniences. Sara watches Jane. "Mama, why aren't you eating? Don't you feel well?"

"Maybe I sampled too much while I was cooking. I'm not very hungry." She shivers and coughs.

Sara sets her fork down. "I'm finished too."

"Come now, you've only eaten a little. You can do better than that." Jane stands as close as she can to the stove without burning herself. "I'm cold is all. Must have caught a chill when I went out to the root cellar for pumpkin. Eat up now; you know how you like pumpkin pie for dessert."

"Mama, you're sick. Your face is red."

"It's from the hot stove." Jane cannot confess to the source of her blush, but does not deny the dizziness in her head. She must sit down on the sofa where she can lean back and pull her feet up. "I'll rest a bit and be well in no time." This new life in her womb is testing her properly at such an age.

Roland and Janet also leave the table, and Roland covers her with an afghan she and Janet made from crocheted squares. Sara brings a comforter from the bedroom.

"I'll make some tea," says Janet.

"No, darling, I don't want anything. I'll just lie a spell."

Roland brings the sitting room stove to full blaze, his own faded eyes ablaze with fear. By now the whole world knows the symptoms. He crumples the Free Press, with its latest flu statistics, for kindling. Sara and Janet dart nervously around the house. They had been playing nearby when Auntie Marjorie rubbed her forehead, and that was the last they ever saw of her. Jane's bewildered smile contemplates a different source of warning signs.

"Mama, Janet will cut up some onions."

Understanding now, she laughs at Sara offering her sister's services. "Oh no. If it is the flu, it won't last long. I'll see to that."

She believes her words, since she has never been sick in her life other than blood poisoning. But Roland, frantically stoking the fire in the kitchen stove hears them over the crackle as "I won't last long." His thin neck swivels jerkily and he begins to pace. Talk everywhere is just this. How whole families are found lying on the floor, unable to feed themselves or tend fires. How two women went out dancing at night and one was dead in the morning. How new vaccines are not working against the virus, and isolation proves just as useless. How Aspirin powder is now being sold by the Bayer Company in tablets and helps with aches, but is not a cure. How last week he took his lunch break with a fellow miner who three hours later had to be carried out of the mine. He's getting better, Roland has heard, and so will Jane. So will Jane.

From the couch, she recognizes her husband's powerful need of a drink. Not just the diluted beer he's been imbibing, but something stronger from the blind pig at the harbour. "Roland, I'll be fine, if you want to go out. My nurses here will take care of me." Sara has brought a pillow for her head, and Janet is pulling her father's warm woollen socks over her mother's lisle stockings. Jane loosens the garter belt that has become binding around her waist.

His cheek twitches in surprise. "Well, awright, I might just do that, if you think you can manage. And I'll pick up some camphor gum and Aspirin at the chemist. Could be quinine's back in stock." Blinking now with justified purpose, he starts out of the overheated house. Then he turns back.

Jane says it for him: "You'll need more money. Camphor's gone up from ten to fifteen cents an ounce. And we're almost out of carbolic."

He jingles the change in his pocket, wanting to cover his wife's medicine, but his thirst causes him to reach for the money tin. He returns it empty to the shelf and leaves.

From the pillow, she issues more instructions to her daughters. "Get the masks from the press in the bedroom. They're clean." Ideally, masks were to be changed every two hours, but usually by then they were cast aside. "And we need to wash hankies."

"I'll do it," says Janet. "I know how."

"You'll need fresh water and use just a few drops of carbolic until

Papa brings more. Pour out the soak pail water, and mind you don't touch the hankies when you put them in the fresh. I'll drop mine in when you're ready."

Sara in a pink tunic and Janet in blue move like Rose Red and Snow White through the house with masks, throwing supper remains in the slop pail and wiping the counters with bleach. Two pumpkin pies remain untouched in the pantry. Jane wants to tell them to sit down, that she will be all right, but in truth, the pounding in her head has become blinding. Unbidden, Sara lays cold cloths on her forehead, and after tending to the handkerchiefs, Janet brings willow bark tea, then a cup of hot water containing a few drops of liniment. Both know the remedies, not only because of what their mother did for Aunt Marjorie, but from friends at school before it was closed. Everyone has a stricken relative. On such hearsay, Sara has taken an enamel bowl and the fire tongs to the open stove until Jane stops her.

"But Mama, brown sugar and kerosene on hot coals will cure you."

"You've done enough for now, dears, both of you. Get into your nighties and to bed so you'll have strength for tomorrow if I require your help again."

Janet heads obediently to the bedroom, but Sara starts to cry. "The fire will go out. Papa won't be home for hours and you'll get cold."

Jane knows she can't win against Sara's will, and her own is failing fast. She cannot raise her head from the couch to crawl into her own soft bed. "All right. Put on your housecoat and slippers and bring the cot and blankets. You can sleep in here if you keep your face at the other end away from mine."

Most mine houses possess fold-up cots for extra sleeping space in small areas. They are made of heavy canvas with a thin, flexible mattress on a metal frame. As Sara snaps it into place, Jane resists thinking of it as her bier. Marjorie and all the other women she has provided with food ended up on cots in their cramped kitchens. And there they lay down and died.

Is this it, then? Is this the unknown realm she has cried over as a helpless bystander? Can she make her daughters and Roland understand that the weakness overrides all the alternatives that terrify them?

That her position is not easier but clearer. From the centre of the co-coon that will release her, she must leave them outside to guess with dread and fear at its mystery. But how did it happen so fast? Just hours ago, she was reading her son's letter with a dripping nose. And wasn't it only yesterday she was running up the green hills of Wales picking wild pansies?

Janet emerges from the bedroom in a long blue flannel nightgown. She whimpers when she sees Sara installed on the cot next to their mother. "I can fit too."

Jane is firm with Janet, knowing she will listen. "Not tonight, sweet-heart. It's too crowded and no one will sleep well."

Her daughters settled, she drifts in and out of the pain in her head. It crests like a hundred hammers until fitful sleep stills the swell briefly. The prospect of Aspirin consoles, but not in the state it will be deliv-ered by Roland. When he is away at night, she leaves the coal oil lamp barely lit on the kitchen table to prevent him crashing into furniture on his return. Tonight it is just enough to see the bright eyes of Sara on her whenever she becomes restless. More than once, she hears her rise quietly to add more coal to the stove.

What will be the added cost for heat if they go over their limit of fuel from the company? Instead of the anxiety she expects from such ex-travagance, the thought opens a memory of Chase River. Her mother is telling her she must quit school because the extra coal needed to bake and cook in the pre-dawn sleeping household is setting Thomas back too much. It unfolds like a scene in a play without the crushing disap-pointment she felt at the time.

Either the unaccustomed heat or the fever is turning Jane's limbs from blocks of ice to shafts of fire. She kicks her covers to the floor, startling Sara.

"Mama?"

"I'm warm now, darling. Go back to sleep."

Jane tries to lie as still as possible, directing the heat in her body to consume the throbbing in her head. As she does, patches of memories pull loose from a wall that has confined and protected her for twenty-four years. Chase River grows clearer through the widening cracks.

She sees a curing shack, primitive, dark, filled with dead meat and weapons. A proper stench, if she could smell, but she cannot. She observes only. In hiding, her thumb catches on a rusty hasp and bleeds while her friend, her dead friend, lies in the dark. She cannot feel the horror of that night in the forest but sees it in a bundle of clothes in the snow, her blood spilling onto his. Back home, she collapses from her wound. Her mother catches her, administering the touch and scent of love and of Wales in a bottle of iodine.

Sara's adenoidal breathing grazes her reverie but does not puncture it. It blends into the grey and leaden weeks she lay lifeless, to be miraculously awakened by her first kiss. A kiss from a golden prince. The scene is clear: the cabin of her friend Louis, her dead friend. She has stolen away from her mother's care for a walk in the fresh March air. Adam is there packing his father's few belongings. Alone. Adam is alone and Jane is alone. Until they are not alone, but two becoming one. She cannot tell him of his father's murder because her high fever has trapped and sealed all traces of it. Was a second high fever its only entry?

Jane does not feel the rapture, but she sees it in Adam's wondrous face and soft gaze. She cannot hear the tender words on the old porch later, but sees their blush in the lilac bush next to it, bestowing tenderness upon all lilac blossoms and anything lilac-coloured. She knew back then that magic is fleeting and most often an illusion. And they both knew this magic would vanish. Jane Owens and Adam Strong were not meant to be a couple beyond the rough edges of a log cabin soon to be demolished for the Extension mine.

But the bloom did not vanish, and Jane did the only thing she could think of: walk into the open arms of Roland Hughes. She cannot feel the betrayal or revulsion of that moment, but can see it in the nervous eager tic in Roland's cheek. Nothing was said when the plumpest, bonniest baby she has ever held arrived six weeks earlier than expected — the question she feared about complexion becoming nothing against the fear of his irregular breathing. And how did she bear the horror of watching that breath stop altogether, blaming the midwife for not slapping him hard enough at birth? She cannot feel the bottomless anguish in her seventeen-year-old heart, but sees her favourite cat Velvet in the cradle and wants to strangle her for not being her baby.

Except for sight, all sensation and emotion have been leached from the pictures. Even then Jane views them behind her eyes and not through them. The image of her lost baby causes her to cry out. Sara leaps to her mother's side.

"Just a bad dream," Jane whispers. Sara lays a cold cloth on her forehead. She holds her hand until a punch on the warped door just before dawn announces her father.

Sara springs to her feet, but Jane does not have the strength to mediate in his drunken entrance tonight. She wishes only for Aspirin. Her headache has dulled and given way to a heaviness in her chest: as if the sofa were on top of her and not the other way around.

Roland shouts, "What the hell happened to the fire? Do I have to supervise every minute in this house or it falls apart? Your mother is sick, or haven't you noticed?"

Jane says quietly in short breaths: "I told her to let it burn down because I was warm with fever. She's kept it going all night."

"Some job she did." He stumbles to the coal box, scoops a few pieces into the scuttle, dropping as many as he grabs. Sara nestles up against her mother on the couch for safety.

"Did you get the Aspirin, Roland? And carbolic?"

"Just my luck, the chemist was closed. Guy I ran into later says there's no quinine to be had in Nanaimo. Where are the onions? Doesn't anybody do anything when I'm away?"

He lurches to the kitchen where he has not chopped an onion in twenty-three years, brandishing a knife he has found after slamming all the cupboards. Jane tells him the girls will look after it. Janet has been wakened by the commotion and comes out hurriedly in her nightgown and housecoat to begin chopping. Sara huddles closer to her mother until Jane sits up abruptly with her head back, blood streaming from her nose.

"Get some rags from the sewing room."

Janet begins to cry because she has not taken the clean handkerchiefs from the laundry line in the kitchen, inadequate as they are now for the flow. She starts toward them, then turns back fretfully to the onions, not knowing which to do first.

With a handful of clean rags, Sara whispers to her mother: "Papa's a beast."

"He's scared," says Jane. "He acts worse when he's scared."

"I'm scared too, but I'm not mean."

"No, you're not, and I want you always to stay this way. Papa didn't have a mother to tell him not to be mean."

"But we have you, Mama, and we always will, won't we?" Sara begins to cry and lays her head on Jane's lap.

Masks forgotten, she strokes her daughter's hair and removes the rag from her nose long enough for a quick breath-held kiss on her head. "And I'll be with you even if I'm not with you."

She knows the signs, as sure as those of birth, each a mysterious, unalterable step to the transition itself. The cough, the aches — head, back, joints, chest — the bleeding, the short breath, and the final suffocation from mucus in the lungs. Some say bleeding noses help with recovery, but not in Marjorie's case. And if she is with child, as Marjorie was, it's well known she is more susceptible to the pernicious virus. How poignant that another man's son should start her life with Roland and his own seed should hasten its end. She must trust the strong fibre that has served her so well for forty years to accomplish her final mission.

"Sara," she speaks through the rag to her daughter still sobbing on her lap. "Please move the cot to the kitchen. Soak a sheet in whatever carbolic is left, wring it out, and hang it on the laundry line. Janet will help you."

Roland has passed out in the bedroom to everyone's relief. As her daughters set up her corner in the kitchen, Jane rises from the couch and moves slowly toward her sleeping husband. Raucous snores insure that he will not see his wife step out of her brown hopsacking skirt and petticoat, pull her bloodstained white blouse and shimmy over her head, slip into a clean cotton nightgown, and change her underwear. No man has ever seen her naked. And only three midwives. Even alone she does not prolong the changing or bathing process, at times ruing her innate modesty because her body is firm and trustworthy.

She stuffs her clothes into an old pillowcase and carries them out to the porch to be burned.

The exertion causes Jane to collapse on the cot. Having piled the clean handkerchiefs neatly on the counter, Janet steps outside for fresh water to wash the sheet. Jane calls Sara away from the onions.

"Please bring me my writing tablet and pen from the desk." While Sara fetches them, she props herself up against pillows in readiness for her task.

At that moment a coarse cough precedes Roland's sluggish footsteps into the kitchen. He spies Sara with the paper and pen and snatches them away. "Is this what you do for a sick woman? Tax her strength with foolery? To draw pictures, I s'pose." He stuffs the writing paper into the cookstove. "Make yourself useful for a change. Make your dear mother some violet tea, get some soup into her, and finish that poultice."

Sara chokes back tears, having learned from her mother that explanations only inflame her father's rants. Jane says quietly: "Roland, the stores will be open soon. Would you try again for carbolic? We're fresh out." She is too weak to ask if he has any money left and no solution if he doesn't. Hangovers from bootlegged liquor are as vile as its other stages. The open air is best for him.

"I s'pose that's a reminder I didn't get the Aspirin too." He stops short, seeing his wife's heaving chest, takes the jacket he has flung over a chair, and escapes.

"Sara," Jane whispers when he's gone. "Bring me the scribbler you use for your lessons. Papa dropped the pen over there. It's important."

Sara runs quickly to her bedroom and brings back a lined notebook.

"I want to write a letter to my sister Catherine in Wales. It's my heart's desire that you will meet her and Margaret and your cousins someday."

"Don't talk, Mama. Save your strength until you get better. We can take you to our school where there are nurses and doctors."

Jane shakes her head. The makeshift hospitals offer more hope than remedy, and she is beyond both. Janet comes in from the porch with a damp sheet in her hand, disinfectant fumes escorting her.

"It's wrung out, Mama. Sara can help me hang it up." She sees the scribbler in Jane's trembling fingers. "Sara! Mama can't be helping you with lessons now. She's too sick." Her tone carries a burst of hostility — finally warranted — toward lessons.

"It's all right, Janet," Jane says quietly. "I asked her for it. I need to write a letter to your Aunt Catherine. Sometimes words are necessary."

Unable to withstand two attacks, Sara retaliates against the sober one. "Leave Mama," she shouts at her sister for the first time ever. "You don't love words the way we do."

Janet drops the wet sheet on the oilcloth table cover and runs sobbing into the bedroom.

"Sara," Jane says as emphatically as she can. "You must never fight with your sister. She's your heart and soul."

Sara nods and Janet returns. Wordlessly, they hang the damp, pungent sheet on the laundry line, sealing their mother off from the rest of the house, and worse, from them. With the unison of twins, they take knives and finish chopping onions for the poultice. For once, Sara's strokes are more precise and focused than her sister's, allowing Janet to shed enough tears for them both.

Behind the curtain, Jane develops a rhythm to ration her diminishing reserves. Write, rest, breathe. Increasingly, she must struggle to raise her head from the pillows between scrawled sentences. No time to feel remorse over bad penmanship. Urgency stokes dying embers, releasing a flare-up of words. All the books she loved so much to read offer their language in a last rite, sometimes in her mother's Welsh rhythms. The letter will set her story down, but not here, not where it could hurt Roland, who gave his name in good faith to the child she was carrying. Nor does she want a new image of herself altering any detail of the perfect love she shares with her children. Sweet Cassie will receive Jane's words of atonement for the silence she has held so long about her friend Louis Strong. His kind face visits her feverish brain.

Please forgive me Louis for not coming forward at the trial. My mind turned in on itself when I was so close to death.

Of his doomed grandson no one ever knew, not even the baby's father. How we both loved Adam. Stickiness oozes from her ear and she dabs more blood on the rag already red from her nose and sputum.

Along with bodily fluids, the infection releases senses frozen from the pictures just hours ago, and for twenty-four years before that. Her longing for Adam momentarily revives her breath, the same way he stopped it back then. By leaving her alone as agreed, he protected her from gossip. Later she heard that after Henry Hargraves was acquitted of the murder of their father, the Strong brothers moved to the mainland. Ruby returned to Salt Spring Island to take a teaching position and to care for their mother. Where were they now? Would any of them have understood her silence?

"Mama!" Janet cries. "Why so many pages? You must rest yourself."

A loud sigh issues from Jane's throat. The pen drops on the blanket after she makes a faint squiggly version of her name at the bottom of the letter.

"I'm done," she says, summoning her twins to her side. She includes Janet in this sacred task by asking her to fold the five pages, bring an envelope from the desk, and seal it. This twin will have no curiosity about the contents.

"I'll write the address, Mama," says Sara, crowding her sister's hand in the drawer, as she seeks the address book. "And lick the stamp."

"Thank you, my beauties. Please mail it later today."

At the stove, Janet heats the pan of onions, mixes salt and enough flour to prevent juices from seeping. Sara adds a large scoop of goose grease before stepping back to let her sister's deft fingers seal the hot mixture in red flannel and lay it on their mother's chest.

"Promise me you will always try to find the good in people," Jane murmurs. "Especially your father."

Weeping, Sara interrupts what sound like parting words. "The poultice will draw out the poisons, Mama."

"Give Mrs. Krall our provisions and she will cook food for you. You're my angels, you know that..."

Janet's sobs drown her out. "Llewyllyn is going to come home from the war and help with everything to make you strong again."

A wave of surrender swamps Jane's aching heart and body. More farewells will only upset her daughters. She can do nothing else for them. They know their few keepsakes — the photos, her bracelets — are in the sachet pouch, now empty of coins since she stopped taking in so much sewing. How she prays they are spared the sight of the death wagon.

"Mama," Sara exclaims, "your skin is turning blue. You look like a Negro lady."

Janet yanks at Sara's arm to be quiet, but Jane smiles at the comparison; she wonders if she resembles Ruby Strong. She prefers Sara's description to cyanosis, its clinical term.

"I'm thirsty. Could you get me some water, Janet?" Her lips are swollen and parched. Because of the washing, Janet must again run outside for a pail of clean water from Milt's pump. Jane's inhalations are strained, but her nostrils clear; a deep and cleansing breath of lilacs has just erased a brief whiff of the same stinking brew of rotten meat, foul breath, brackish flower water, and privies she smelled outside the butcher's cabin.

"Sara, please come close."

Sara climbs onto the cot and presses herself tenderly against her mother's shoulder. Jane blinks away a mist dimming her vision. She sees someone walking toward her through the nebula — a straight, tall, dark man with a wide smile extending his hand. Behind him is a shadowy figure she cannot make out — someone younger, perhaps. Is it her son? He has no place to cry alone. He is surrounded by soldiers in splashing mud, gas masks, bayonets, and bullets. Short of a thumb, his fingers fumble on the trigger. She longs to hide him but she has no time left. The outstretched hand is coming closer and she takes it: sturdy and work-worn, a familiar hand she trusts.

Sara must put her ear to her mother's lips to hear: "If you ever have a son, please call him Louis." So feebly spoken the last syllable of the name is indistinct. "His name must be honoured because he was a fine and gentle man. And he had no one to help him."

A smile starts across Jane's cracked lips but is cut short by something more private and enigmatic. Sara kneels next to her, staring. She looks up only when Janet's screams wrest her from her mother's captivating secret.

THREE MEMOS LANDED ON MY DESK before the date sank in: February 13. Dad and I had survived birthdays and Christmas without Mom, but Valentine's Day would mark a year since her death. I felt bad the anniversary had almost slipped my mind, especially since Dad would be thinking of it every minute and would never dream of reminding me in my important busy schedule.

The first memo was a court notifier setting the trial date for Andy Lambert's testimony on April 5. Dex was the primary on that and should be arranging to bring him over from the island. The second was a court lens for a prelim on March 15 for my own case versus the two young offenders for attempted murder. Crown prosecutor was Ray Kelsey, and his name caused neither the flips nor the flops it once had. The third sheet did bring more of a physical response: a note from Wayne that the diary date on the Kubik investigation was overdue. *Please review this file and provide an update.* It was a routine procedure to us all, but I felt responsible for the standstill in the case, given my access to the Kubiks. I had left a message awhile ago for Selena to call me but she hadn't. I wanted to talk to her alone about Greg McGimpsey.

I dialled Dad's number. Big flakes of snow were drifting past the window and melting on contact. I mouthed his words along with him when he picked up: "Did you see the snow? I hope you'll take your time driving home tonight. This city isn't equipped for slush."

"Yes, Dad. Anything planned for tomorrow?"

"Thought I'd walk to the two parks to visit your mother and mine."

It was not surprising that Sara had always been specific about having her ashes strewn around the giant weeping willows in Douglas

Park she loved so much. But Mom, for all her organization, left no instructions for her death. More remarkable was that Dad made a decision immediately as to where we would dispose of her cremated remains: Queen Elizabeth Park. It had been one of her favourite running routes, close enough to home that it became a mere appetizer before supper. The winding ascent up Little Mountain built lung power while the rock gardens distracted from its pain. Dad was firm that he and I would scatter her ashes alone at sunset sometime after her big funeral. He singled out a sequoia tree at the bottom of the hill close to a pond. I told him he had ruined the possibility of a family plot by burying them ten blocks apart, but he insisted the birds and bees would link the two final resting places. Both women deserved to rule in their domains.

"I'll leave for Douglas at four."

"I'll meet you there at four-thirty."

"Supper at Seasons on the Park is on me if you don't have any exciting plans for Valentine's Day."

"Not so far."

When I hung up on Dad, both my phones rang. My cellphone was an unknown number, so I answered the call of duty.

"Constable Dryvynsydes?" said the only voice I knew that throaty.

"How are you, Selena?"

"I am managing, thank you. You called?"

"I wanted to talk to you about something."

"New evidence?"

"Maybe. Has your husband gone back to work?"

"Yes, I am alone."

"Is tomorrow morning at ten convenient?"

"I will see you then."

On my cellphone was a message from Warren. Did I have plans for supper tomorrow? I asked myself what Retha would do and heard a distinct answer: both. I called Warren and explained the situation with Dad, agreeing to meet him at an upscale restaurant on south Granville at seven. I then called Dad and trimmed our agenda. No guilt was exchanged.

Colleen Street was deserted compared to the last time I saw the crescent filled with cruisers and media vans. It seemed odd to have the door opened by Selena in charge of her own home.

"Happy Valentine's Day," I said,

"Valentine's Day — is it? Happy, no."

She was wearing a black Lululemon jogging suit, the spandex making her frame look like a skeleton. Her sleek hair was held back at the neck with a silver clip; the olive tones of her skin had become sallow except for darker patches around her eyes. She gestured me toward one of the leather sofas and asked if I would like a cup of coffee. Usually, I refused any beverage when I was on duty but just as she offered it, the sun broke through the filmy curtains on the bay window, reflecting a glint of colour from the raku bowl sitting on the pewter shelf. Once again, I was enticed into Selena's world and nodded.

Not surprisingly, the coffee was as strong as espresso; I felt like a peasant asking for milk. She sat on her Bauhaus chair and stared at me until I spoke.

"Greg McGimpsey."

Her expression became cautious but not startled; it occurred to me that Vlasta or Marek might have called. "What about him?"

"You know him."

"Yes."

"He drives a white Porsche. He knows you. What can you tell me about him?"

She sipped her coffee and licked her lips. "What did he say?"

"I asked you first," I said lightly, as I would to a friend.

She stood up and circled her chair with the cup in her hand. "We were in a drama group together. We were good friends."

"Could he have had anything to do with the homicide?"

"You spoke to him. What do you think?"

"I don't recall mentioning that I spoke to him."

She turned sharply to me. "You said he knew me. How would you find that out without speaking to him? Unless you are going on the word of my sister and brother-in-law."

That opened it up. When I said "We should have you on our team," she gave me a half-smile, the kind Marek Kubik said was worth a month of grins from anyone else. "All three said the same thing. That you were friends from the theatre group."

"So what else do you want to know?"

We were going in circles. "My original question. Did he or his car have anything to do with Anton's death?"

She sat down on the chair, crossed her legs, stared out the window, and shook her head with emphatic disdain. The sun had retreated, and her black outfit made her look like a shadow against the slate-coloured space inside and out.

"Would you confirm that for the record?" I spoke again almost lightly because I was not taking notes.

"The answer to your question is no."

"He was not the one who came to your door in a white Porsche?"

"Constable Dryvynsydes." Her voice rose in exasperation. "Why would Greg McGimpsey want to kill my baby?"

"I'm not saying he did. I'm just trying to connect the dots. We have someone you know driving a white Porsche."

"Would it not make more sense to look for white Porsches driven by people I do not know? Greg McGimpsey would not want to hurt my baby."

She opened a narrow, flat drawer in an end table and pulled out a pack of cigarettes and matches. She slid one out and offered it to me conspiratorially, as if we were at a teenage slumber party. I was strangely tempted, even though my last smoke had been with Gail the night before her wedding. I shook my head.

She lit hers, using an oblong jade bowl on the end table as an ashtray. "Did Greg McGimpsey give you cause for suspicion?"

Would anyone but Selena repeat the last name of a friend like this? She spoke as if I were in the dock and she were questioning me. "Not particularly. He said he called with condolences when he saw it on the news."

"I missed his call." She turned her head to the side to blow a ring of smoke. "He might have spoken to Jan."

"When last did you see him?"

She took another deep drag and looked away again. "I can't remember."

"Did you go to any theatre productions since you quit?"

"Last fall, yes. And I saw him once downtown since then."

Their stories meshed. "Was his girlfriend with him?"

"Why do you ask that?" She stood up again, went to the kitchen and returned with the coffee pot, which was narrow and sculpted — like her.

"I'm a cop, a nosy one. Why not?"

"He was alone. I had Anton. But I saw her in the play. She joined after me."

"They're engaged," I said, holding my cup for her to pour, then pulling my hand back quickly when coffee overflowed onto my fingers.

"I am very sorry," she said, reaching across and rubbing my hand in a comforting massage as she blotted the coffee with a cocktail napkin from the cigarette drawer. "Did you meet her, the fiancée? Is that why you bring this up?"

"No, but she called." As soon as I said it, I remembered I was not here to gossip. Selena had a similar realization and lowered her gaze. She opened the drawer again and brought out a small yellow candle. I resisted the urge to ask her what other smoking paraphernalia were in there — a hookah, maybe? I inhaled appreciatively.

"Pineapple. It is a subtle scent and hard to find."

Like you, I thought again. "And your husband won't smell the cigarettes."

She gave me another half-smile.

"How is he?"

"On the outside he is the same — dutiful and protective — but he has a big empty hole inside."

"I can't imagine your loss." I knew from experience that Selena's surge of engagement was over and would not come back. Once more, I was coming away with nothing but undercurrents, nothing that could implicate Greg McGimpsey or anyone else in the death of Anton Kubik. I stood up. "We're not much further ahead, are we?"

A trace of wistfulness crossed her face at the thought of my departure, but she collected herself. She walked me to the front door.

"Your sister and brother-in-law care about you and Jan. They want to help."

"Vlasta and Marek are both very sweet. We know that. Thank you." She shivered at the chill in the air. "It feels like snow again."

I paused for a moment on the threshold. The perfect order of the house almost masked the turbulence submerged in this woman's gaunt frame. And as soon as her husband came home, it would be buried beyond detection. "You'll hear from me. Take care of yourself in the meantime."

She nodded and closed the door.

When I got back to the office, Wayne and Tessa were helping the Sex Crimes unit with the assault case. A teacher, age forty, was charged with sexual exploitation of a fourteen-year-old student. He denied the accusation, claiming the girl had been provocative — asking for help unnecessarily, lingering after volleyball games — and was getting even with him. Didn't he watch TV and read the papers? All the high-profile cases of teachers, both male and female, molesting their students should have kept him on his guard, even if he were telling the truth.

Sexual assault charges were often the hardest to untangle. An allegation of molestation against either herself or one of her children was the most damaging act of revenge a woman could commit. But the real thing was so despicable that every accusation had to be investigated thoroughly. No one remains assigned to sex crimes units for long because of the stress involved. Homicide sounds more dramatic, but dead victims can't lie or manipulate.

The teacher, Mr. Naylor, was married with two kids, and had a clean record in that school for six years. Tessa had been doing interviews with other kids, teachers, school board members; even Sukhi had been called in to talk to a shy East Indian boy who was a friend of the victim. Not much evidence supporting the girl's case had turned up, besides her emotional testimony and that of her parents. The newest lead came from Calgary, where he had taught before moving to Burnaby. Seems there was a smudge on his file at the Calgary School Board: allegations of sexual exploitation with no charges pressed. The thirteen-year-old girl and her family had not wanted to come forward. Naylor had also denied it on that occasion and had moved to B.C. shortly after. The girl would be nineteen now and might be willing to talk.

Wayne turned to me. "What are you doing tomorrow?"

I shrugged.

"There's a force plane leaving at 7 AM if we can schedule an interview with the girl."

My mind blanked. "Why me? Why not Sex Crimes?"

"They want to send a female and theirs are tied up."

"I'd go," said Tessa, "because I have a feel for the guy, but I'm leaving for Guyana with my dad the next day."

"What's your feel?"

"That he did it. But young girls are hormonal and easily influenced, so we don't have anything firm. The Calgary girl might just tip in our favour."

My head spun, inventing possible excuses. Having just come up empty at Selena's, I said, "Okay, I'll go."

Wayne smiled. "The girl does pedicures downtown and we'll set up an interview. I'll brief you on the case."

I spent the rest of the afternoon going over the file to get an idea of what to ask. It helped to look for patterns. The next time I checked the clock, it was four: time to change for my two dates. I had brought good clothes to work — a short tweed skirt, white blouse, and sweater vest. As I pulled on my brown tights, I thought of Sara insisting a woman's legs were flattered by high heels, but the kitten heels on the copper-coloured Mary Janes I stepped into were as high as I got. At least I wouldn't have to worry about towering over either of my escorts tonight.

Dad was already at Douglas Park when I got there. He was holding a yellow and white rose, sitting on a commemorative bench next to the ball diamond. The plaque read "To A Wonderful Father Who Loved This Park." I wish I had thought of it first, because Dad spent hours here through the summer watching baseball with the willows in the background. Then I reminded myself its recipient was dead.

"Did you ever think how confusing it's going to be when our time comes?"

"You can divide my ashes," he said rising from the bench and starting toward the willows with me. Just then the late afternoon sun broke through the heavy clouds as it had at Selena's this morning. What other city opens from a dark, damp oyster shell into such a glistening pearl? The bright sky felt like a sacred dome above us, the smell already in the air of Japanese plum trees about to burst into gaudy pink blossoms. Warmed by the short walk, we stood under the lofty trees where we had recycled my grandmother in her chosen corner eight years ago. Mom, Janetta, Lawrence, Lenny, and Doug were part of the ceremony. I had been surprised at how the ashes — which might have looked like white fertilizer to a passer-by — took more than a week to be absorbed into the soil and moss. Of course, dispersal of human remains in public places is against the law, so we did it in the evening. One of the practices a law enforcement officer can rationalize as being illegal but not immoral.

Dad wedged the yellow rose in a cleft in one of the branches. I'd parked my car on Heather Street and we started back toward it. Last year we might have walked to Queen Elizabeth but Dad had already walked from home and was looking stooped. We drove the few blocks to RCMP headquarters, where I decided to leave the car in the parking lot and walk from there. I took Dad's arm to cross Cambie, but as soon as we were on the road starting up Little Mountain, he led the way to the burial site. Ringed by ferns, Mom's sequoia was marked by a brass plaque identifying the species. The lowest branch was out of reach, so Dad set the white rose at its base.

"Your mother would be happy for a bird or bee to make use of the flower."

Traffic was swelling behind us and I was thankful not to be joining the stream heading up to the restaurant, and then being forced to park halfway back down on the road.

We found a bench near the pond and sat watching the sun make its exit over the city Mom and Sara loved so much. Sunsets were bittersweet at the best of times, and sometimes I wondered if I should simply allow Dad's mind to idle in melancholy rather than try to rev it up, as I was now, babbling about work. But he was interested to hear of my trip tomorrow — even giving speeding tickets was enough to impress him.

"Calgary? That's quite a jaunt to see a witness." He never asked for details. "Will you get a chance to see our cousin?"

"I hadn't thought of Mona Mingus. Thanks, Dad. I'll call her. Don't you wonder about Jane Hughes coming back to fill the gap left by Mom and Sara?"

"A full circle." He looked at his watch and stood up. "We had better get going if you're to meet your young man. You can drop me at Wendy's. I'll walk home from there."

Wendy's was not far from south Granville, but for the second time today I was later than my date. I waved as I passed Warren standing outside the restaurant on Granville. The closest parking spot was at the end of a side street; I ran back as fast and gracefully as I could in my kitten heels.

Couples were milling on both sides of the entrance. "Relax," he said, "I made reservations. A week ago. Easier to cancel than book late for Valentine's Day. Call me an optimist."

"Or a Boy Scout. Always prepared."

We were ushered to a table against the wall. During the Ray years, I had sampled a few of Vancouver's fashionable restaurants but had never been to this one. Slim leather chairs, bronze-coloured plates that looked like pottery. I thought of Dad, eating his senior's chicken burger, as I studied the appetizers: ravioli of quail, black winter truffle, seared foie gras with candied grapes.

Warren ordered a beetroot salad and I decided to go straight to the main course. I passed over the fennel and pepper-crusted yellowfin tuna, not wanting to be guilty of depleting overfished species. I couldn't remember if Arctic char was also in dwindling supply, but Warren ordered it anyway. It came with smoked salmon caviar, honey mussels, neon squid, and littleneck clams; he said I was welcome to sample them all. The neon squid convinced me to settle on something safe like Virginia's organic redbro chicken with twice-cooked leeks.

From the restaurant's wall of wines he ordered a bottle of Okanagan white. As the waiter poured it, the old queasiness started up. Every time I saw him, Warren Wright got better-looking. From scruffy barfly clothes to hospital gown to running gear, he now sat across from me in a sports jacket and checked shirt undone at the neck. His thick hair was trimmed but not short. I wondered why some model type wasn't with him in this expensive restaurant, and when he would discover his mistake.

"Happy Valentine's Day." He raised his glass. "Stranger."

He said it fondly, but he was right. We *were* strangers. I still really knew nothing about him. Had he been — or was he now — married? Did he have kids? Had he just broken up with someone?

He had obviously been thinking the same thing. "I've been giving you your space, but I feel as if I'm in a cat and mouse game. Or is it cops and robbers?"

I smiled and sipped my wine. "My schedule's been crazy lately."

"It's more than that. Will you ever trust me enough to tell me where you live? I wanted to pick you up tonight, like a real date."

"I was already in the area," I said feebly.

"And next time? You'll be in that area too."

"It's my work. We have to take precautions."

"It's three months, Arabella. Have I given you cause for suspicion — beyond that arrest?"

"None."

"Then do I have to sign over three cows to your father? What's expected of me?" He was becoming more attractive by the minute as his face flushed with frustration.

My shoulders crumpled. I heard myself almost whimpering at yet another romantic disaster. (*The trouble with you, Bella, is that you're too independent.*) "I don't know much about you, I guess."

"That's why people go on dates. To get to know each other. For the record, I've never been married, though I was close once, if that helps. She was an artist and moved to the States after six years together. I didn't try hard enough to follow or keep her here." His beetroot salad arrived at that moment and he pointed his head and fork to my bread plate, as if it were common for him to share with a dinner partner. "And you? I don't know anything about you, much as I keep trying."

"Same. My relationship broke up after three years." I didn't offer that he found someone else. "And my mother died not long after."

"Yes, it must be hard for you today."

His expression of sympathy made me realize that I had been using mourning as an excuse for too long. It had been a whole year, for God's sake. Here was a normal, red-blooded male, whom I fantasized about alone, only to freeze up when he was actually around. "I'm sorry to be so difficult."

He sat back with an exasperated sigh. "Let's drop it for now and enjoy the evening. I don't want to pressure you into anything."

Just then, our meals arrived and were intriguing enough to keep our jaws moving in one way or another. My appetite had deserted me, and I forced myself to finish my expensive food. He clearly did care about me, and I had no explanation for my yo-yoing emotions. Or control over them. Seeing I had knocked the wind out of him was now knocking it out of me.

After an hour of strained small talk, we got up and left. Outside, we stood awkwardly together. I turned toward the side street where my car was parked; it was usually at this point that he would say goodbye and jog off home. He stood close to me without moving and looked directly in my eyes.

"Would you care for a nightcap somewhere? My place, maybe. It's close."

I caught my breath at his nearness, but the faltering creature I had become spoke without warning. "I'd love to, but I have to catch a plane tomorrow morning at seven. For work."

His eyes lingered on mine before he stepped back. Then he shook my hand and said, "Thanks for a pleasant evening, Arabella. Give me a call sometime." He turned quickly and walked down Granville.

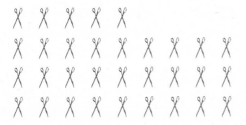

ON THE DARK TARMAC, raindrops conveniently masked my tears. Four other members were boarding the twelve-seater, each of us with Tim Hortons coffee, and all but me with a muffin. I still had no appetite. They were on their way to Edmonton via Calgary to take a course together, so after the usual small talk, I left them alone and opened my notes.

For all the sleep I got in my off-limits apartment, I could have gone to Warren's and taken a chance on a new adventure. How did I keep messing up? Given more opportunities than most, I always seemed to blow them at the last minute. Men aside, the unsolved Kubik case niggled at me constantly, and here I was on my way to collect critical evidence in a sex assault file. Would I lose my edge again?

The sound and vibration of the small plane's engine put an end to self-recrimination and concentration. My eyes clamped shut on the ascent and reclaimed the sleep they had missed in the night. No sunrise over the Rockies for me. I first saw daylight as the plane coasted into the Calgary airport. The pilot announced that it was minus twenty-five outside, but the number meant nothing until I stepped into the prairie air. Dad had advised me to dress warmly, and I had on a thick turtleneck, pea coat, scarf, and high boots, but it was my bare legs under dress pants that felt the cold most. Mom and Dad had brought me to Alberta a couple of times as a kid, once for the Calgary Stampede, and once on a trip to Red Deer and to Gull Lake where Sara and Grandpa had owned a cottage and Dad and Janetta spent their summers growing up. Both were in July; this was February. Snow covered the foothills and frost coated the airport buildings and roofs of the sprawling suburbs. Behind me, the four members came down the metal stairs noisily, reacting to the cold in unquotable language. At least the crisp air woke me up and dried my damp cheeks.

It was ten-thirty Calgary time. The interview with Robin Basa was scheduled for noon at the city police station, where rooms were made available to us. I was booked into a downtown hotel with shuttle service that would get me back to the force plane tomorrow morning at ten on its return from Edmonton. Wayne told me to cab it anywhere else I needed to go during my twenty-four-hour stay.

Before looking for the shuttle, I found a pay phone and called Mona Mingus.

"This is Arabella Dryvynsydes. I spoke to you in January about our family connect—"

"I remember who you are."

"I happen to be in Calgary and am wondering if you'd have time for a short visit later today."

Pause. "That might be possible. My stories finish at three, so you could come at three-thirty."

"Stories?"

"Days, All My Children, General Hospital. I've got a bit of time before Wheel of Fortune."

I thought of Dad and Jeopardy! and their shared DNA. She told me she was on the north hill just off 16th Avenue and gave me her address. I promised to be there on time.

"I've been thinking a lot about Mother's picture."

"It's in my purse," I assured her, then to give her time to produce her item for the barter, added, "and I'm looking forward to reading my great-grandmother's letter."

Luckily my shuttle was at the curb and I hopped on. Half an hour later, I was checked into my hotel, thinking I should eat something. Not because I was hungry, but I didn't want a headache to complicate my agenda. The police station was only a few blocks from the hotel, they told me at the desk, so I set off on foot and found a Starbucks along the way where I warmed up and satisfied a few protein requirements with a jumbo pecan cranberry muffin and a cup of steamed milk.

The Calgary City Police headquarters were in a grey cement building about twelve storeys high. A friendly woman at the front desk led me to the interview room I would be using and did a routine explanation of the audio/video equipment; she said there would be someone in the adjoining room monitoring it as well. Before I had my jacket off or tape recorder out, the door opened again and a tiny young woman came in quietly. Standing next to her, I thought of Sara's expression "knee high to a grasshopper," with me as the grasshopper. I shook her hand, thanked her for coming, and offered her a chair across the little table from me.

Robin Basa's appearance was Goth meets salon: choppy black hair with a maroon streak, diamond nose stud, dark purple lipstick, muted eye makeup. Under her black leather coat she wore a hot pink midriff-length sweater over a black tank top, black jeans rolled up to the calf, and pointed high-heeled boots. Several fingers bore silver rings, the only part of the outfit her customers would see under a white smock. I pushed my notebook to the side, turned on my tape recorder, and asked if she knew why she was here.

"Sort of."

"We'd like to know more about the complaint lodged against Mr. Frank Naylor when you were his student in Grade Seven."

She blushed. "Yeah, like, we never laid a complaint, you know."

I nodded. "Why not?"

"My parents didn't want a spectacle or anything. They're, like, from the Philippines. Mom came as a domestic and brought Dad and me over a few years later. She wanted to bring my grandmother over, and uh, they thought a police record might, like, make them look twice at our family." She made a nervous sound close to a laugh.

"Thank you, Robin. You've just told me a lot."

"Uh, like what?"

"Like the fact that you haven't said you didn't charge Mr. Naylor because he was innocent."

Her flawless skin turned pink again.

"I know how uncomfortable this is for you, and we really appreciate your courage in being here. But if a man did something that still makes you feel this uneasy six years later, don't you think he should be stopped from doing it again?"

She nodded.

"Tell me how it started."

"He told me what a good artist I was. Like I should be encouraged to do more."

Our Burnaby victim alleged that Mr. Naylor asked her to help design a poster for an upcoming volleyball tournament, and while she was at the computer he began stroking her hair. He told her what a beautiful strong body she had, that he would like to take pictures of her in shorts, then digitalize them for the poster.

I nodded.

"Like, he wanted me to stay after school to help with ideas for a poster," Robin blurted out. "I was like, 'Why me?' and he goes, 'Because you're so artistic.'"

"And did you?"

"I was scared not to. My parents were strict. Teachers and priests, like, they were the highest."

I wondered what her parents thought of Robin's look and lingo now. She must have broken out of her shell somewhere along the way.

"And then?"

"Uh, he said I was pretty, and then he goes, 'When you get into art school, they'll want you to model.'" As she spoke, she smoothed her hair with the flat of her hand then fluffed it up from underneath using her fingers. I stayed quiet. "Like, my hair was long then and he would take it and roll it into different styles, and pretend, like, it was for the modelling."

"How did you feel about that?"

"It grossed me out." She gave a nervous shriek of a laugh. "I was shy. But I didn't want to fail my class."

"How many times did this happen?"

"Three. He told me, like, what a beautiful body I had, and that third time he goes, 'They will want to see your whole body, you know, for modelling in the art school.'" Her face was hot and alive with the thought. "And then he, like, started trying to take my blouse off."

"Was the door closed?"

"Yeah, he always closed the door."

"What did you do?"

"I was freaking out. But I was, like, frozen — you know?"

I nodded sympathetically. "Go on."

"I was saved by the janitor. She opened the door to clean and, like, there we were. Mr. Naylor told her to come back later, that we were working on an art project. Yeah, he quickly bent over the poster and picked up a marker. But the janitor had seen enough and got me outta there real fast."

"The janitor reported it?"

"Yeah, she called the police and my parents. Like, she had daughters of her own."

"What did you tell the police?"

"Nothing. I couldn't speak. Too ashamed. Especially in front of my father. And like, I didn't want other kids knowing." She lowered her eyes and pulled her arms tightly around herself, remembering.

I asked her if that was the end of it, and she said in her household it was. It was never mentioned, but her dad got stricter than ever, keeping her home after school like a prisoner. She ran away once and got in with the wrong crowd until she took her esthetician's course. The janitor stopped her later and said she understood about different cultures and would respect her parents' wishes about keeping it quiet. But the school board heard about it anyway.

"Is it any easier now talking about it?"

"Yeah. I've learned there are lots of creeps like that out there. Like, they're the creeps, not me." Robin pointed dramatically with her finger away from herself, then to her thin little chest.

"Would you be willing to testify?"

She made a face. "My dad'd freak out."

I patted her hands, which were now stretched out on the table. "Let's hope we won't need you in person. But I can't tell you enough how helpful you've been, Robin. You could be a hero to a few young girls."

She smiled and combed the back of her hair with her fingers. Then she handed me her card. "Like, if you ever need a pedicure."

I gave her mine and thanked her again before she left.

I sighed with relief. This should help snag the teacher who didn't show much originality in his tactics. I hadn't seen the other girl, but Robin's vulnerable size made him seem more despicable. Try it on someone as big as I was — except at that age, any girl in similar circumstances might react the same way. I turned off the tape recorder, jotted down a few notes, then talked to the guys in the next room about the interview. They gave me a DVD and VHS to take back to Burnaby. They told me it was a good job, leaving me hopeful for a change.

The midday sun had warmed the atmosphere enough to walk for a while; only my ears felt a sting. After a couple of blocks, I came to the Bay, the same white marble building as in Vancouver. Its familiarity lured me inside where I found a bargain bin full of woollen toques. I bought a black one. I could now continue my exploration of the city. Chinatown had caught my eye on the way over, so I turned back in that direction. It was only a few streets long and interesting enough — no, I wasn't comparing it to Vancouver's — but the bigger attraction was the bridge ahead. Lions carved into stone gazebos made me want to cross it. Mona lived on the north hill so I would see how far I could get.

On the middle of the bridge, I stopped. Standing under the stone lions gave me a personal perspective of Calgary. Forget spreading suburbs, skyscrapers filled with the country's wealth, and even revolving towers — they could be anywhere — but this vision of a powerful city rising out of the ice mist of the frozen river got to me. As if it had started small and was still stretching to reach the haughty little hill that would always be looking down on it. From now on, the word *Calgary* would conjure up this image for me.

At the top of Centre Street, I turned left and followed the scenic route along the brow of the north hill. Sixth Avenue did not come all the way through, however, and I soon had to leave the river vista and Crescent Road mansions behind to connect with it. Mona lived in a neighbourhood not unlike Dad's in Vancouver filled with working-class houses from the thirties, now worth half a million dollars. Many homes had been enlarged and gentrified, but Mona's was not one of them: a small brown stucco bungalow with white trim around the windows. I was five minutes early, so I walked once around the block before ringing the bell.

Mona's appearance did not match her drab voice, even when the two came together in a fleeting smile and an invitation to enter. She was about Janetta's age — early seventies — trim, and more agile than I expected. As with Janetta I sensed a casualness that would not have been there during her professional years. She would likely have never received a visitor in the mauve fleece jogging suit she was wearing now. Her hair was short, white — naturally wavy — her eyes pale blue, and her lips glossed in pink. She showed surprise that a newcomer like me would walk from downtown — or at least as much surprise as she could muster. She led me into the small living room, which was joined by an archway to a dining room with a left turn into the kitchen. All the furniture and ornaments had belonged to her mother, she informed me. Was she a younger, more functional version of Laura Owens with her shrine?

She gestured me toward the worn blue velvet sofa and asked if I would like a cup of tea. When I said yes, she brought in two full mugs, then came back with a creamer and sugar bowl. She stood while I added milk and returned them both to the kitchen, next time appearing with two plates, each holding half a buttered scone. The final trip produced a jar of marmalade and spoon: I was to spread my half with the marmalade so she could carry it back promptly to the kitchen. It appeared she had few guests, and even fewer trays.

"You're here on a visit?"

"Work."

"Police work?"

"Yes." I quickly opened my handbag to dodge any explanations. "Here's the picture."

She studied the two little girls for a long time. "Can't imagine how it got left behind with Cindy."

"And I can't imagine the path that's taken me here, bringing it back to you."

"I guess you could say that." Mona's face was softening now that I had presented my credentials. "Did you know I was named Sara Monica, but my father shortened it?"

I nodded. "And my aunt — Sara's daughter — is Janetta. The twins never forgot each other."

Like Wendell, like Dad, Janetta, even Gail and Monty, we spoke of the great injustice done to them by their aunts in keeping them ignorant of the other's existence. I asked Mona what her mother remembered of Sara and their mother Jane.

"Mother didn't talk much, and I didn't ask. She was cozier with Wendell about family matters, because he loves to gab."

"So neither of you ever went through her things when you brought her to Calgary?"

"She was getting forgetful by then, and I didn't want to disturb anything. Though I did go down to the trunk this morning after you called." She got up and took two yellowed envelopes from the dining table and handed them to me. When she continued to stand, I wondered if I was to read them quickly and give them back like the milk and marmalade. But she sat down and sipped her tea.

I opened the one tied with a blue ribbon. It was a bangle and handkerchief identical to the ones Janetta gave me. I told her so. If she thought this was as remarkable as I did, she didn't let on.

"I opened that envelope but didn't get around to the letters."

"Did your mother ever say anything about them — when you were growing up, I mean?"

"Just that they were all she had from her mother, along with the picture." She sniffed. "And to think Cindy had it."

The other envelope was bulkier. Inside were six sheets of paper: one was a letter on fine stationery from Catherine Williams in Wales, and the other five were lined sheets torn from a notebook and written in a scrawled hand I didn't recognize. My throat was dry; I swallowed some tea before I started.

March 22, 1947
Llantrisant, Glamorganshire

Dear Lizzie,

Though I have never had the pleasure of your

acquaintanceship, I hope you will be familiar with my name from your departed husband, my dear brother Thomas.

My health is failing and there is something I want to accomplish before it deserts me completely. Yours is the only address I possess for any of my Canadian relatives and I ask your assistance in carrying out this mission for me.

Enclosed is a packet of letters from my beloved sister Jane written from Vancouver Island to me in Wales. We always prayed that one day we would meet again, and after her death and that of her son Llewyllyn and her sweet Janet, I had hopes of meeting with Sara and presenting the letters in person. This was not to be. I did receive three letters from young Sara written from your address but it seems my replies did not reach her and she stopped writing. Thomas advised me of her marriage to Miles Dryvynsydes and her move to the Canadian prairies but no address was included. I continue to cherish the picture of the two little girls, but I believe it is time to relinquish custody of my sister's letters to her only daughter.

I will be ever grateful if you would kindly forward this packet to Sara Dryvynsydes. I will die in peace knowing they have ended up where they belong.

I hope you and Laura, and my other nieces, Edna and Myrtle, are keeping well.

My sincere thanks to you, dear sister-in-law, for aiding me in this special task.

Yours truly,

Catherine Williams

The most astonishing part of the letter was that it hadn't been read. If it had, someone might have noticed that Janet was presumed dead and Sara was still alive. So it was not just Lizzie keeping the twins apart; one twin was herself an unwitting accomplice. What were the odds of the uncurious sister receiving the letter with all the clues and then passing it on to the uncurious daughter? If it had fallen into Wendell's hands, the Mingus family might have started a search for Sara Dryvynsydes somewhere on the prairies.

If, if, if.

When I looked up, Mona was drinking tea in the same recliner where her mother had sat in Wendell's picture. I controlled my tone. "Would you like to take a look at this now, Mona? It's fascinating. Aunt Catherine was also led to believe your mother had died as a child."

"Is that so?" She checked her watch with *Wheel of Fortune* in mind. "Maybe later."

Clearly Mona's only interest in words was one vowel at a time. Thoughts of little Sara writing to her Aunt Catherine in Wales grieved me. How did she express herself? Did she confide how much she missed her sister? Did she beg her aunt to get her out of Lizzie's home or did she use the same restraint her mother did in her letters, allowing her unhappiness to escape between words? Did Lizzie tear up Catherine's replies? My hands were shaking as I unfolded the brittle bundle of lined pages. The writing was almost illegible, and certainly not the careful hand of Jane Hughes that I knew. To make sure, I checked the last of the five pages and saw a faint signature: "*Your loving sister Jane xxxx.*" Those kisses comforted me as I sank back into my great-aunt's sofa to decipher each scribbled word in her mother's letter.

October 27, 1918

My dearest Cassie,

I started life with you at my side and now I send a final farewell to you with my sweet daughters next to me. In my mind I have shared all my trials and blessings with you, always in the hope of speaking them one day in person. That will never happen on this earth.

The Spanish flu is stealing my breath as I record the sadness that has burdened my heart since I left Chase

River. To you I direct my story because here in Nanaimo it might cause hurt where none is deserved. The fever now consuming me has opened a passage to another high fever almost 24 years ago on the most terrible night of my life.

Dear Cassie, I was witness to a brutal murder of a friend I held in high esteem. You might recall me speaking of my favourite laundry customer, a Negro gentleman. Louis Strong was killed because he refused to sell his orchard that lay over rich deposits of coal. The murderer was a butcher, skilled in the bludgeoning of animals, and required only one blow to my poor friend's head, thereby making it difficult to prove blame when his body was found at the foot of a bluff as an accident two days later. The biggest clue was a bundle of clothes he dropped outside the butcher's house. Can you imagine that he was bringing them to me to launder when he was struck down?

You may wonder what I was doing there on a dark night. Based on hearsay from another customer, I was on my way to his cabin to warn him that the butcher who acted like a friend was not to be trusted. But I was too late. Mama believed I had gone in search of a lemon for Gomer's croup and never knew better. And I myself lost memory of it because that night in hiding I cut my thumb on a rusty hasp and almost died of blood poisoning. When I recovered, the land had been claimed for the Extension coal mine which would soon provide a livelihood for my husband, our brother and Mama, so you will understand, dear Cassie, my grave dilemma in coming forward. Maybe it was fortunate my fevered brain locked away details of that gruesome night or I could not have forgiven myself when the butcher was charged for the murder, then later set free for lack of evidence. Only now I see things clearly.

There is more. Your little sister is not who you think. My first baby son Owen born just before I turned 17 was not from my husband Roland but from Adam Strong, the son of my murdered friend Louis. A chance meeting after my convalescence landed me in his arms and never have I known such a beautiful man before or since. Our baby has been my secret alone, and now yours. Tragically, he stopped breathing within hours of his birth. Was he meant to be a sacrifice for his mother's sins? Suspicions of his origins were buried with his ruddy skin, and with him a piece of my heart.

You have read unkind references to Roland Hughes from my own pen, dear sister, but I was the false-hearted one in encouraging marriage for my own motives. He came from a motherless home with a drunken father and there is goodness in the man when not in the clutches of alcohol. How can I now bear the thought of Sara and Janet in the same predicament? Oh Cassie, if only you were closer to raise them as I would. My best friend has just died of the flu and our brothers' wives would make life more miserable for them than being abandoned. I can only hope Llewyllyn returns whole and mature from the battlefield soon to help care for them.

I am failing fast and must close. I ask God's mercy in judging me for my sins against Roland and the Strong family and against our decent Owens name. But it is strange my head is only filled with the bliss I have known — of my childhood in Wales with you and the others, of the miracles of Llewyllyn, Sara and Janet, of an afternoon in a log cabin, and of many everyday moments we do not recognize as such at the time. I pray you will meet my children one day and present me well. Go you with God.

I had a vague sensation of a TV being turned on. Was it in this room or in the house next door? Latitude and longitude no longer applied.

Jane Owens Hughes: the finale. Images crowded out one another: the fairytale twin girls, in their bows and dresses from the photo, weeping at their mother's deathbed; a sunlit porch with two perfect lovers — doomed and therefore more perfect; the broken-hearted young mother; a decrepit but noble Roland Hughes in the background. Without a photo trail, my imagination was free to assign my own features to them all. I even pictured myself bursting into a courtroom waving the letter as last-minute evidence. What would my uniform look like then?

I sat up straighter on Janet's couch, my shoulders squared in respect to our matriarch casting her pages to currents that would deposit them, four generations later, into my hands. How Sara would have feasted on this letter! How did Janet miss her chance?

Eventually I noticed Mona sitting in the room. But she was now oblivious to me. I waited for the commercial before asking, "Would you mind if I made copies of these letters — for my father and Aunt Janetta and me? If there's a copy shop around, I could take a cab and be back in no time."

"There's one at the Sears mall. I'll drive you." Her eyes returned to the screen.

Why didn't it surprise me that Mona would not let these precious possessions out of her safekeeping, even without knowing how precious they were? I thanked her and excused myself to the bathroom while *Wheel of Fortune* finished.

"I can take you back to the hotel from there," she said, as we walked to her old stucco garage at the back, alone in its original state among new double garages.

A clear dismissal. So much for any notions of looking through family albums to put a face to Janet. Wendell would have to supply those someday. And I had already hit the jackpot.

At the mall, I made copies of the two letters — for Dad and me, Janetta, Monty and Gail. Then a final one for Wendell; despite access to the originals, he'd receive a copy sooner from me. On the way to the hotel, Mona talked about Calgary growing too big and how she didn't drive anywhere beyond the north hill anymore. I thanked her for making an exception in my case, though it was a small sacrifice to get rid of me. "And thank you for sharing the letters. Maybe we'll meet again."

"Maybe," she said, checking her watch, likely for sitcoms she never missed. She drove off with the family treasures to be returned to the guarded trunk. Until they disintegrated or she did.

The evening air chilled my intentions of searching for a trendy restaurant for supper. Room service would do just fine for me to go over the letters again; maybe I'd call Dad and Gail later with the news. Back in my room, I flopped on the bed to digest the day. Warren had been pushed out by Robin Basa, Mona Mingus, and Jane Hughes. No wonder that's how he felt. Sara said there were no accidents, so this bad timing might not be entirely my fault.

Two cases wrapped up in one day. Robin Basa had given us a lot in confirming Frank Naylor's M.O., and Jane Hughes put a lid on the Strong cold case. What were the historical implications? Should I notify the textbooks to add a footnote to their next editions? Or at least inform Professor Barnwell to set the record straight in future classes?

Sleep overruled my appetite, and I awoke two hours later feeling groggy and hungry. I was too tired for any phone calls other than room service. A Greek salad and teriyaki chicken wrap arrived as I was arranging the pages into five sets. Propped against pillows, I set Jane's letter on my legs and tried to eat as I reread it. Each sentence burst open another cell of my great-grandmother's locked world. The will required for this final act humbled me to the bone.

Something in the paragraph about her baby grabbed me. I forgot to open my mouth for a forkful of Greek salad my hand was delivering. Olive oil dripped down my chest, barely missing the page. That she and Adam Strong could not be together was a given Jane felt no need to explain to her sister. Raising a child as a single mother in her society, especially a black child, must have seemed more daunting than explaining him eventually to Roland Hughes, which she might well have done had the poor thing lived. Her trust in her husband was deeper than we imagined.

Unplanned pregnancies today entailed fewer secrets.

Or did they?

The oil was soaking through my sweater. I pulled it off and got a facecloth from the bathroom. My last Greek salad had been in a hotel room with Selena Kubik just after the brutal death of her baby. I was so hungry I had eaten her garlic bread as well as my own. I wiped the oil from my skin.

Suddenly cold, I got into the fleece pyjamas I had brought to this frigid province. I picked up the letter and read once more: *Our baby has been my secret alone, and now yours. Tragically, he stopped breathing within hours of his birth. Was he meant to be a sacrifice for the sins of his mother? Suspicions of his origins were buried with his ruddy complexion, and with him a piece of my heart.*

I set the tray with my food on the dresser, the chicken wrap untouched. My head fell back against the headboard. I lay perfectly still, barely breathing. Had my great-grandmother's letter solved another murder?

THE WEEKEND PASSED in slow motion. From the time I got off the plane Saturday until I arrived at work Monday morning, my mind was at once in a daze and clearly focused. Words and scenes circled over and over, dislodging more words and scenes. Even my dreams, when I was lucky enough to sleep, trapped me in one of those banked cement velodromes for sprint cycling.

I made a few attempts at distraction, like going for a run/walk along False Creek. A pathetic teenage ploy: put yourself coyly in the neighbourhood of the guy you like in the hope you will/will not see him. Of course, I didn't. I wasn't up to the grown-up gesture of a phone call yet. My future was on an hour-to-hour basis.

I also called Dad to recount my visit with Mona Mingus and read the two letters over the phone. He suggested supper at Wendy's or at the house, but I declined. With my thoughts in such turmoil, I was in no mood for conversation, even with my number-one fan. Perhaps that was part of my problem. Mona and Laura were perfect examples of where excessive parental attachments could lead. Dad would never knowingly abet my arrested development; it was up to me to keep the bonds loose enough for someone else to enter.

In my present state, I also decided Gail and Monty could wait for the update. Especially since there might be another shocker to add.

On Monday morning, I was first to the office, having slept little the night before. In the past four days and three nights I might have logged eight hours total. Dex arrived a few minutes later, then Sukhi, then Wayne, and once we were all set with coffee in hand I put the DVD of Robin Basa's interview into the machine. When it was over, Wayne put his arm around my shoulder.

"Good work, Dryvynsydes. This should go a long way in nailing the bugger."

"You can thank Robin Basa. She could have held out."

"Not against our Bella's persuasive powers." Sukhi gave me a fist bump. Dex was already occupied in printing off fresh weekend e-mail Fwds and nodded. I looked at my watch. Eight-thirty. Jan Kubik would have left for work by now. I cleared my throat. "Who wants to make a house call with me?"

Hands shaking on my coffee cup, I put forth the theory that had been consuming me for three days. Wayne's and Sukhi's eyes widened; even Dex stopped his printouts. "It's still guesswork," I said, "but who's in?"

"I'll go with you," said Sukhi.

Since most of my meetings with the Kubiks had been solo, my dread hit full force as I pulled up to the house on Colleen Street in an unmarked car with Sukhi. At the door Selena's dark eyes darted back and forth between the two of us, then fixed on me. Her thick black hair hung lank and greasy. I introduced Constable Ahluwalia.

She offered us a seat, but we remained standing in the foyer. In the living room I noted the sun catching the sheen on the raku bowl — this time with no effect. Sukhi looked at me, waiting.

"We believe we have new information. I'd like to talk to you some more about Anton at the police station. About your part in what happened the day he died. We can take you there now, or you can use your own car."

Selena opened her mouth as if to catch her breath, then said quietly, "I will go with you."

"I can help you change."

This was the point in movies — and often on actual calls — where someone under suspicion makes a swift move and produces a gun or knife. That's why we go in twos. I had no fear in Selena's case, her spirit having been replaced with embalming fluid. I walked behind her, as she clutched the banister mounting the stairs.

The master bedroom was done in the same minimalist style as the lower floor: mud-coloured walls, sleek leather king-size bed with a soft lime-green duvet cover and lime-green and grey striped shams. I turned my head as she slipped out of her lounge suit and into a turtleneck and pair of jeans. If my hunch was right, she would soon have no privacy at all; it seemed proper to extend this courtesy to her, like a last meal. She folded the outfit, put it into a perforated stainless steel laundry hamper, and pulled her unwashed hair back at the neck with an ivory barrette. She held up a cosmetic bag and asked: "Will I be coming back soon?"

Naïve questions like this brought back the hotel room when I was there for her comfort. I couldn't shake that feeling even now.

I shrugged. "Hard to say. But you won't need anything."

Back in the foyer, she put on her leather car coat, then made a quick detour to the living room for her cigarettes. Sukhi was at the car and guided her into the back seat. No one spoke on the way. The face I watched in the rear-view mirror displayed no emotion, but it had aged a decade since I first looked at it from this angle six weeks ago.

Just as I was thankful then at the hospital, there was no one around when we pulled up to the back entrance of the detachment. Inside, Sukhi went next door to the interview room we would use to set up equipment. I informed Selena that she might like to call her lawyer because she was now a person of interest in this case, and anything she said could be used against her. I showed her a phone where she could make the call; she asked if I could look up Tomas Svoboda in the phone book because she had trouble seeing fine print. As I stepped away to give her privacy, I could not avoid hearing her low businesslike tone in Czech, as if she needed the lawyer to sign a real estate deed. When she finished, I asked her if she was satisfied with her phone call to counsel. I could be called upon in court to testify as to the occurrence and length of this call.

She nodded, and walked ahead of me into the interview room where an ashtray, a tape recorder, and two bottles of water awaited us on a table. I sat down across from her.

"You've been going through a lot, Selena."

"My lawyer says I should not speak to anyone."

"And that's good advice, but I know you and care about you. I think it might help to talk."

"That's what you said in the hotel room, Constable."

"And would it not have been easier then to spare yourself the past six weeks of torment you've been living with?"

She lit a smoke. I pressed RECORD.

"Here's how I see the situation, Selena. You'll have to correct me if I'm wrong." I took a deep breath. "There never was an abductor, was there?"

I didn't expect an answer and continued. "And Anton was Greg McGimpsey's baby."

Her forehead jerked visibly into her scalp. "What proof do you have for such a statement?"

"A soother was picked up next to the pond. Do you think its DNA will match Greg McGimpsey's?"

Pink blotches were forming on her cheeks, but she said nothing. Each drag of her cigarette was as deep and vital as a respirator inhalation.

"Let's go through it together. Greg was the perfect lover for you — artistic, spontaneous, passionate — though you knew he would not be the perfect husband. Jan was that, despite being too possessive and inflexible. Greg never asked for more; in fact, the thrill of the affair probably suited him. He believed you were taking precautions with him, so the baby had to be Jan's. You let him think that way. And only you will ever know whether it was an accident or staged. How am I doing so far?"

Selena's continual puffs created a veil of smoke like a beekeeper's netting over her face. She listened without a word.

"The pregnancy changed the equation for you, didn't it? You were still in love with Greg, but you had to cut him loose. The prospect of a baby brought you back to Jan — your history, shared dreams, and so on. Still inflamed over the forbidden love, Greg kept calling. You thought the loyalty of both men would last. And you're not alone; we all think that of our men.

"At the theatre production last fall, you noted Greg's interest in the new cast member. His calls became less frequent, but by now Anton was in the picture and you were engrossed with him. Neither you nor your husband was prepared for the delight the baby would bring. But here's the catch: although you and Jan had renewed your bond, Greg was more than ever a part of your life because he was the father of this child you loved so much."

Selena sat as rigid as a wire sculpture, her eyes red and liquid.

"You're skilled at living on several levels, Selena. From hiding your true feelings under a dictatorship to nurturing fantasy in a stifling marriage. After a long and lonely Christmas holiday with Jan away, you indulged in the fantasy of you, Greg, and Anton together someday. Please stop me if I get too far off track."

Her anguished face had become almost unbearable to watch. I had to finish.

"Then who should appear in your daydream but Greg McGimpsey himself? When you saw the car, you believed he was here to say he couldn't go on without you. But when he came to the door on January 2nd, it was to tell you he was getting married. Did he taunt you with the news or did he do it kindly?" I paused. "This was too much for you. You had a chance to tell him Anton was his, but you didn't. Instead you imploded. He had destroyed your dream and you destroyed the only part of him you had left. His baby."

A howl like that of a snared wolf filled the small interview room.

"It was an accident," Selena cried. "When I dropped him in the pond, it was an accident."

Her face was a mess of wet, smoky streaks. I dug for tissues in my bag, handed a wad to her, and used some to wipe my own eyes, my nose, and my clammy hands. When I could speak again, I murmured, "How I hope that's true."

She was still wailing, at first muttering in Czech, then between convulsive breaths: "I have wiped us all out — my baby, my husband, and myself."

Her cigarette fell from her limp fingers to the floor, and I got up quickly to retrieve it for the ashtray. With her face contorted in wretchedness and her body heaving, I put my hands on her bony shoulders. When she had settled down to intermittent snuffles, I walked back to my side of the table. Before I sat down, I said, "Selena, I'm placing you under arrest for the second-degree murder of your son, Anton Kubik. You have the right to call your lawyer again to inform him of this charge."

She shook her head, waved her hand, and did not move. Her voice, thick from tears, was a croak. "It is already too late for more advice. He will find out soon enough. What I want to know is how you did it, Constable."

"I heard of another love child whose paternity was never known. It died too. Of natural causes. But that spark brought to light the other clues that weren't giving us anything on their own."

"Like?"

"You asking me in the hotel room if I'd ever been betrayed, for one. Your tone was too raw to be thinking of a stranger. How you clammed up when I asked if it was the man in the Porsche. And the way you and Greg spoke so nonchalantly of each other. Too cool by a mile. Things kept coming together. Like the expensive Keith Holmes painting in Greg's hippie pad filled with posters and masks — did you buy it for him?"

Her eyes said yes.

"But I still have a couple of gaps. How did Greg McGimpsey end up at the Van Dusen Gardens when it was a private memorial?"

"I do not know. He left a message of sympathy on our machine. His concern was sincere. I did not return any of his calls. Jan spoke to him — he knows him from the theatre. He might have mentioned a closed gathering at Van Dusen to be polite. Jan is more polite than I am."

"And how did you come up with a Kosovar?"

"That country was in my head and he had to be a foreigner. In case Greg was implicated."

"You thought fast."

"I did not think. If I had, I would not be sitting here. I only reacted. Like a wounded animal."

I knew Selena would withdraw again soon. Maybe forever. "It's your turn now."

"It is unspeakable."

"I'm preparing you for the questions you can expect."

She groaned. "I am already a carcass. The vultures will pick my bones. I no longer care about myself, but I fear for Jan. He will disintegrate. And Greg will — how do you say — detonate? — when he hears the truth. I am not without a heart, Constable."

"I've never believed you were. Passion can take over all our organs. But the pond, Selena. What happened at the pond?"

Bending and speaking slowly, she lit another cigarette. "Greg's news hit like a lightning clap — or is it a thunderbolt? I did not say much to him, but slammed the door and began to pace around the house with Anton in my arms. My distress frightened him and he began to scream. I tried my best to console him, but he would not stop. I walked around the house, bouncing him, stroking him, showing him his toys, all with no results. When I gave him his soother, there were a few moments of peace, so I took him outside to distract him — he liked watching birds in the yard. But soon he spat it out and screamed even harder. He turned blue trying to catch his breath — " She paused. "And then I do not remember anything beyond a helpless feeling without a bottom. My arms went limp. He slipped from them into the pond."

I thought of the cigarette falling just now and imagined the baby. She began crying again.

"I do not know how long I stood. My brain went blank. I do not believe I was punishing myself and Greg by discarding what I loved most, as you suggest, Constable. I do not know what to believe." She put her face in her hands, the cigarette bobbing unsteadily between her fingers.

I let her cry. After a few moments, she raised her head. Her nose was dripping, but she continued.

"When my mind cleared, I saw my precious baby in the pool, as if for the first time. I became hysterical and dialled 911. You know the rest."

I handed her more tissues from my bag and stood up. "I'll let you collect yourself for a moment. You're doing well, Selena, under such circumstances."

I left the room and went next door. Sukhi was shaking his head in disbelief. Mine too felt dizzy, and I let out a big sigh. "Anything you want to add?"

He gave me two questions which I took back to Selena. "How did Greg know Jan was away that morning?"

Her head was again in her hands and her words barely audible. "I do not know. Jan travelled often for work and sometimes Greg phoned the office anonymously to make sure."

"And wouldn't Greg wonder about an abductor so soon after he was here? The time and details were all over the media, although we kept the Porsche out of it. Didn't he see your fury?"

She mumbled. "He saw my shock but he did not see my fury. I do not know what he thought because I did not return his calls. He probably wanted to ask me about the abductor. But he would never reveal to anyone else that he had been here, for his own protection as much as mine."

I stood up and offered my hand to help her out of the chair. I signalled Sukhi through the one-way glass that I would meet him upstairs. "Thank you, Selena, that's enough. I have to book you into cells until your appearance in court tomorrow. Until then you will not be allowed access to anyone other than your lawyer."

On the way out, I asked her if she would like me to speak to Jan. Their lawyer would have informed him where she was.

"Would you please, Constable? I cannot face him yet. He did nothing to deserve this but love me."

"And Greg will be a witness."

"You will need a padded cell for that encounter. He is very emotional."

At the door leading to the cell block, she turned to me. "What if I deny everything in court?"

"You won't. It's eating you up too much."

The clank of the heavy door behind us caused her to flinch without changing expression. I led her down the women's corridor. Loud snoring came from one cell we passed; empty trays sat on the floor outside three others. At the end of the passageway the matron sat behind a large desk playing computer solitaire, a room with monitors of all the cells nearby. Today almost all of them were filled with women who had seen better times — or was that the case with all prisoners? The matron took Selena's name and listed her offence on a book-in sheet. A big woman from Trinidad, she was both practised and unruffled enough not to react even to a murder charge. She did not look up until she nodded to me that Selena was ready for the strip search. I did it quickly in the private room designed for it. I had more or less watched her change, after all, and anything illegal would have created an obvious bulge on someone as scrawny as she was. Neither of us looked at the other during the procedure, even when I was obliged to take her bra to prevent her from doing herself harm. It would go into a basket under the counter with her jacket.

After the matron took her picture, I suggested she call her lawyer again in a small room for that purpose. She seemed even more aloof after this conversation. The matron escorted her to the cell, unlocking the steel door with her cantaloupe-sized hand. "Your B&B for the night, honey."

Selena paused briefly at the threshold of the cement cubicle, which contained only a mattress on a built-out ledge and a stainless steel toilet with a drinking fountain attached to the back. When the matron locked the door, I thought I saw more colour in Selena's face, but maybe it was just the blotchy patches blending. If confession wasn't good for the soul, at least it could not have been any worse than what she'd been holding in. And I too, through my nausea and fatigue, felt a welcome freedom, though little triumph.

Back in the office, Sukhi had supplied Wayne and Dex with the details. Our angry sergeant was pacing the room.

"What a lying bitch! Holding us hostage while we're working our asses off trying to find a killer. You especially, Dryvynsydes. How many hours did you waste with her, interviewing relatives, making sure she was all right? Jesus Christ! Why couldn't she have said it was an accident from the start? Aren't you madder than hell?"

"Sadder than hell." I had no problem understanding the why of not coming forward, knowing everything else that had to come out with a confession. Wasting police manpower wouldn't have come into her calculations.

But Wayne was more agitated than I'd ever seen him. He had two kids, and I was looking almost as loony as Selena to him. "You're sad about a woman who kills her own child? Not because she or the baby has a life-threatening disease, or anything like a mercy killing. No, because she has the hots for some guy she can't have."

His words stung more than expected. He had summed up the crime correctly, but the woman herself was more complex than one action. If I'd said that, he would have come back with "All killers are," and been right again. I had no defence for it — or for her — and could only feel queasy at the thought of the seeds of emotion we all carry swelling so far out of control. It was just the first of the contempt that would greet Selena's name at every turn. I'd have to get used to it. "Despair like that is so ugly I don't like thinking about it. And the remorse must be worse than death."

"You're verging on Stockholm syndrome," Wayne said, still steaming. "Attachment to the criminal."

Dex came between us. "I believe you mean Lima syndrome, Wayne. Stockholm syndrome is a morbid attachment of captive to captor; Lima syndrome is when the captor becomes sympathetic to his or her victims. It was coined when the guerrillas who took over the Japanese embassy in Peru let some of their hostages go." Then he turned to me. "What tipped you off?"

"A precedent, you might say."

I wasn't about to explain that two cases obsessing me had erupted in a "eureka" moment. Like the earth's plates shifting into each other. Cracking open and forcing light on what's underneath. If I got the attention of my three partners for that, I would surely lose it — Wayne's at least — in extending the plate-shifting theory to Selena's obsessive brain. Same upheaval, different results — in her case a tsunami. "A supercop friend of mine once said there are no reliable procedures in police work. Always be open to an outcome you'd never expect."

Just as I poured myself a cup of coffee, my phone rang. Jan Kubik was downstairs at the desk. My stomach lurched at the prospect of this assignment, and the face of Roland Hughes — haggard but fine-featured like Sara — accompanied me on my way to meet him. At least he was spared the news I was about to deliver to Jan.

"Constable Dryvynsydes," he said anxiously, shaking my hand. His leather car coat was a sootier shade than Selena's. "I want to see my wife."

I told him he wasn't allowed any contact until after court tomorrow. "But I would like to speak to you, Jan." I didn't reciprocate the surname formality. "To prepare you for what Selena is facing."

He followed me to a small private room and made himself as comfortable as he could on the edge of a padded chair.

"Your wife has been charged in the death of your baby son."

"Yes, yes, our lawyer has just told me that."

"You aren't stricken by this news?"

"Of course I am, Constable Dryvynydes. How could it have happened?"

Anticipating a stunned silence, tears, or fury, I said quietly: "She confessed, Jan. She said the baby slipped from her arms into the pool, and she did nothing until it was too late. There was no abductor."

He stared at me. Was I wrong in detecting impatience in his expression? That I should get on with my story and tell him something he didn't already know. "Selena killed your baby," I repeated.

Jan Kubik lowered his head. "It was not my baby, Constable Dryvynsydes. Did she confess to that too?"

Now I was stunned into silence.

"Of course, she does not know that I know. That would have broken the spell for her. My wife required an excitement I could not give her. My complicity in her affair with Greg McGimpsey would have sucked the air out of it."

I struggled to think of a response. "Your delicate orchid."

"She always will be."

"And you had the last laugh over Greg, because he didn't know."

Jan nodded. "Greg is raw material, I am refined goods, and as you know, they are not encouraged in our diets. My wife craved both, but her early hardships would never allow her to choose the lifestyle he offered. Not just from a materialistic point of view, but because of her European culture, which I share. Nor would Greg have wanted my wife on a permanent basis. You are aware of his new woman from the theatre — someone much younger, with whom he can hike on weekends. Can you see my wife with a backpack? No, I was as certain she would not tell him as I was of his paternity. I am a precise man, if nothing else, Constable Dryvynsydes. I recently had myself tested and I am sterile. Being also a proud man, I had denied the possibility for many years. So you will understand that Anton was the supreme gift for me, thanks to Greg."

"And Anton's death? Did you know about that too? I should warn you that you might be facing obstruction of justice charges."

"I did not know. None of my suspicions made sense. The white Porsche led to Greg, but that was out of the question. And Selena's story seemed confusing, given all the co-ordinates. I knew I would get nothing more from her. But she was never a suspect in my mind," he said emphatically.

"So is this a relief?"

Jan looked at me cynically, then caught himself. "I think perhaps release would be a better word. Like an open wound from a tight blister. But I would like to thank you, Constable Dryvynsydes, for your considerate manner toward my wife and myself. If there is nothing else, I will contact our lawyer as to how we should best proceed."

"She's lucky to have you."

"I hope she will finally feel that way."

I did not add that he too had what he wanted: a helpless, grateful Selena, removed from New World temptations. Exclusive rights shared only with the Crown. Was it worth a child?

He followed me out the door and I told him I would see him in court the next day. I was suddenly starving and wanted to be alone. A Caribbean restaurant in Metrotown would provide time and space to think, along with the best curry and roti I knew. Love stories played out in many variations. Selena and Jan's might be in the same category — in reverse — as the woman marrying the man who had lye thrown in her face. And where did Jane and Roland fit? At the moment, Adam Strong and Greg McGimpsey, the men of passion, seemed the lesser players. But they were all love stories.

THE VULTURES WASTED NO TIME in picking Selena's bones. By next morning, news of the arrest had appeared in print, on TV, and the internet. My bones, on the other hand, finally got some rest. When I returned to the office from lunch, Wayne, restored to his cool self, took one look at the bags under my eyes and gave me the rest of the afternoon off — and today too, if I needed it. I shut off my phone and slept for twelve dreamless hours. No more velodromes.

Messages from Dad and Gail wanting the inside scoop would have to wait. As soon as I surfaced from my underground parking, it started to pour so hard my focus couldn't handle both road and conversation, even on a Bluetooth. At the office, my team toasted me with Tim Hortons roll-up-the-rim coffee, and a congratulatory e-mail from Tessa in Guyana made it complete. I appreciated their praise, but did not feel in the mood for celebration. As gruesome as the offence was, and however justified its retribution, this case was giving me no satisfaction. Today Sara's belief in karma as cause and effect suited me more than the Criminal Code. She disliked the moralistic spin on crime and punishment, sin and virtue. Compared to what? According to whom? If virtue is its own reward, Selena's act had taken its own revenge on her.

Before my old qualms about career choice had a chance to take over, a memo on my desk reminded me of my worth to society. The Mitchell Pogue trial had been postponed until May. Visions of Andy Lambert, broken and condemned to live in hiding, made me weak with fury. Wanton, deliberate brutality on an innocent deserved nothing less than the long sentence I hoped Pogue would get. But wouldn't the headline on Selena read the same — minus "deliberate," if she was telling the truth? Why did the thought of baby Anton provoke tears and Andy rage? To a lesser degree, I felt the same about the two other cases coming up: the amateur thief who had shot my foot and the teacher who preyed on young girls. One delinquent, the other odious.

Dex read my next thought. "What about McGimpsey? Someone better tell him he'll be called as a witness."

"I told Selena I'd break the news to him about the baby."

Dex straightened up to his full height. No longer the dedicated robot who slept with his badge, he looked at me with the same soft expression he had used for Andy Lambert and his smelly dog. "You? You've done more than your share, Arabella. I'll talk to him. He's likely to go ballistic when he hears it was his baby, but he won't act out the same way with me."

My partner's strong, broad shoulders brought a rush of gratitude for this job I had just questioned moments earlier. Would I have felt such support working in a tearoom?

Selena's first appearance was at nine at the Provincial Court on Main Street in Vancouver. It was not obligatory for the arresting officer to attend, but my involvement had carried me too far not to see it through. Wayne might think I was showing symptoms of some syndrome or other, but he didn't know it was curiosity about other people's lives that had caused me to join the force in the first place.

I'd have to leave right away to get through the downpour during rush hour. With Wayne's offer of another free afternoon to sleep, I took my own car. Luckily, I hit all the lights on Boundary and Hastings, but parking near the courthouse was impossible because of media vans. The most eager reporters were sharing umbrellas with cameramen, hoping to catch a soundbite from Jan or their lawyer on the way in, making me think they hadn't arrived yet. This was the heart of Vancouver's downtown eastside, where an estimated five thousand people inject or inhale drugs every day. Only time would tell if the Woodward's project would accomplish any urban rehabilitation by providing market and non-market housing along with shops, medical, and social services all in the same giant complex. Reluctantly, I left my car two blocks down

Cordova Street in the hope it wouldn't be sold for parts by the time I got back. The alarm and club on the steering wheel wouldn't do more than slow down the pros. I grabbed an umbrella from the back seat and made a run for the courthouse.

Inside, there was even more traffic. Dockets outside each courtroom door listed the cases for the day; well-dressed lawyers were easy to spot among the shabbier family members and friends of the names on the sheets. Selena was up first. Before I could read any further I felt a tap on my shoulder.

"Nice work, Bella."

Ray. Tanned from a winter vacation. I thought of Blondie in a bikini. Red for some reason.

"Thanks."

"Word is you solved the whole thing. From a dream or what?'

"Word is I don't divulge my sources."

After explaining he was here for a theft case at ten, Ray nodded toward a cluster of three lawyers in conversation behind us. I knew two of his colleagues from Crown Counsel, but not the third man who was short, bald, and animated.

"Svoboda. Maybe a plea to manslaughter for a deuce less?" He shrugged. In lawyer talk, he meant Selena might get two years less a day, which would mean a provincial sentence to be served in the Alouette River Correctional Centre in Maple Ridge. Anything more than two years was federal and would be served in the Fraser Valley Institution in Abbotsford.

"Or maybe infanticide, if she pleads guilty." He was still guessing. "Five years max but most likely a lot less, and served at home. The baby was under a year and they might make a case for a disturbed mental state resulting from the birth." He shrugged again. "Or maybe she'll walk."

I'd been witness in enough cases never to predict a court decision. "Or it could go to trial and she'll get second-degree murder with a minimum of twenty-five years — parole at ten, day parole at seven. Like Robert Latimer killing his daughter, but without the protest faction for a mercy killing."

For a moment, I forgot I no longer shared my opinions with this man who had once shared my bed. His awkward grin told me he hadn't forgotten.

"I just found out I've been recused from your case. Past history a conflict of interest."

Something lifted at the sight of him squirming over the nostalgia of our connection. Were bonds breaking and floating away? I smiled broadly and said, "That's too bad, because you would have done a good job, Ray."

I watched the strain on his face transform into a bewildered expression as I excused myself to talk to the Kubiks, who were trying to get through the entrance of the courthouse. As Marek Kubik, now flanking Vlasta O'Brien with Jan on the other side, said in so many words: we cannot expect to stay with the first person we kiss. Or even the second, third or fourth.

Wet reporters and cameramen closed in on the threesome with mikes, each hoping to get something out of one of them before they reached the safety of the threshold. But they sidestepped the media deftly and paused inside the lobby to shake their umbrellas. Vlasta's eyes were red and swollen. She wore a camel-coloured cashmere cloak and a burnt orange nubbly scarf tossed stylishly at the neck, attracting attention from all the suits, male and female. Spotting a familiar face, they moved toward me; Marek and Jan offered their hands. Marek was no longer the magnetic bundle of energy Tessa and I had interviewed in his office, but there was warmth in his greeting. On Jan's arm hung a Gucci tote bag.

"Our lawyer says there is a chance that Selena will be granted bail. She will need her trenchcoat to get to the car in this rain."

Jan's optimism for bail at the first appearance was unfounded, in my experience. I didn't think Svoboda would lead him on, but he might well be hearing what he wanted. As Marek glanced sadly at his brother, I searched for similarities in the two of them. Both had thick white hair and a direct gaze from brown eyes. But Jan was taller, his lips thinner, and his posture military next to Marek's mobile, almost slouchy body.

Tomas Svoboda broke away from the other lawyers to join us. He embraced Vlasta, then offered me his hand. "Your reputation precedes you, Constable Dryvynsydes." Apart from my usual discomfort with short men and with defence lawyers who would later be grilling me on the stand, I took it as a tone of respect. My work was done on this case, and both sides would now skew it to their own purposes.

We moved as a block through the courtroom door but inside, Svoboda led Selena's relatives to the front and I took a seat near the aisle on a back bench. After all, I was a witness for the prosecution. One small consolation, if it could be considered as such, was that my sympathy in this case was confined to one set of observers. Deciding whether I felt worse for the family of the victim or the accused wasn't always a given. Imagine sitting in court as the parents of a kid charged with beating up an old woman in a home invasion, cringing with both dishonour and loyalty.

The presiding judge was Madge Konkin, one of the most reasonable on the circuit, but also regularly late due to a smoking habit she couldn't break. As we sat waiting, Ray appeared again at my side. "Do you mind?" I slid down the bench to make room for him. "I've got some time before mine comes up. This is high-profile."

"We won't get much today."

"You look tired, Bella."

"Gruelling few days. I'll be all right."

"Cracking this case was more than just police work. How did you do it?"

"Maybe because I'm more than just a police officer."

A familiar bout of blinks told me he had interpreted a dig I didn't intend: that he had failed to appreciate the woman I was. An hour ago I would have intended it. But now I said, "How are you, Ray?"

"Good days, bad days."

"You've been in the sun."

"Mexico. Went down with Craig for some scuba diving."

He looked toward his colleague on the Crown Counsel team at the front. Craig was single. Was this his way of telling me he was also unattached again?

Just then, the clerk came in and called the court to order. We all stood for the entrance of Judge Konkin, an attractive, redheaded woman in her fifties. Both lawyers bowed to her, and she did the same to the courtroom. We sat down when she instructed the Crown to call its first case. Craig stepped forward.

"I'm calling case number one on your honour's list in the matter of Selena Kubik on the charge of second degree murder of Anton Kubik on January 2, 2008."

As soon as Svoboda introduced himself as counsel for the defence, the sheriff brought Selena in through the side door to the dock. Vlasta gasped loudly and Marek shifted in his seat. Only Jan remained silent and rigid. In her turtleneck and jeans, Selena cast a half-smile in their direction.

Svoboda declared his intention to apply for bail for his client in the Supreme Court. The judge fixed a date a week from now for the hearing of his application for judicial interim release, and pounded her gavel. Selena was led out of the dock through the side door by the sheriff. From here, she would be transported to the Surrey Pretrial Services Centre, where she would remain until the bail hearing. As Svoboda and the Crown lawyers vacated their spots at the front for the next case, he was no doubt explaining to Jan, Vlasta, and Marek that they would have access to her in Surrey. They could also have some realistic hope that she would be granted release on a surety — my guess would be $100,000 — which Jan could probably come up with, and if not, Marek was sure to chip in. She was not a flight risk, had no criminal record, and was not likely to re-commit.

So that was it. I stayed seated as the four of them passed down the aisle, like the family exiting the pews first in a wedding or a funeral. Each acknowledged me again, the unnecessary raincoat swinging from Jan's arm.

Ray and I stood up to follow. A sudden sensation of us as a couple again hit me. A fleeting titillation. We'd had our chance to make it work. I didn't believe in trying relationships again unless something beyond our own human weaknesses had broken it in the first place. Like a war, an earthquake, or an extended coma. The birthmark that looked like a hickey peeked out from under his dress shirt collar when he turned his head a certain way, the same mark I had duplicated many times on the other side of his neck for symmetry. Strange how the outside of people didn't change and you could be deluded into thinking the same was true of their insides. Or maybe the delusion lay in the hope that the inside had changed.

I patted his arm. "Good luck with your case."

"Thanks, Bella. With the judge's smoke breaks, it could be awhile yet."

I felt him watching me walk out of the courthouse. Yes, he was good-looking. I couldn't take that away from him.

The rain had stopped, and I gulped a mouthful of fresh air. The deepest swallow I'd had in ages. The hookers and other street people had been driven into doorways, cafés, and lobbies of cheap hotels by the heavy downpour, so my car was safe. Disabling an alarm in weather like that can be even trickier than they are.

I reached in my purse for my keys and pulled out some loonies instead. I fed them into the parking meter. My hands had decided for me: before heading back to my bed, I'd take a stroll through the soft, humid air of Gastown. These inhalations were too purifying to be squelched inside a car just now. I thought of Calgary — was it only four days ago? — and its icy brightness. Bracing in its way, but only Vancouver wrapped you in silky mist like this. I turned onto Water Street at the first corner, inhaling the strong saltwater aroma of the inlet shimmering nearby.

Soon the barred and boarded-up windows and littered sidewalks were behind me. That Gastown and its cobbled streets and pricy tourist quaintness bordered the poorest postal code in Canada no longer seemed a contradiction. Maybe because I stood equally in both worlds. I thought back to Wanda's grungy household where I realized how a postal code had saved me from her version of blame and self-pity. But as familiar as her territory had become to me, these shops and fashionable eating places were just as familiar. Mom and I had often met for lunch here, and had then taken our time going through all the boutiques and art galleries. And for Ray and me, a reservation at Aqua Riva was not enough, unless we got a table on the water. They were happy, privileged times. Not to be mourned or regretted.

I wondered if Jan, Vlasta, and Marek had beaten the paddy wagon to SPSC. Would they be in Jan's Mercedes or Selena's Jaguar? Wherever she ended up, none of them would forsake her. Jan would be present at every visiting session, regardless of number.

I paused under the antique steam clock, Gastown's crown jewel. Across the street I spotted a rack of scarves in the window of a boutique carrying Asian and African items. I went over to inspect them. A clerk informed me they were knitted in India from silk scraps of sari material left on the cutting room floor: long streamers in a blaze of shaggy, multicoloured threads. I chose the one with the most turquoise in it, feeling a sudden desire for that shade. I paid the woman and wrapped it twice around my neck, letting the ends fall over my oregano jacket. I didn't look as classy as Vlasta O'Brien, but I could pretend I did.

I stepped out of the shop onto the corner across from the clock. It would soon be belching steam and whistling the hour in its famous Westminster chimes. Any tourists out on this February day would gather around it in delight. And now my feet made the decision to stand and wait to hear it as well.

Without warning, my fatigued mind took flight. Rooted to the corner of Cambie and Water Streets, my head filled with visions of pedestrians walking in step around the square of the intersection and across the diagonal. All passing by me as if I were a traffic cop with a whistle directing the choreography. Jane Hughes nodded her thanks for being allowed to cross first. Wiping her nose with a lace handkerchief, she was taller than I expected. She had a large, open face, and her hair was the same no-name brown colour as mine. Her long, full skirt and green woollen cloak made her look as if she belonged under the steam clock when she reached it. Roland Hughes crossed on the other diagonal, stooped but light on his feet, bowing toward me as he passed, then joining Jane under the clock. Louis Strong stayed on the square, plodding around the four corners and tipping his hat at each of them. Adam Strong followed his father with a spring in his muscular body — Yeah, Jane was all I could say. Sara walked against the flow, disobeying signals and winking as she did. Janet, following the stream, met her coming the other way, and they fell into each other's arms on one of the corners. Grandpa followed with Sara's coat and stood smiling behind the twin sisters. In a power walk, Mom strode the square, then the two diagonals, blowing me kisses without changing her pace. Dad tried to catch up to her with his deliberate steps, but couldn't.

Suddenly the intersection became overrun with people crisscrossing every which way: my two work teams marched through, then Janetta, Lawrence, Mona Mingus, Laura Owens, Gail, Monty, Ray, Wanda, Terry, Selena, Andy Lambert, Marek, Jan, Vlasta. I lost track. Rhythmical stops and starts on the corners, middle X moving in harmony with the square, then a sudden reversal of direction. The musical ride without horses.

Just then, the steam clock burst into vaporous foghorn song. One shrill honk, and all but one disappeared from my giddy reverie. Across the street, Warren Wright leaned against a wrought iron lamppost with its bouquet of white globes, watching. Then as always, he walked away.

Once in motion, my feet lurched across Cambie Street. And they didn't stop.

"ROLAND HUGHES?"

Trust Monty to pick out the one dangling detail after more than an hour of Jane Hughes and Selena Kubik.

Hoarse from talking, I sighed. "I'd hang up on you, except Gail's on the other phone. What about him?"

Amplified by the extension, Monty's bear roar blasted our ears until Gail told him to tone it down. "Thought you were a detective, Bella. We know from Laura Owens that he remarried, but nothing more."

"Nice talking to you, Commissioner."

He snickered again, then hung up to let Gail and me finish the conversation.

Monty's laughter had reached Dad standing at the sink washing dishes. Sleep deprivation in check, I was once again sane enough not to see the world as a conspiracy and had accepted his third supper invitation. Time spent with him was not only valuable but hardly responsible for my messed-up love life.

"What was that all about?"

"Monty says we left Roland Hughes out of the investigation. What became of him and his second wife?"

"That shouldn't be too difficult to find out." As usual, the sight of his bent neck reaching for a high cupboard saddened me.

"What do you mean?"

"We can check him right now on the computer. B.C. Vital Statistics." He folded the tea towel, hung it on the oven door, and started toward the basement. I followed his slow steps in slippers down the stairs. He turned on the computer and offered me the swivel chair.

"Your fingers are faster than mine. Start with B.C. Archives."

He pulled another small upholstered chair over next to me. This was Dad's first den; he and Mom often ate supper and watched the news here after she did a run on the treadmill while he watched *Jeopardy!* Eating upstairs began as a concession to my broken ankle, then became a habit. But I believe he preferred it down here with his memories of Mom — even in full view of the empty space where her exercise equipment had once stood before I impulsively got rid of it.

There were two listings for Roland Hughes. One died in Vancouver in December 1942 at age sixty-nine, and the other in Comox in 1975 at the age of sixty-four. It had to be the first. With a few more clicks, we established that Roland Hughes married Jane Owens on May 2, 1895 and Katherine Odgers on December 24, 1926, both in Nanaimo. More searches determined that Katherine MacDonald was born in 1882 in Nanaimo, and in 1901 had married Harold Odgers, who died in 1918 at age forty-five. Was he too a victim of influenza? Eight years later Kay and Roland tied the knot.

"Grandpa was fifty-three in 1926. More than ready to come up from the mine, if he lasted that long."

I looked at Dad, who had not realized he'd said "Grandpa," so I didn't point it out. My guess was that Roland Hughes had never been referred to so fondly.

Unless.

I kept clicking and produced more on Kay. B.C. birth records online were only available until 1903, marriage records until 1931 and death up to 1986. Luckily for our purposes, Kay and Harold had a daughter Maria born in 1903, who married Victor Shybunka in 1925 in Nanaimo. Though no more births were listed, Marie and Victor could well have had children who grew up at Grandpa Roland's bony knee. We did discover that Kay survived Roland for twenty-nine years and died at age eighty-eight in 1970 in North Vancouver.

Seeing these names officially with a microfilm number beside them made them much more real. As if all our other information might have been made up until proven with statistics. Vital Events, as they were called, could not supply us with the particulars of when or why Roland

and Kay moved to the mainland. Did Maria and Victor lead the way and they followed to be near the grandchildren?

Three cheers for uncommon names like Shybunka and Dryvynsydes. We would have spent weeks searching for Williams, Hughes, or Thomas, but only two listings for T & C Shybunka appeared in the lower mainland, both in North Van where Kay ended up. I checked the national phonebook and found fewer than ten Shybunkas in the whole country, so even that number was doable, if these didn't yield anything. It was worth keeping Monty off my back for good. But not tonight. I was ready for bed and had to stop yet for gas on the way home.

Pushing the swivel chair back, I noticed an envelope on the computer desk in Dad's own writing.

"What's this? "

He looked embarrassed. "Oh, it's just my book returned. I expected this."

The envelope was slit, and I pulled out the contents. A form letter from an editor said they were not accepting any new submissions at this time. Nothing personal, nothing promising.

"I've got more publishers to try."

"And what's this?" I picked up another sheet from under the envelope.

Dad tried to grab it from me. "Nothing. Just a little song that came to me. More like a poem because I can't write music."

"For your next book?"

"Kind of a musical. Not that I'd ever get anywhere with my old-fashioned ideas. But the words just popped into my head."

"And your finger gave you permission."

He smiled. I began to read, as he shifted uncomfortably in his slippers.

> When frustration has a stranglehold on all of your senses
> And your best means of expression is a scream,
> Try to realize
> It's only a disguise
> For a signal that you're closer

To your dream.
Without friction there's no motion,
Watch the ships upon the ocean,
Or the seed under that heavy weight of earth
You can't grow without resistance,
And might I add persistence,
So take my word for what my word is worth.

"Hmm. My father, the lyricist."

He snatched the page away and put it in a drawer. He clearly did not want to discuss his work any further. And what did I know about writing a book or a musical? So many plots were confusing my brain that I couldn't imagine weaving any of them into even a simple storyline like Sissipuss. I yawned, walked ahead of him up the basement steps. He never trusted me to turn off the computer, power bar, and basement lights at the same time. On the way through the upstairs den, he pulled out Tess of the D'Urbervilles from the shelves of Sara's books.

"I've been meaning to give you this. Talk of these poor lost babies brought back a memory of Mother giving it to Janetta and me to read when we were in school. She said her own mother had treasured her copy growing up."

"Didn't Jane's teacher give it to her when she quit school? Next you'll have me signing up for an English course."

"Not a bad idea."

On Dad's note of bravery giving me even that much advice, I took my leave. Halfway to my apartment, I stopped for gas. The pumps were all occupied and I pulled up behind a minivan where a tall young man was just finishing.

Crane Reese. As he replaced the nozzle, a woman got out of the driver's seat and walked with him into the gas bar. It was Marla, our classmate, who had jumped on my barstool next to him when I vacated it at Squires after our last class. She had her arm around his waist, pushing open the door. The cashier was close to the window, and I watched Marla open her wallet to pay. Crane brought some snacks and drinks to the counter, and Marla paid again. His contribution to the transaction was a neon smile both to Marla and the cashier.

Crane exited behind Marla and got into the passenger seat with the drinks and snacks. I kept my head down as they pulled away. Would it be me ferrying Crane everywhere he wanted to go if I had stayed on that barstool? Stools and chairs he so gallantly pulled out for you. Marla was welcome to the job.

Back in my apartment, I flopped on the bed without undressing. I had a bad habit of waking up fully clothed, as if I were in a homeless shelter, afraid someone would steal my jeans. Flat described my mood best. Was this what those cards meant when they went on about the journey being more important than the destination? Or what painters and writers referred to as process? Were my thumbs actually twiddling when I wondered "What next?" Business as usual could hardly apply after a week where nothing could be considered usual again.

My great-grandmother had taken up residence inside me. I was not on her shoulders as that image of ancestors goes, rather her life was steeping into all my cells like tea leaves. I could never presume to steal the strength she gained from all she went through when I had faced no such challenges — a shot in the foot didn't come close. Nor could I claim Sara's early trials or her knowledge and wisdom as my own. Or Mom's drive for perfection. How then could I qualify? I felt like the painted wooden Russian doll housing the smaller ones inside her — I was the biggest but also the most hollow.

My self-pity was ambushed by a crazy dream of the image I had denied. A wobbly totem pole of Jane, Sara, Retha, and me trying to balance on one another's shoulders.

I jerked awake, laughing, and sat up on my bed.

I didn't have to compete. As the living representative, I held all the power. They now existed only through me, so how could I feel unworthy, when I had full responsibility? If Sara was right — that ignorance is the only sin — was awareness then enough of a mission? Of my lineage, of lost babies, of the misguided and the inspirational? Or even of the sound of willows swishing in the breeze, or the smell of plum blossoms in the air? If so, I wouldn't need to take over a soup kitchen just yet to insure a sense of purpose. And if nothing was permanent — as Sara also claimed — my co-ordinates just might be on track until further review.

I changed into my sleep shirt, brushed my teeth, got into bed and picked up Tess of the D'Urbervilles. It fell open at: *So the baby was carried in a small deal box, under an ancient woman's shawl, to the churchyard that night, and buried by lantern-light, at the cost of a shilling and a pint of beer to the sexton, in that shabby corner of God's allotment where He lets the nettles grow, and where all unbaptized infants, notorious drunkards, suicides, and others of the conjecturally damned are laid.*

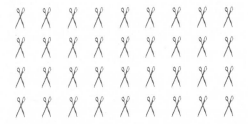

AS PREDICTED, Selena Kubik was granted bail on a surety of $100,000. Her trial date was set for October, eight months away. I did not attend the hearing, and if there were a plea bargain in the meantime, I would not be required to testify at a trial. My association with the Kubiks could well be over, unless I decided to buy new furniture from Vlasta O'Brien. Of course, I'd follow Selena's case — and life — with interest, but I believed she would survive whatever sentence she was given, and in her own way, grow from it.

Tessa was back, looking relaxed and more exotic than ever after a visit to her homeland. Heritage will do that for you. She said her father didn't produce an eligible Guyanese man for her, but she had soaked up the heat and soft, lilting accents, eaten her fill of tropical fruit, and drunk coconut water from the husk every day at the outside markets. That her new guy in polygraph had texted her constantly made the homecoming to rainy Vancouver easy.

Wayne handed me the phone number of Jennifer Ward, the mother of the young offender who had shot me. She had called to say her son wanted to see me before the trial next month. Should she bring him in? I phoned to say I would meet them downstairs.

Tyson Ward lived in one of the mansions on Government Road. When he and his mother arrived at the front door of the detachment, I took them into the same room where I had spoken with Jan Kubik. In her crisp white shirt and blonde ponytail, Jennifer Ward looked as if she had come from a home with vaulted ceilings, decorated in pale yellow, cream, and seafoam. After the introductions, she left me with Tyson, dressed in oversized designer garb. He mumbled something I couldn't hear, and I asked him to speak up.

"I'm sorry I shot you." He looked down, and I couldn't tell from his expression if he expected me to say "That's okay."

"That makes two of us. My ankle will never be the same, but it's functional again. Your consequences are just coming up."

What sounded like a fit of sneezing turned out to be staccato sobs. I had already seen his face crumpled in tears from the ground, but I had been summoned for this performance and let him carry on. Every crying style was known to me, both the physical technique and degree of sincerity. Yet a polygraph for tears — a lachrygraph? — would be useless, because even the remorseless ones can be genuine at the time; certainly they regret the situation they're in.

The gun used had been taken from his scruffier friend Billy's uncle — well-known to us for drugs and theft — but it was good-looking Tyson who pulled the trigger. The rich kid needing diversion. Life was too boring and easy: why not try a break-in? Just to see how it felt. Tyson's house possessed two of everything that was in the house they targeted, but what a mega rush to force entry into a perilous situation. And Billy's family could have used the loot. The gun was no more than a prop that Tyson took charge of. Neither of them planned to pull the trigger, especially on a cop.

Would that reckless decision scar him permanently, or would the thrill of violence become a habit? Too soon to say. Tyson Ward was distinguished from Terry Dean only by cleanliness, affluence, and lack of excuses for his behaviour. How closely we're all connected. I hated the phrase "I hope you've learned your lesson" and when the crying stopped, out popped: "May the force be with you." Once again, I spoke before thinking, and this time I chuckled at the double meaning.

Jennifer Ward reappeared and thanked me for coming. She did not try to comfort Tyson or lecture him, nor did she apologize for him by saying he got in with the wrong crowd. When they left, I felt he might have a chance.

I spent the rest of the afternoon on paperwork. Back in my apartment after supper, I sat down with my phone. I dialled T Shybunka first. An older voice said hello twice, as if he were hard of hearing.

I stated my name, then in a non-telemarketing tone, tried to keep him on the line long enough to ask if he were related to Katherine Hughes.

"Who's calling?"

I repeated my name and explained that I was doing a family history; I believed Katherine Hughes might have been married to my great-grandfather. I hoped this would be a Wendell and not a Mona Mingus conversation.

"Kay Hughes was my grandmother."

"And I am the great-granddaughter of Roland Hughes and his first wife Jane."

"Is that a fact? Granddad thought his family was lost. Wait till I tell the kids. Too bad Rilla's gone — she would've loved this." I sighed in relief that it would be a Wendell encounter. "Who did you say you are again?"

I asked if I might come to visit on the weekend. Did he have any pictures?

"My daughter keeps them. I'll get her over here. When did you say you're coming?"

I set a time for Saturday afternoon and told him my father would be with me. I didn't need to check with Dad about meeting the interloper who had robbed him of his Grandpa.

As with Wendell, the two old men proved compatible. Tim Shybunka lived in a seniors' apartment in North Van, two blocks from his daughter Dorothy, where he could show up unannounced any time he felt like it. His son Daryl and his family also lived in North Van, farther away in Deep Cove. Dorothy was with her dad, waiting to receive us with homemade muffins and coffee. I took an immediate liking to the woman — plump, energetic, fiftyish — because she dispelled my doubts about being too attached to a parent at the expense of a life of your own. Seeing her kiss her dad's bald head or pat his shoulder when she passed his recliner shamed me for thinking otherwise. She had two careers: music therapist in a hospital and bookkeeper for her husband's plumbing business. Their two kids, one a deep sea pilot, the other a teacher, also lived within walking distance with their spouses — this was a family that wanted to be close.

Dorothy picked up the box of photos and began dealing them like a deck of cards, setting aside the few that might interest us. "I keep telling Pops we should put these pictures in order. We never knew much about Granddad before he married GG."

She handed me the wedding photo. "GG tinted that herself. She made extra money colouring for a photo studio when she was on her own raising Grandma."

A strange wash of emotion came over me as I stared at the tinted black and white studio photo, my first glimpse of Roland Hughes. There was no such record of him with my GG. Roland was the same height as Kay and half her size, his thin neck almost lost in the stiff collar of his dress shirt and suit jacket. A full dark moustache partially made up for the missing hair on his head, and he had a jaunty stance that showed his small frame to advantage. On his lined face was an apologetic smile, but a craftiness in his eyes kept him from seeming pathetic. Was Sara right in saying she had a lot of her father in her?

Kay looked anything but apologetic, grinning at the camera with warmth and confidence in a pink wedding suit and a matching cloche hat. Her corsage was the same red as their lips and cheeks, the tincture tubes probably limited. Like the wedding picture of Thomas and Lizzie, Kay clearly came across as the spouse in control. But the similarity ended there, because Kay's face and posture held an ease and merriment that were completely absent in Lizzie. To have bred such an affectionate line, she must have been that way herself. A contrast to Mona Mingus, Laura Owens, even Dad, certainly no less dutiful or caring but physically undemonstrative. And was I the final link in that chain of inhibitions?

I passed the picture to Dad as Dorothy handed me another picture of Roland bathing a baby in a tub. "That's Pops," she said proudly.

When Tim didn't hear, she repeated cheerfully, and he chuckled. "Granddad told me later I was the first baby he ever bathed."

Seeing Dad's and my faces might have caused him to add: "He felt guilty about his drunken ways with his first family. Grandma told us when she came to live with my mother — Maria was her name — that she rescued him from drinking himself to death. Saw something worth saving, I guess. Never took another drink after he met her. Smoked a pack a day, though."

Dad asked it first. "Did he ever mention the twin daughters he left behind?"

"Not to me. I was fourteen when he died. But Grandma said it ate away at him all his life. Being sober made it worse."

Tim Shybunka's memory only held so many highlights of a step-grandfather who died seven decades ago, so Dorothy took over. She had spent a lot of time with her great-grandmother when she lived with her grandmother, again nearby.

"GG loved to talk about the early years."

I thought wistfully of what I might have learned, having Jane as well as Sara.

Kay Hughes had said it was painful for Roland to speak of Sara and Janet. How they were taken from him by his wife's brothers, and he was declared unwelcome to visit in his derelict state. Even the brother-in-law who had been his friend got in touch only once to inform him one of the twins had died of influenza. He moved to a rooming house in Nanaimo and started gambling after that. Kay Odgers met him at a dance. Said her first impression of him hooked her because he was such a good dancer. Light on his feet and too busy with all the women in the hall to drink too much that night. He wanted to see her again. She told him he'd have to quit drinking and gambling first. When he appeared two months later, shaky but sober with some money saved, she didn't turn him away.

Timing and karma. Were they the same thing? Was Jane an unwitting accomplice to her own misery? Was she an enabler? Are we all? Did she believe she had to suffer Roland's alcoholism to atone for the false start to their marriage? She spoke of sins in her deathbed letter — at last in a voice of freedom. I felt sure Sara would have been thankful to know her father found peace with a loving woman, having found the same thing herself with Miles Dryvynsydes.

Dorothy went on. "GG felt bad about that daughter of Granddad's. She said they went to the island to her uncle's funeral to see if they could find out where she was. He'd been her guardian, but his widow said she'd moved to the prairies and left no address."

"You've got a good memory," Dad remarked.

Tim heard enough to add: "My grandmother was that kind of woman. Made you want to listen to her."

Dorothy handed us three more photos: Kay and Roland at Niagara Falls with Marie and her husband Victor Shybunka; Roland with Tim and Rilla as children on a ferry; Roland alone with a birthday cake — that one had a couple of lines written on the back: *March 29, 1938, age sixty-five.* The wizened face still carried an apologetic smile under unshrinking eyes; were they the eyes of his twin daughters that looked past each other on a street in Medicine Hat around the same time?

"Oh, and here's one you might like to have. It ended up with Granddad's things." Dorothy spoke casually, tossing a picture of two little girls with bows in their hair onto Dad's lap. Dad's utterance came from such a deep place I could see the hairs on his neck stand up. Dorothy sat back and watched us as he passed it to me. "You know this picture?"

I nodded. "That makes three out of four. The other is somewhere in Wales."

Between us, Dad and I filled Dorothy and Tim in on the history of the photos, Dorothy sitting close to her father to repeat when necessary. At the end both were speechless, until Dorothy sprang up and coaxed us to stay and have homemade borscht with them. "Pops eats so much borscht, perogies, and cabbage rolls, you'd think he was a full-blooded Ukrainian, when his name is the only Ukrainian thing about him." Tim Shybunka strained to hear what his daughter was saying and smiled.

It had been a long afternoon and we declined politely. When we stood up to leave, Dorothy offered to have copies made of Roland's photos; we accepted on behalf of Janetta and Wendell as well. We promised to meet again soon.

Traffic crawled on the Lions Gate Bridge. Dad nodded off next to me. In the middle of Stanley Park, he sat up straight.

"Dreaming?"

"Maybe. Mother used to talk about the songlines in Australia among the aborigines. She read books about them and couldn't contain her wonder at how they kept their stories alive for thousands of years, all orally. Each generation sang their sacred paths to life through rocks, trees, landmarks. I think I just had a dream about those songlines. Except the landmarks were all these people we've unearthed, including the ones under it. Each of them has offered scraps of memory to the same songline, thereby preserving it. Is this our sacred path?"

"Well said, Pops." I gave him a light punch on his arm, as we turned off Denman to Davie, finally moving at a normal speed. "I've had an overactive imagination myself. Blamed it on lack of sleep." I didn't try to explain the circus I envisioned in Gastown.

When I dropped him at his house, he asked me in for supper. "Thanks, but I've got places to go. And you need a nap. Then open a can of sardines and get back to your musical."

He slapped the air dismissively and got out. Maybe someday he'd get a kiss on his head — from Dorothy, for sure.

Within minutes, I was in the maze of False Creek streets off Spyglass Place and found a parking spot not far from my target. I stepped inside and pushed the button for 315, my stomach churning. The voice spoke, and I said "Arabella" into the speaker, wondering if the buzzer would sound. When it did, I pushed the lobby door open and took the stairs. At 315, I knocked. I would have deserved the half hour it seemed to take someone to answer, but it was only a second or two. Warren Wright stood in the open doorway, looking bewildered. Inside I could see sun streaming from the west through all the space he had chosen to leave around his few pieces of furniture.

"Come in," he said, gesturing me past the galley kitchen and into the sunlit living room.

I stood fast on the sisal mat next to the door and shook my head. "If you're not doing anything, I'd like to invite you to my place for supper."

A smile started to curl one side of his mouth.

If bad timing were responsible for misplaced letters, photos, affections, and even sisters, this family was long overdue for a change of course. "You might want to bring your toothbrush."

ACKNOWLEDGMENTS

Extensions is a work of fiction, although I have drawn upon many reports of the coal mining world around Nanaimo in the late nineteenth/early twentieth centuries for its creation.

For inspiring my interest in this era, I credit my late aunt Olive Harper, who, thirty-five years ago, gave my family a copy of Ghost Towns and Mining Camps of Vancouver Island by T.W. Paterson and passed along the four letters she possessed in her mother's handwriting. My ensuing vision has relied on many sources. Lynne Bowen, author of Boss Whistle, has provided not only a primer on coal miners, but also personal encouragement. To the late Peggy Nicholls I owe a great deal for sharing her vast historical knowledge and genealogical findings. Other helpful books and publications were Go Do Some Great Thing: The Black Pioneers of British Columbia by Crawford Killian, Old Square-Toes and His Lady: The Life of James and Amelia Douglas by John Adams, several essays on Sir James Douglas by Charlotte Girard in B.C. Studies, The Dunsmuir Saga by Terry Reksten, America's Forgotten Pandemic by Alfred W. Crosby, The Great Influenza by M. Barry, The Silent Enemy: Canada and the Deadly Flu by Eileen Pettigrew, Flu by Gina Kolata, as well as various studies online. Among the many references I consulted on the Louis Stark family were articles from the Salt Spring Island Archives, including "Recollections of Sylvia Stark as told to her daughter Marie Albertina Stark Wallace," the B.C. Archives, Nanaimo Archives, Lynne Bowen's Three Dollar Dreams, and The Chronicle of Ladysmith and District compiled by Viola Johnson-Cull.

My own research trip to Nanaimo and environs was made possible by my dear friend Marilyn Martin and my cousins Irene Luknowsky,

Jim, Carla, and Rick Harper acting as chauffeurs, hosts, and enthusiastic explorers. My thanks to them all.

Arabella's story could not have been written without Annelisa Dey Thomas. She has been my daughterlode of information about police situations and protocol, and adjusted the contemporary narrative to reality throughout. To their sister's expertise, Gillian Dunn and Phoebe Dey added discerning questions and comments on several drafts of the book. They were always up for a consensus in a dilemma, despite their busy lives. My gratitude for the three of them and their help goes beyond words.

I am deeply indebted to Carol and Jan Fishman for their patience and willingness to enlighten me on legal proceedings.

John Lebeau deserves high praise for his careful reading of the book and his thoughtful and heartening remarks. I am also grateful to Richard Lebeau and Louise Lacouceur for their suggestions. Others who have contributed prompt answers to research questions or offered relevant debate on various points of the book are Art and Doreen Alexander, Novell Thomas, Pat Gilkes, Renate Williams, Joan Jason, Valerie Richie, and Colleen Martin.

Sincere thanks to my NeWest editor Anne Nothof for her support of the novel from the start and her keen eye thereafter. My appreciation to Lou Morin for her warmth in the NeWest process, to Paul Matwychuk for his easy, knowledgeable manner, to Natalie Olsen for procuring the enthralling cover photo, and to Shawna Lemay for her early guidance.

Finally, I give thanks to my husband Cedric, for balancing my heart and art and keeping me on my grammatical toes.

myrna dey GREW UP IN CALGARY AND RECEIVED A B.A. AND AN M.A. FROM THE UNIVERSITY OF ALBERTA. FOLLOWING RESEARCH IN BERLIN, SHE TAUGHT AND STUDIED GERMAN AT THE UNIVERSITY OF CALIFORNIA, BERKELEY, FOR TWO YEARS IN THE MID-SIXTIES. SHE ALSO LIVED FOR SIX YEARS IN GUYANA. SINCE 1976, SHE AND HER HUSBAND HAVE MADE THEIR HOME IN KAMSACK, SASKATCHEWAN, WHERE THEY RAISED THEIR THREE DAUGHTERS. HER SHORT STORIES, ARTICLES, AND ESSAYS HAVE BEEN PUBLISHED IN *READER'S DIGEST, NEWEST REVIEW, CANADIAN LIVING, THE NATIONAL POST, THE GLOBE AND MAIL,* AND *MACLEAN'S.*